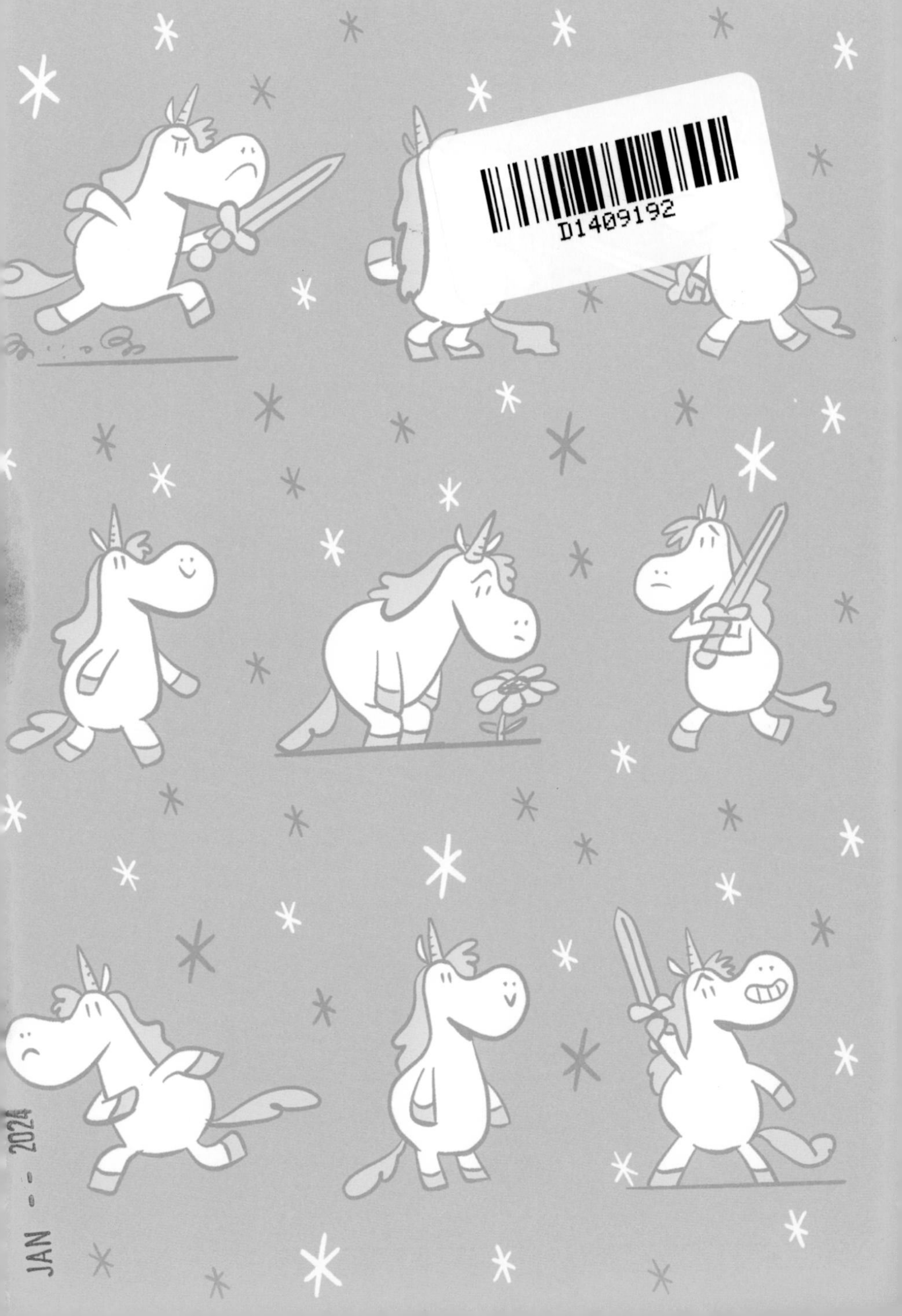

ANDI WATSON

CLARION BOOKS
Imprints of HarperCollinsPublishers

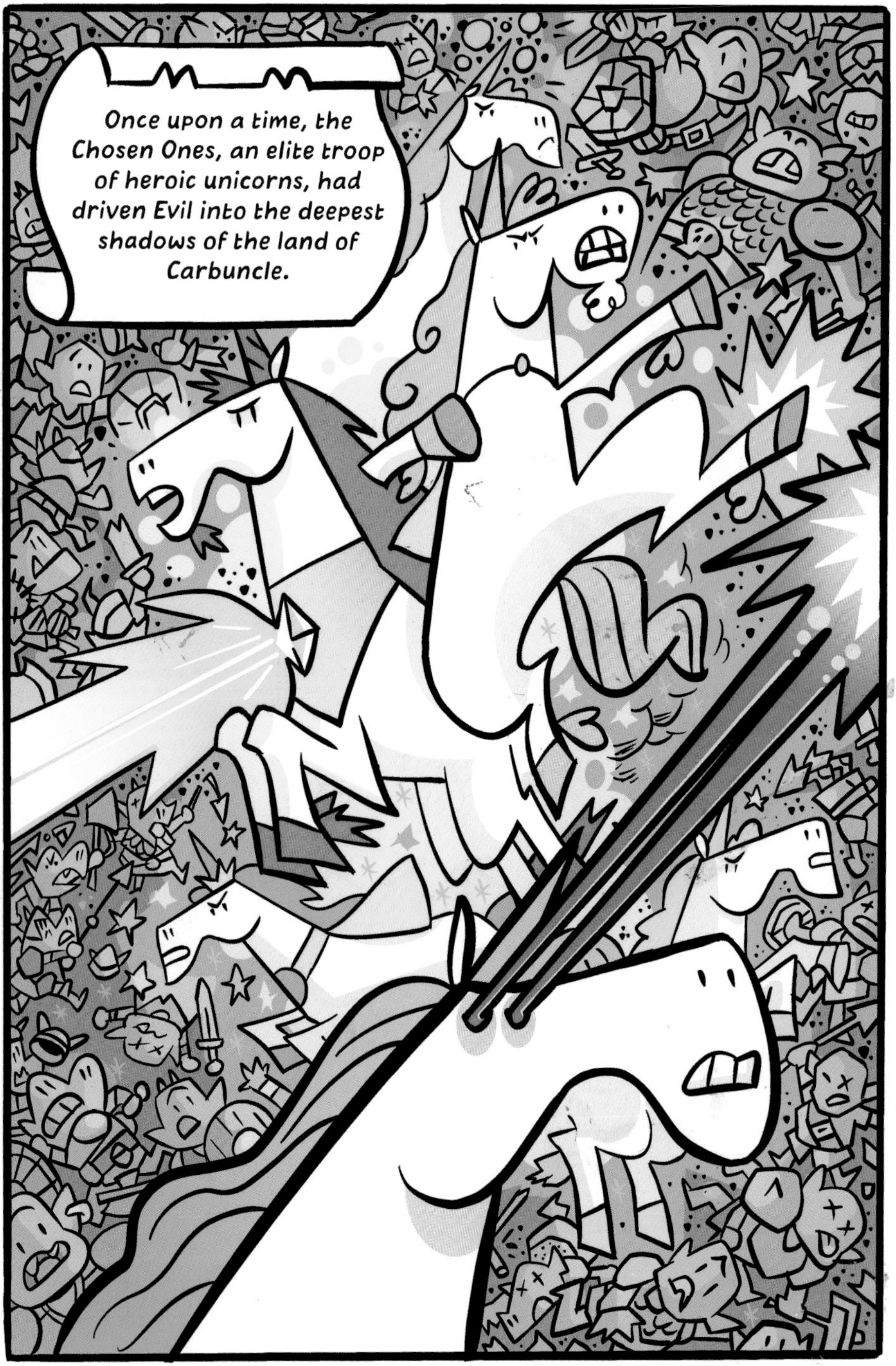
Once upon a time, the Chosen Ones, an elite troop of heroic unicorns, had driven Evil into the deepest shadows of the land of Carbuncle.

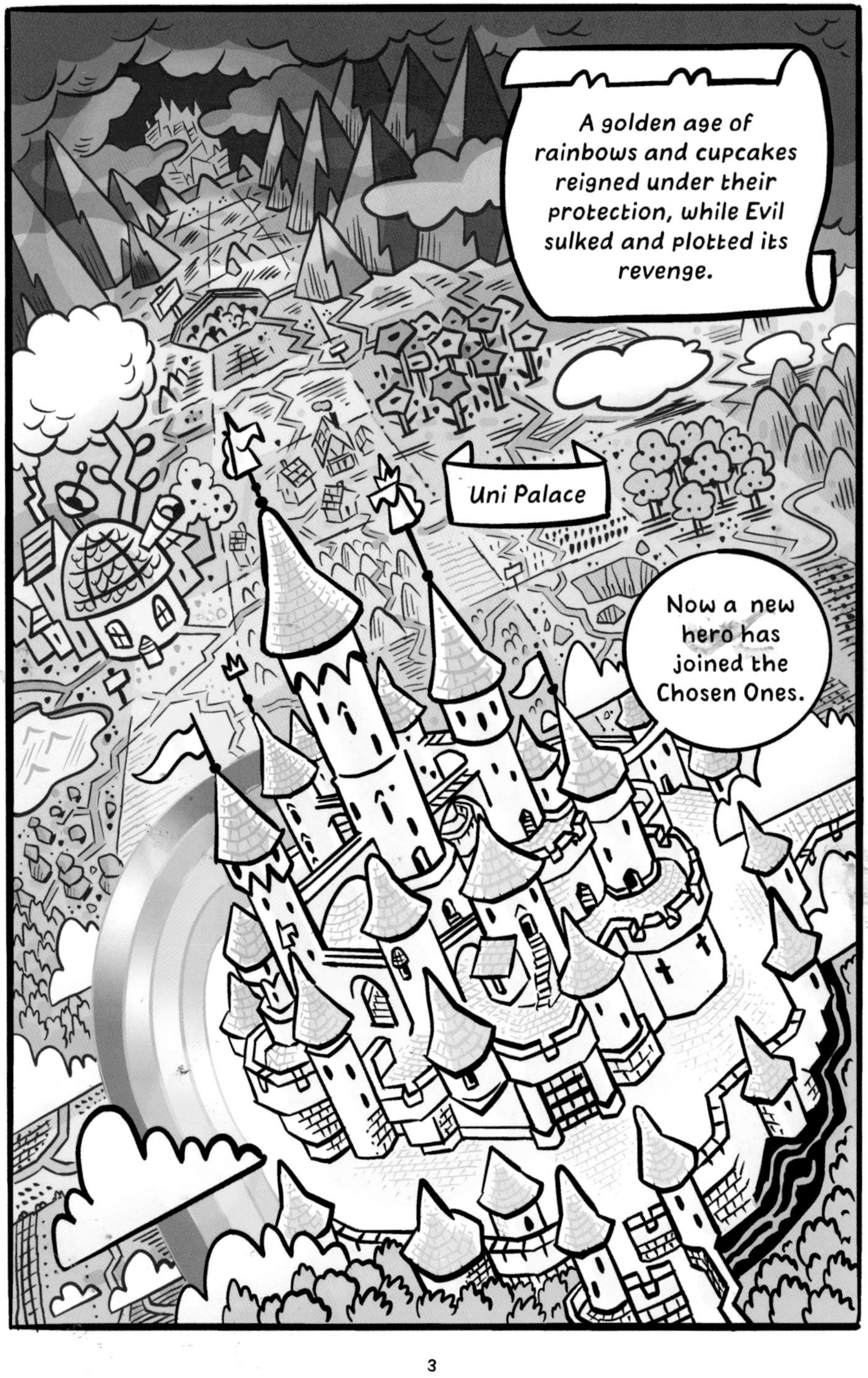
A golden age of rainbows and cupcakes reigned under their protection, while Evil sulked and plotted its revenge.
Uni Palace
Now a new hero has joined the Chosen Ones.

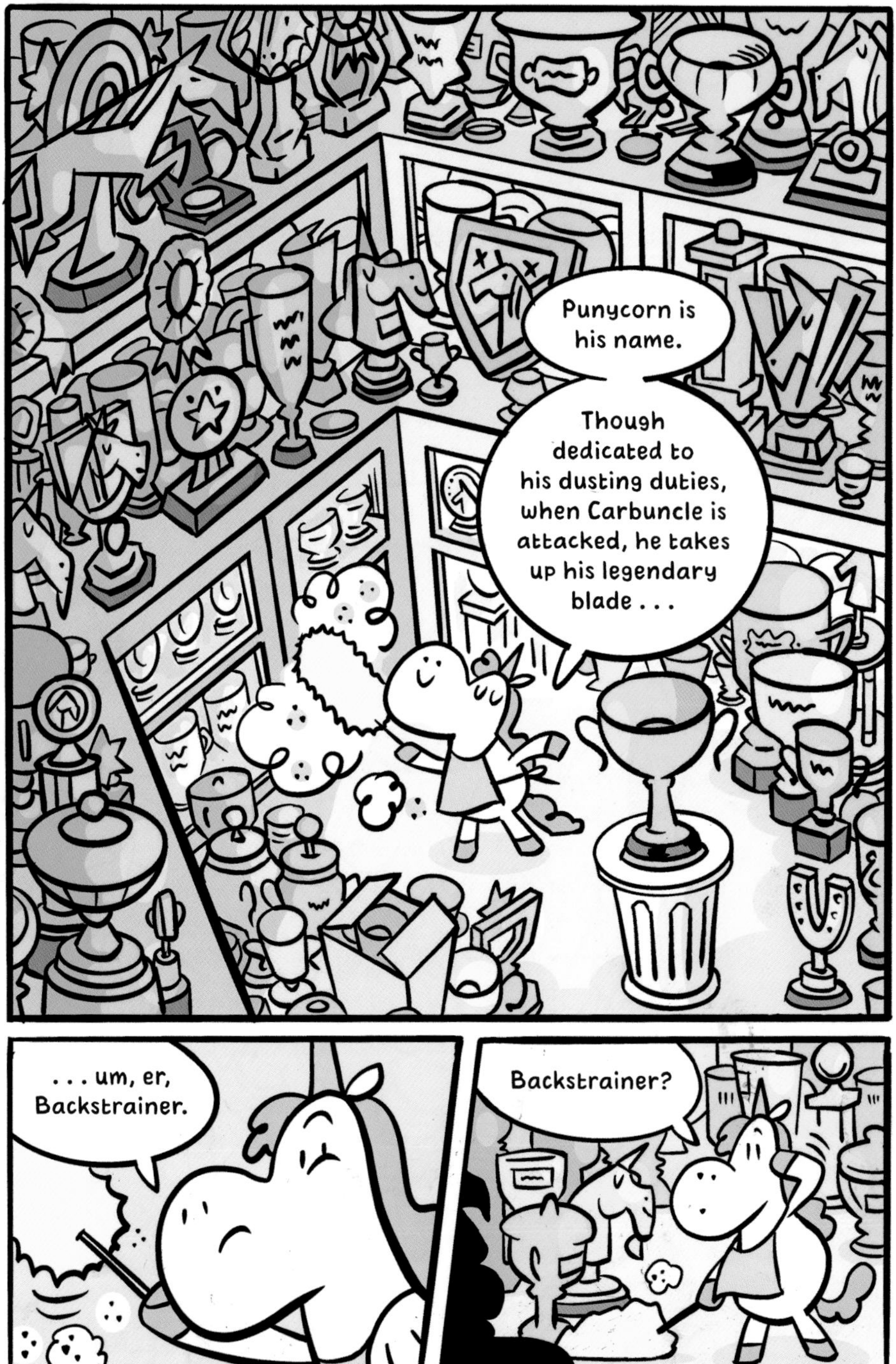
Punycorn is his name.
Though dedicated to his dusting duties, when Carbuncle is attacked, he takes up his legendary blade . . .
. . . um, er, Backstrainer.
Backstrainer?

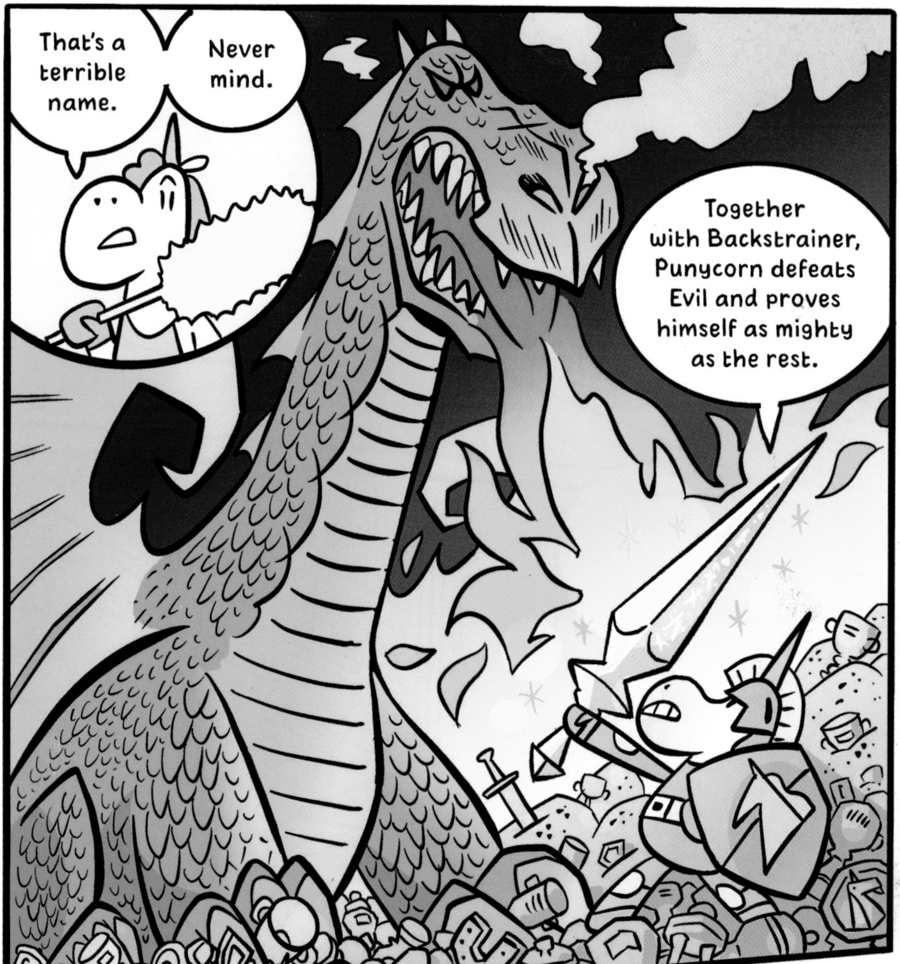
That's a terrible name.
Never mind.
Together with Backstrainer, Punycorn defeats Evil and proves himself as mighty as the rest.

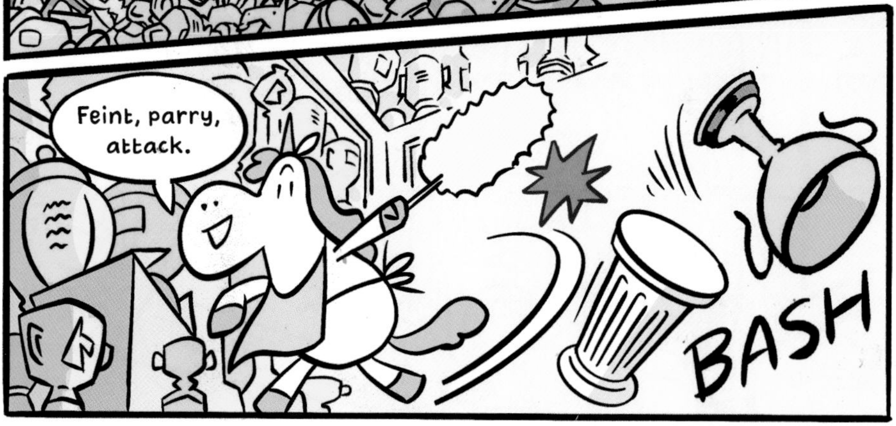
Feint, parry, attack.
BASH

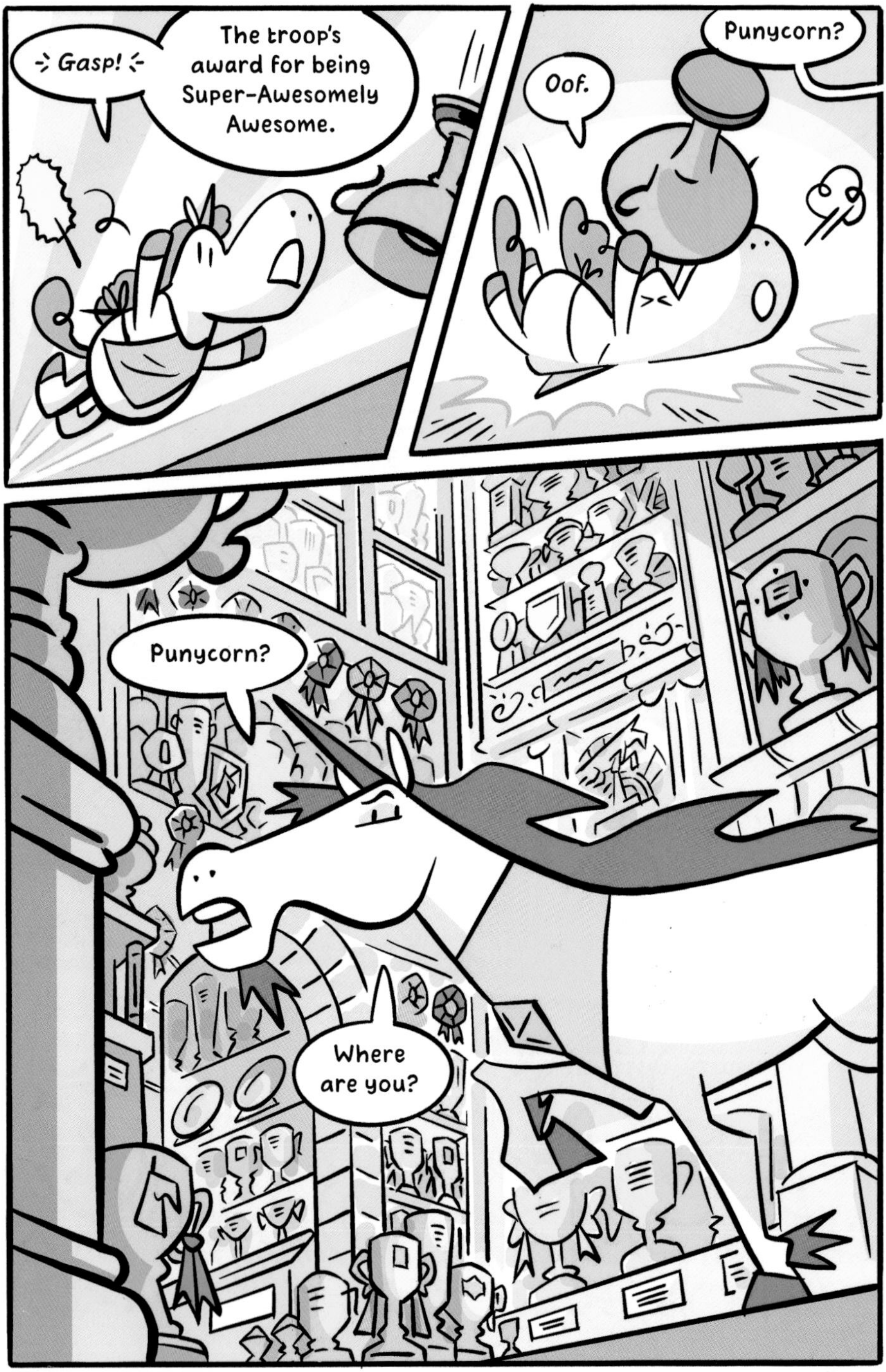

Gasp!
The troop's award for being Super-Awesomely Awesome.
Oof.
Punycorn?
Punycorn?
Where are you?

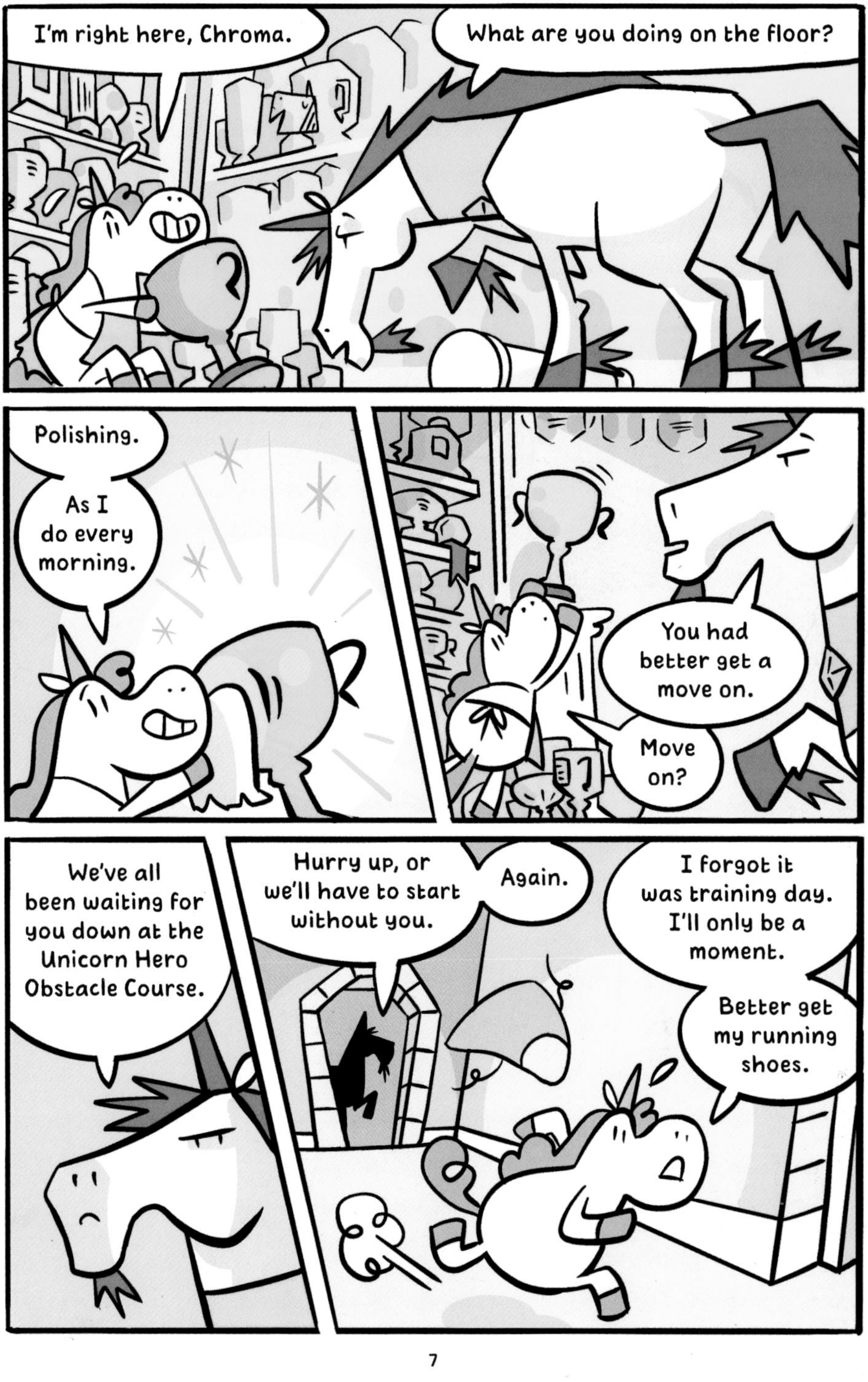

I'm right here, Chroma.
What are you doing on the floor?
Polishing.
As I do every morning.
You had better get a move on.
Move on?
We've all been waiting for you down at the Unicorn Hero Obstacle Course.
Hurry up, or we'll have to start without you.
Again.
I forgot it was training day. I'll only be a moment.
Better get my running shoes.

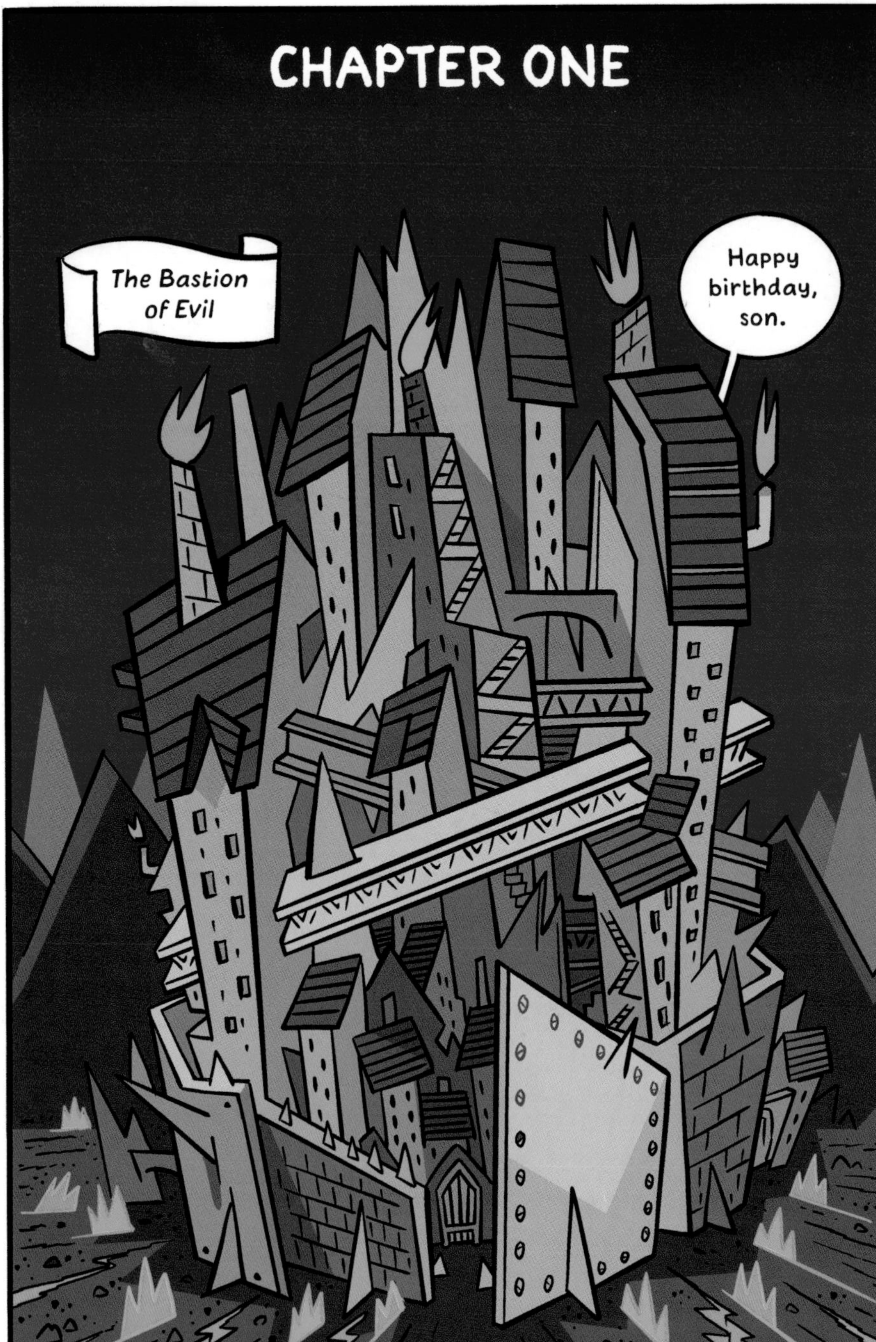
CHAPTER ONE
The Bastion of Evil
Happy birthday, son.

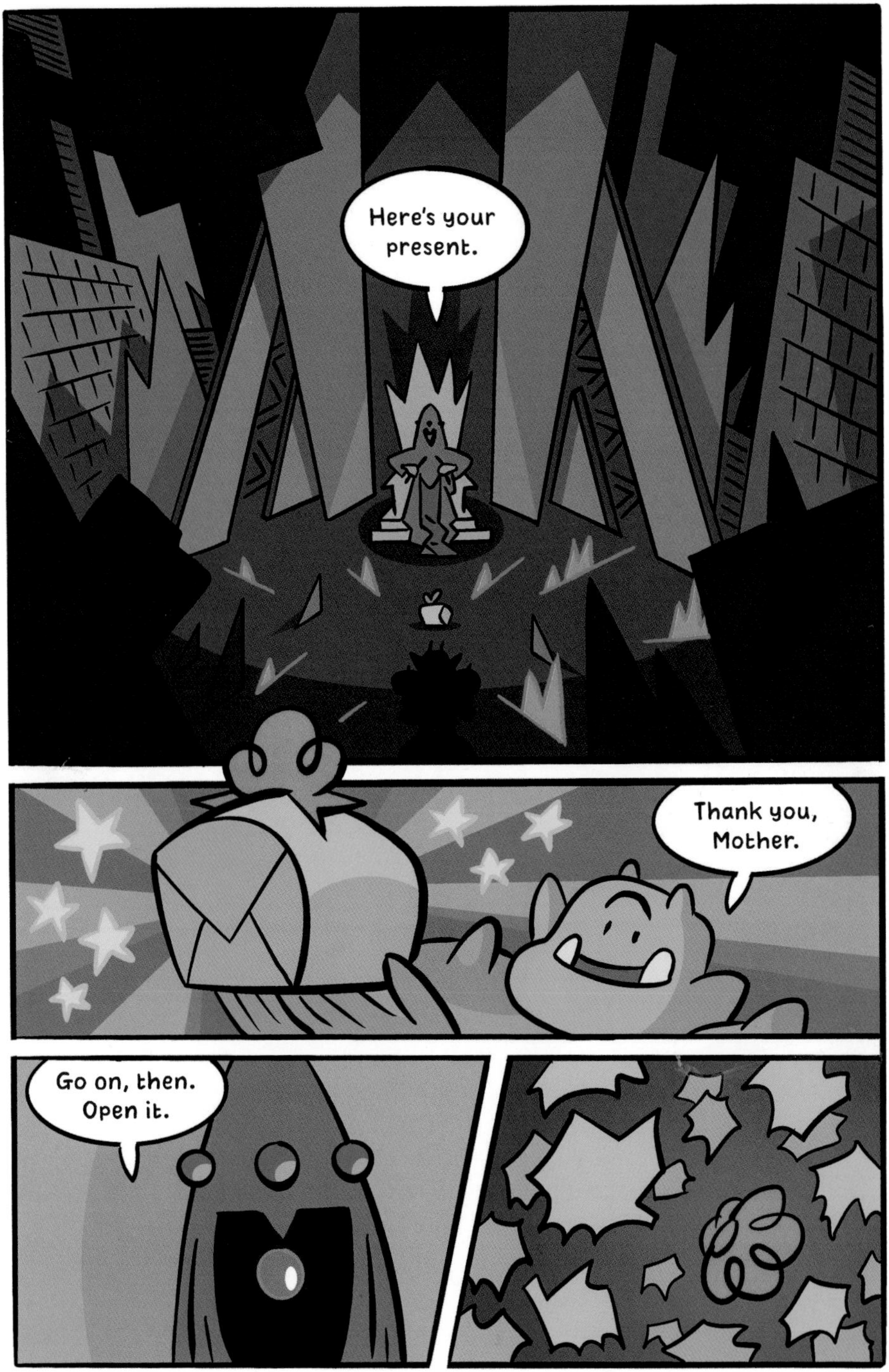
Here's your present.
Thank you, Mother.
Go on, then. Open it.

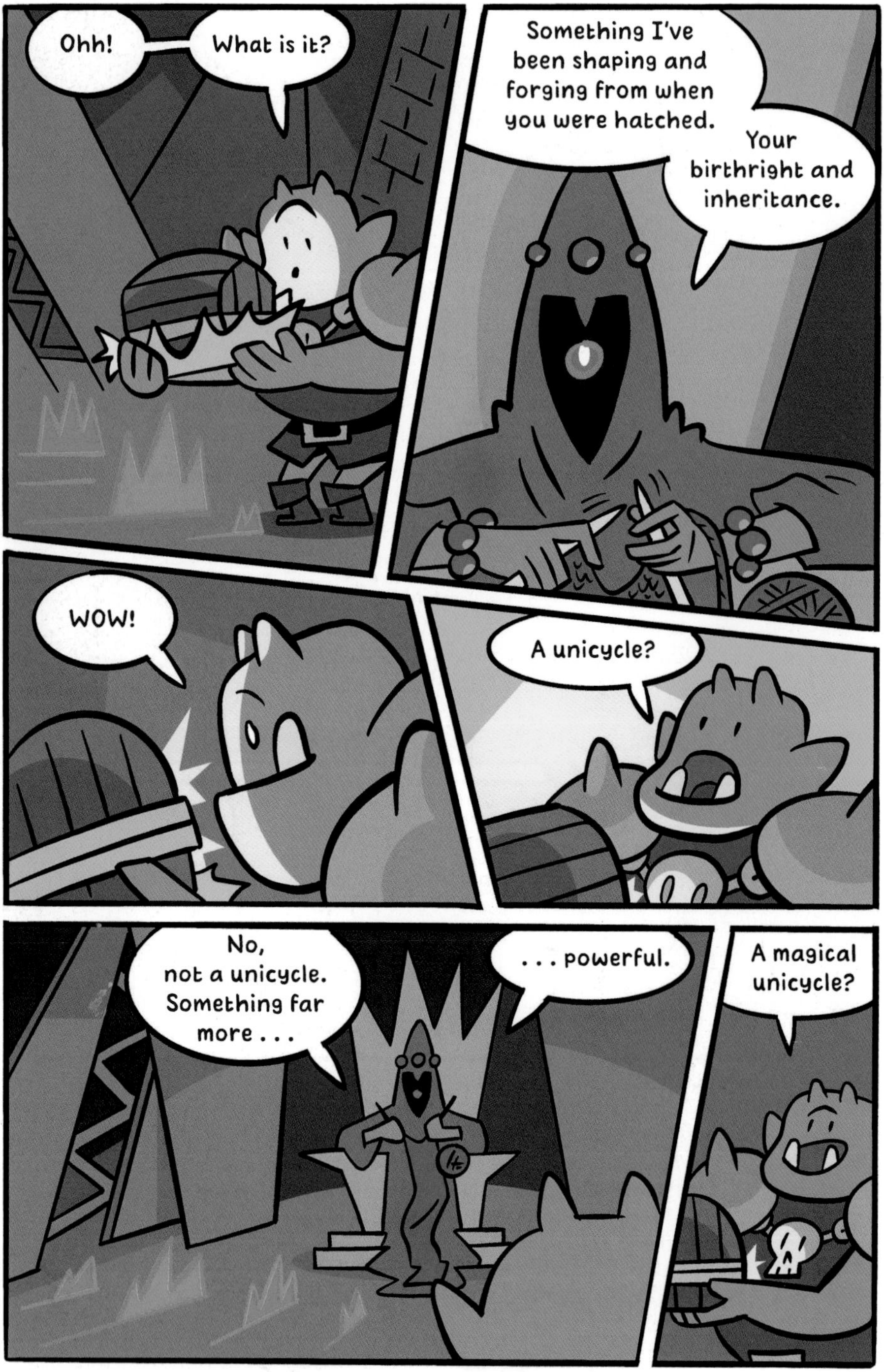
Ohh!
What is it?
Something I've been shaping and forging from when you were hatched.
Your birthright and inheritance.
WOW!
A unicycle?
No, not a unicycle. Something far more . . .
. . . powerful.
A magical unicycle?

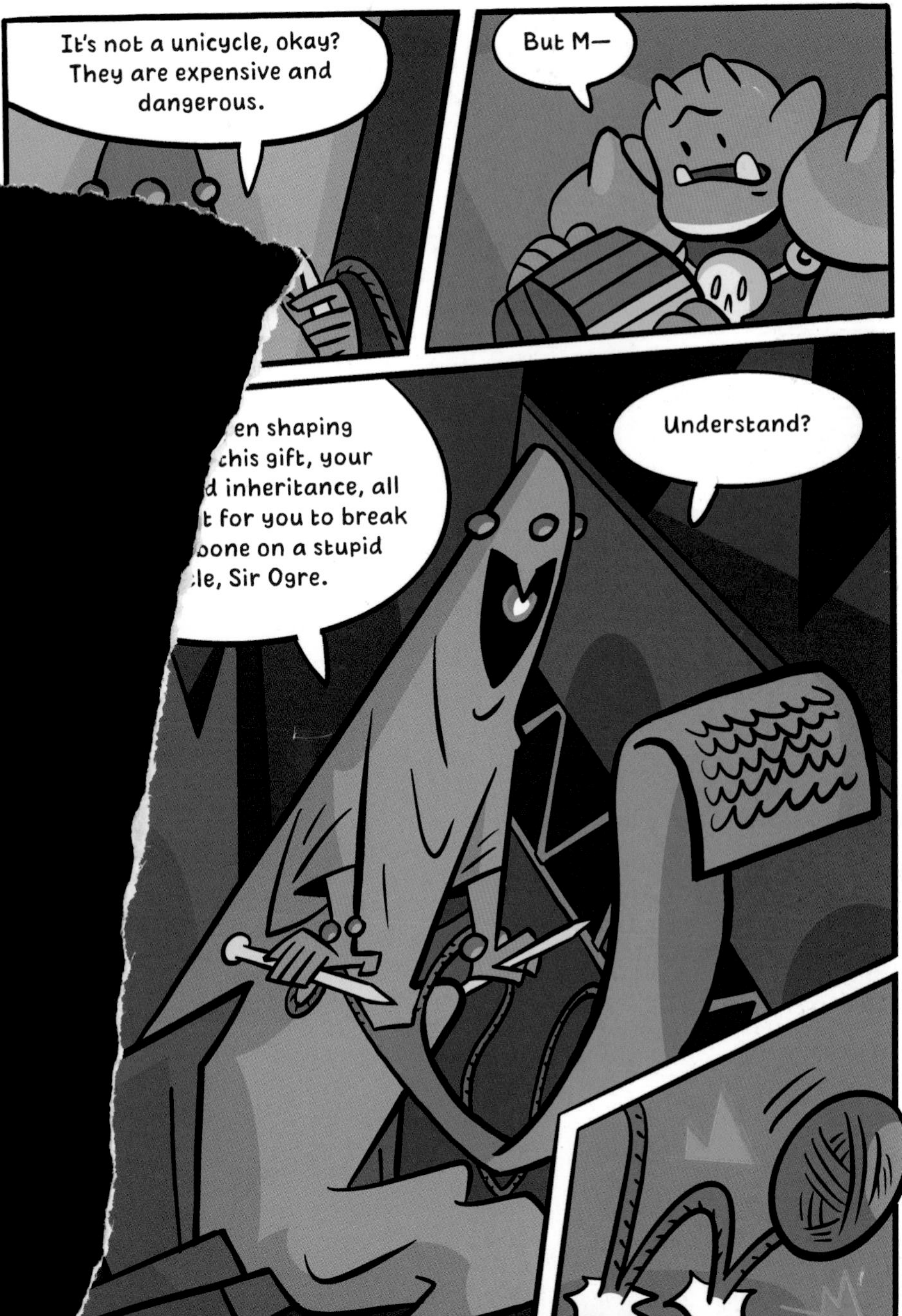
It's not a unicycle, okay? They are expensive and dangerous.
But M—
en shaping
chis gift, your
d inheritance, all
t for you to break
oone on a stupid
cle, Sir Ogre.
Understand?

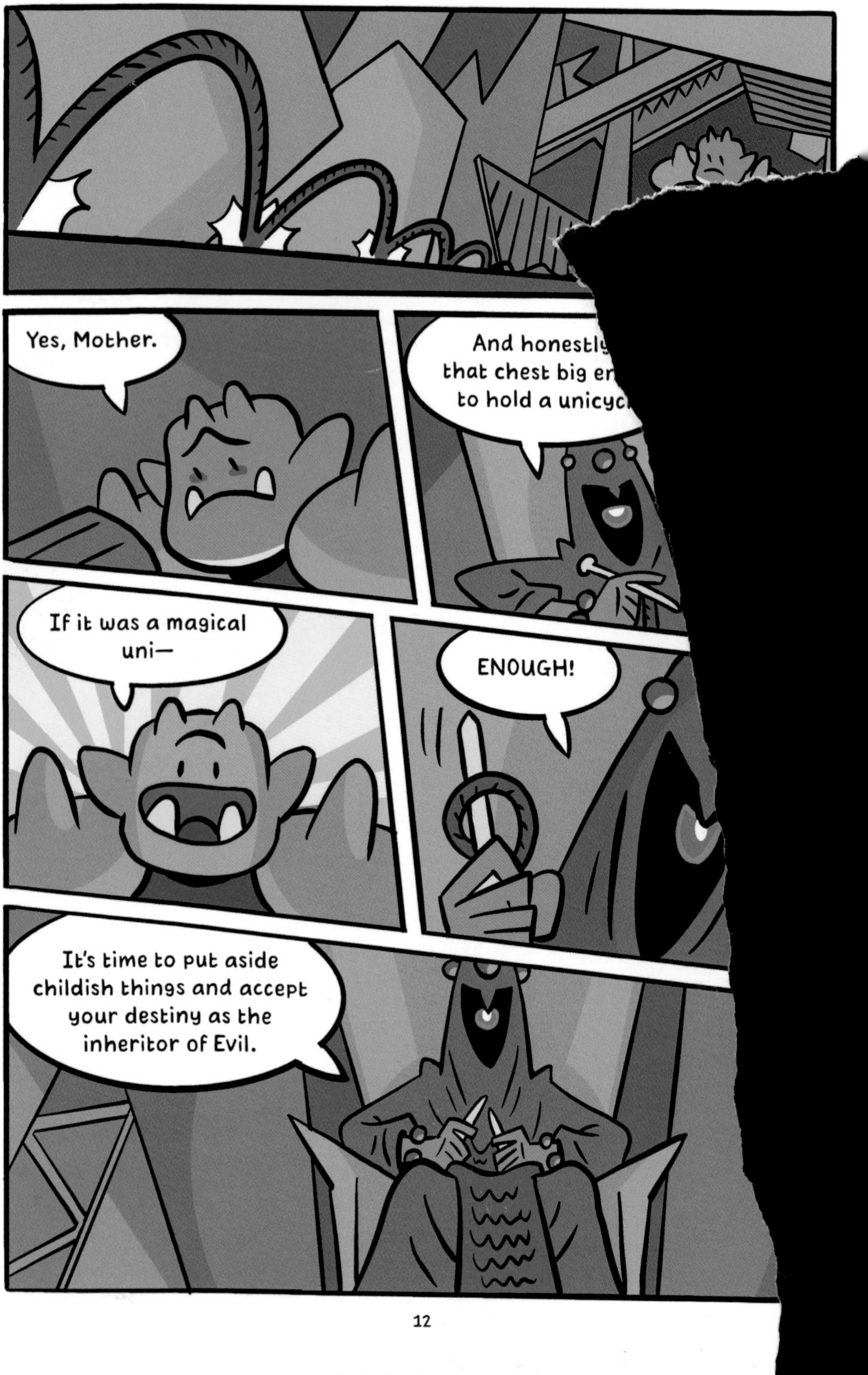
Yes, Mother.
And honestly
that chest big en
to hold a unicyc
If it was a magical
uni—
ENOUGH!
It's time to put aside
childish things and accept
your destiny as the
inheritor of Evil.

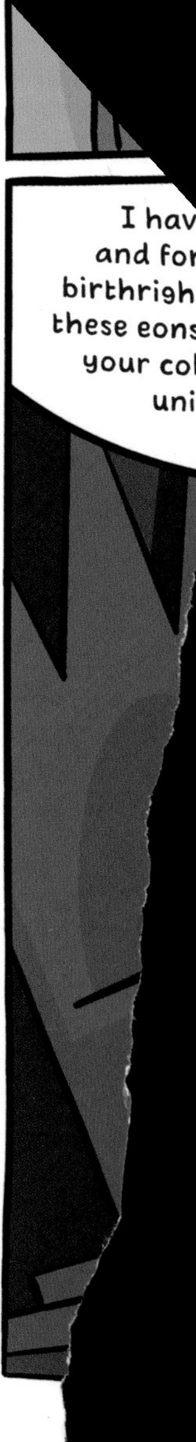
I hav
and for
birthrigh
these eons
your col
uni

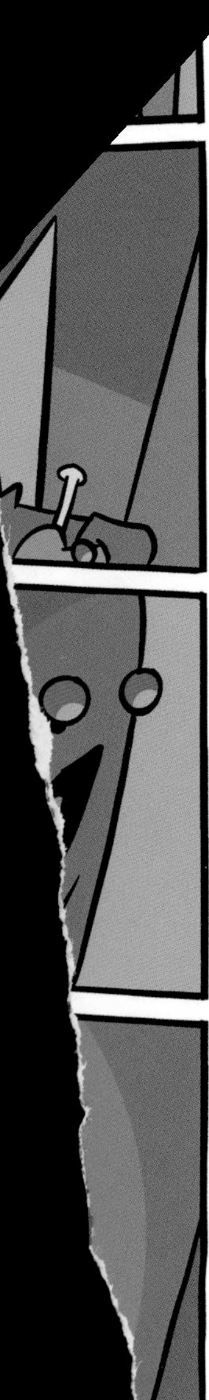

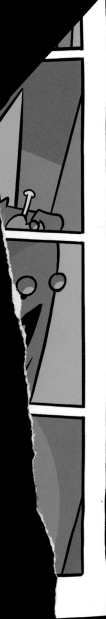

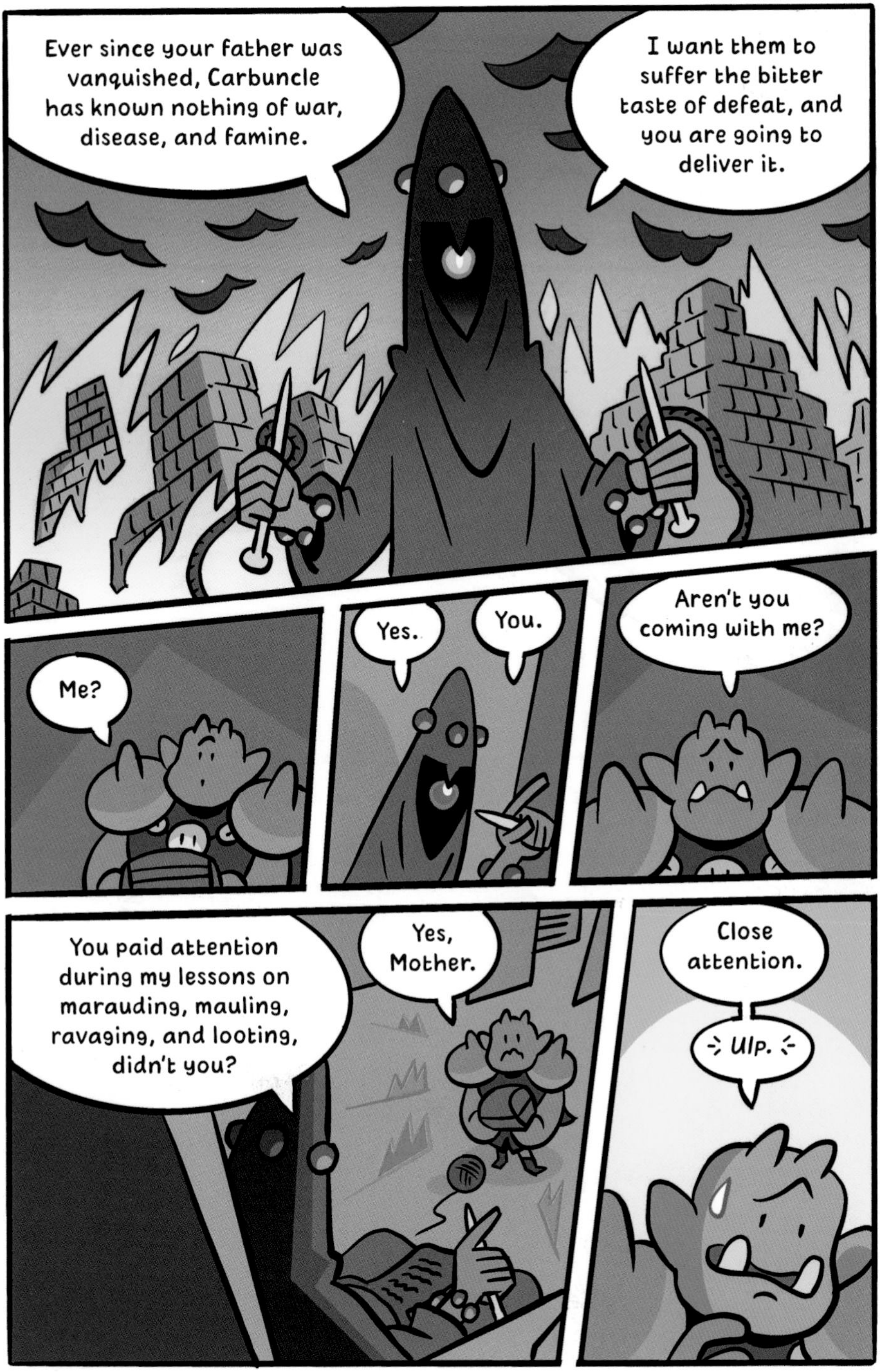
Ever since your father was vanquished, Carbuncle has known nothing of war, disease, and famine.
I want them to suffer the bitter taste of defeat, and you are going to deliver it.
Me?
Yes.
You.
Aren't you coming with me?
You paid attention during my lessons on marauding, mauling, ravaging, and looting, didn't you?
Yes, Mother.
Close attention.
Ulp.

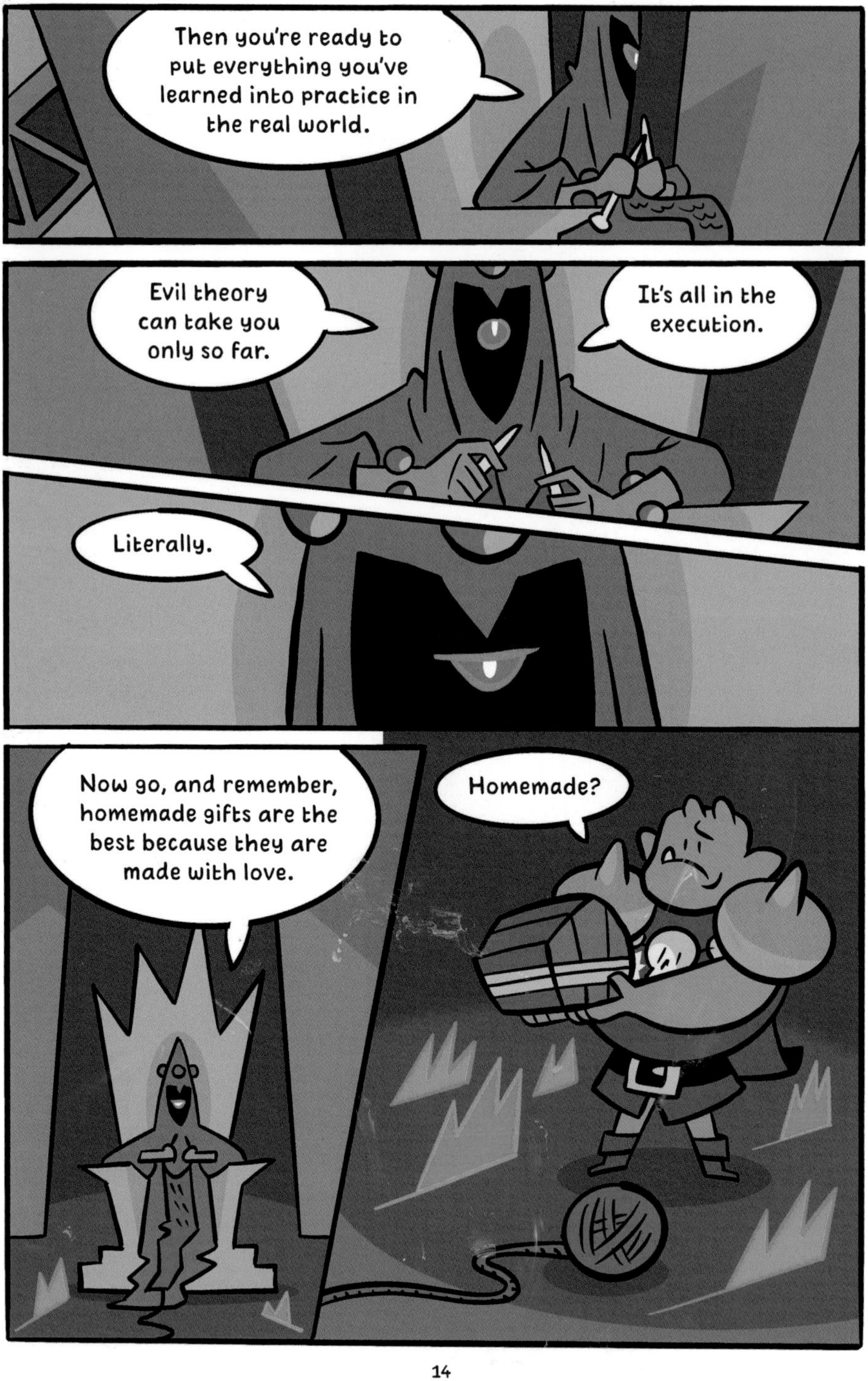
Then you're ready to put everything you've learned into practice in the real world.
Evil theory can take you only so far.
It's all in the execution.
Literally.
Now go, and remember, homemade gifts are the best because they are made with love.
Homemade?

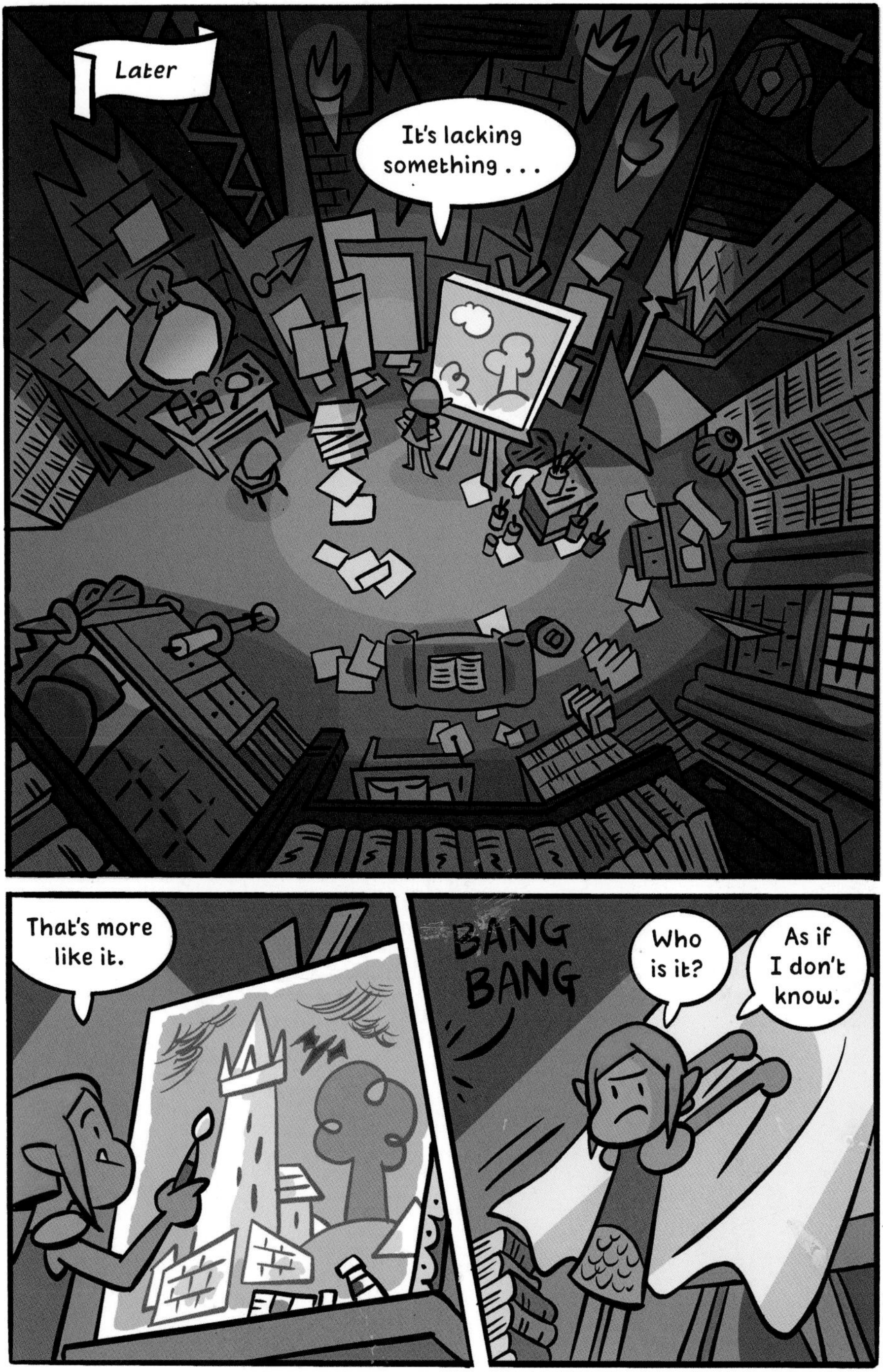
Later
It's lacking something . . .
That's more like it.
BANG BANG
Who is it?
As if I don't know.

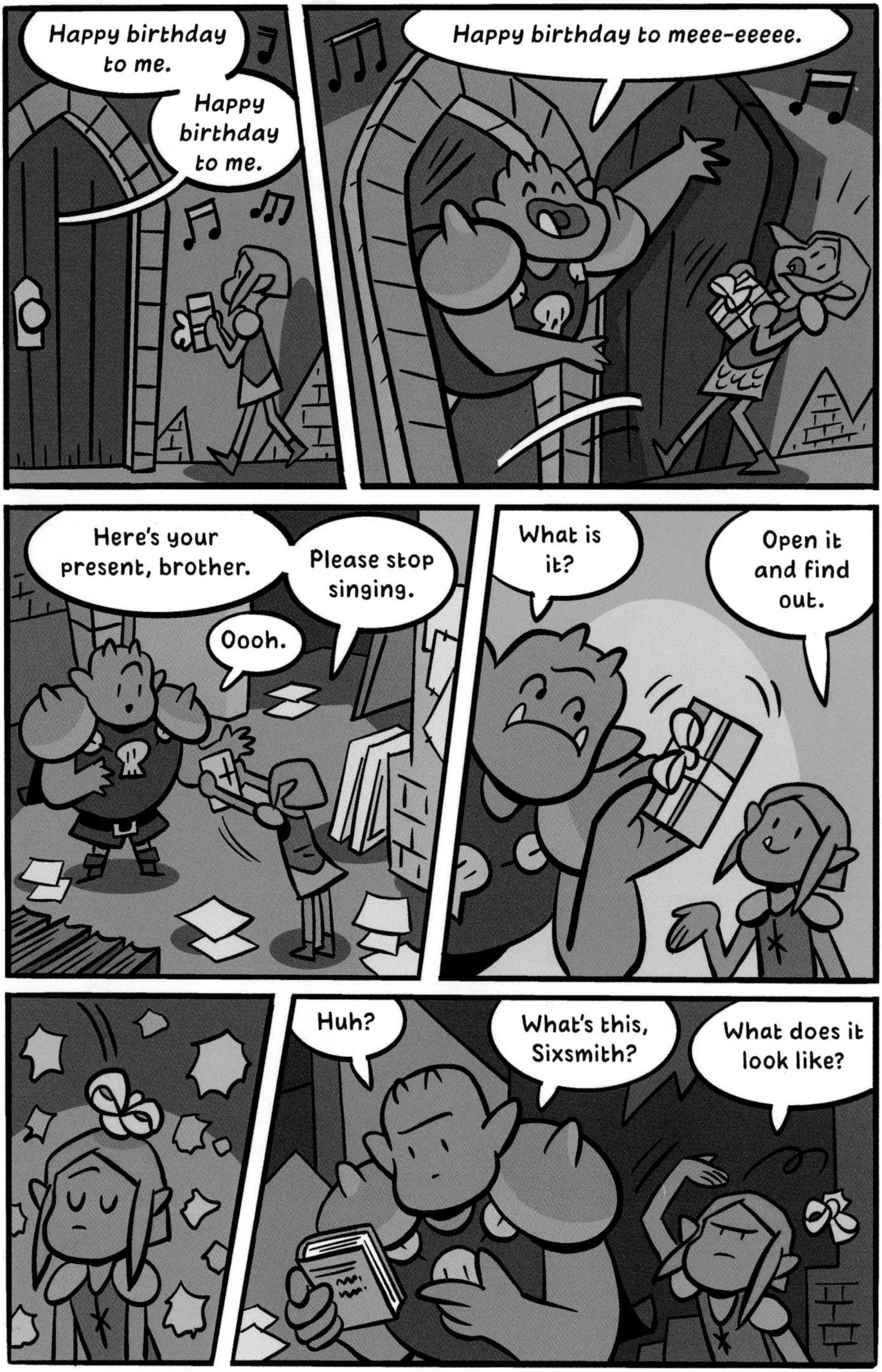
Happy birthday to me.
Happy birthday to me.
Happy birthday to meee-eeeee.
Here's your present, brother.
Oooh.
Please stop singing.
What is it?
Open it and find out.
Huh?
What's this, Sixsmith?
What does it look like?

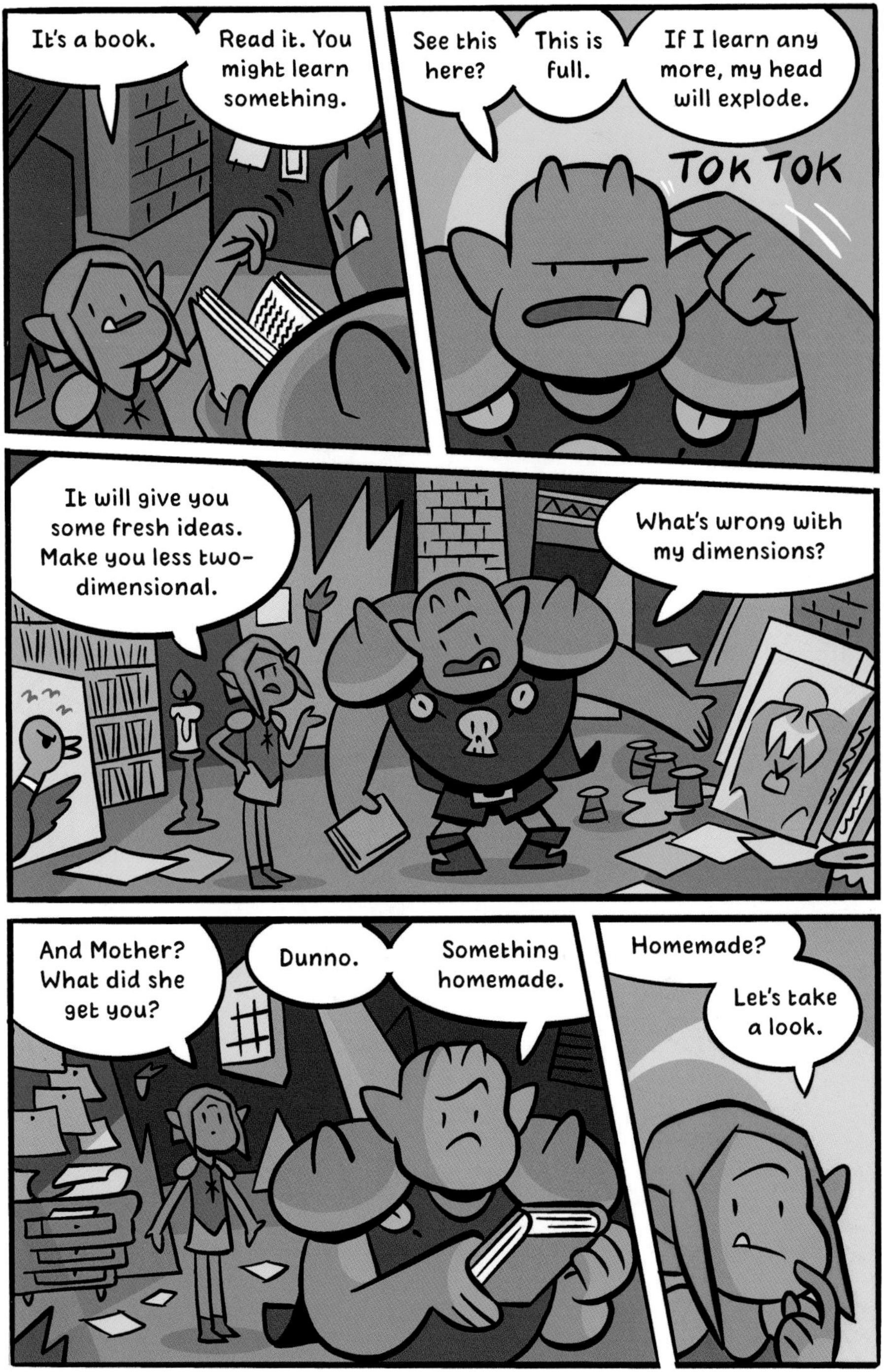
It's a book.
Read it. You might learn something.
See this here?
This is full.
If I learn any more, my head will explode.
TOK TOK
It will give you some fresh ideas. Make you less two-dimensional.
What's wrong with my dimensions?
And Mother? What did she get you?
Dunno.
Something homemade.
Homemade?
Let's take a look.

CHAPTER TWO

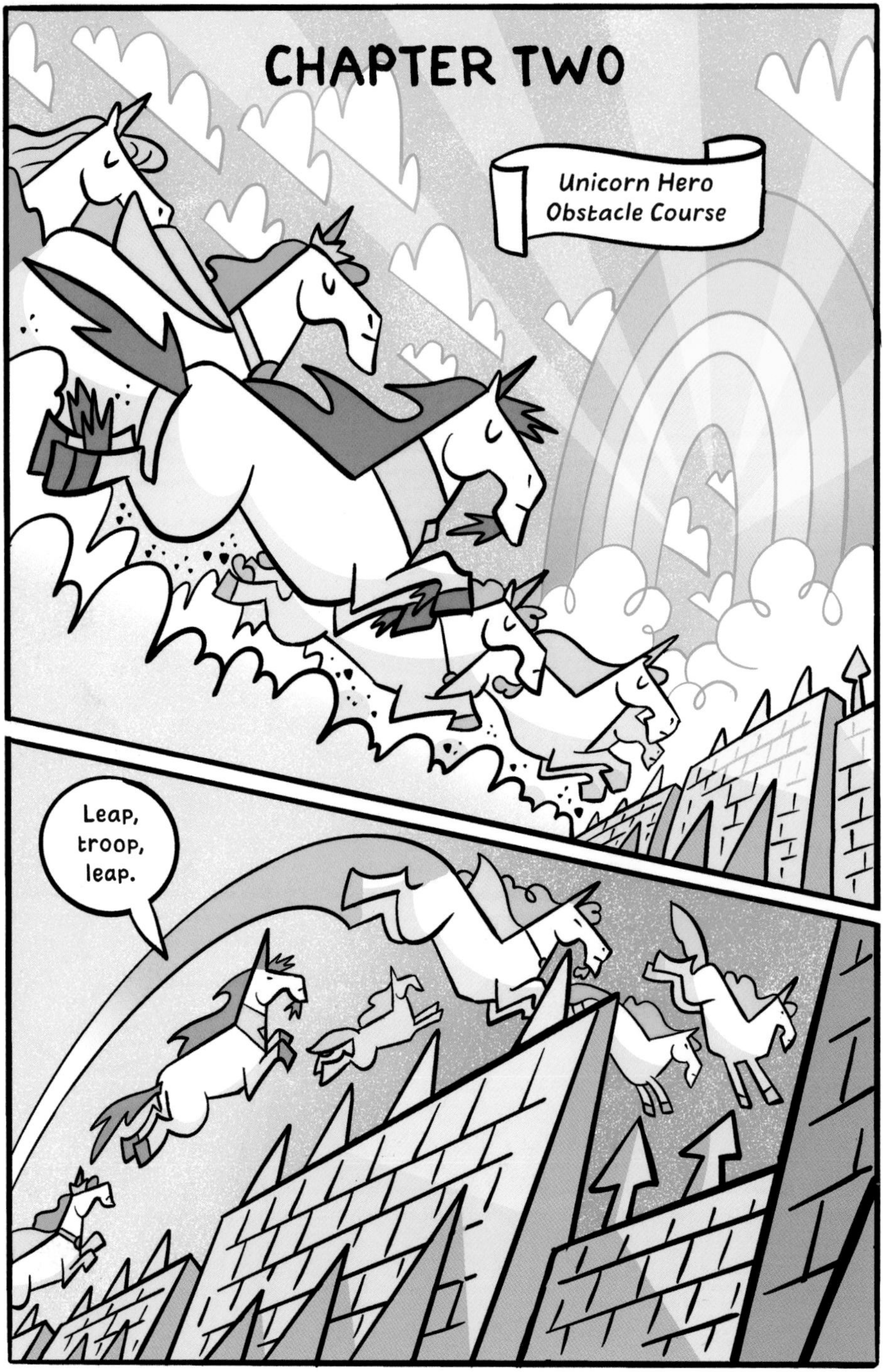
Unicorn Hero Obstacle Course
Leap, troop, leap.

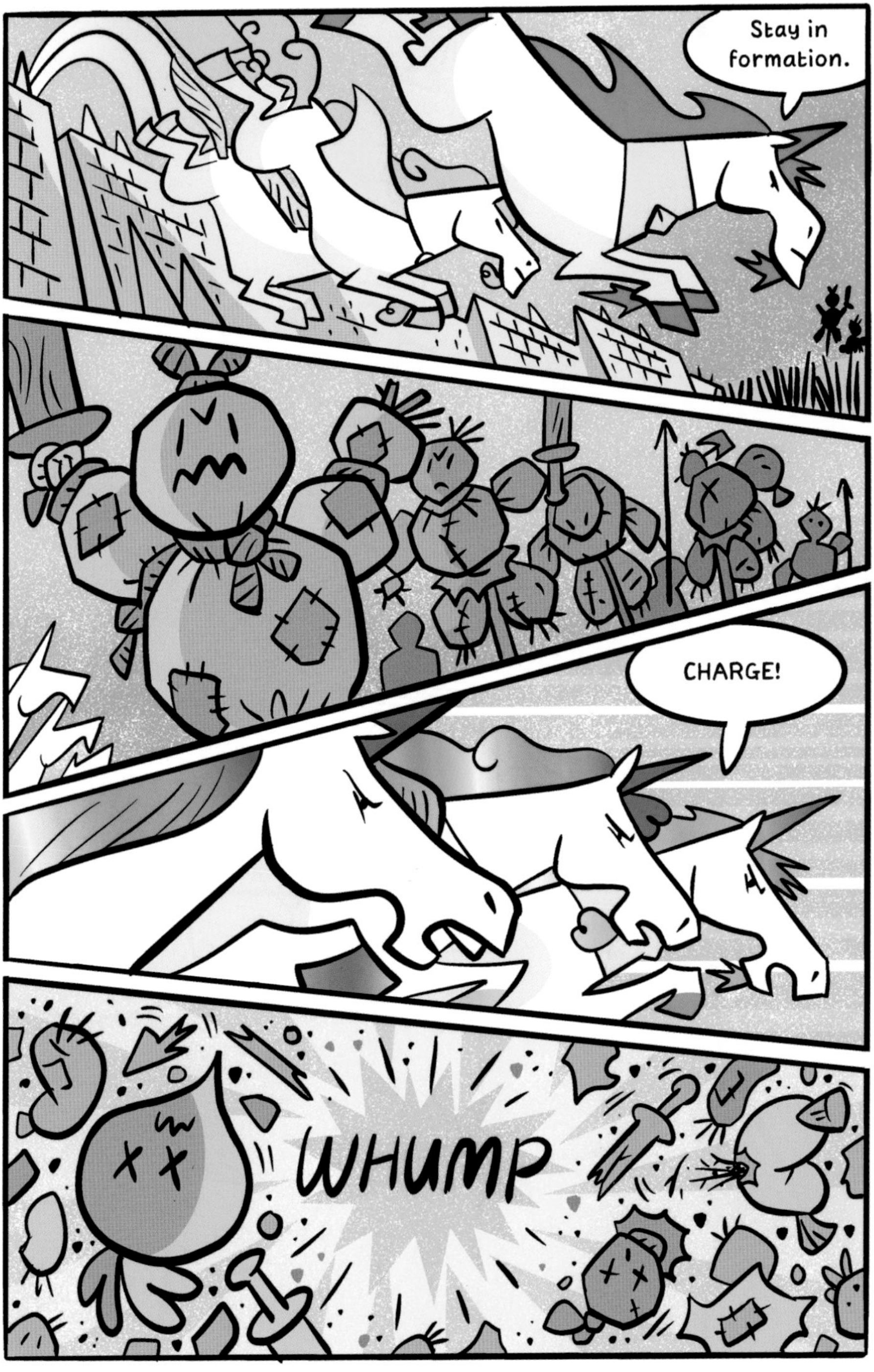
Stay in formation.
CHARGE!
WHUMP

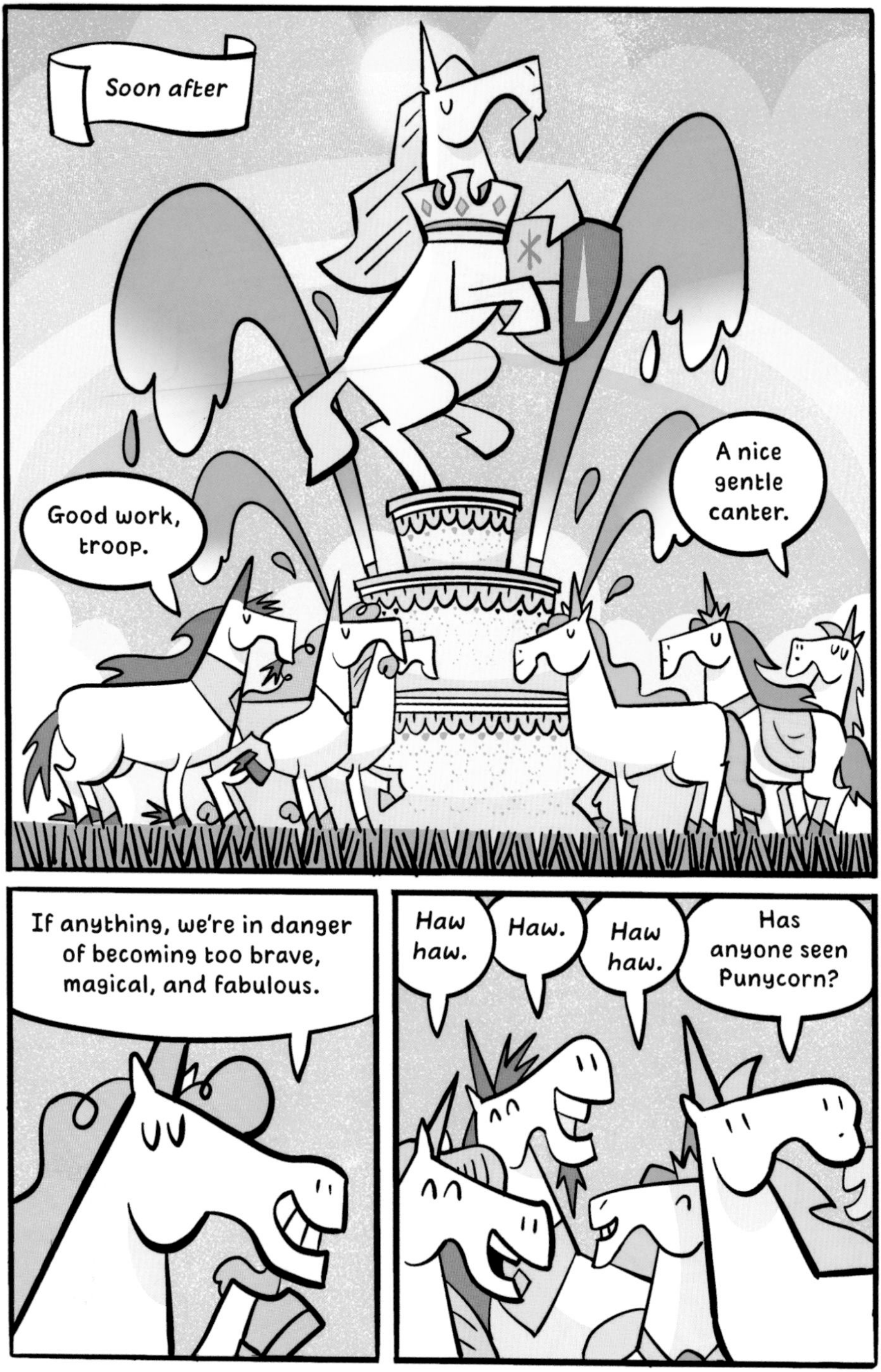
Soon after
Good work, troop.
A nice gentle canter.
If anything, we're in danger of becoming too brave, magical, and fabulous.
Haw haw.
Haw.
Haw haw.
Has anyone seen Punycorn?

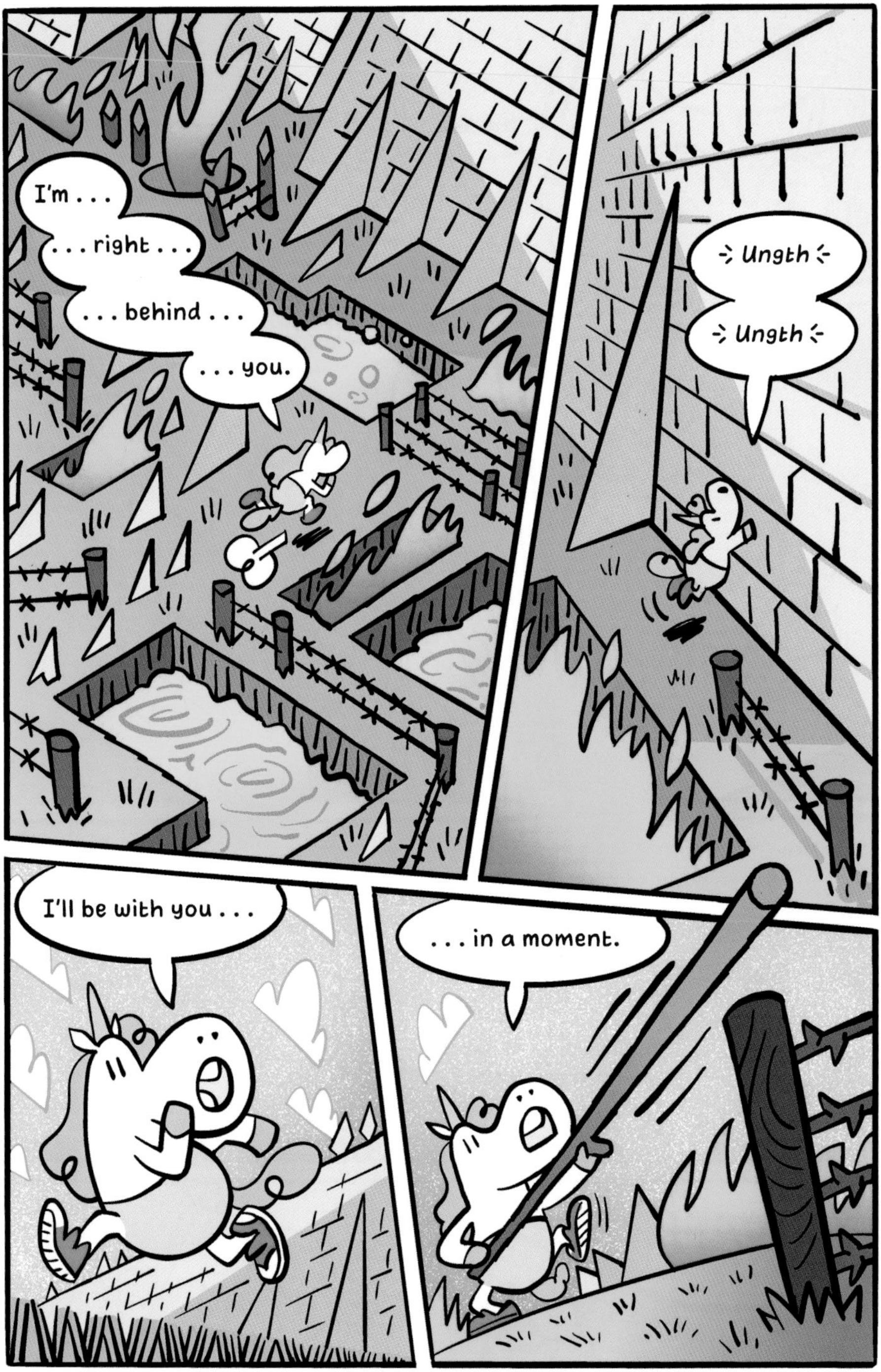
I'm . . .
. . . right . . .
. . . behind . . .
. . . you.
Ungth
Ungth
I'll be with you . . .
. . . in a moment.

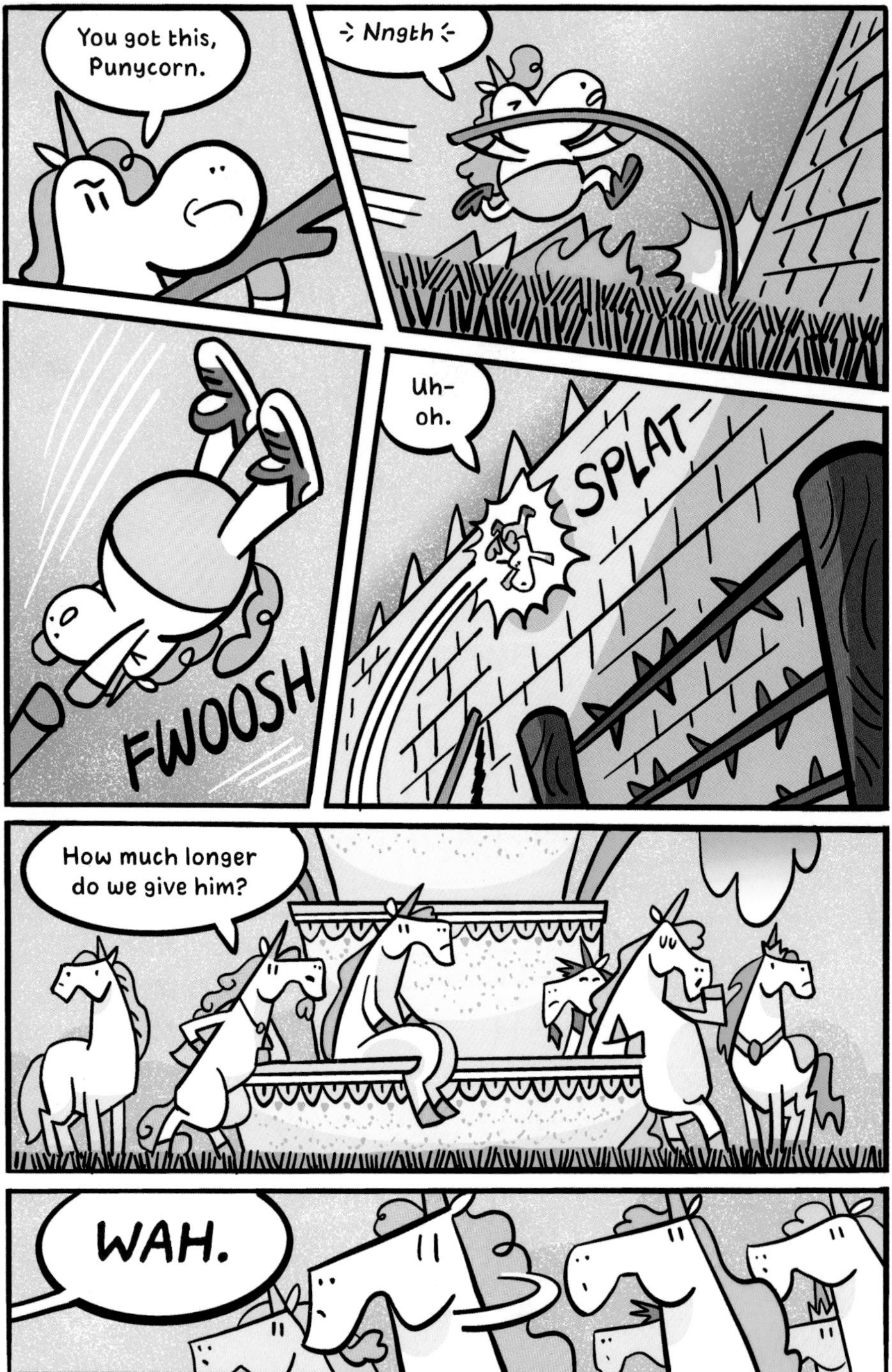
You got this, Punycorn.
Nngth
FWOOSH
Uh-oh.
SPLAT
How much longer do we give him?
WAH.

CHAPTER THREE

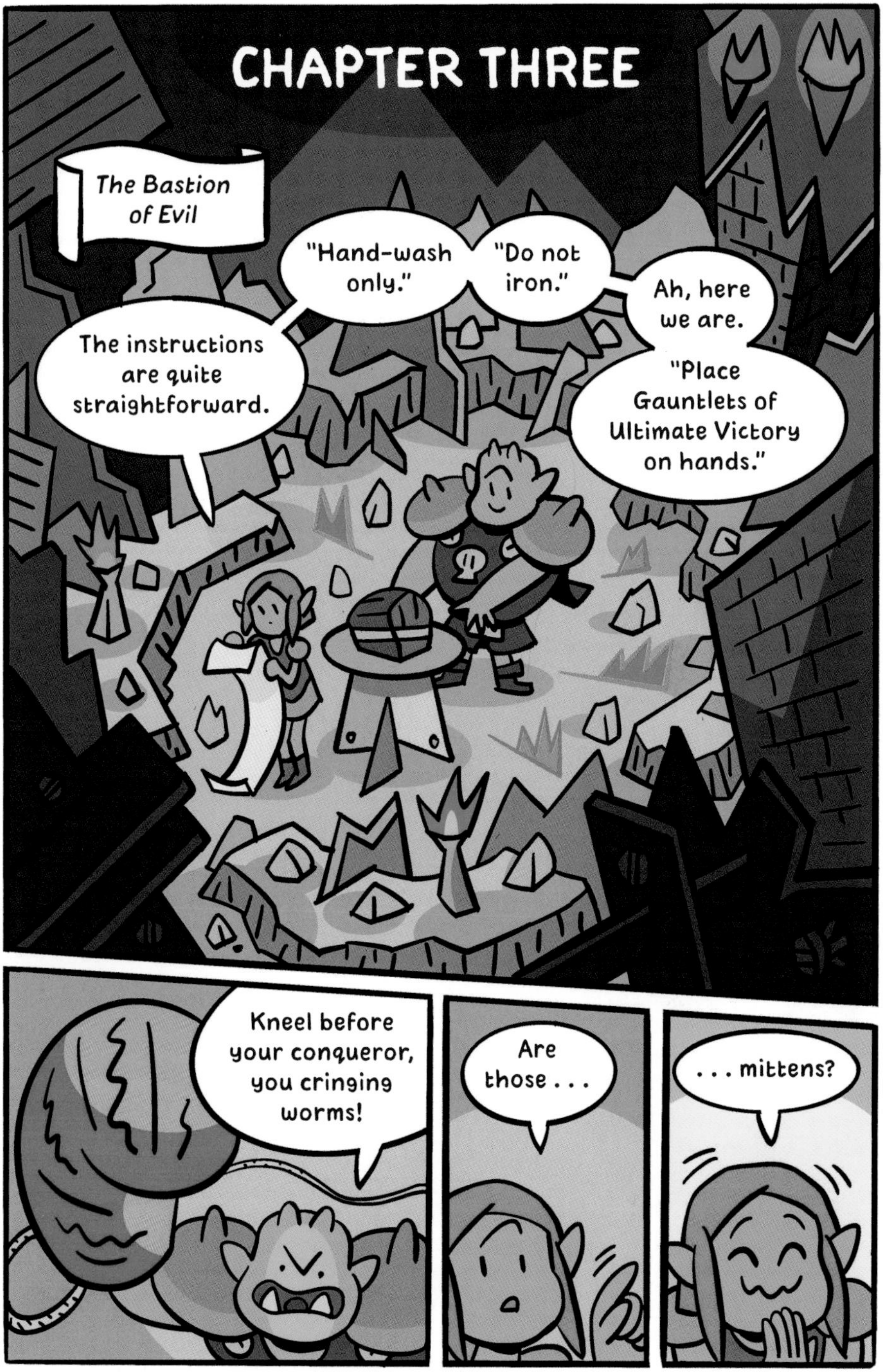
The Bastion of Evil
The instructions are quite straightforward.
"Hand-wash only."
"Do not iron."
Ah, here we are.
"Place Gauntlets of Ultimate Victory on hands."
Kneel before your conqueror, you cringing worms!
Are those . . .
. . . mittens?

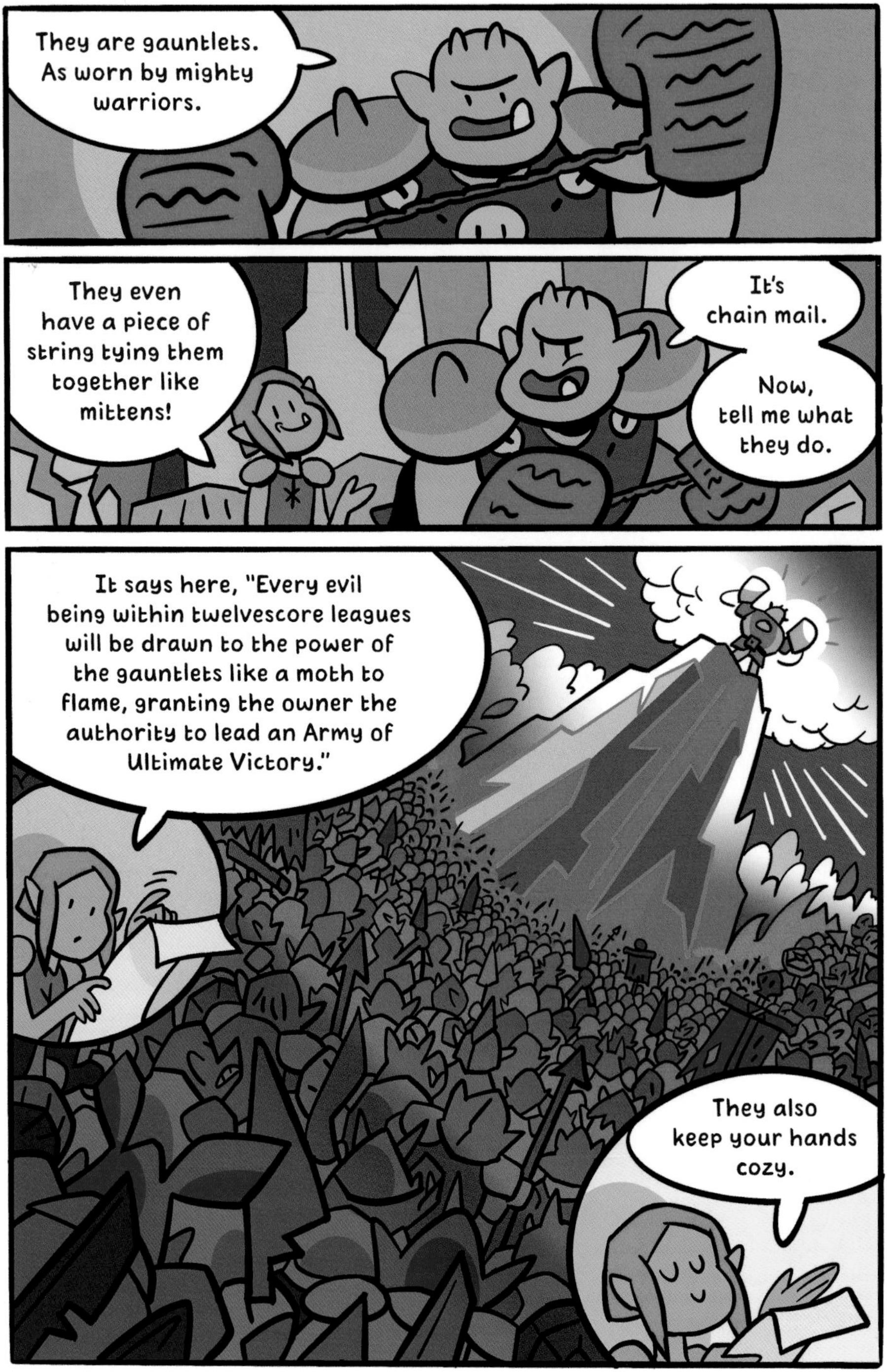
They are gauntlets. As worn by mighty warriors.
They even have a piece of string tying them together like mittens!
It's chain mail.
Now, tell me what they do.
It says here, "Every evil being within twelvescore leagues will be drawn to the power of the gauntlets like a moth to flame, granting the owner the authority to lead an Army of Ultimate Victory."
They also keep your hands cozy.

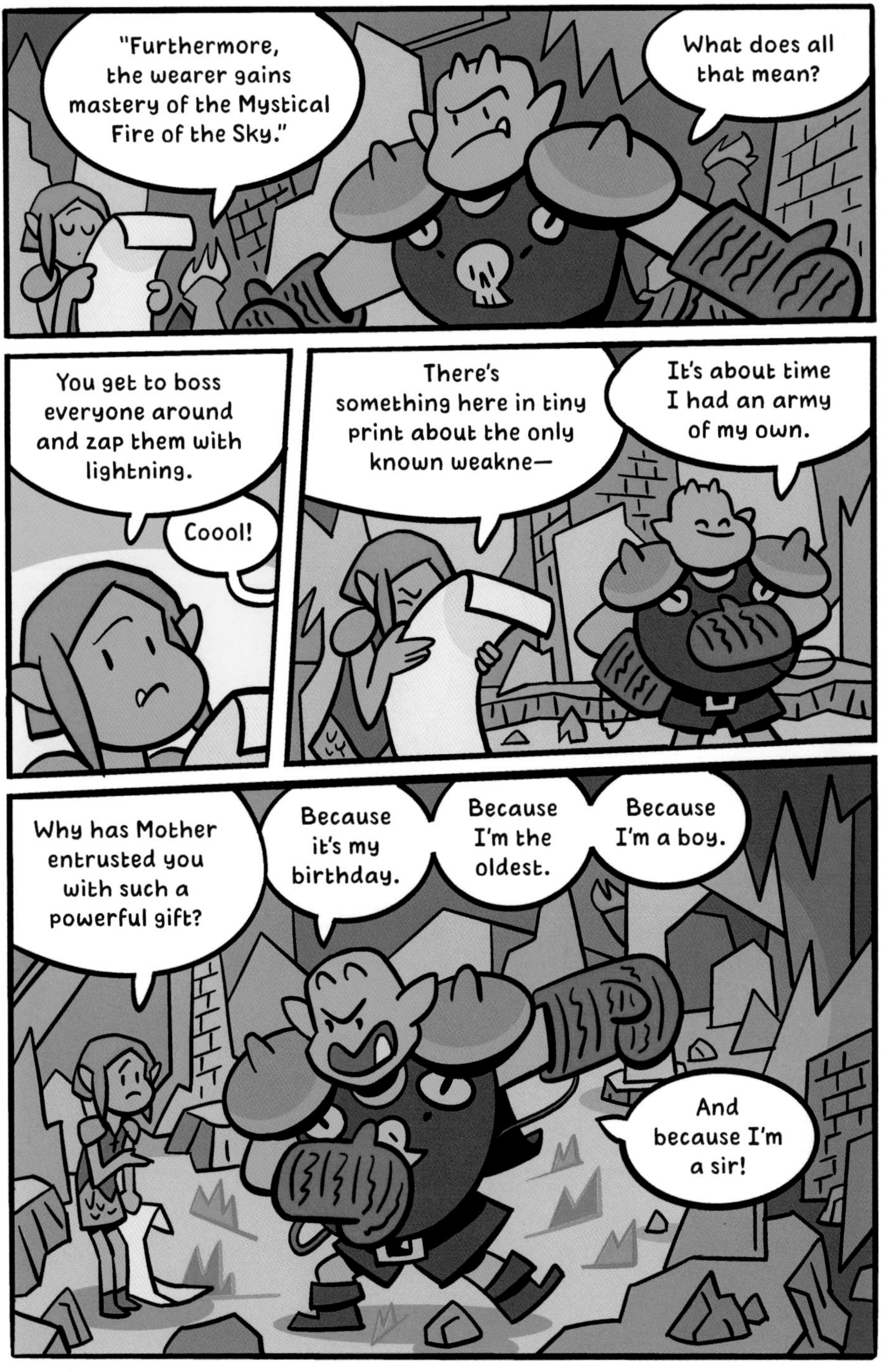
"Furthermore, the wearer gains mastery of the Mystical Fire of the Sky."
What does all that mean?
You get to boss everyone around and zap them with lightning.
Coool!
There's something here in tiny print about the only known weakne—
It's about time I had an army of my own.
Why has Mother entrusted you with such a powerful gift?
Because it's my birthday.
Because I'm the oldest.
Because I'm a boy.
And because I'm a sir!

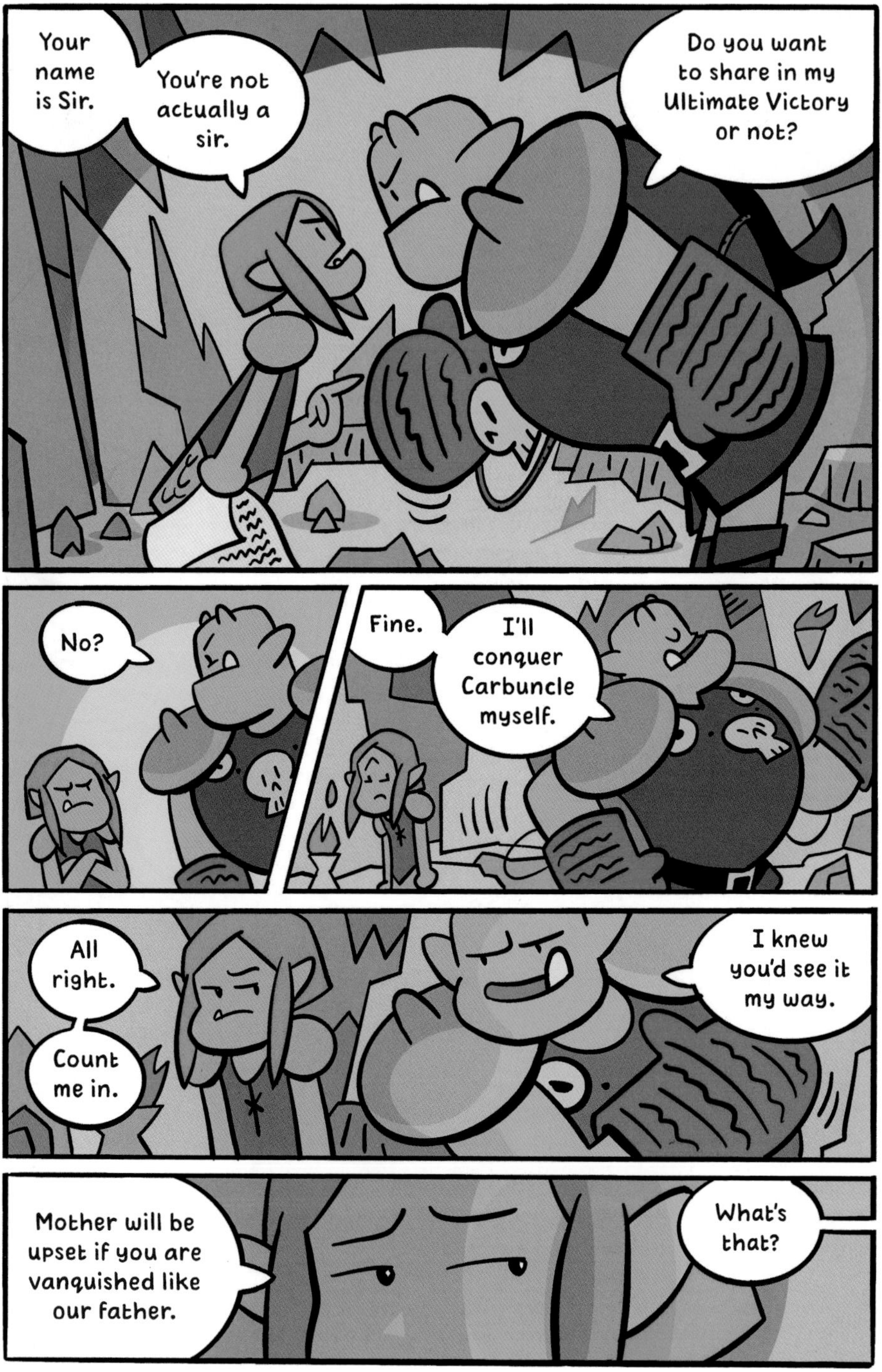
Your name is Sir.
You're not actually a sir.
Do you want to share in my Ultimate Victory or not?
No?
Fine.
I'll conquer Carbuncle myself.
All right.
Count me in.
I knew you'd see it my way.
Mother will be upset if you are vanquished like our father.
What's that?

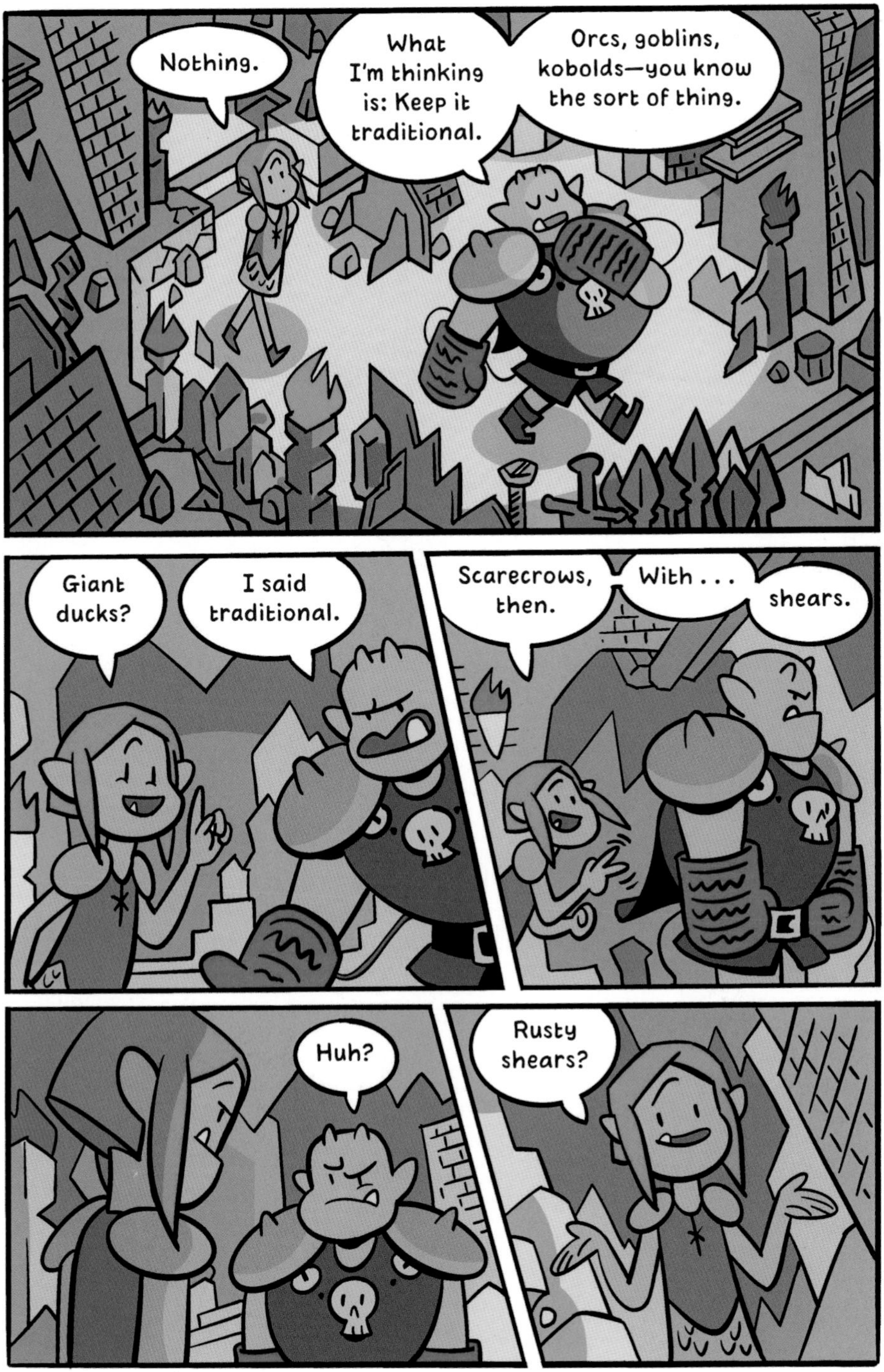
Nothing.
What I'm thinking is: Keep it traditional.
Orcs, goblins, kobolds—you know the sort of thing.
Giant ducks?
I said traditional.
Scarecrows, then.
With . . .
shears.
Huh?
Rusty shears?

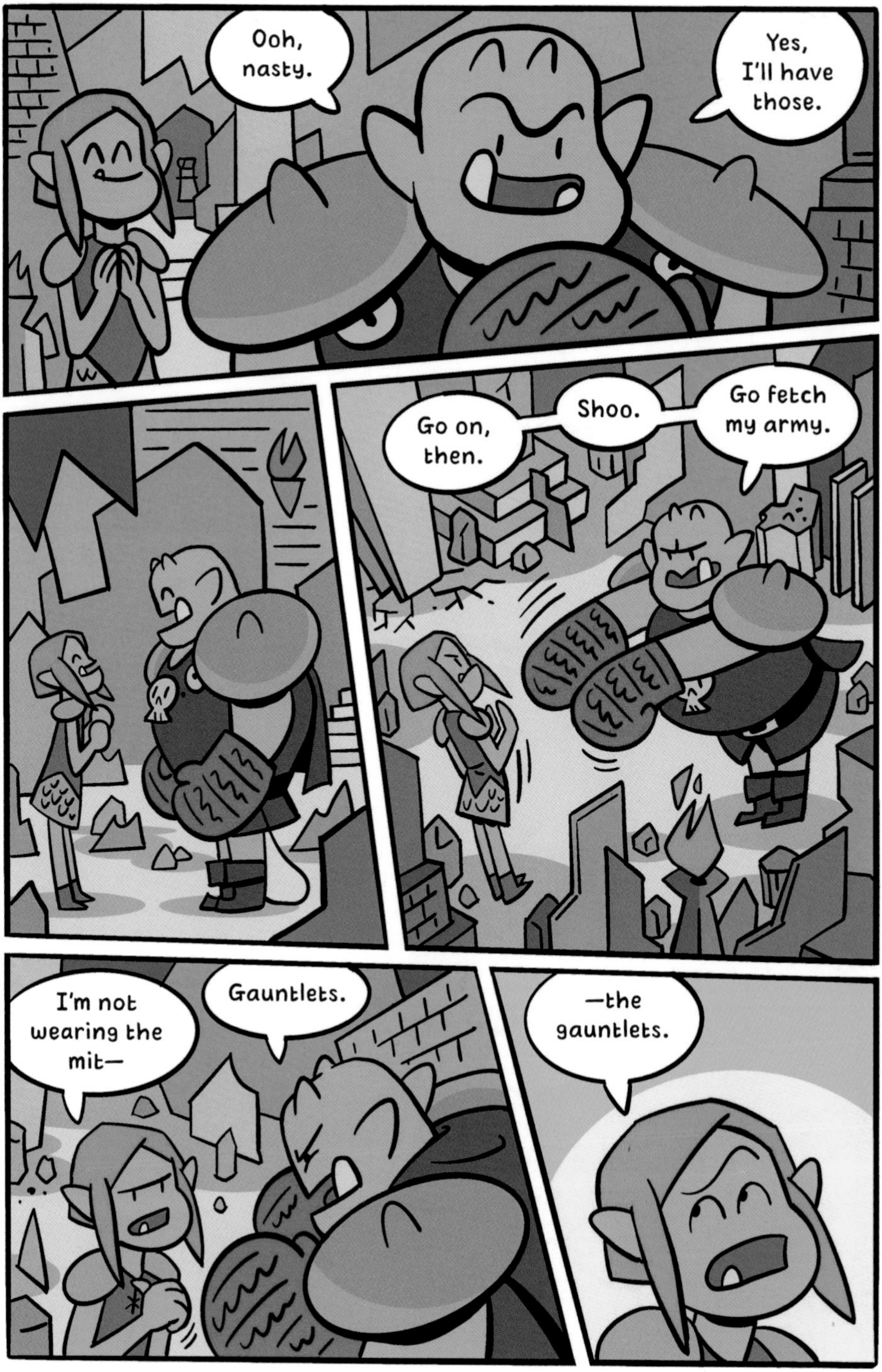
Ooh, nasty.
Yes, I'll have those.
Go on, then.
Shoo.
Go fetch my army.
I'm not wearing the mit—
Gauntlets.
—the gauntlets.

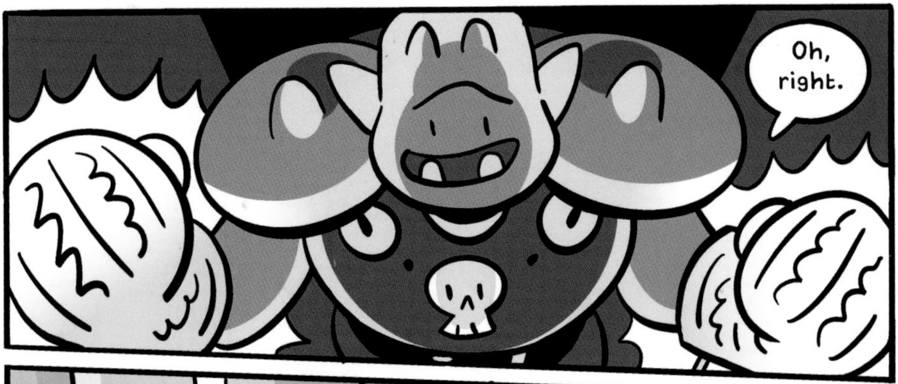
Oh, right.

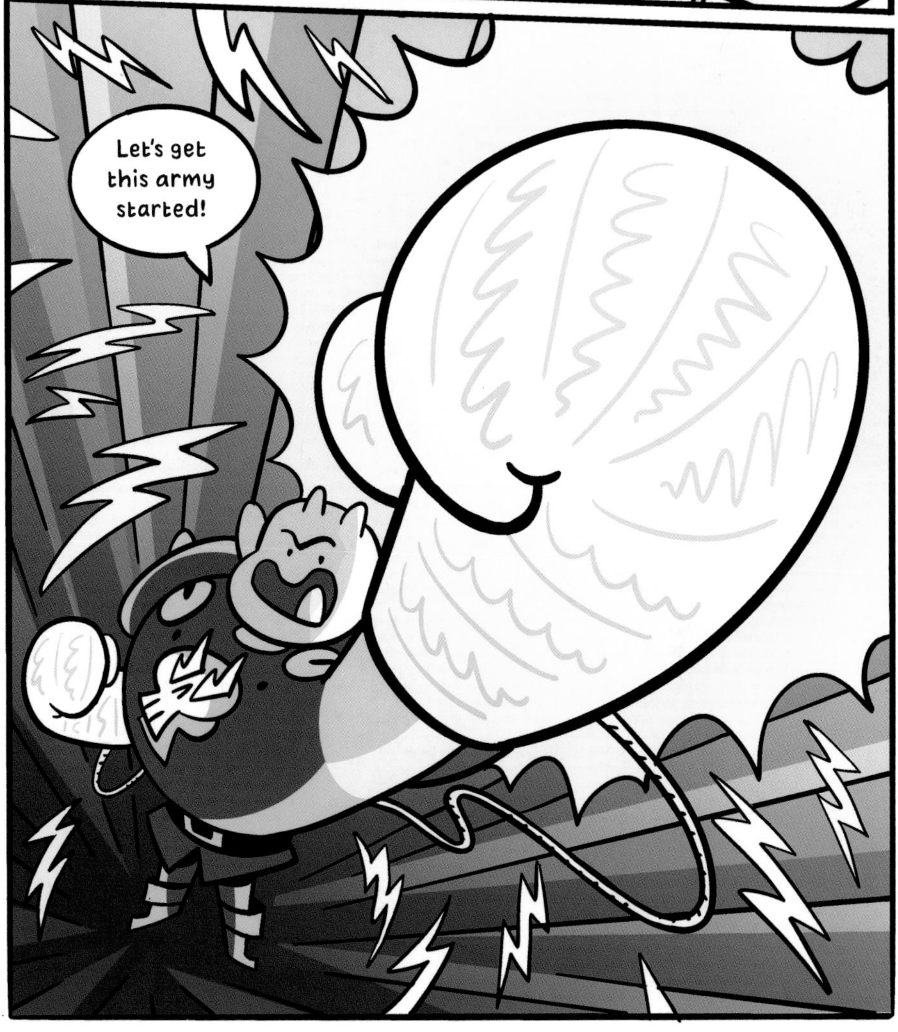
Let's get this army started!

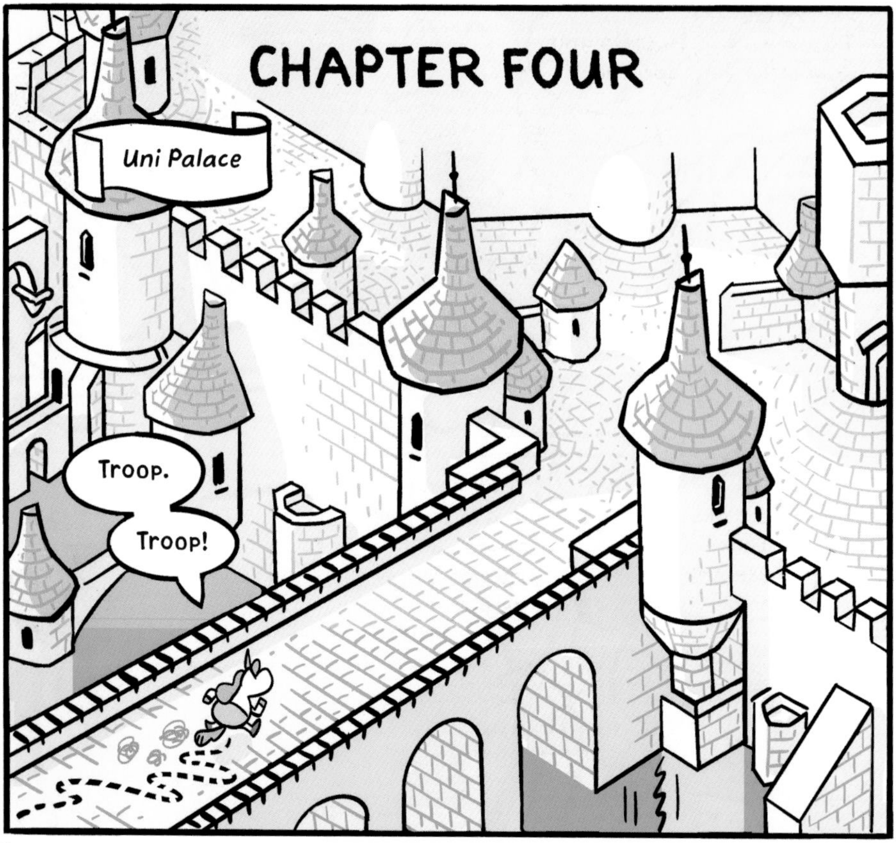
CHAPTER FOUR
Uni Palace
Troop.
Troop!

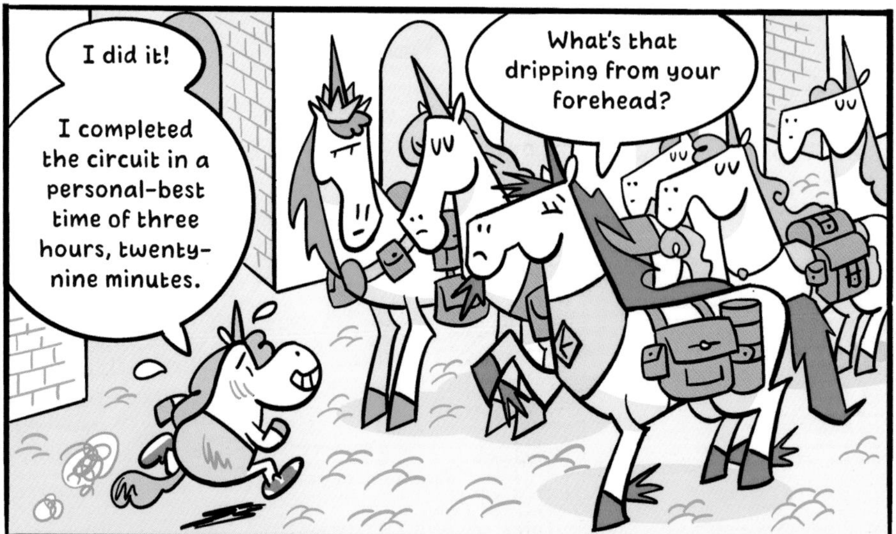
I did it!
I completed the circuit in a personal-best time of three hours, twenty-nine minutes.
What's that dripping from your forehead?

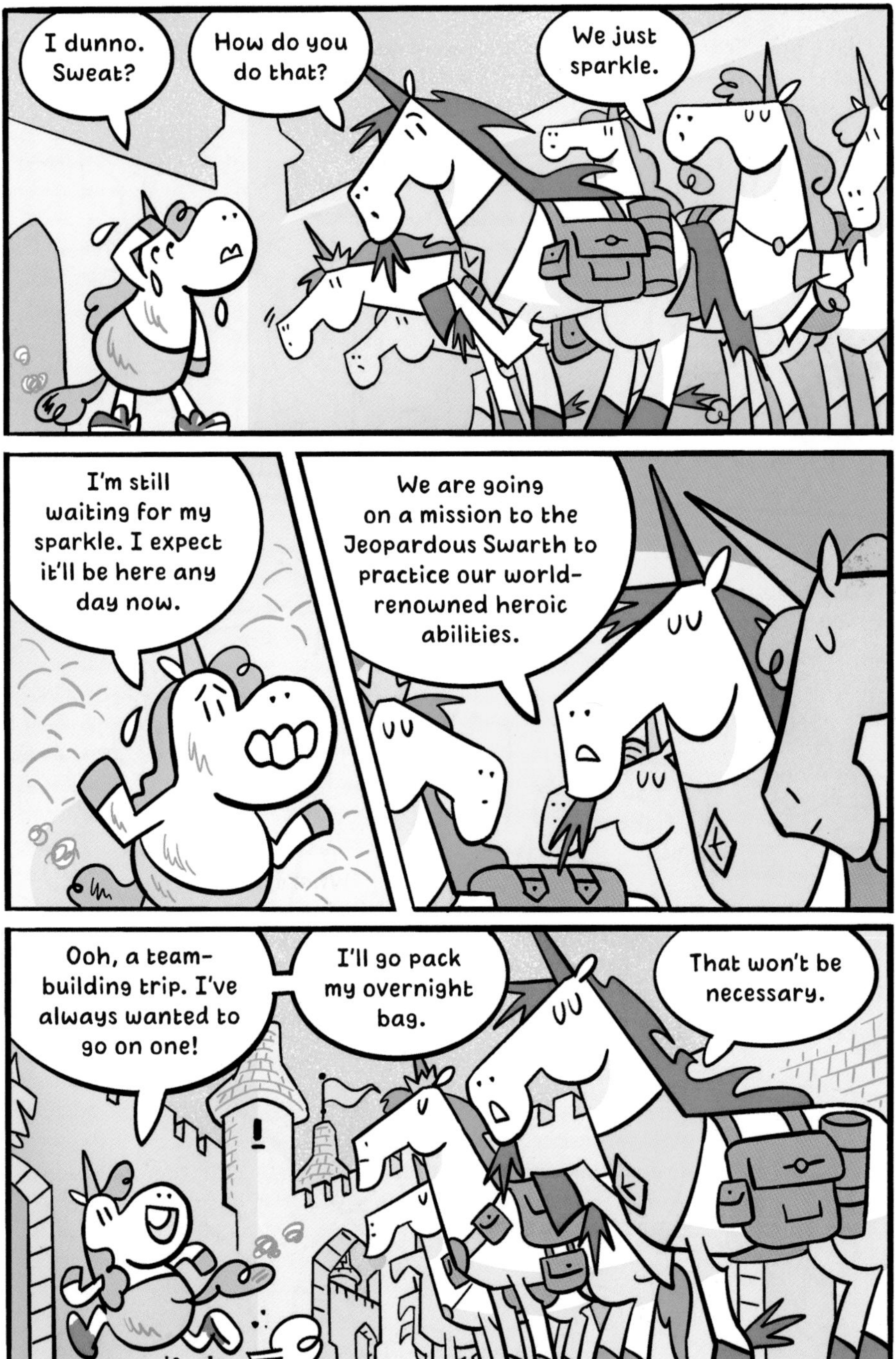
I dunno. Sweat?
How do you do that?
We just sparkle.
I'm still waiting for my sparkle. I expect it'll be here any day now.
We are going on a mission to the Jeopardous Swarth to practice our world-renowned heroic abilities.
Ooh, a team-building trip. I've always wanted to go on one!
I'll go pack my overnight bag.
That won't be necessary.

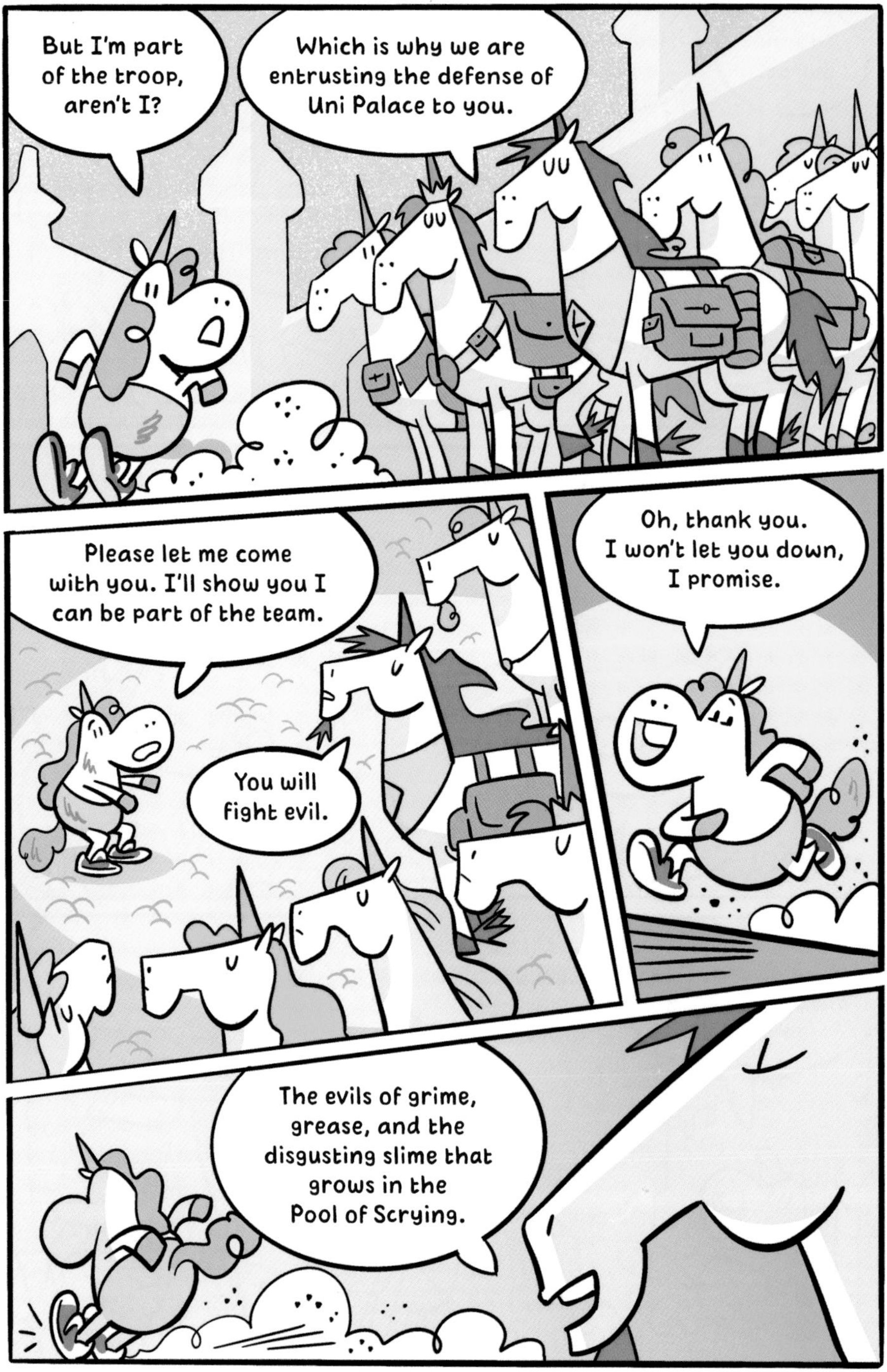
But I'm part of the troop, aren't I?
Which is why we are entrusting the defense of Uni Palace to you.
Please let me come with you. I'll show you I can be part of the team.
You will fight evil.
Oh, thank you. I won't let you down, I promise.
The evils of grime, grease, and the disgusting slime that grows in the Pool of Scrying.

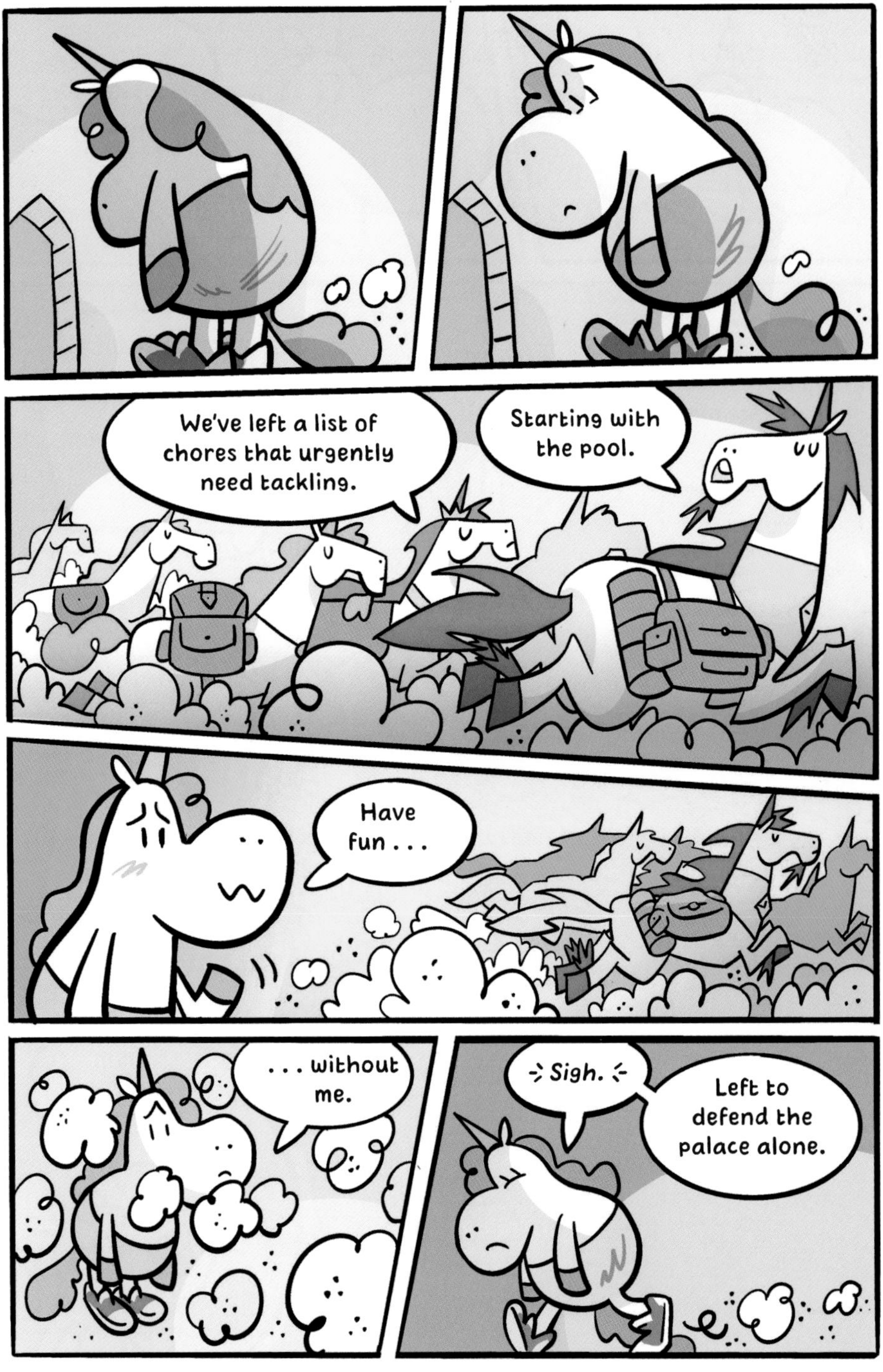
We've left a list of chores that urgently need tackling.
Starting with the pool.
Have fun . . .
. . . without me.
Sigh.
Left to defend the palace alone.

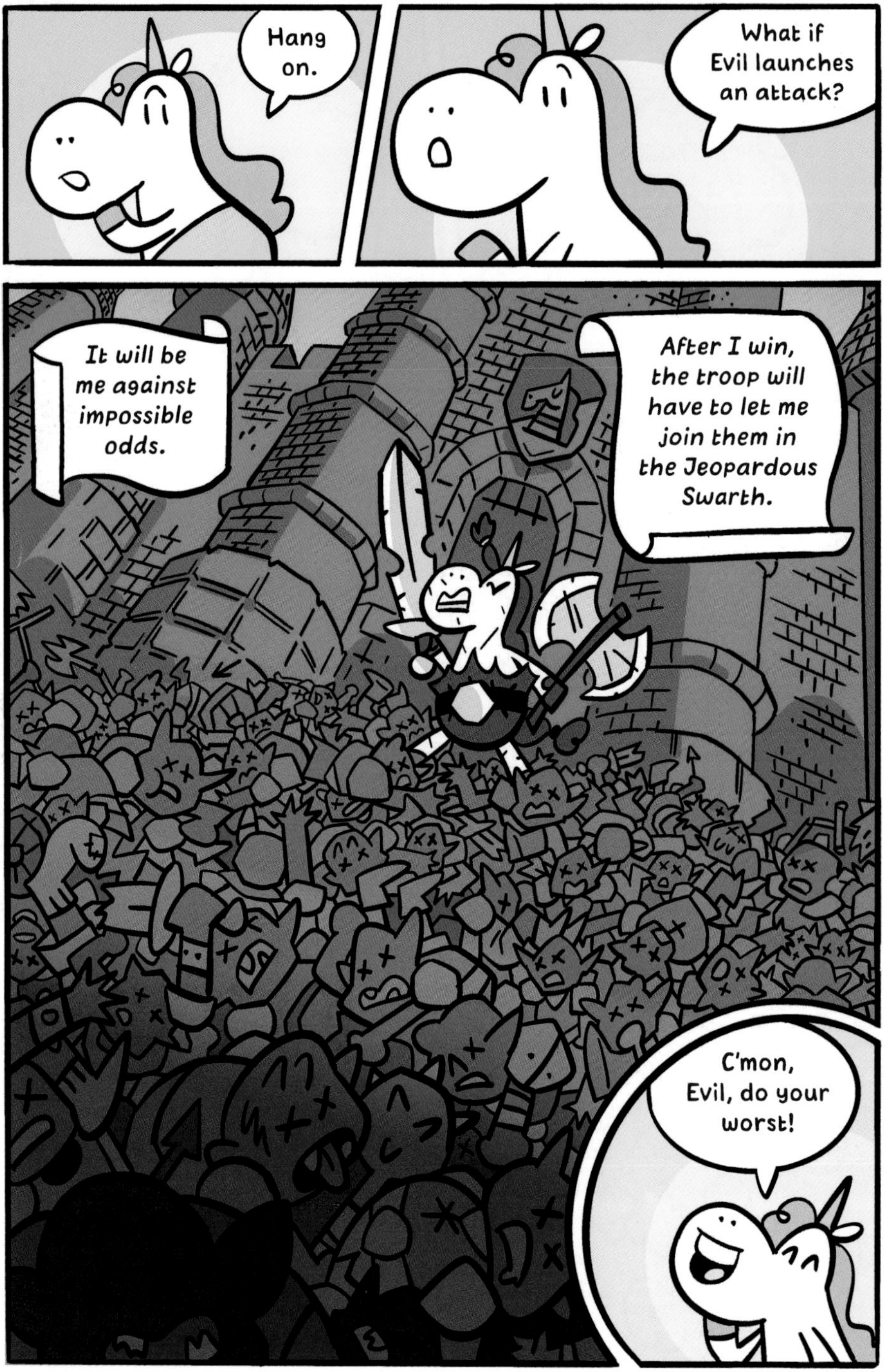
Hang on.
What if Evil launches an attack?
It will be me against impossible odds.
After I win, the troop will have to let me join them in the Jeopardous Swarth.
C'mon, Evil, do your worst!

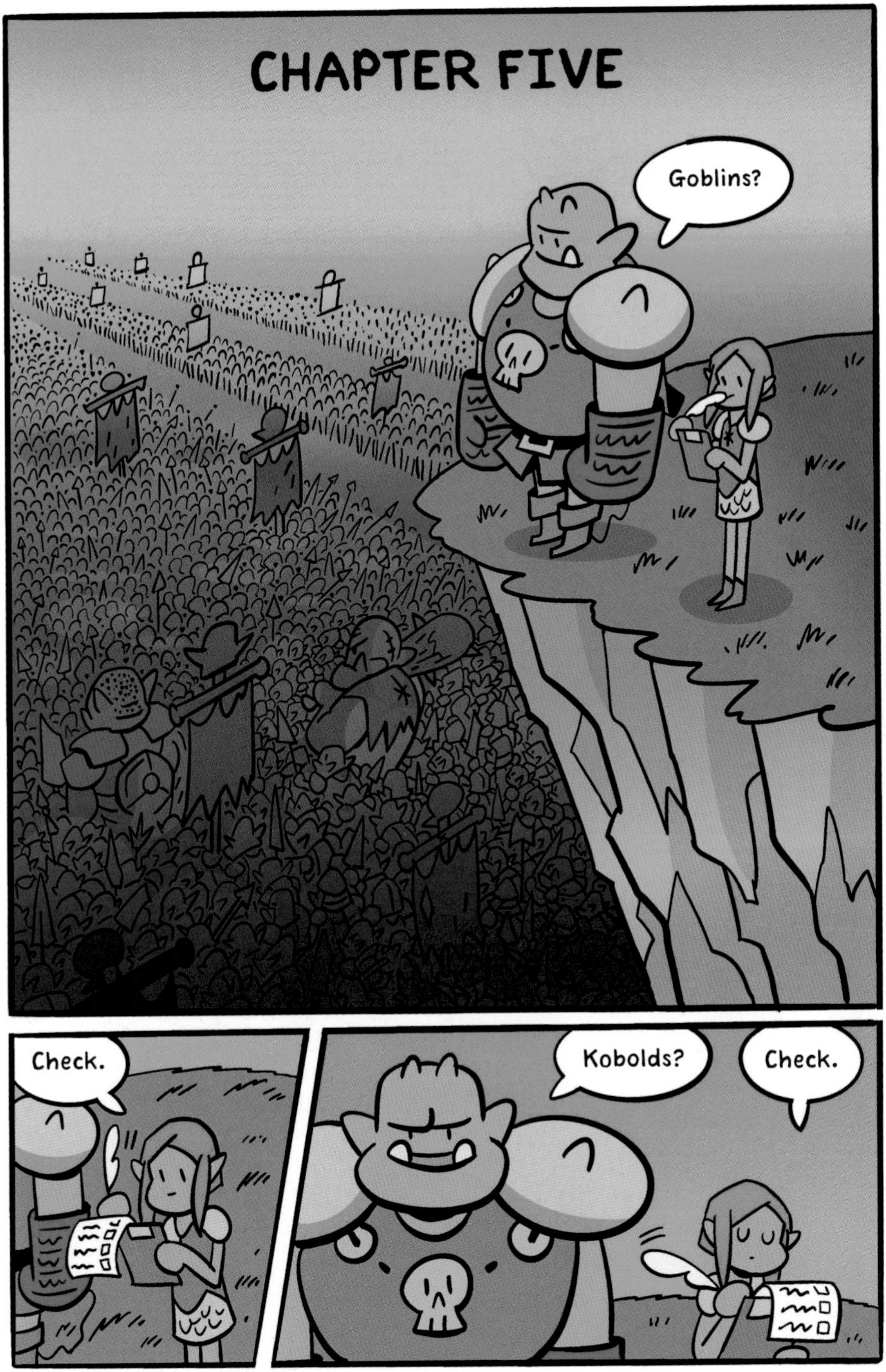
CHAPTER FIVE
Goblins?
Check.
Kobolds?
Check.

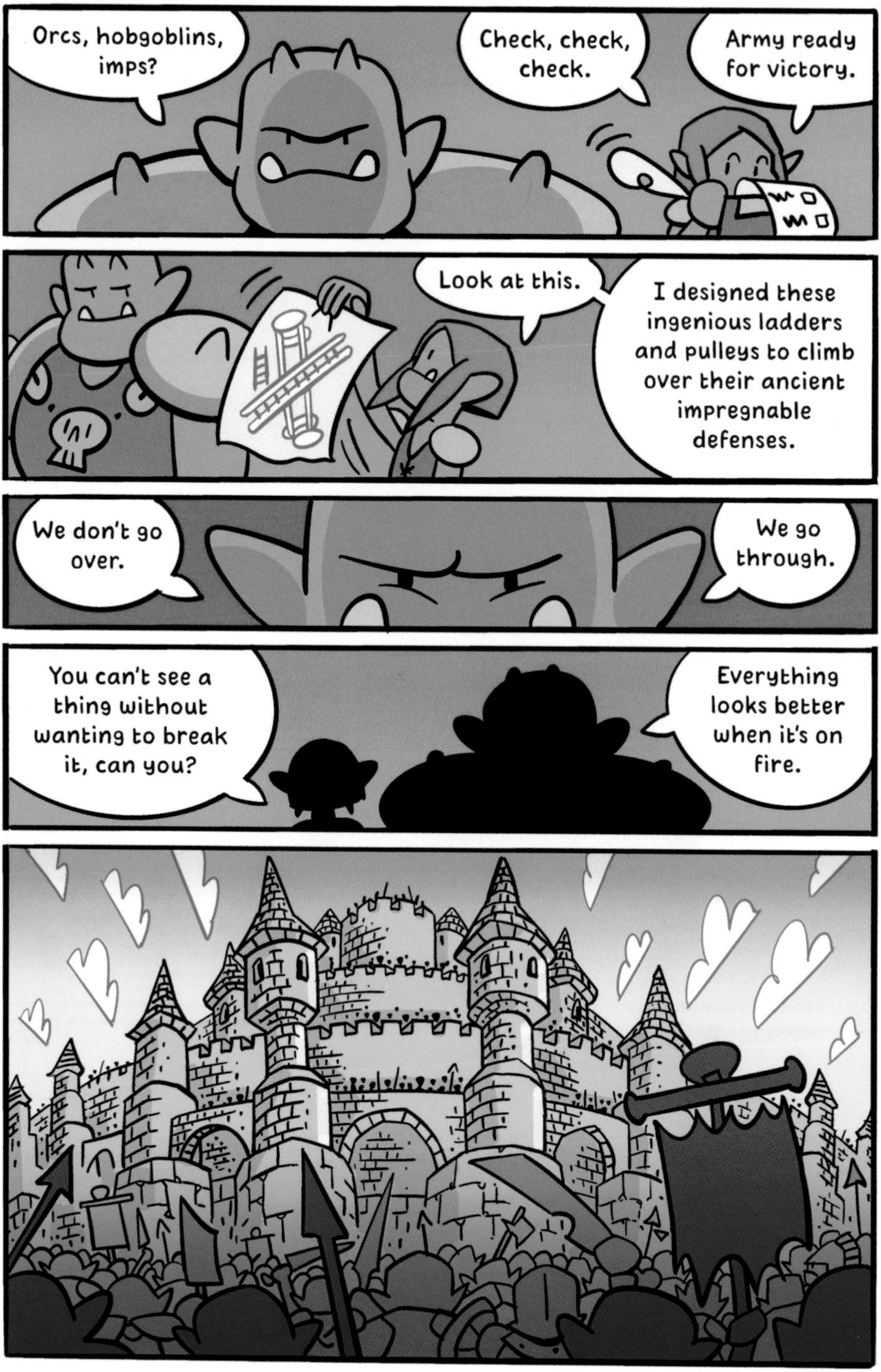
Orcs, hobgoblins, imps?
Check, check, check.
Army ready for victory.
Look at this.
I designed these ingenious ladders and pulleys to climb over their ancient impregnable defenses.
We don't go over.
We go through.
You can't see a thing without wanting to break it, can you?
Everything looks better when it's on fire.

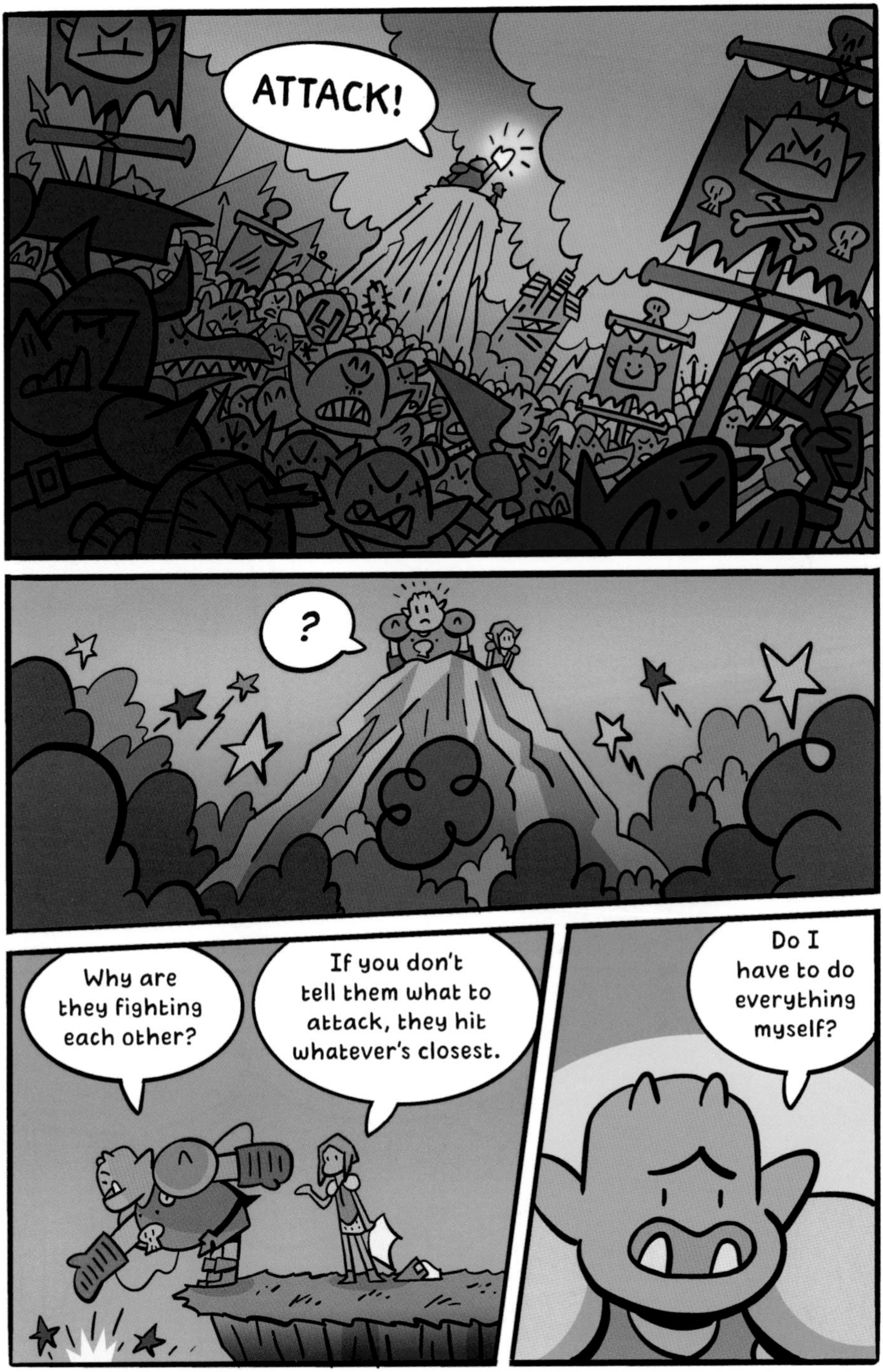
ATTACK!
?
Why are they fighting each other?
If you don't tell them what to attack, they hit whatever's closest.
Do I have to do everything myself?

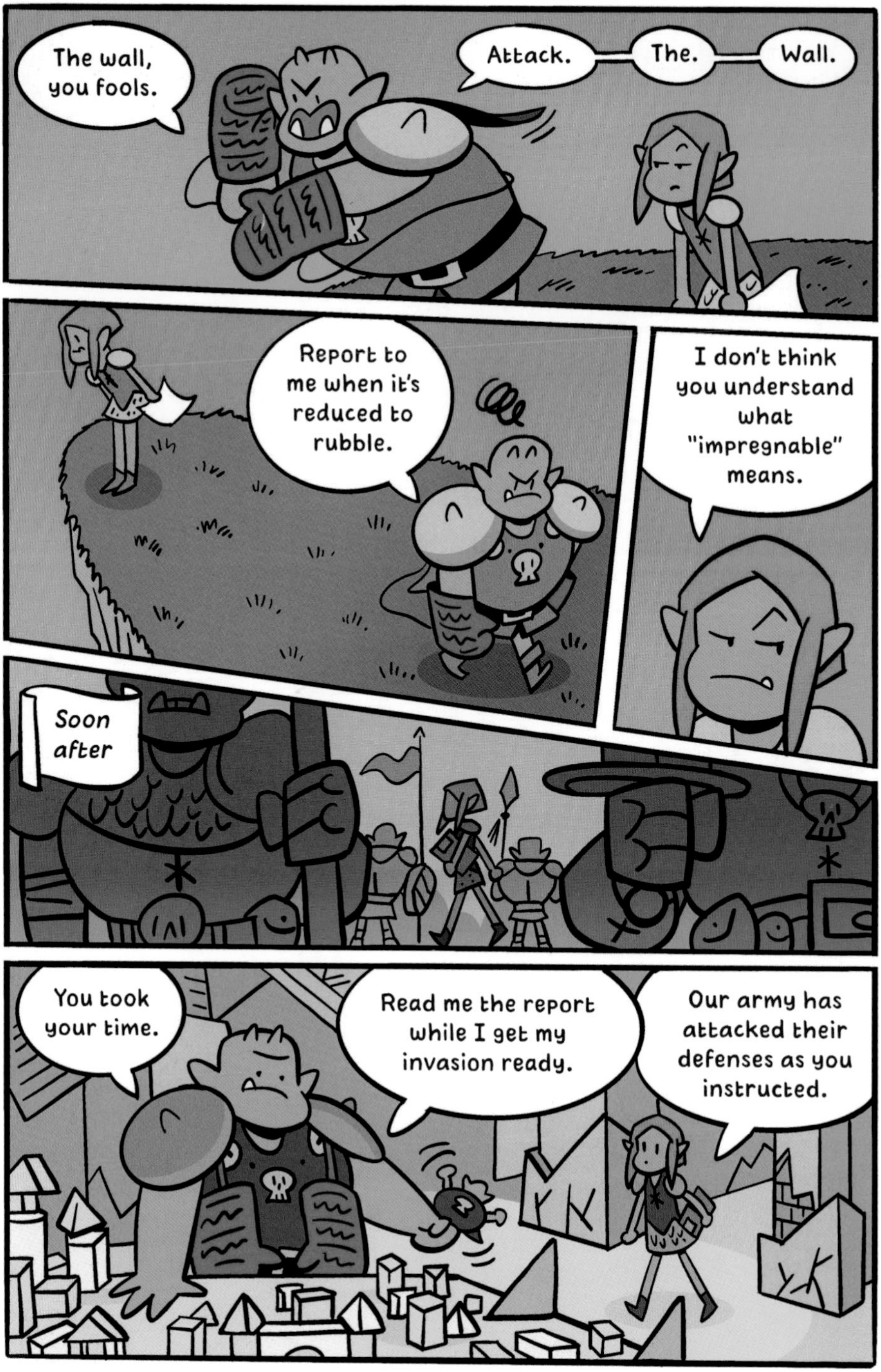
The wall, you fools.
Attack.
The.
Wall.
Report to me when it's reduced to rubble.
I don't think you understand what "impregnable" means.
Soon after
You took your time.
Read me the report while I get my invasion ready.
Our army has attacked their defenses as you instructed.

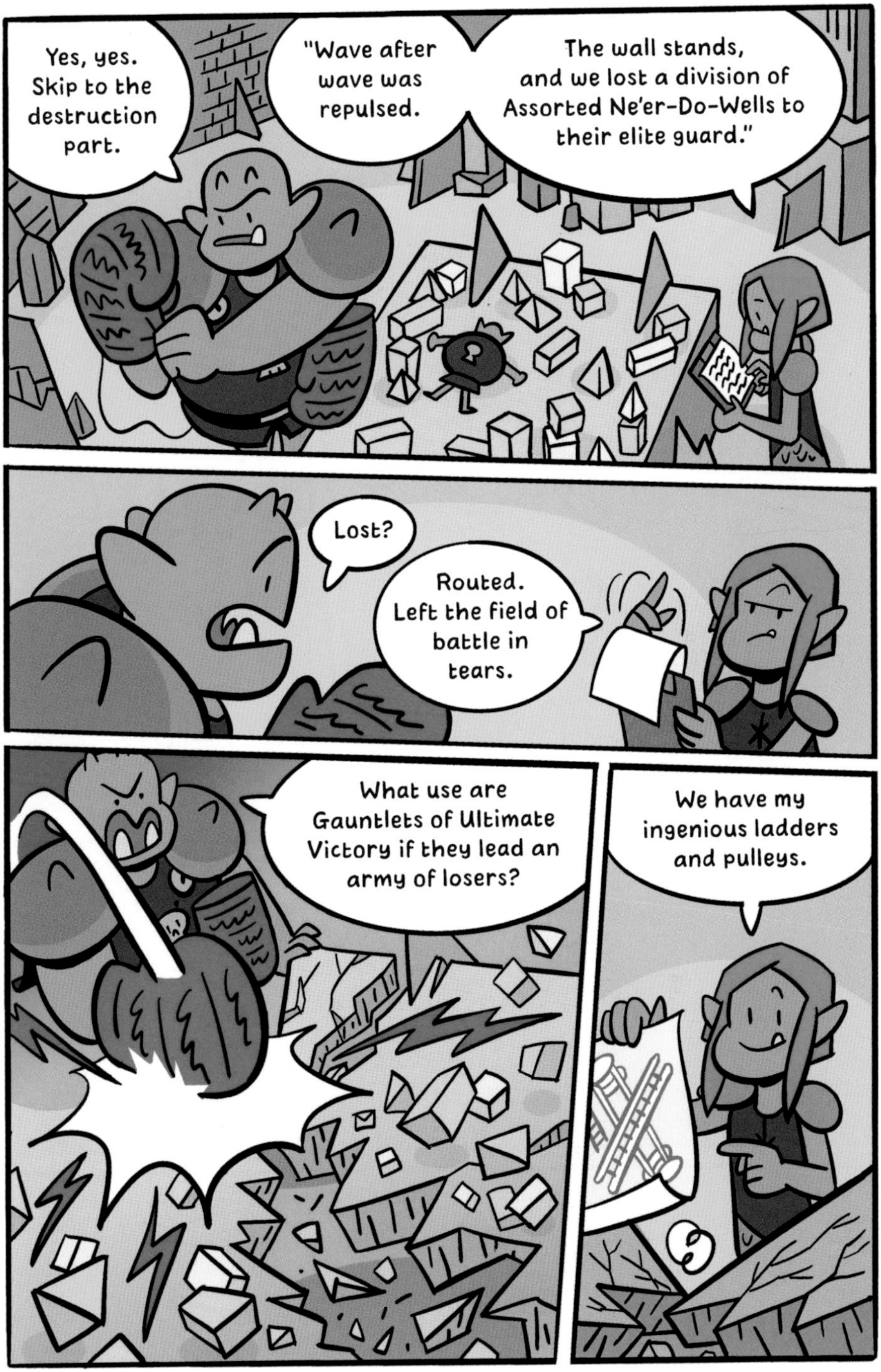
Yes, yes. Skip to the destruction part.
"Wave after wave was repulsed.
The wall stands, and we lost a division of Assorted Ne'er-Do-Wells to their elite guard."
Lost?
Routed. Left the field of battle in tears.
What use are Gauntlets of Ultimate Victory if they lead an army of losers?
We have my ingenious ladders and pulleys.

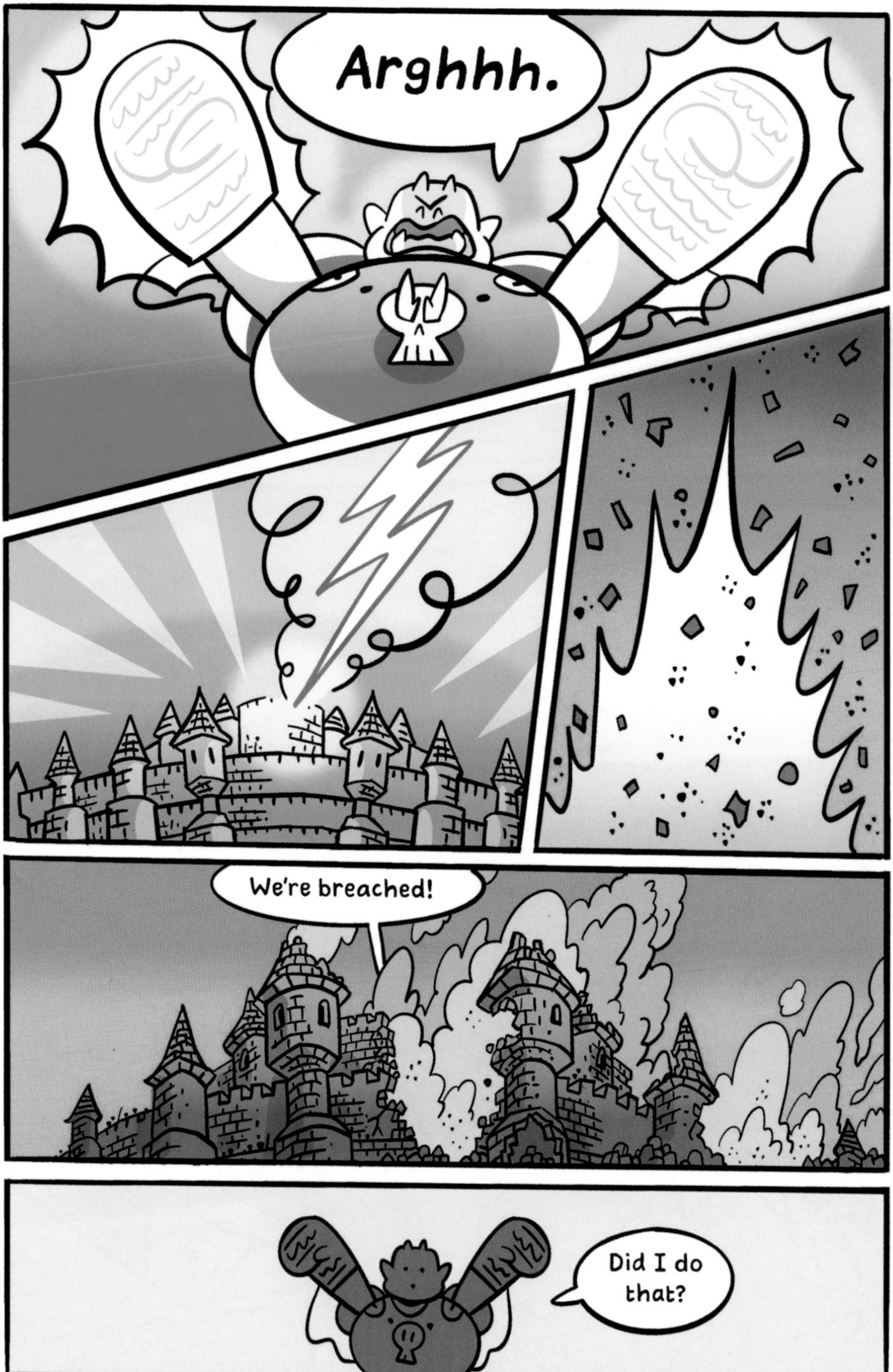
Arghhh.
We're breached!
Did I do that?

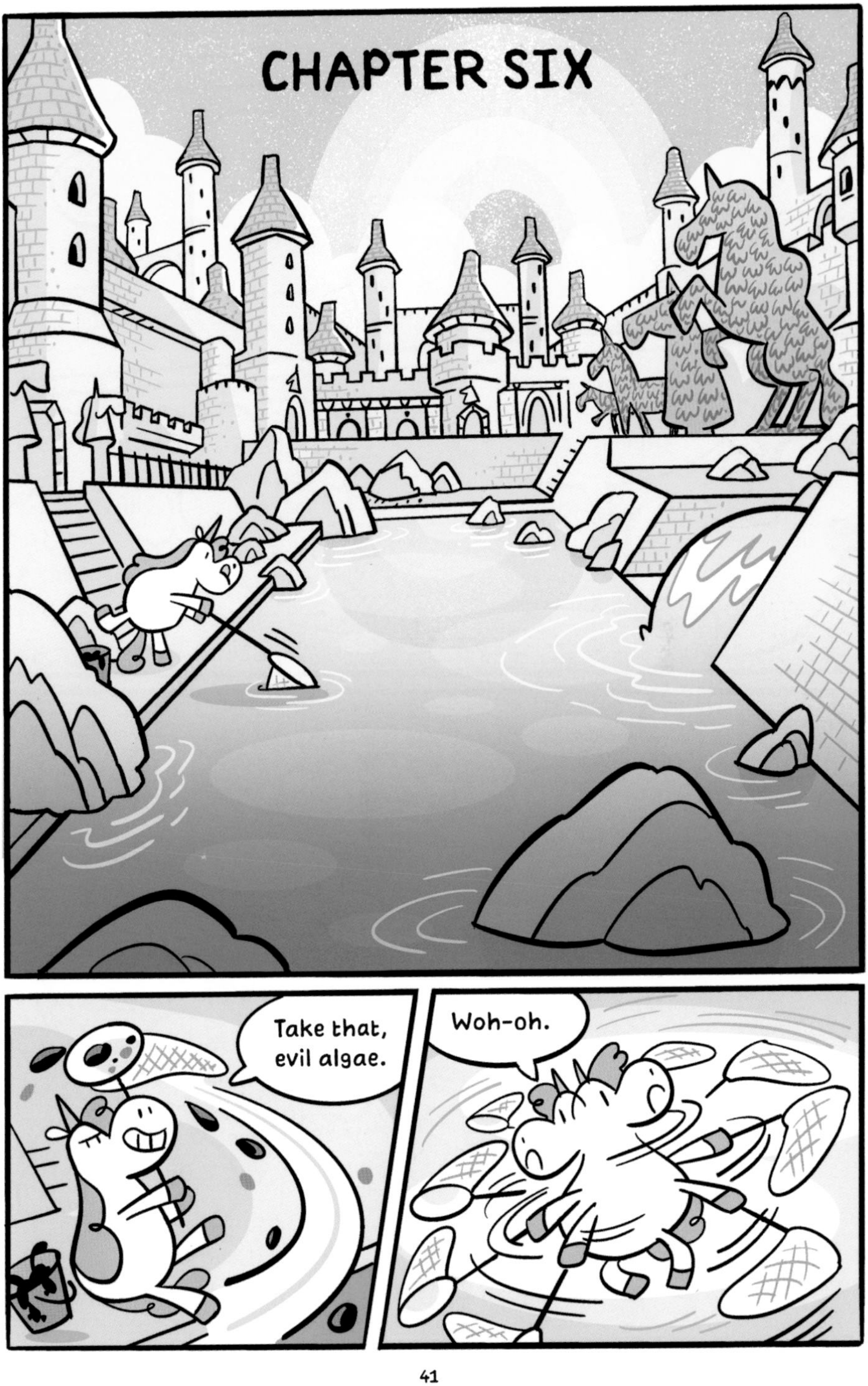
CHAPTER SIX
Take that, evil algae.
Woh-oh.

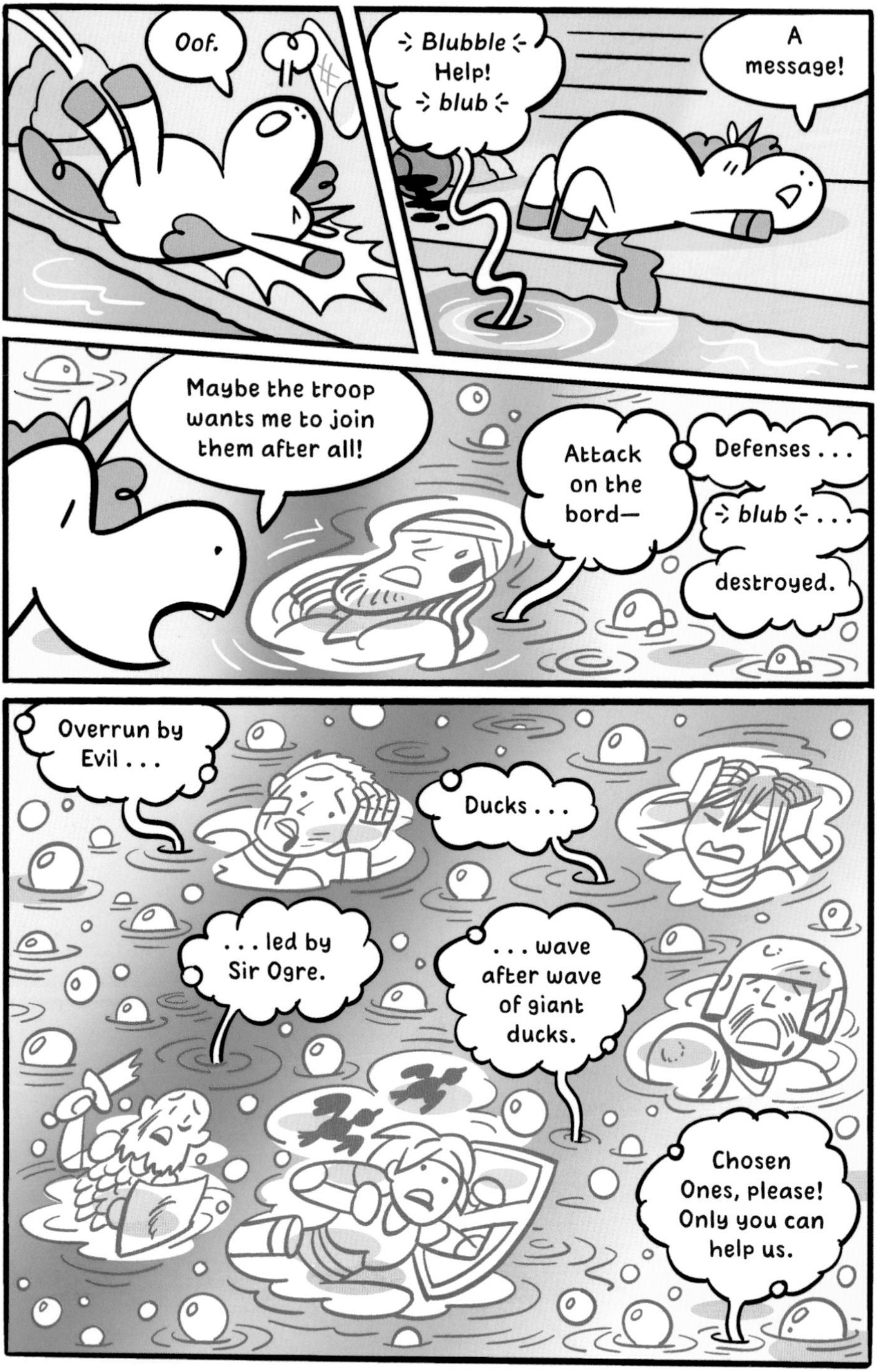
Oof.
-ɜ Blubble -ɛ Help! -ɜ blub -ɛ
A message!
Maybe the troop wants me to join them after all!
Attack on the bord—
Defenses . . .
-ɜ blub -ɛ . . .
destroyed.
Overrun by Evil . . .
Ducks . . .
. . . led by Sir Ogre.
. . . wave after wave of giant ducks.
Chosen Ones, please! Only you can help us.

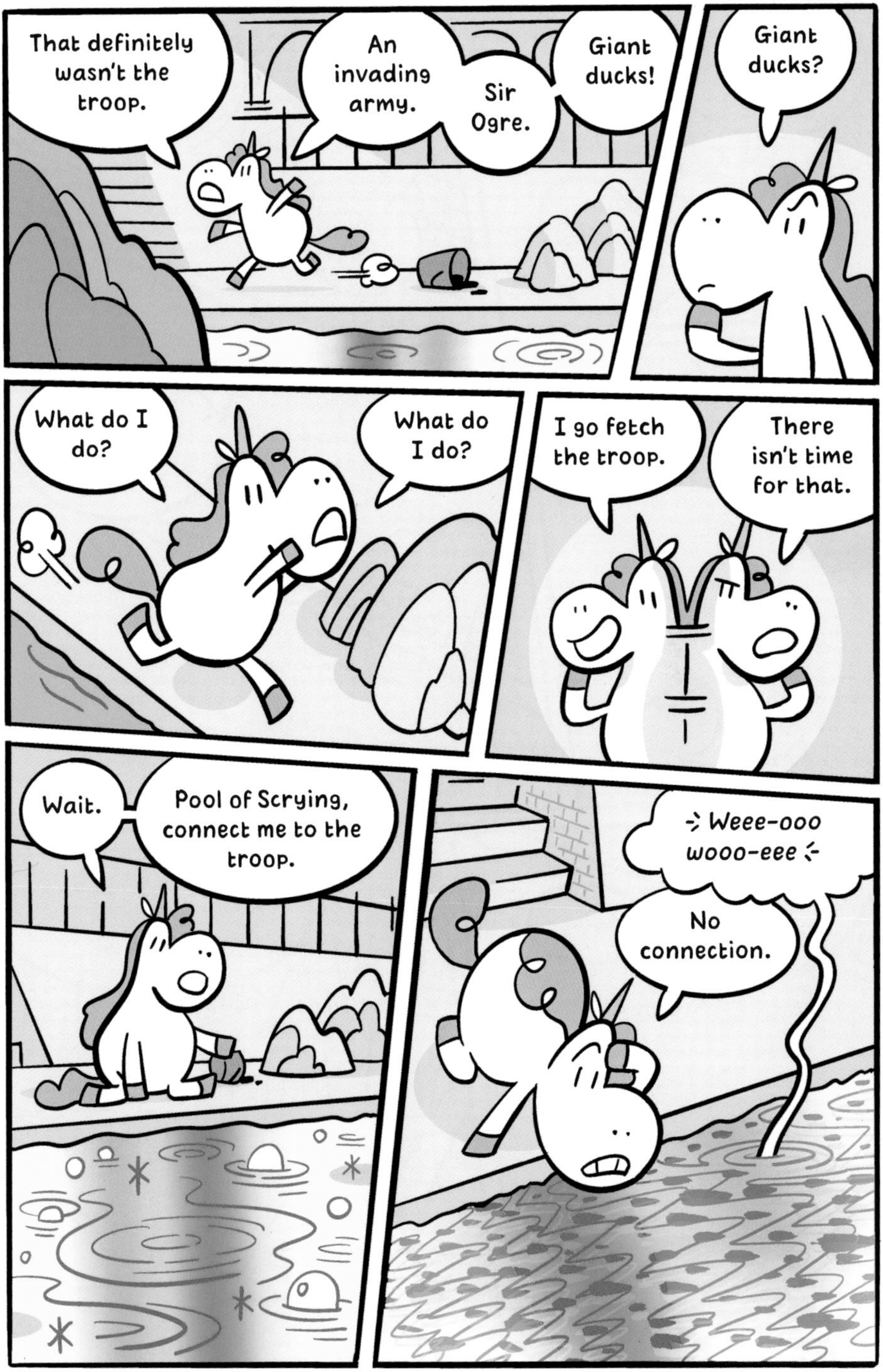
That definitely wasn't the troop.
An invading army.
Sir Ogre.
Giant ducks!
Giant ducks?
What do I do?
What do I do?
I go fetch the troop.
There isn't time for that.
Wait.
Pool of Scrying, connect me to the troop.
Weee-ooo wooo-eee
No connection.

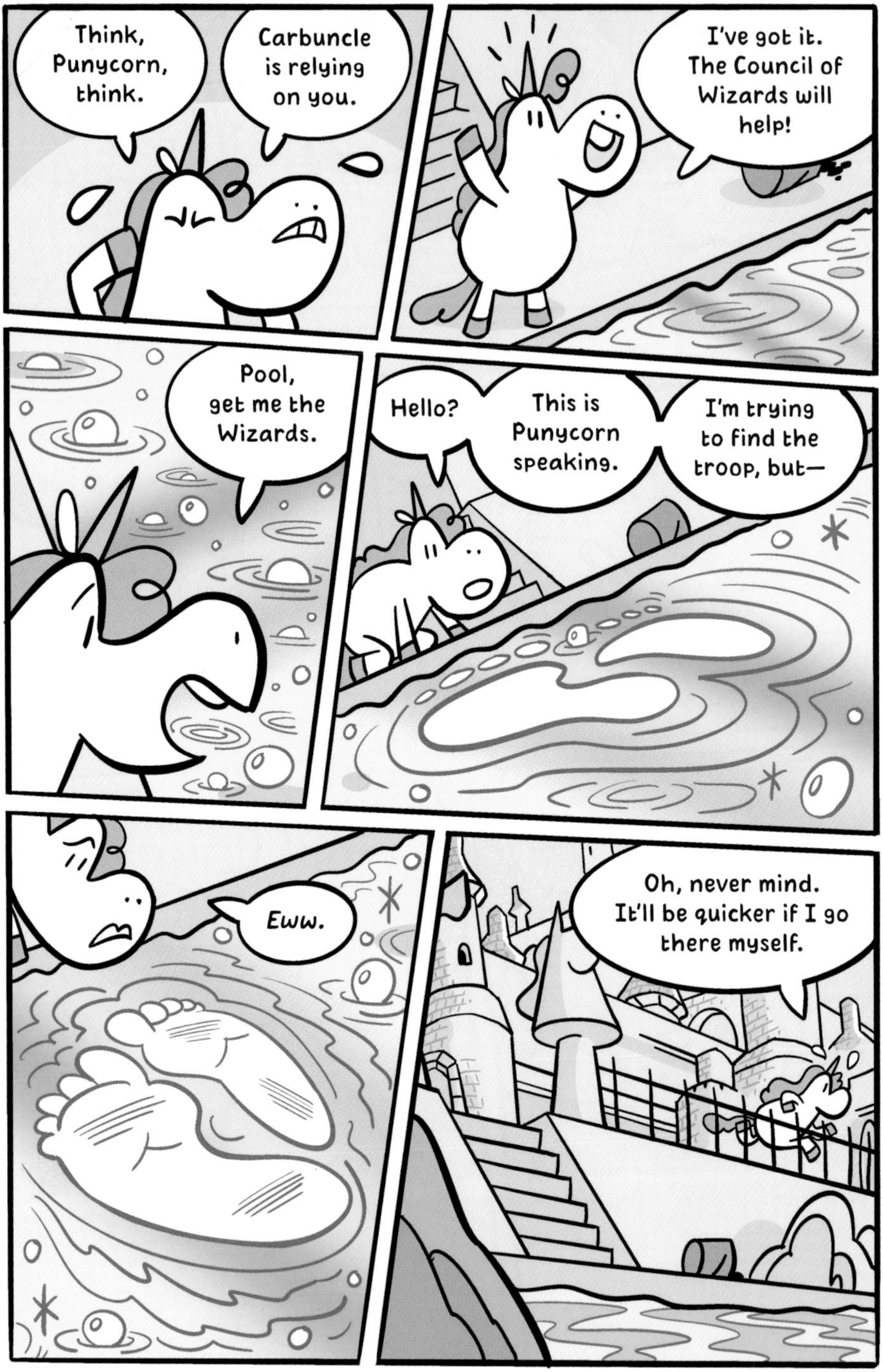
Think, Punycorn, think.
Carbuncle is relying on you.
I've got it. The Council of Wizards will help!
Pool, get me the Wizards.
Hello?
This is Punycorn speaking.
I'm trying to find the troop, but—
Eww.
Oh, never mind. It'll be quicker if I go there myself.

CHAPTER SEVEN

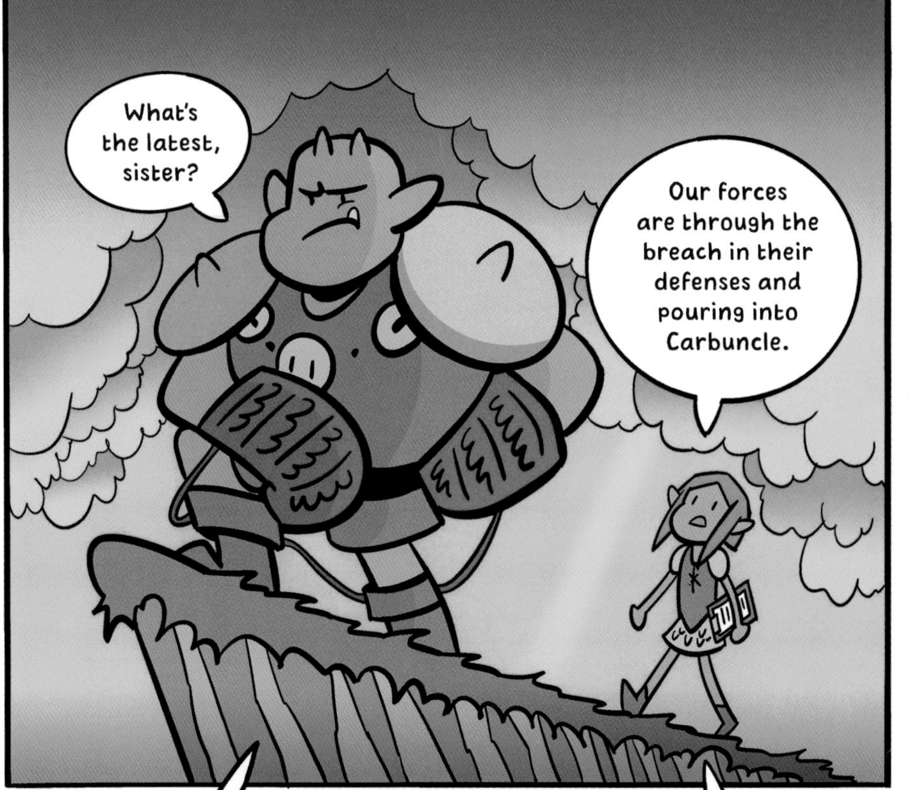
What's the latest, sister?
Our forces are through the breach in their defenses and pouring into Carbuncle.

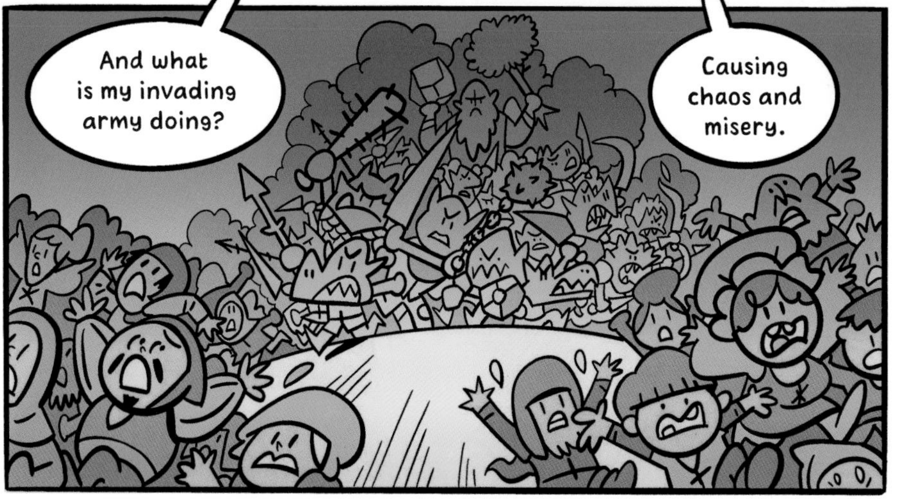
And what is my invading army doing?
Causing chaos and misery.

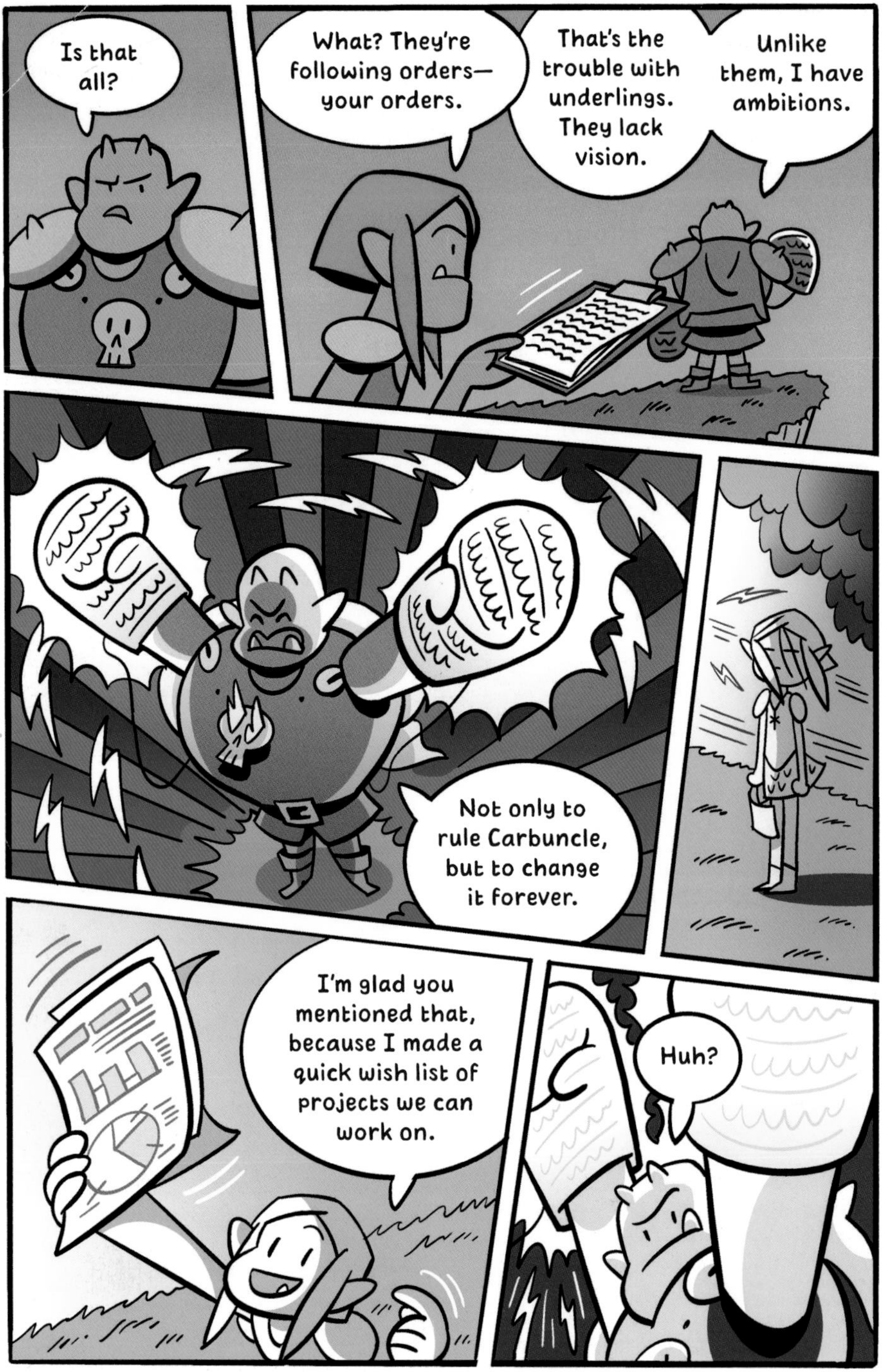
Is that all?
What? They're following orders—your orders.
That's the trouble with underlings. They lack vision.
Unlike them, I have ambitions.
Not only to rule Carbuncle, but to change it forever.
I'm glad you mentioned that, because I made a quick wish list of projects we can work on.
Huh?

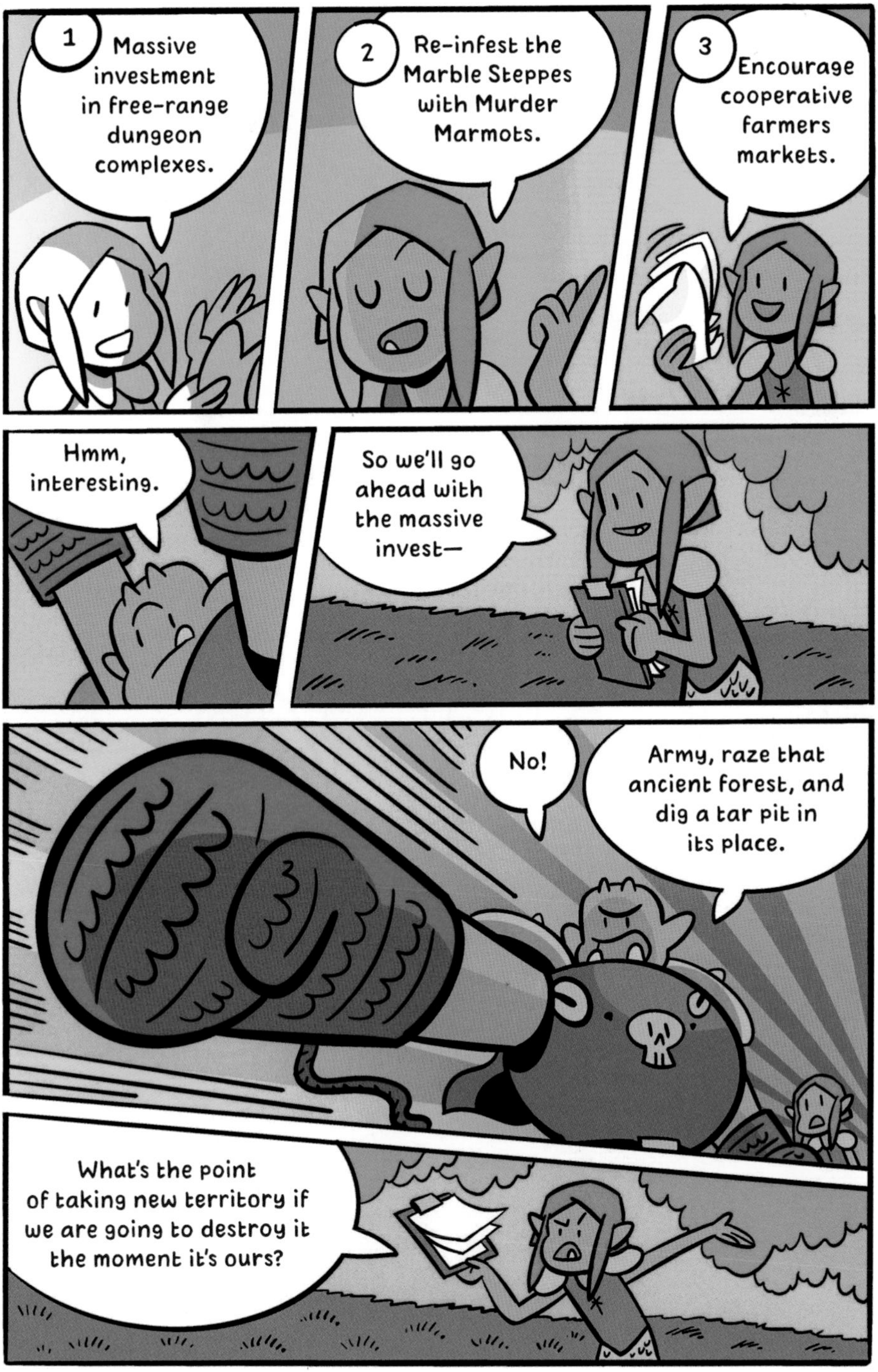
1 Massive investment in free-range dungeon complexes.
2 Re-infest the Marble Steppes with Murder Marmots.
3 Encourage cooperative farmers markets.
Hmm, interesting.
So we'll go ahead with the massive invest—
No!
Army, raze that ancient forest, and dig a tar pit in its place.
What's the point of taking new territory if we are going to destroy it the moment it's ours?

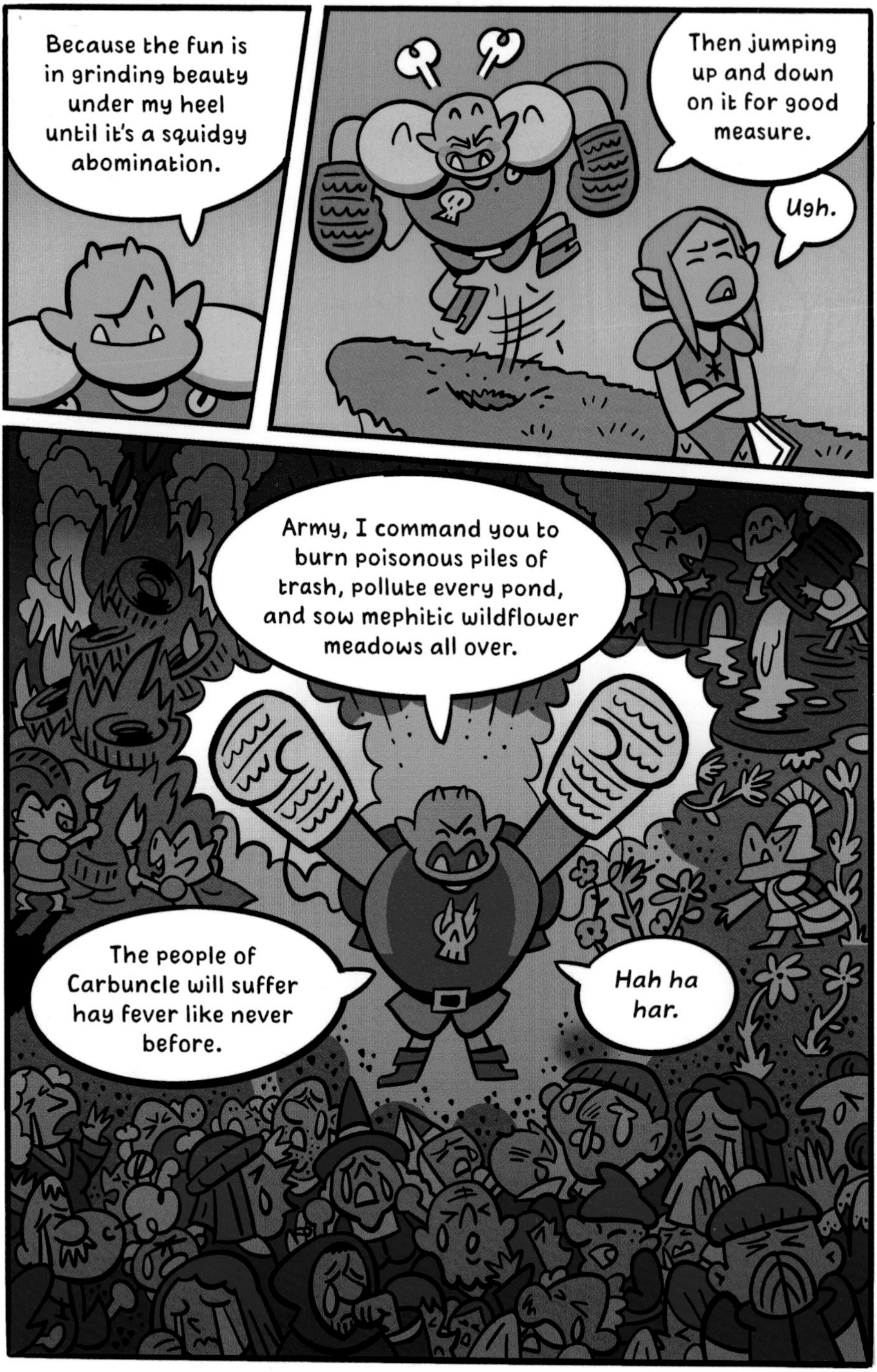
Because the fun is in grinding beauty under my heel until it's a squidgy abomination.
Then jumping up and down on it for good measure.
Ugh.
Army, I command you to burn poisonous piles of trash, pollute every pond, and sow mephitic wildflower meadows all over.
The people of Carbuncle will suffer hay fever like never before.
Hah ha har.

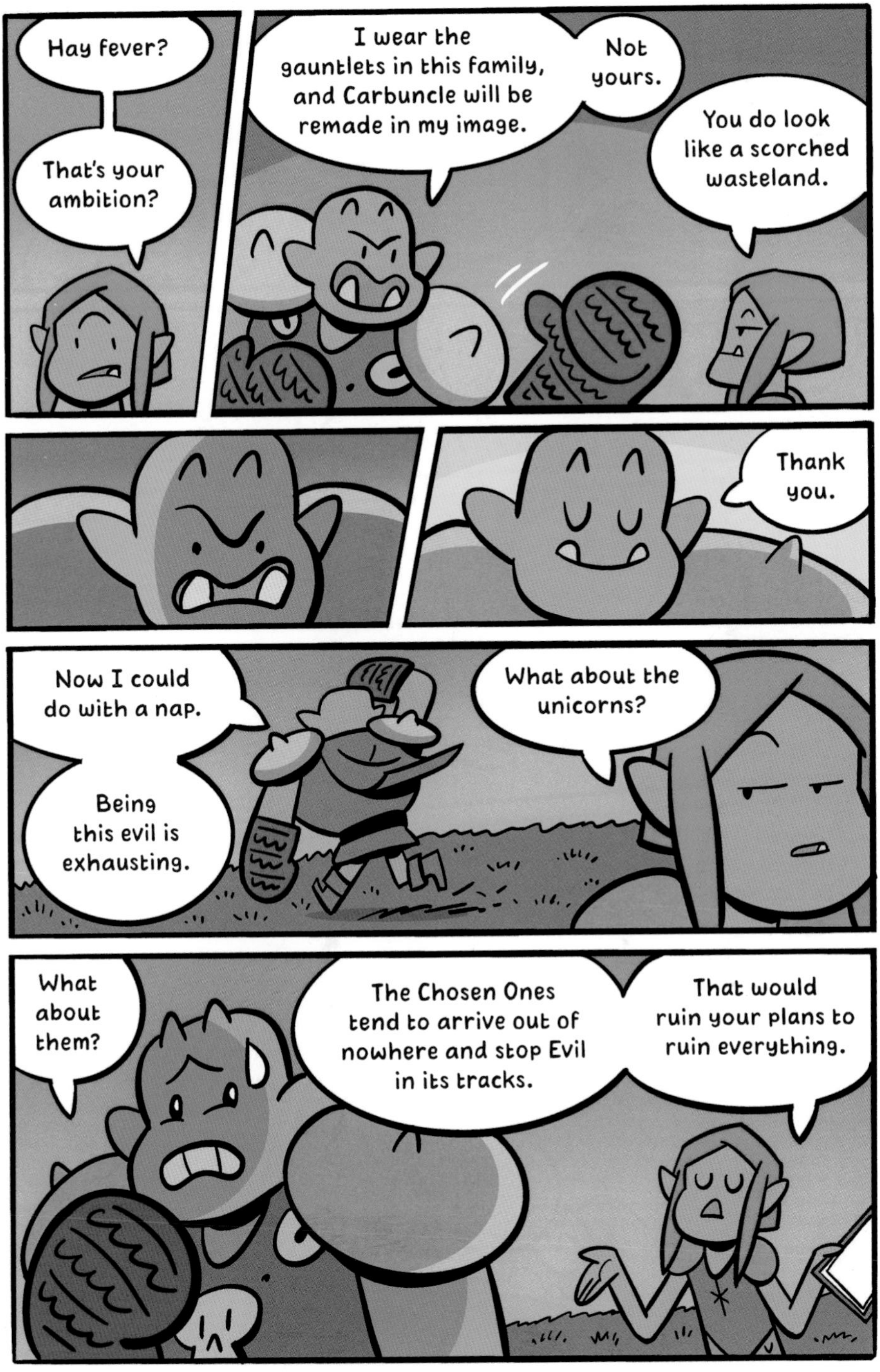
Hay fever?
That's your ambition?
I wear the gauntlets in this family, and Carbuncle will be remade in my image.
Not yours.
You do look like a scorched wasteland.
Thank you.
Now I could do with a nap.
Being this evil is exhausting.
What about the unicorns?
What about them?
The Chosen Ones tend to arrive out of nowhere and stop Evil in its tracks.
That would ruin your plans to ruin everything.

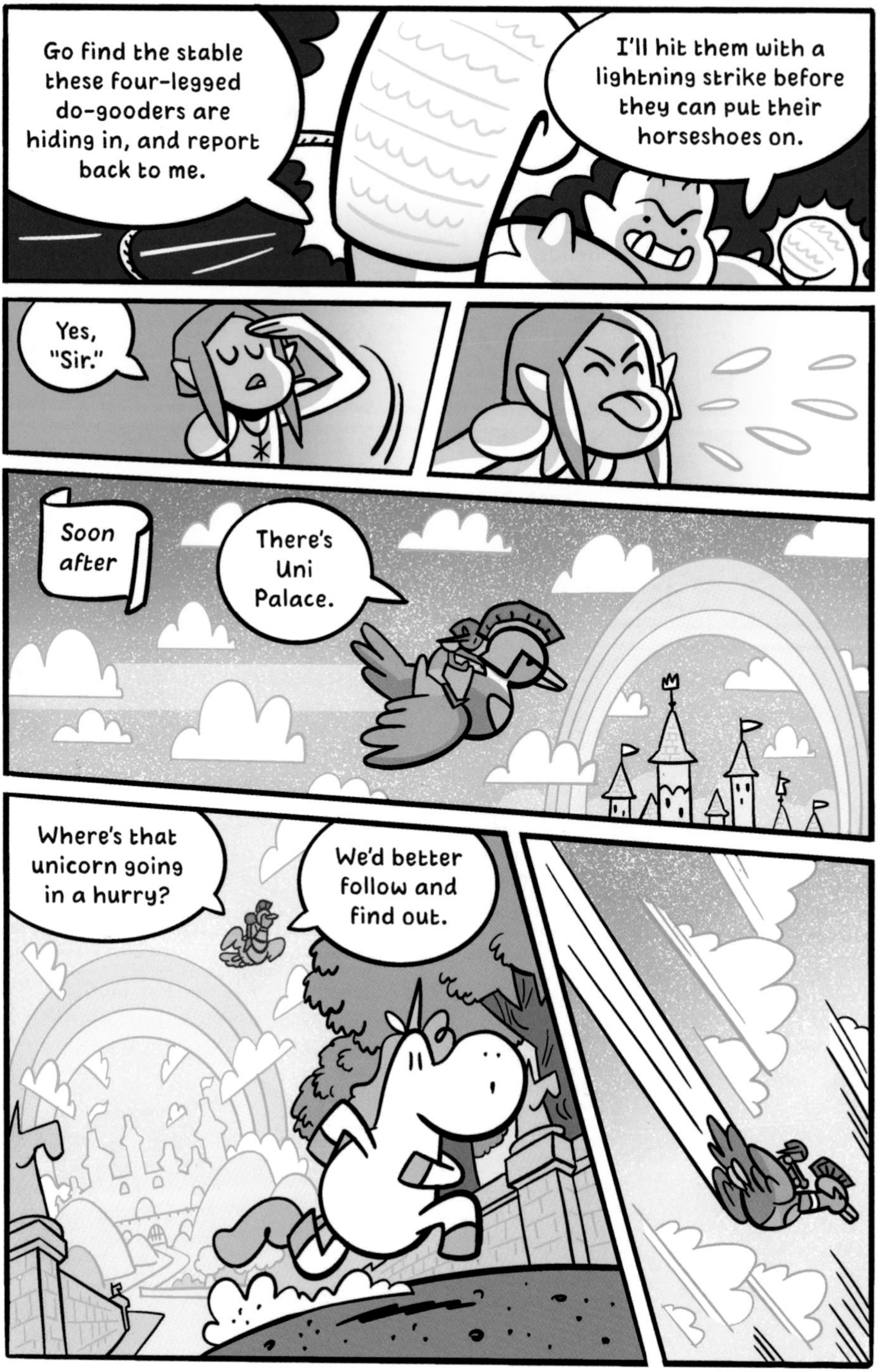

Go find the stable these four-legged do-gooders are hiding in, and report back to me.
I'll hit them with a lightning strike before they can put their horseshoes on.
Yes, "Sir."
Soon after
There's Uni Palace.
Where's that unicorn going in a hurry?
We'd better follow and find out.

CHAPTER EIGHT

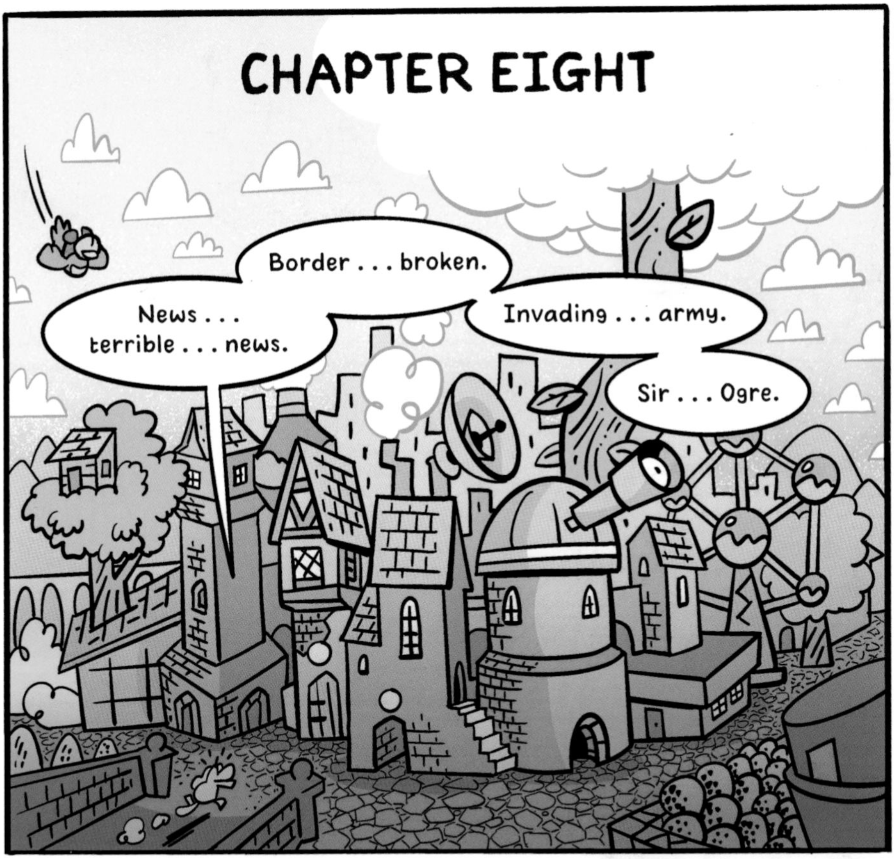

News . . . terrible . . . news.
Border . . . broken.
Invading . . . army.
Sir . . . Ogre.

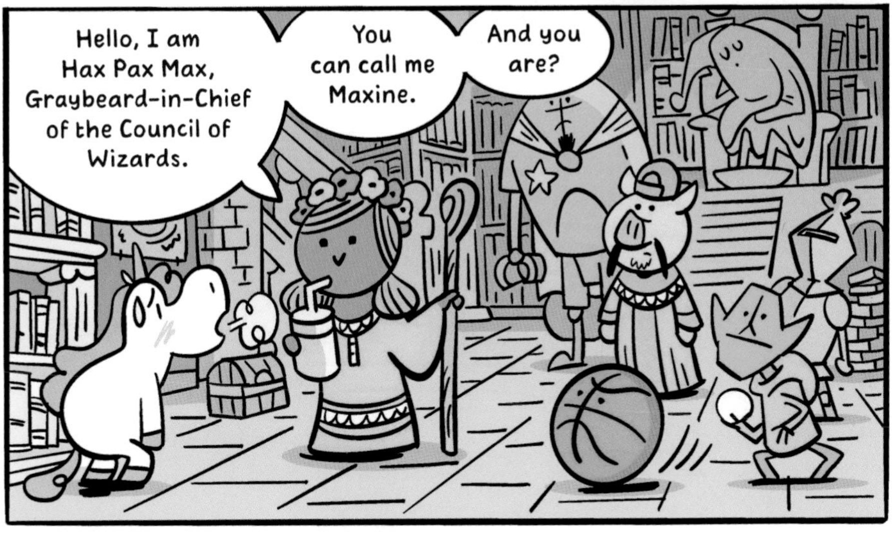

Hello, I am Hax Pax Max, Graybeard-in-Chief of the Council of Wizards.
You can call me Maxine.
And you are?

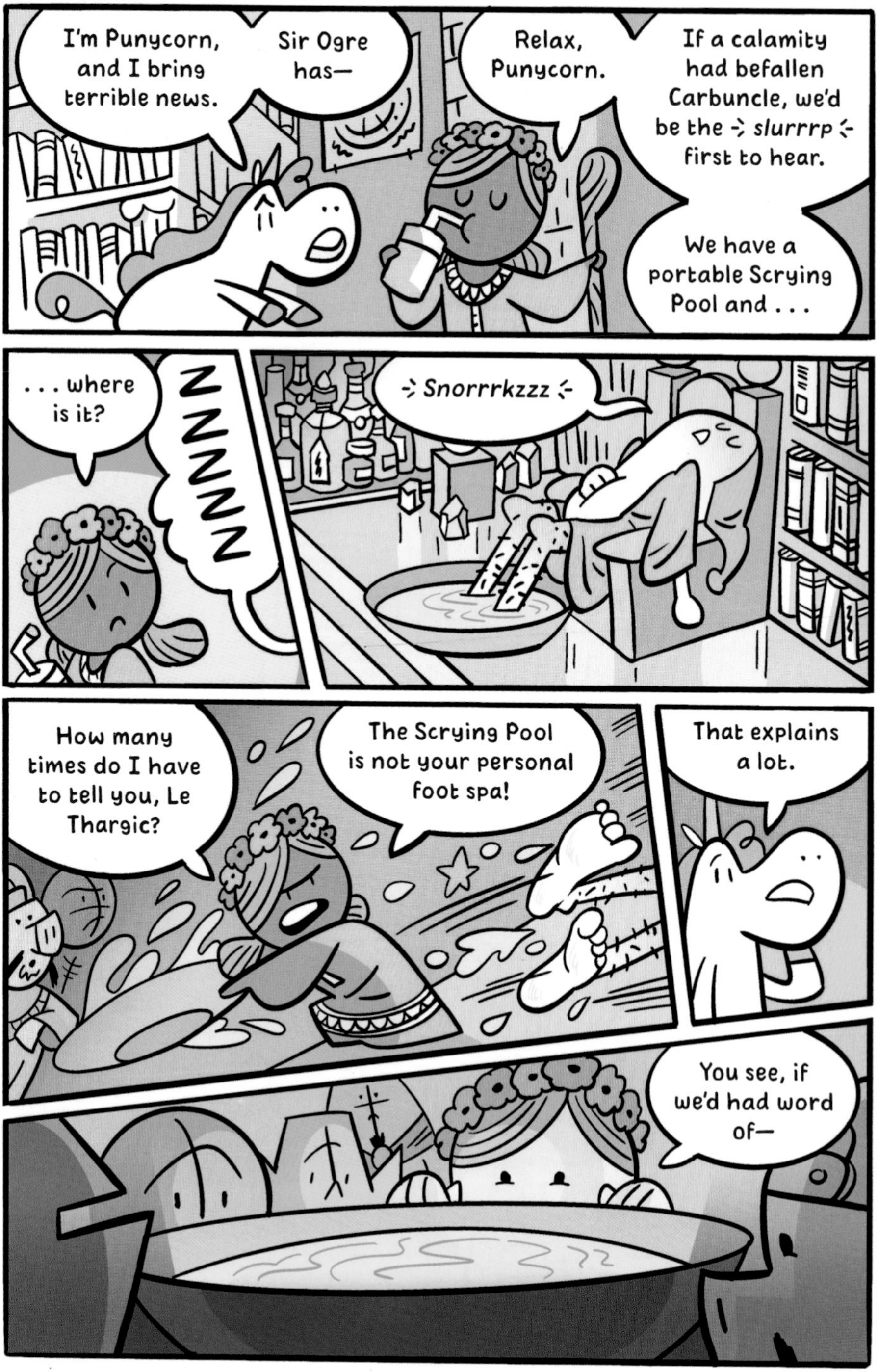
I'm Punycorn, and I bring terrible news.
Sir Ogre has—
Relax, Punycorn.
If a calamity had befallen Carbuncle, we'd be the -; slurrrp ;- first to hear.
We have a portable Scrying Pool and . . .
. . . where is it?
ZZZZZ
-; Snorrrkzzz ;-
How many times do I have to tell you, Le Thargic?
The Scrying Pool is not your personal foot spa!
That explains a lot.
You see, if we'd had word of—

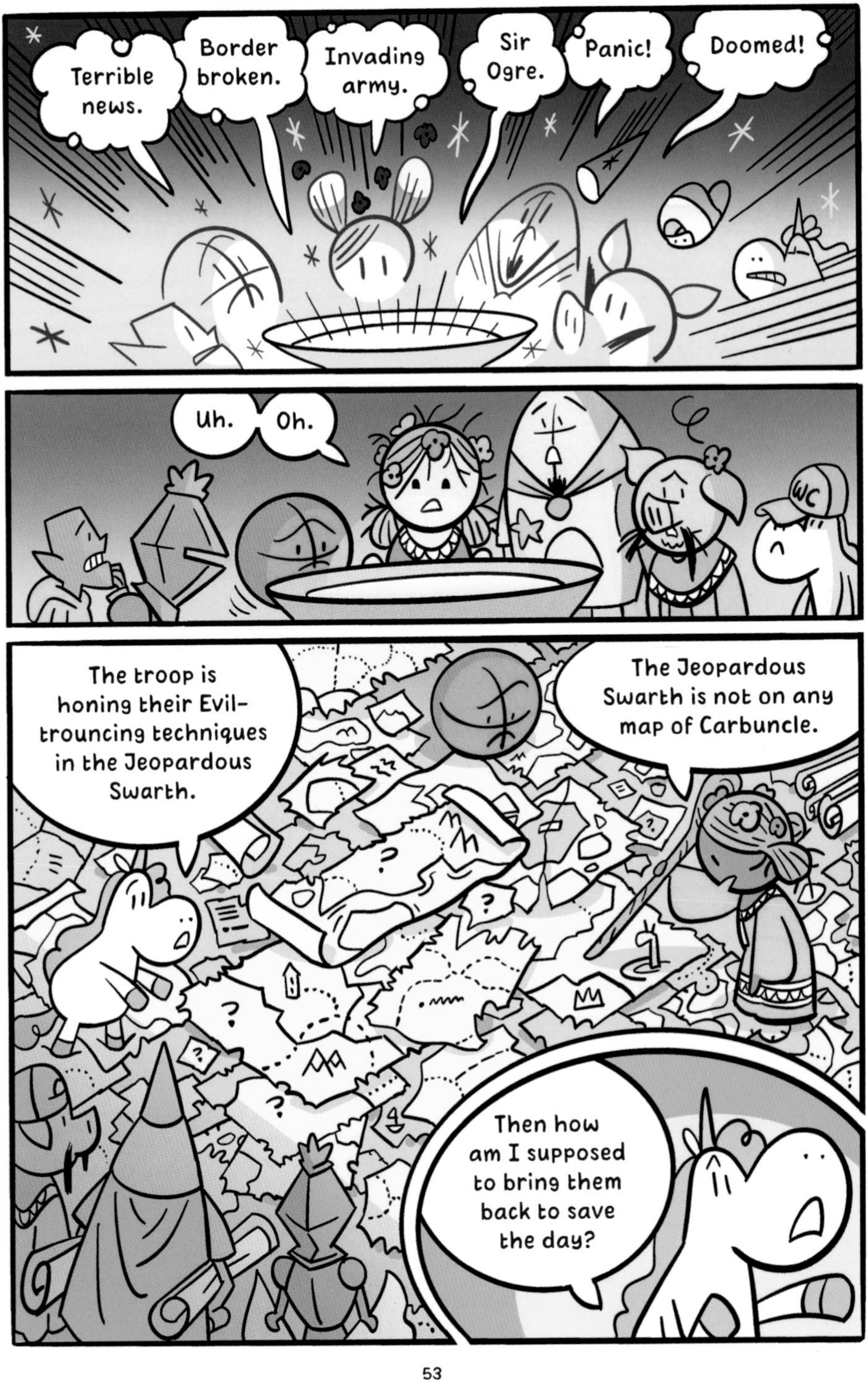
Terrible news.
Border broken.
Invading army.
Sir Ogre.
Panic!
Doomed!
Uh.
Oh.
The troop is honing their Evil-trouncing techniques in the Jeopardous Swarth.
The Jeopardous Swarth is not on any map of Carbuncle.
Then how am I supposed to bring them back to save the day?

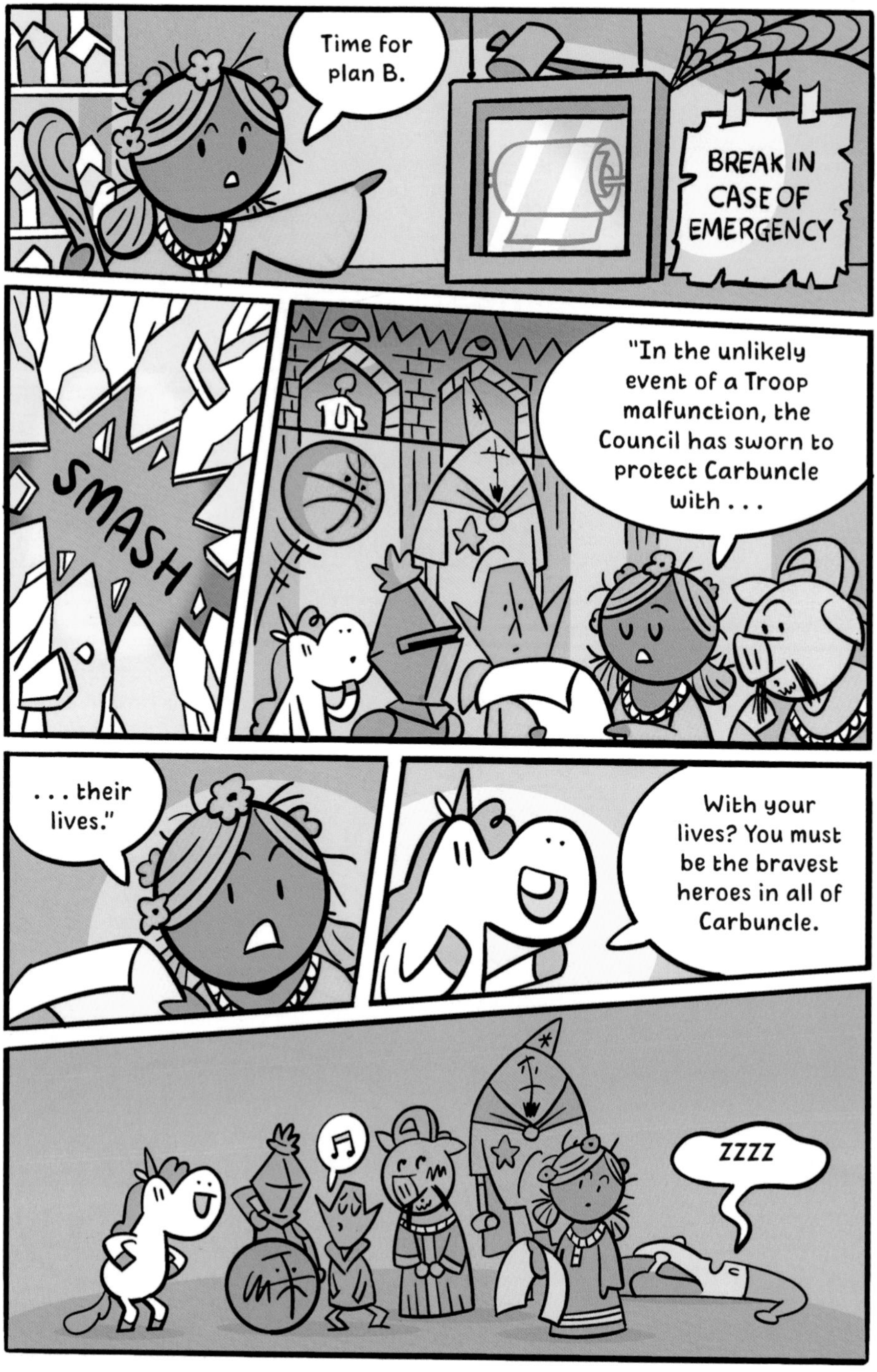
Time for plan B.
BREAK IN CASE OF EMERGENCY
SMASH
"In the unlikely event of a Troop malfunction, the Council has sworn to protect Carbuncle with . . .
. . . their lives."
With your lives? You must be the bravest heroes in all of Carbuncle.
ZZZZ

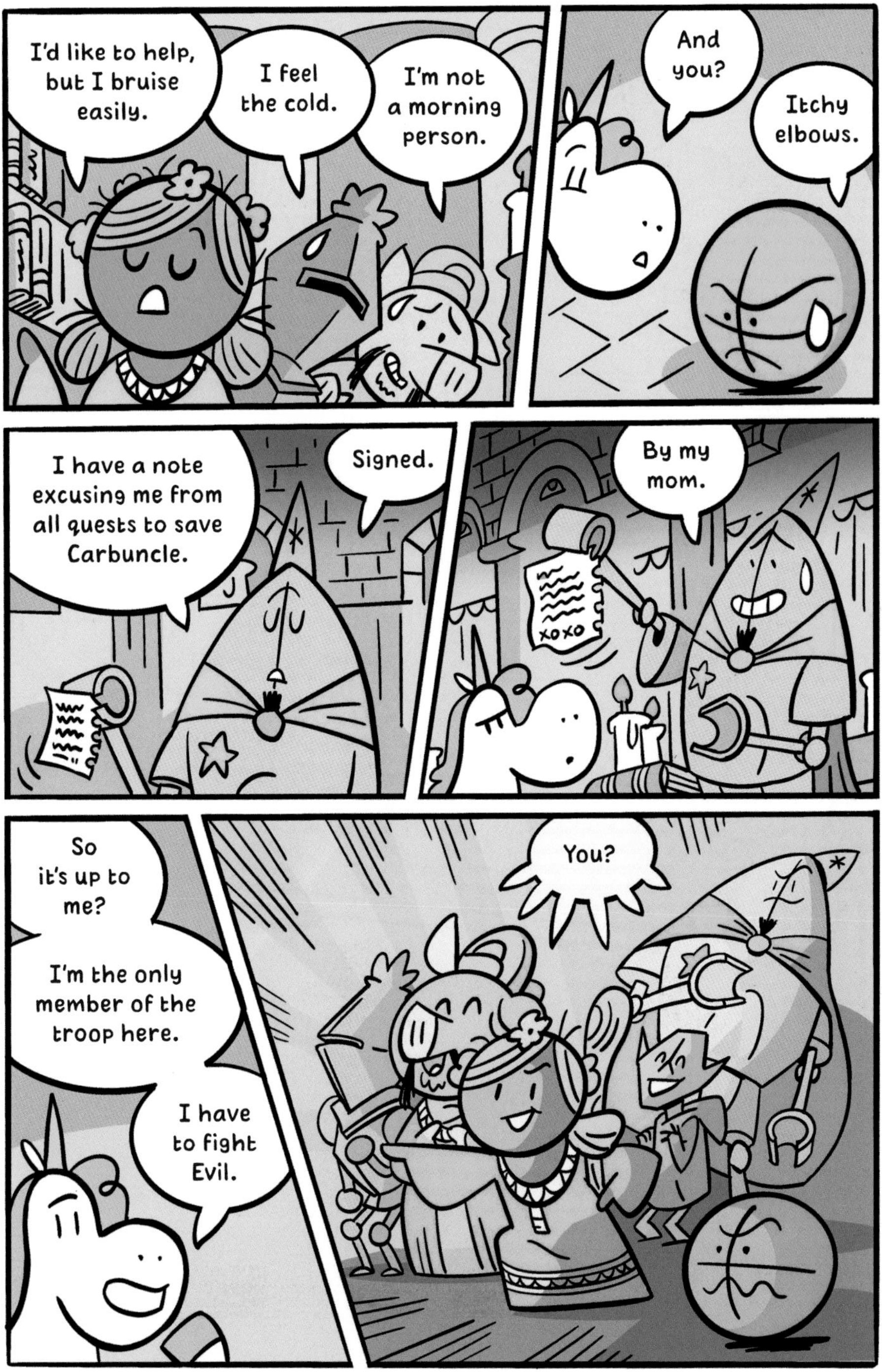
I'd like to help, but I bruise easily.
I feel the cold.
I'm not a morning person.
And you?
Itchy elbows.
I have a note excusing me from all quests to save Carbuncle.
Signed.
By my mom.
XOXO
So it's up to me?
I'm the only member of the troop here.
I have to fight Evil.
You?

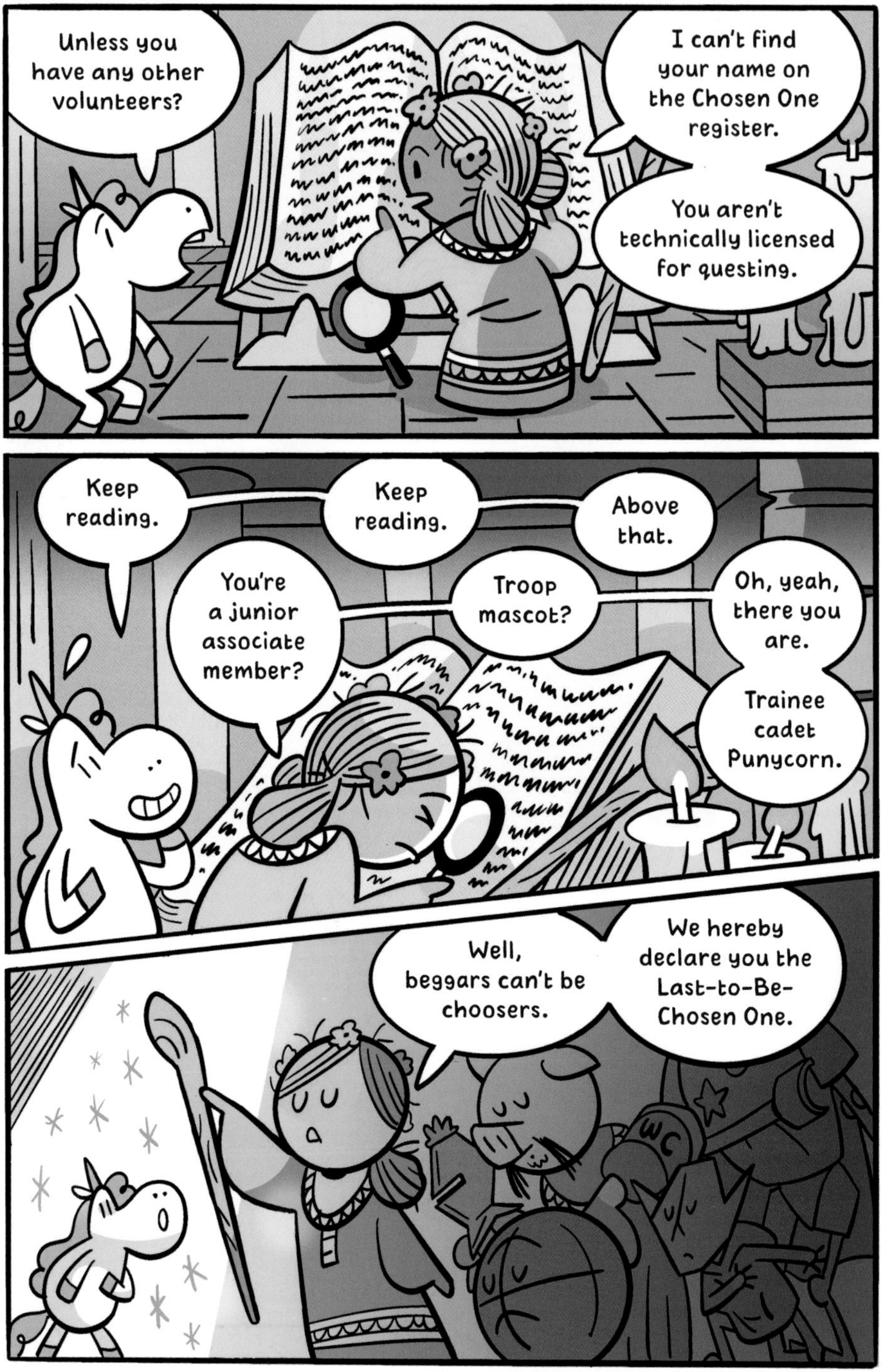
Unless you have any other volunteers?
I can't find your name on the Chosen One register.
You aren't technically licensed for questing.
Keep reading.
Keep reading.
Above that.
You're a junior associate member?
Troop mascot?
Oh, yeah, there you are.
Trainee cadet Punycorn.
Well, beggars can't be choosers.
We hereby declare you the Last-to-Be-Chosen One.
WC

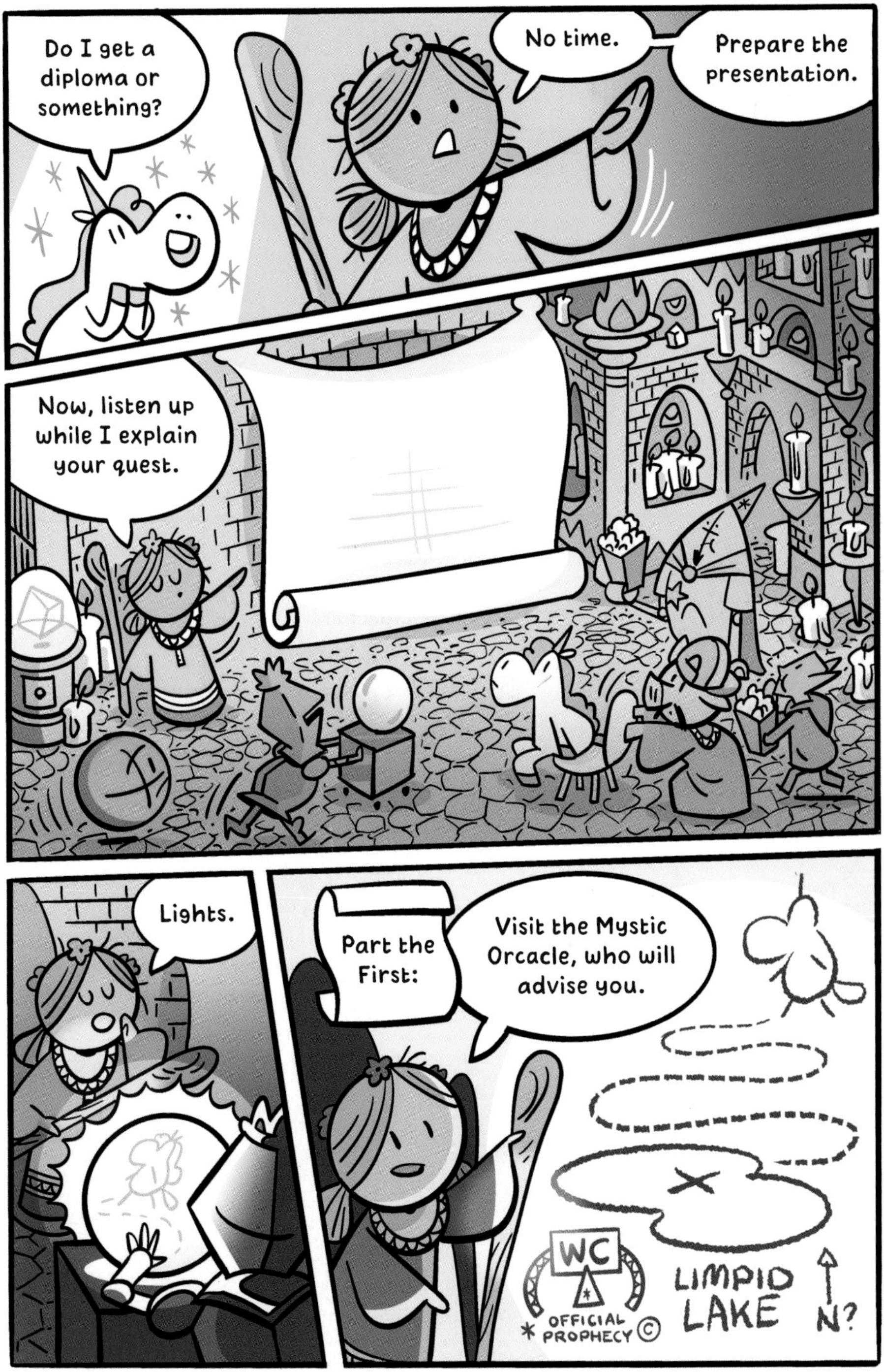
Do I get a diploma or something?
No time.
Prepare the presentation.
Now, listen up while I explain your quest.
Lights.
Part the First:
Visit the Mystic Orcacle, who will advise you.
WC
OFFICIAL PROPHECY ©
LIMPID LAKE
N?

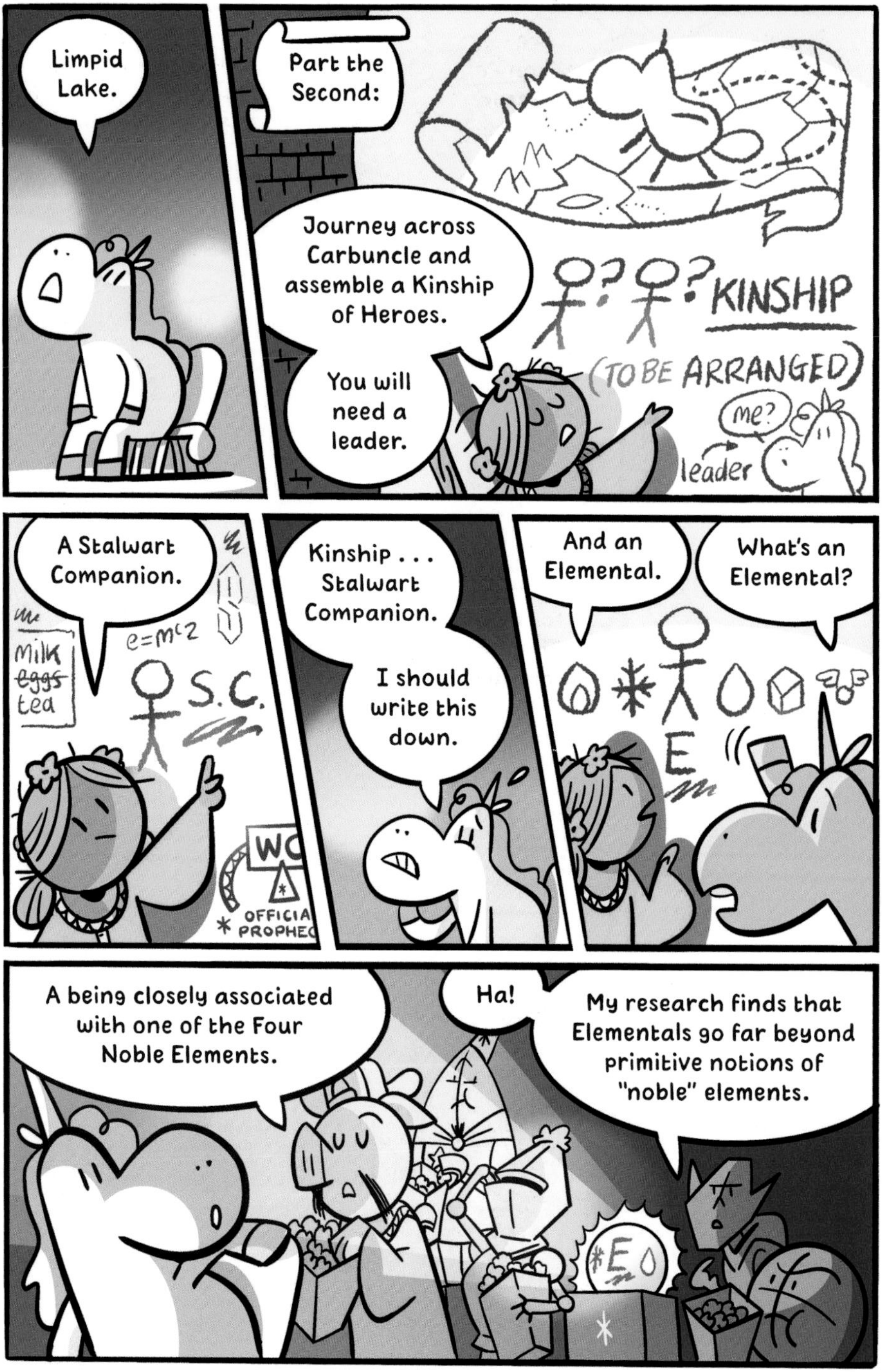
Limpid Lake.
Part the Second:
Journey across Carbuncle and assemble a Kinship of Heroes.
You will need a leader.
KINSHIP
(TO BE ARRANGED)
me?
leader
A Stalwart Companion.
Milk
eggs
tea
e=mc2
S.C.
OFFICIA
PROPHEC
Kinship . . . Stalwart Companion.
I should write this down.
And an Elemental.
What's an Elemental?
E
A being closely associated with one of the Four Noble Elements.
Ha!
My research finds that Elementals go far beyond primitive notions of "noble" elements.
E

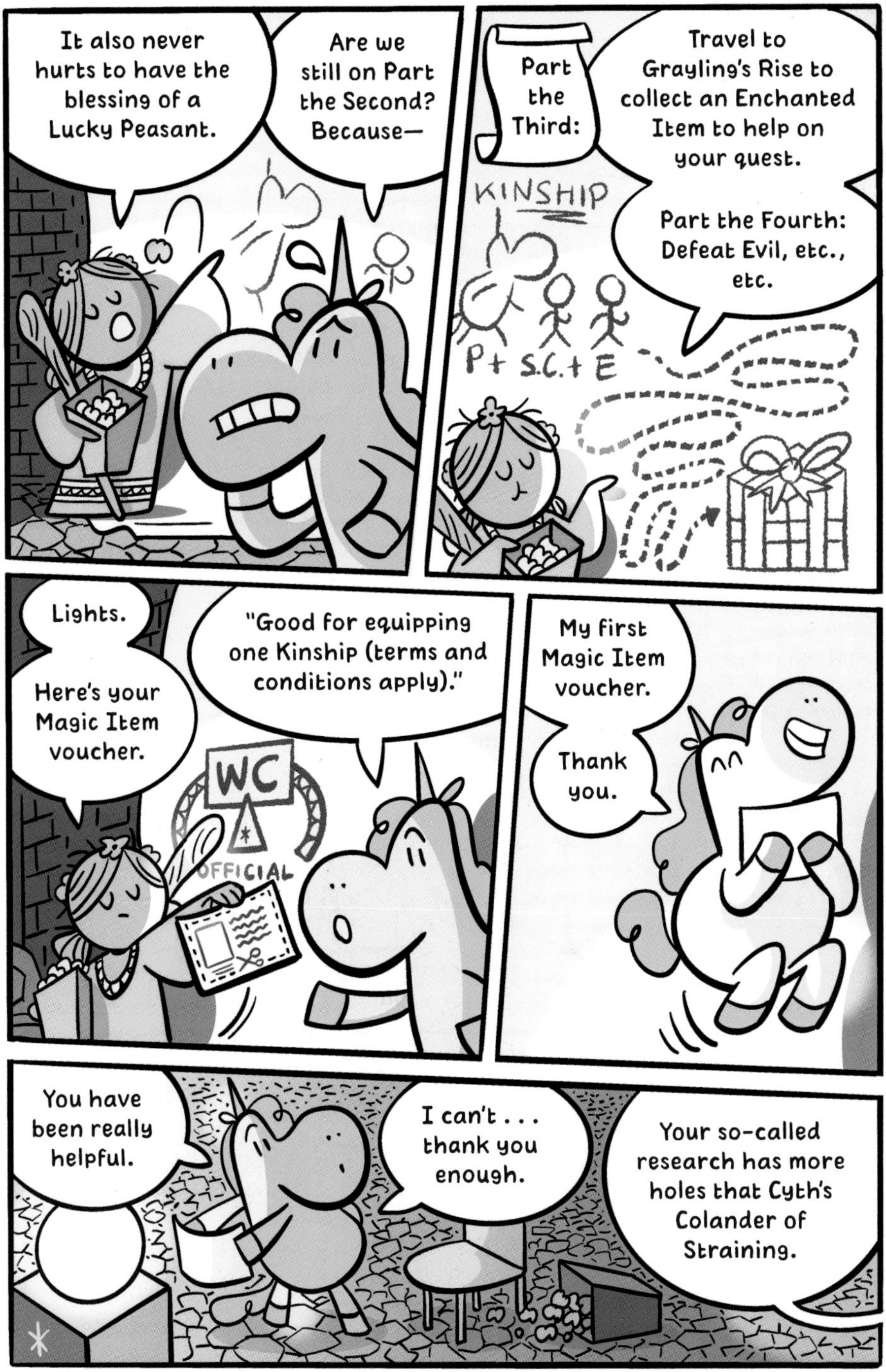
It also never hurts to have the blessing of a Lucky Peasant.
Are we still on Part the Second? Because—
Part the Third:
Travel to Grayling's Rise to collect an Enchanted Item to help on your quest.
Part the Fourth: Defeat Evil, etc., etc.
KINSHIP
P + S.C. + E
Lights.
Here's your Magic Item voucher.
"Good for equipping one Kinship (terms and conditions apply)."
WC
OFFICIAL
My first Magic Item voucher.
Thank you.
You have been really helpful.
I can't . . . thank you enough.
Your so-called research has more holes that Cyth's Colander of Straining.

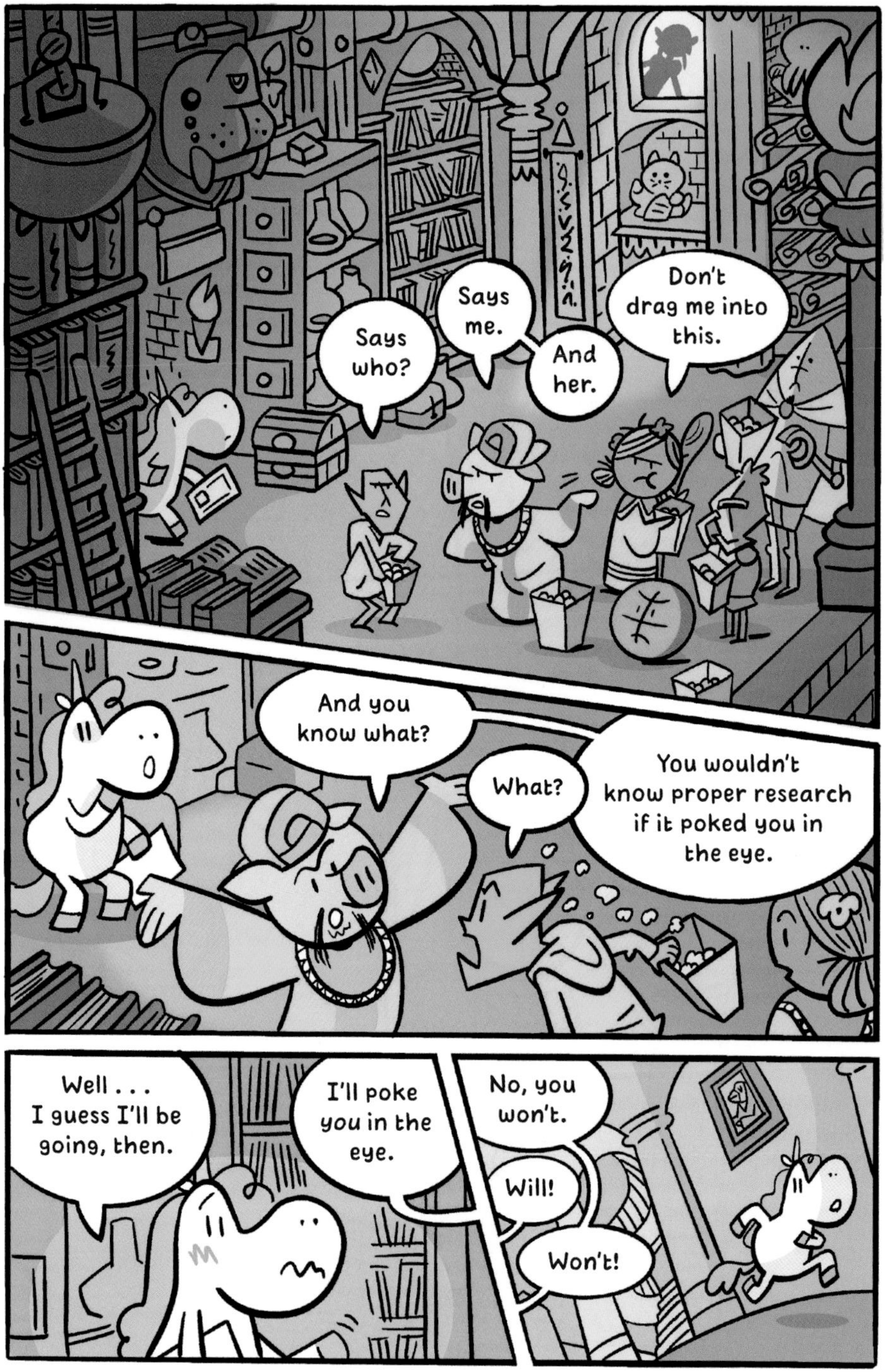
Says who?
Says me.
And her.
Don't drag me into this.
And you know what?
What?
You wouldn't know proper research if it poked you in the eye.
Well . . . I guess I'll be going, then.
I'll poke *you* in the eye.
No, you won't.
Will!
Won't!

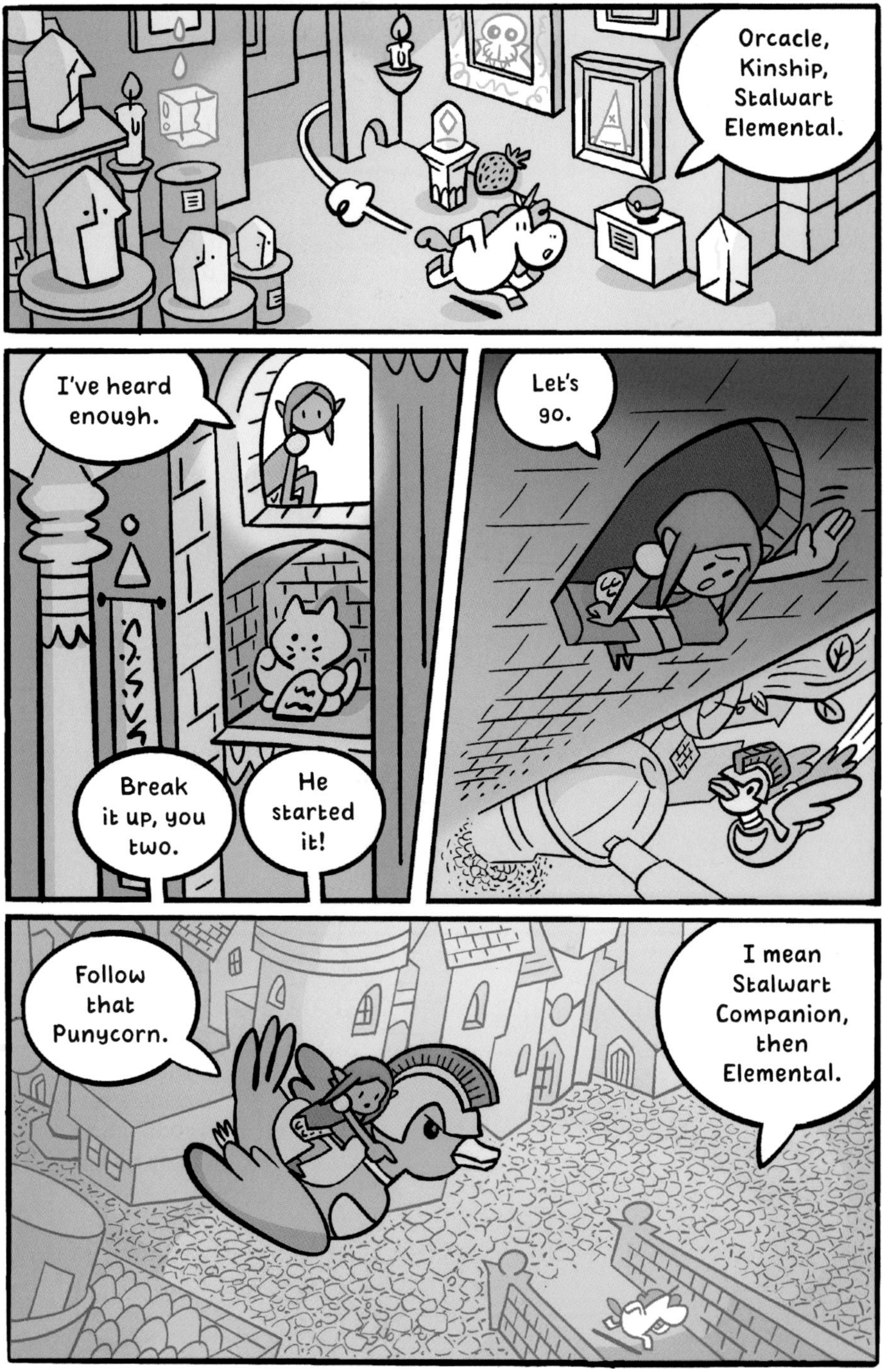
Orcacle, Kinship, Stalwart Elemental.
I've heard enough.
Break it up, you two.
He started it!
Let's go.
Follow that Punycorn.
I mean Stalwart Companion, then Elemental.

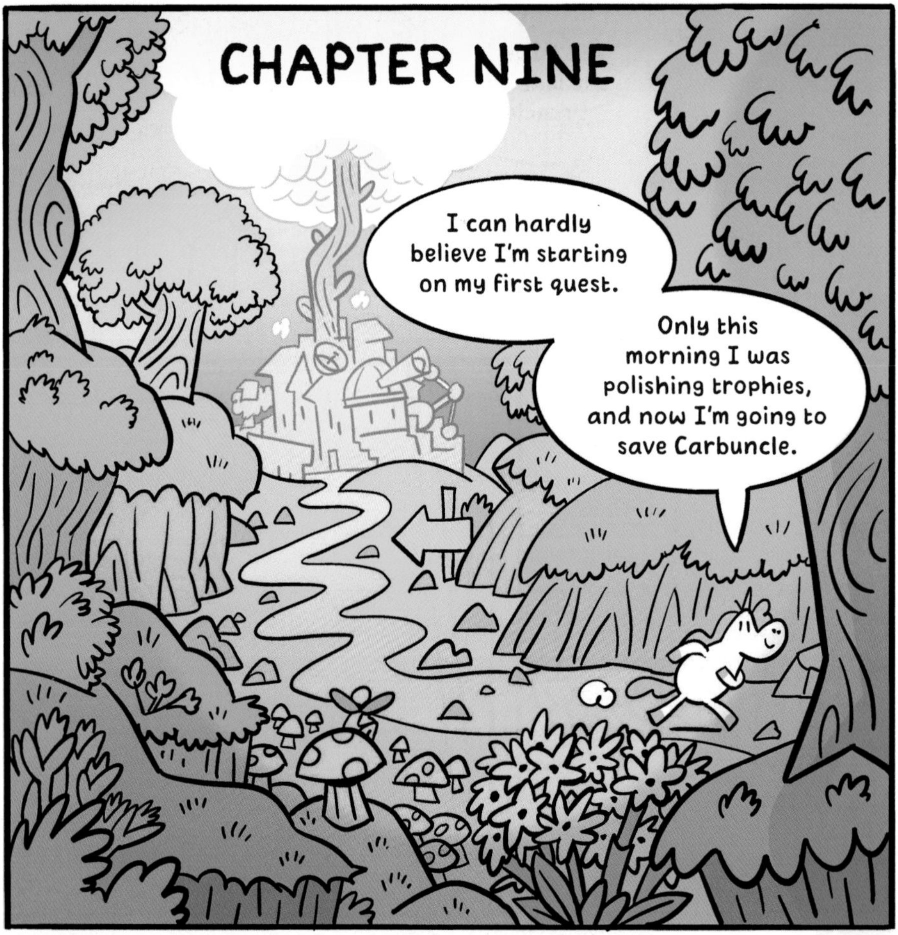
CHAPTER NINE
I can hardly believe I'm starting on my first quest.
Only this morning I was polishing trophies, and now I'm going to save Carbuncle.

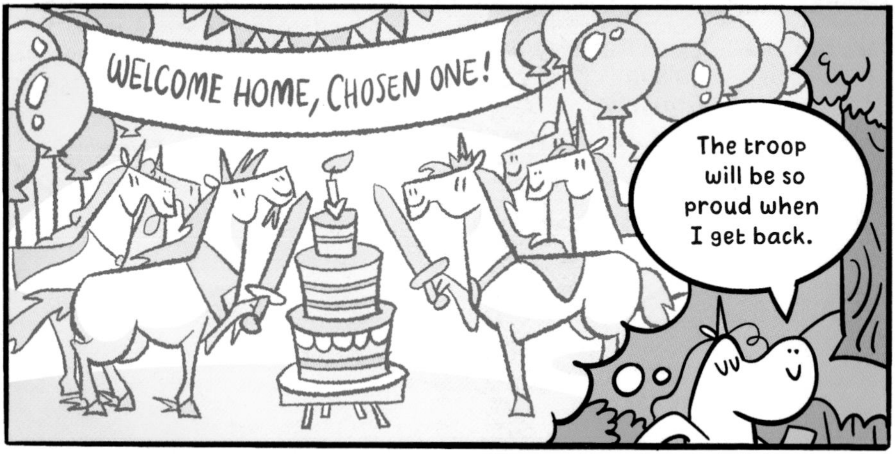
WELCOME HOME, CHOSEN ONE!
The troop will be so proud when I get back.

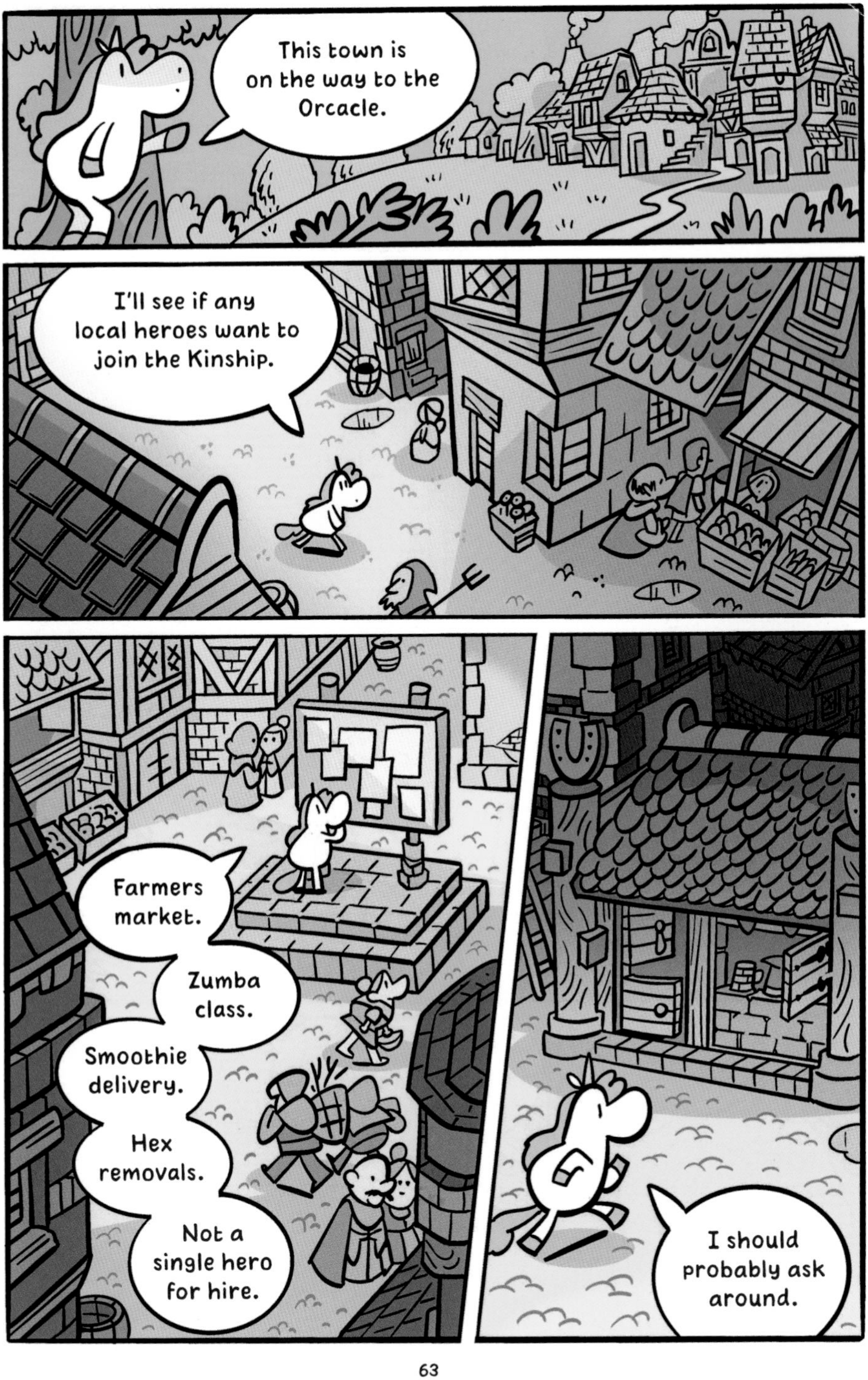
This town is on the way to the Orcacle.
I'll see if any local heroes want to join the Kinship.
Farmers market.
Zumba class.
Smoothie delivery.
Hex removals.
Not a single hero for hire.
I should probably ask around.

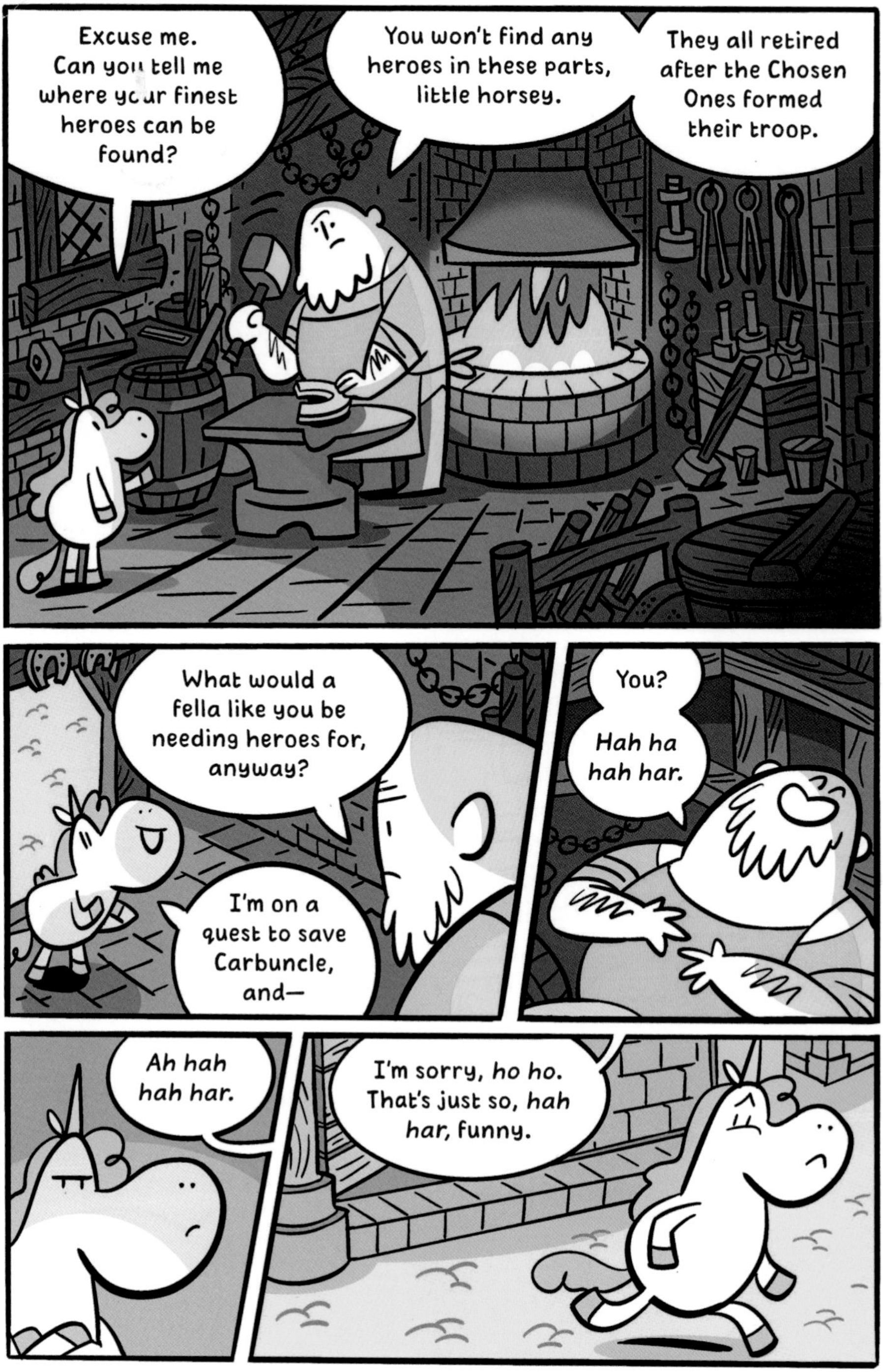

Excuse me. Can you tell me where your finest heroes can be found?
You won't find any heroes in these parts, little horsey.
They all retired after the Chosen Ones formed their troop.
What would a fella like you be needing heroes for, anyway?
I'm on a quest to save Carbuncle, and—
You?
Hah ha hah har.
Ah hah hah har.
I'm sorry, *ho ho.* That's just so, *hah har,* funny.

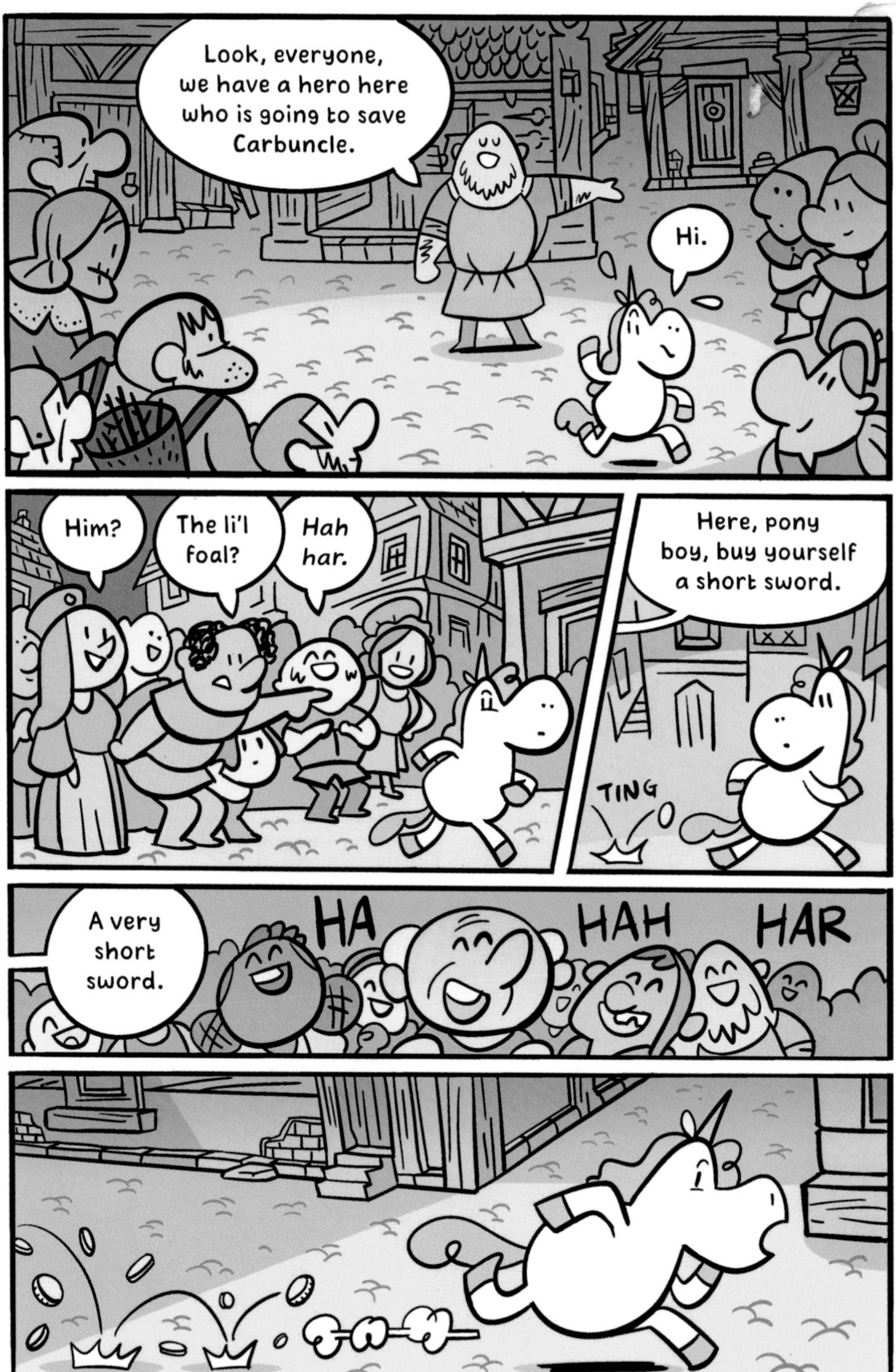
Look, everyone, we have a hero here who is going to save Carbuncle.
Hi.
Him?
The li'l foal?
Hah har.
Here, pony boy, buy yourself a short sword.
TING
A very short sword.
HA
HAH
HAR

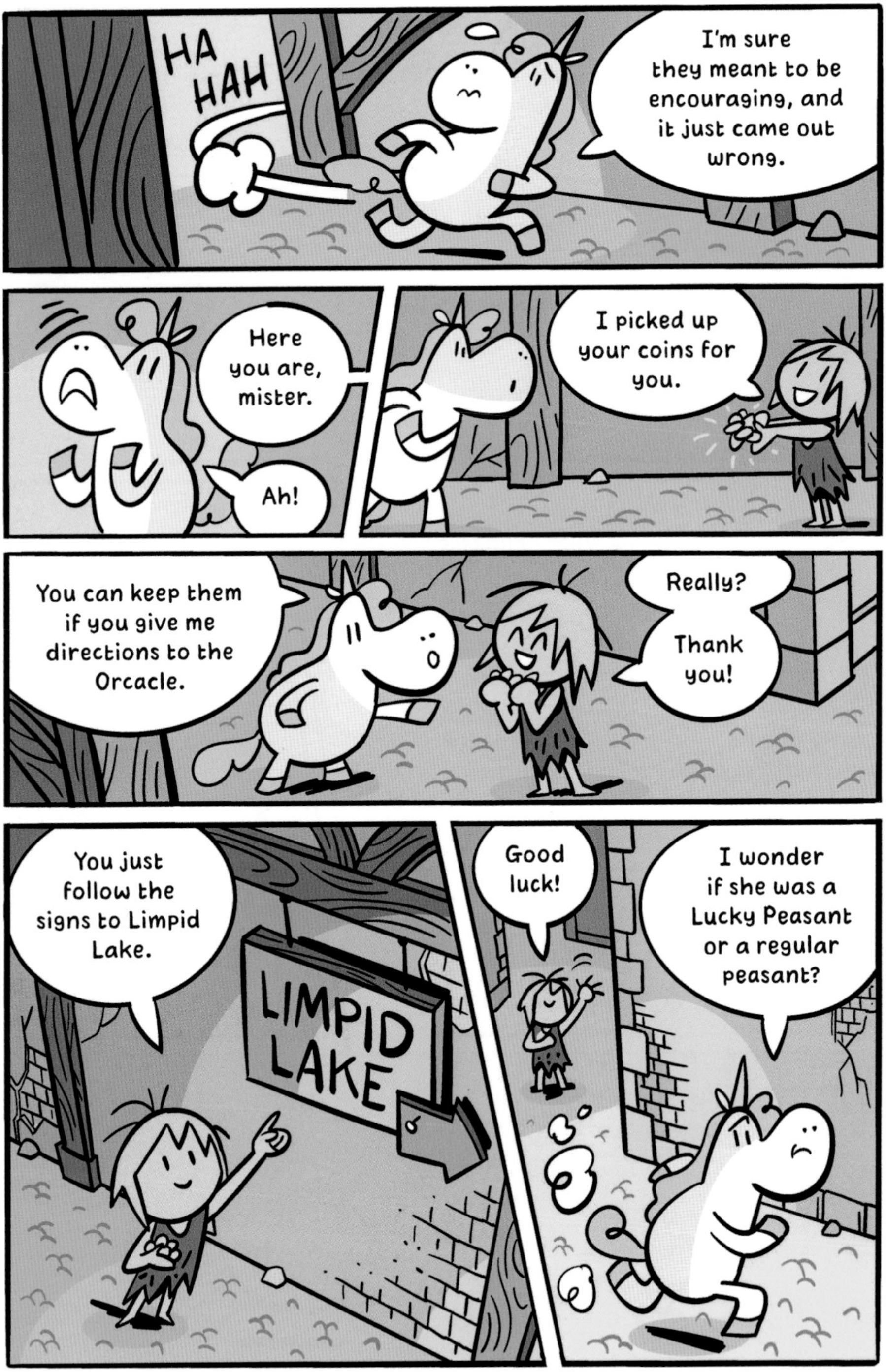
HA
HAH
I'm sure they meant to be encouraging, and it just came out wrong.
Here you are, mister.
Ah!
I picked up your coins for you.
You can keep them if you give me directions to the Orcacle.
Really?
Thank you!
You just follow the signs to Limpid Lake.
LIMPID LAKE
Good luck!
I wonder if she was a Lucky Peasant or a regular peasant?

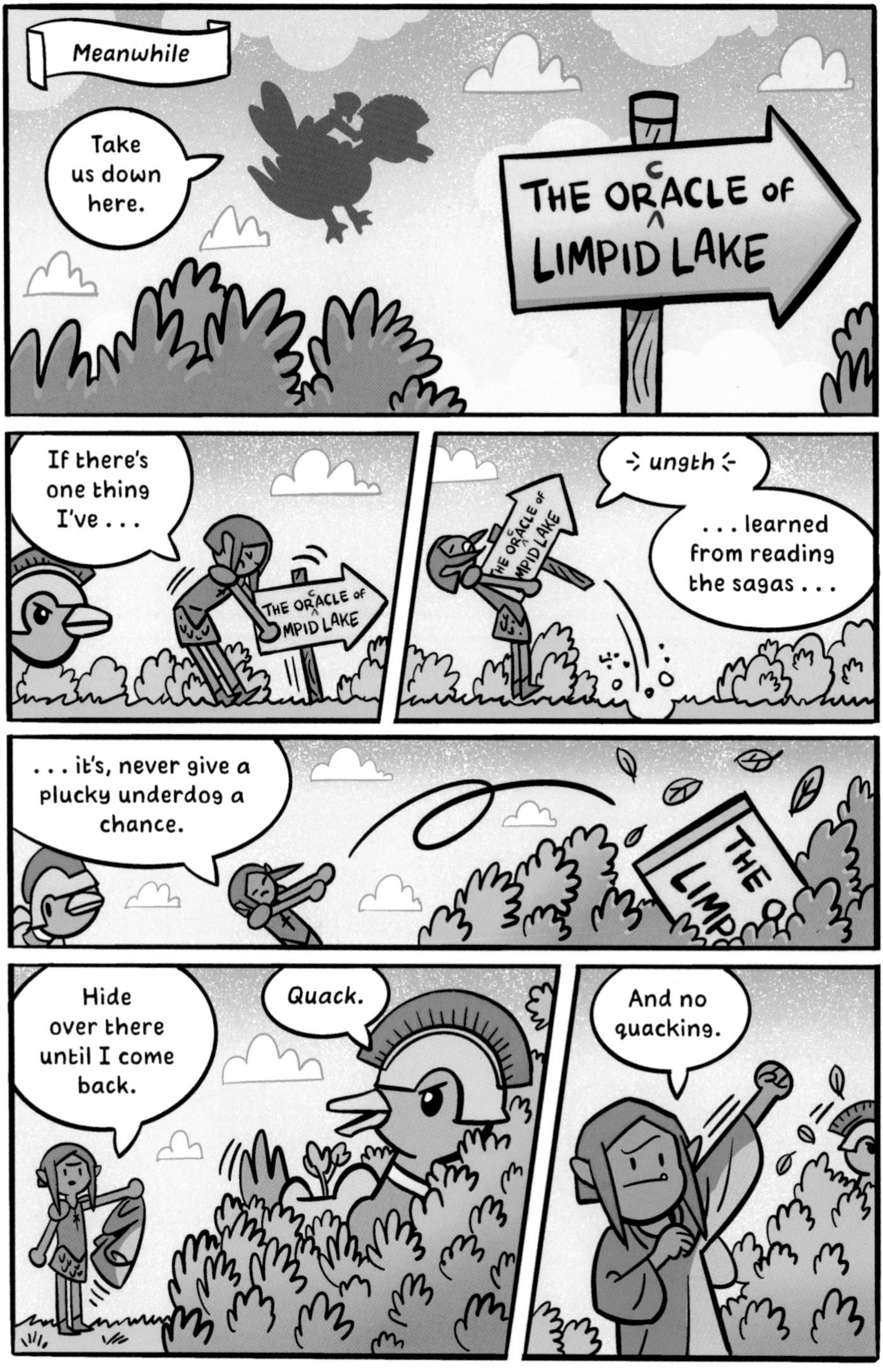
Meanwhile
Take us down here.
THE ORACLE OF LIMPID LAKE
If there's one thing I've . . .
THE ORACLE OF MPID LAKE
THE ORACLE OF MPID LAKE
ungth
. . . learned from reading the sagas . . .
. . . it's, never give a plucky underdog a chance.
THE LIMP
Hide over there until I come back.
Quack.
And no quacking.

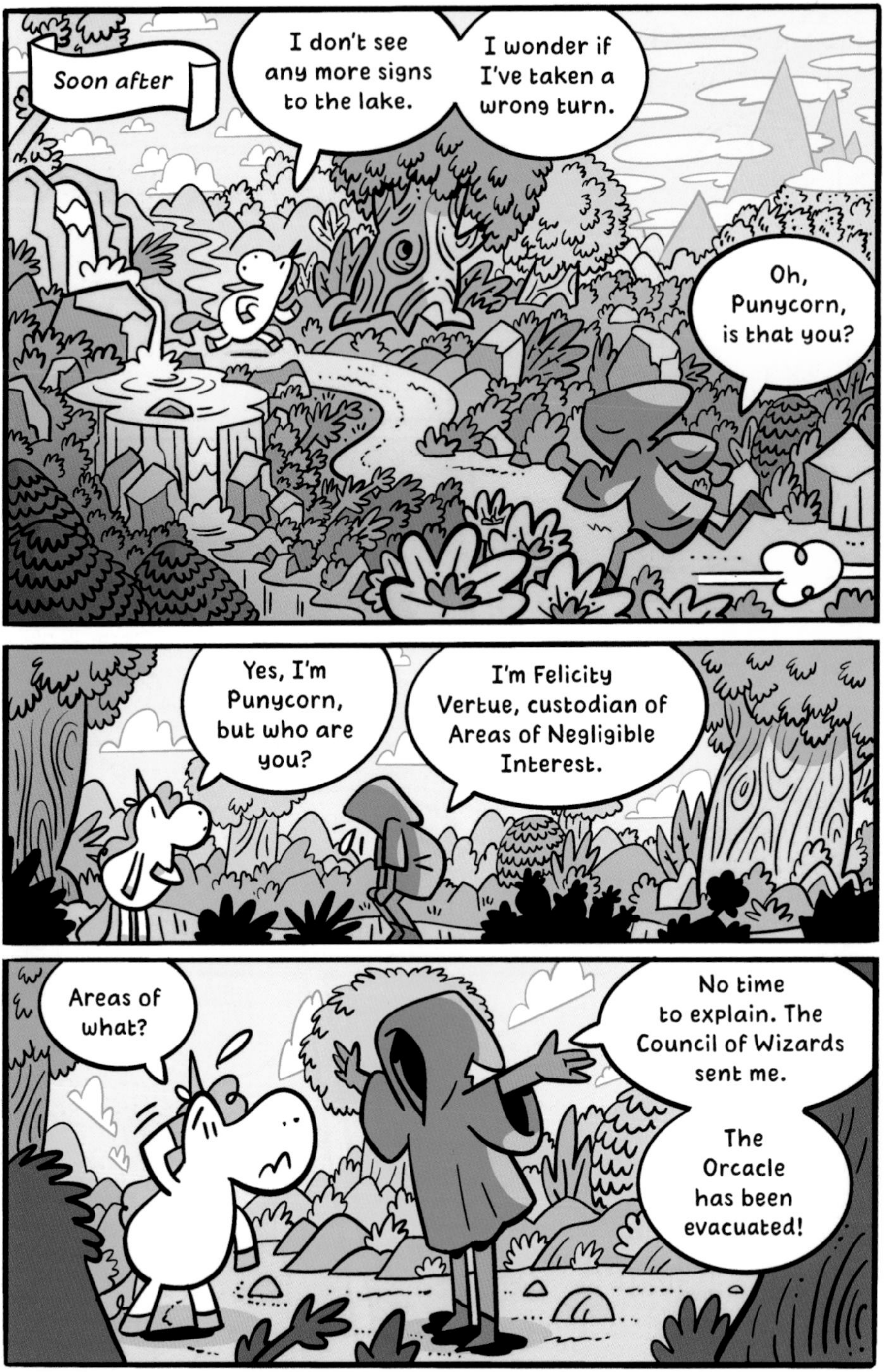
Soon after
I don't see any more signs to the lake.
I wonder if I've taken a wrong turn.
Oh, Punycorn, is that you?
Yes, I'm Punycorn, but who are you?
I'm Felicity Vertue, custodian of Areas of Negligible Interest.
Areas of what?
No time to explain. The Council of Wizards sent me.
The Orcacle has been evacuated!

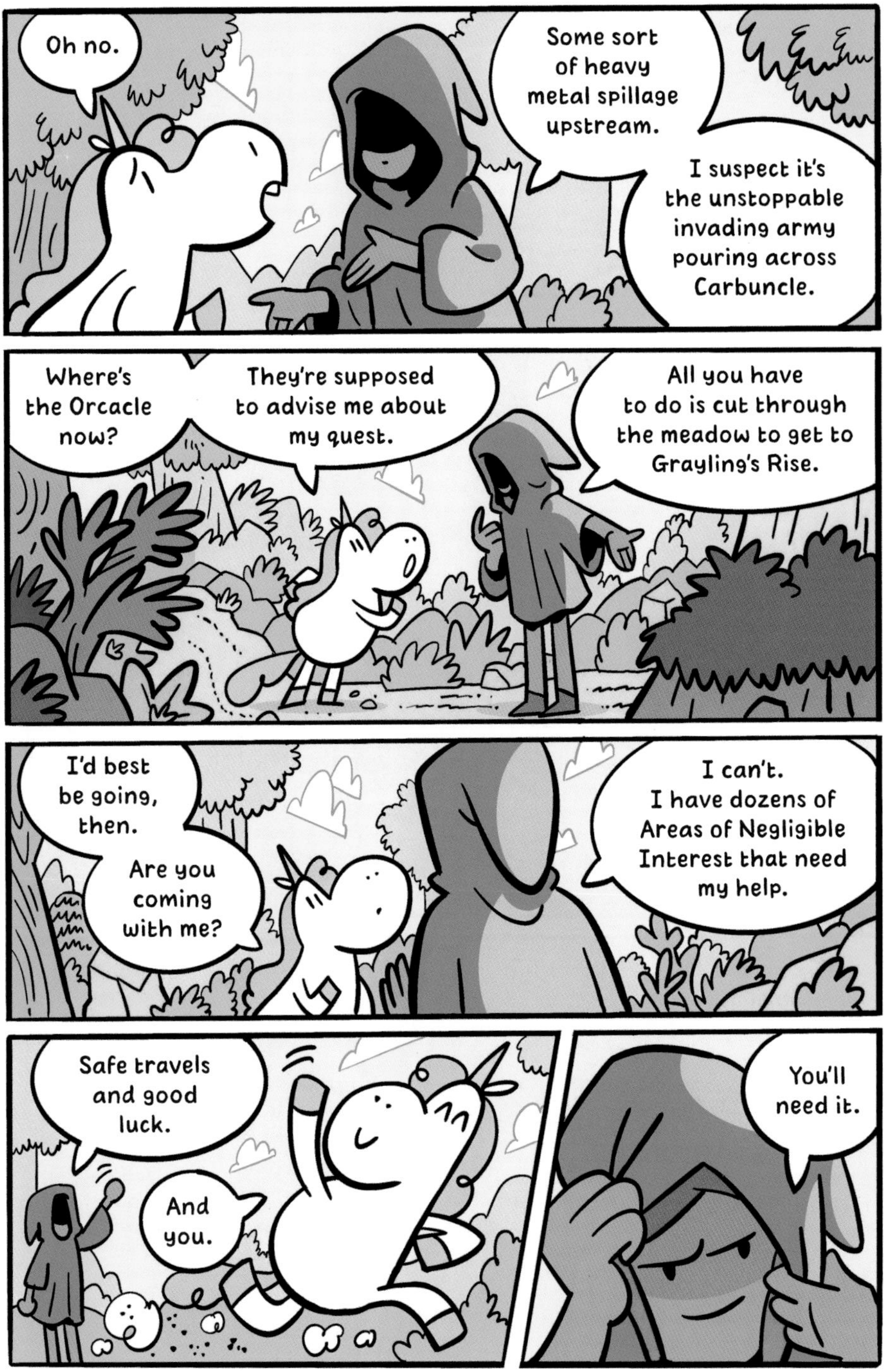
Oh no.
Some sort of heavy metal spillage upstream.
I suspect it's the unstoppable invading army pouring across Carbuncle.
Where's the Orcacle now?
They're supposed to advise me about my quest.
All you have to do is cut through the meadow to get to Grayling's Rise.
I'd best be going, then.
Are you coming with me?
I can't. I have dozens of Areas of Negligible Interest that need my help.
Safe travels and good luck.
And you.
You'll need it.

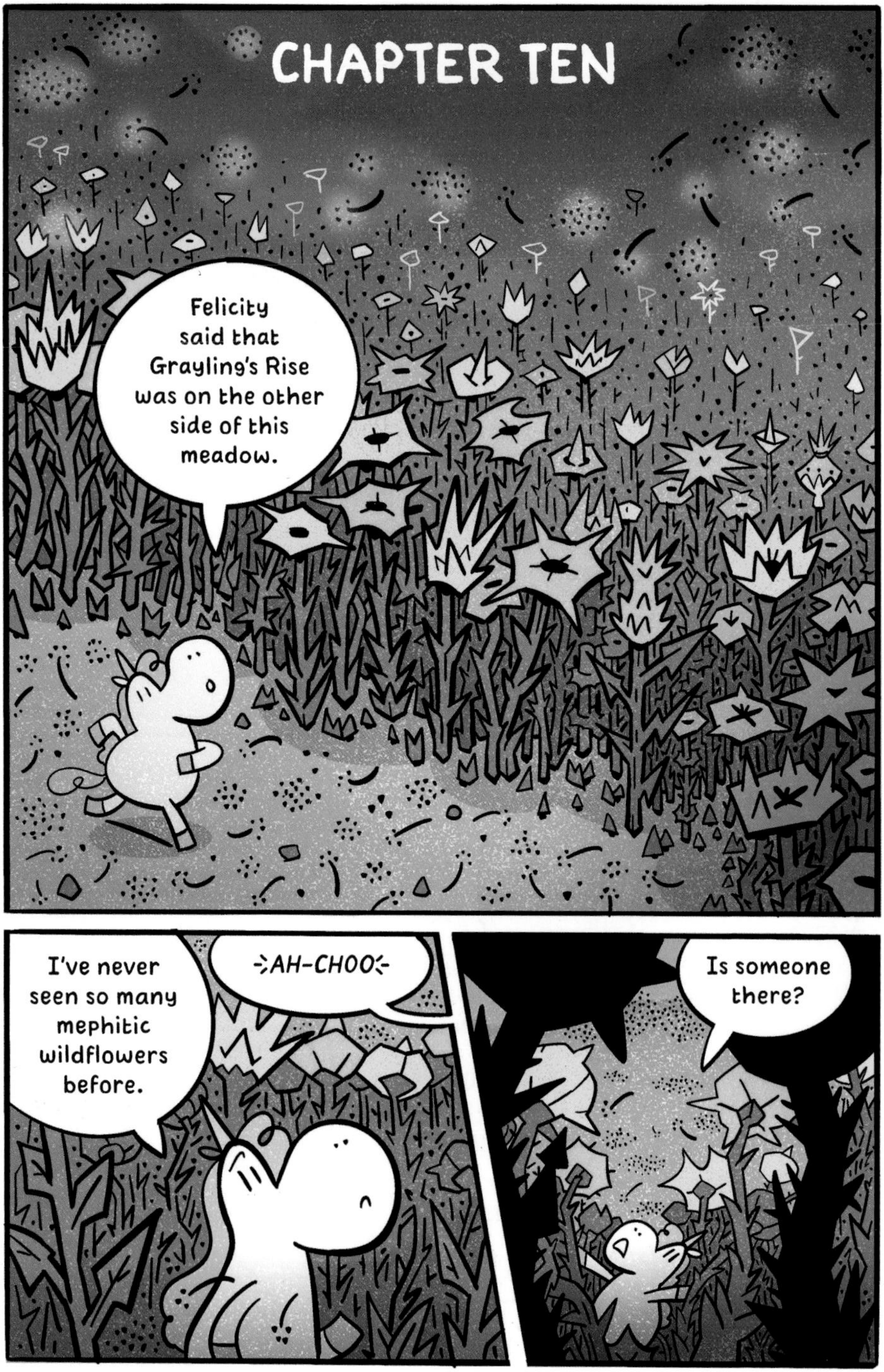
CHAPTER TEN
Felicity said that Grayling's Rise was on the other side of this meadow.
I've never seen so many mephitic wildflowers before.
AH-CHOO
Is someone there?

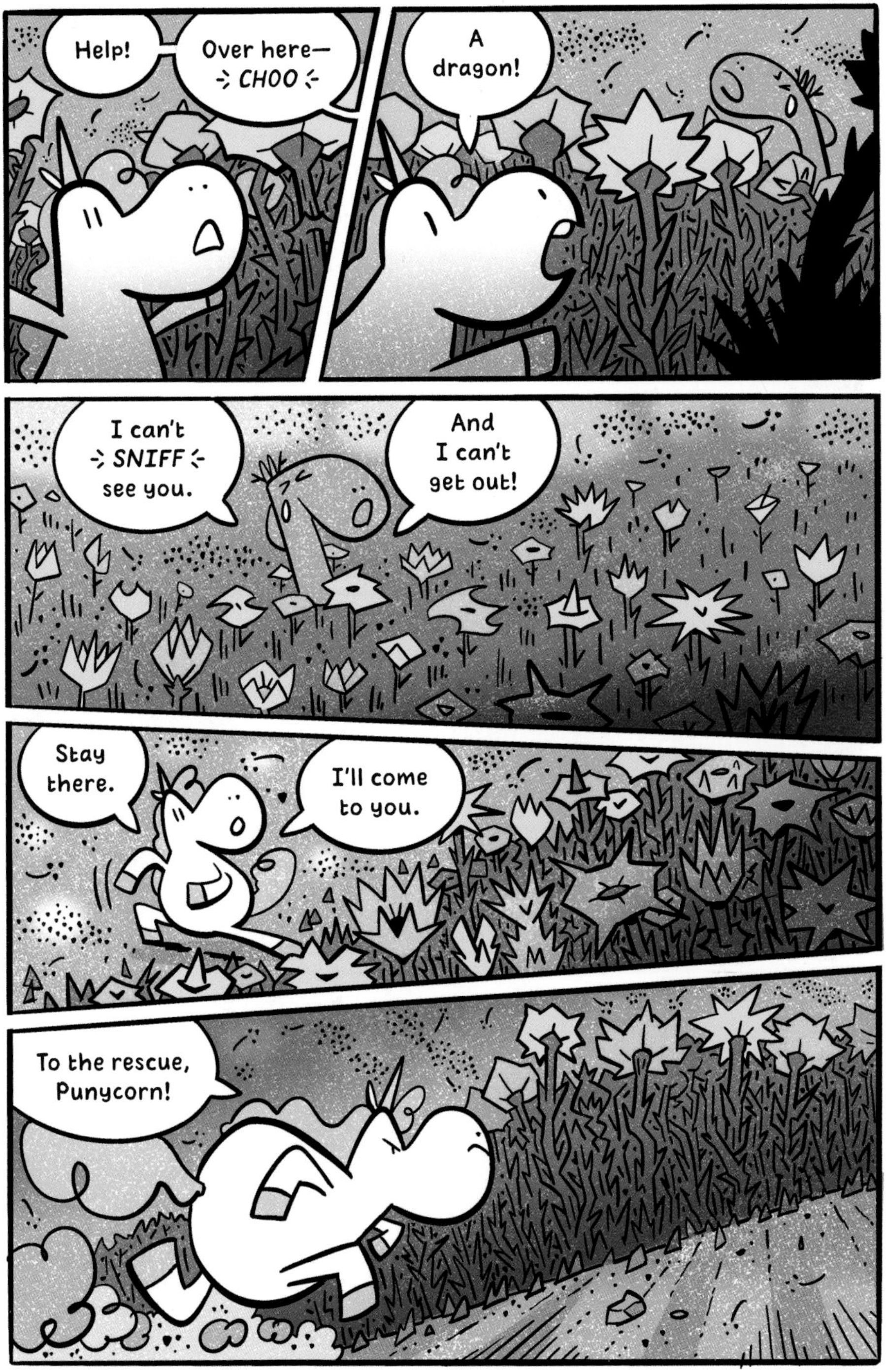
Help!
Over here— CHOO
A dragon!
I can't SNIFF see you.
And I can't get out!
Stay there.
I'll come to you.
To the rescue, Punycorn!

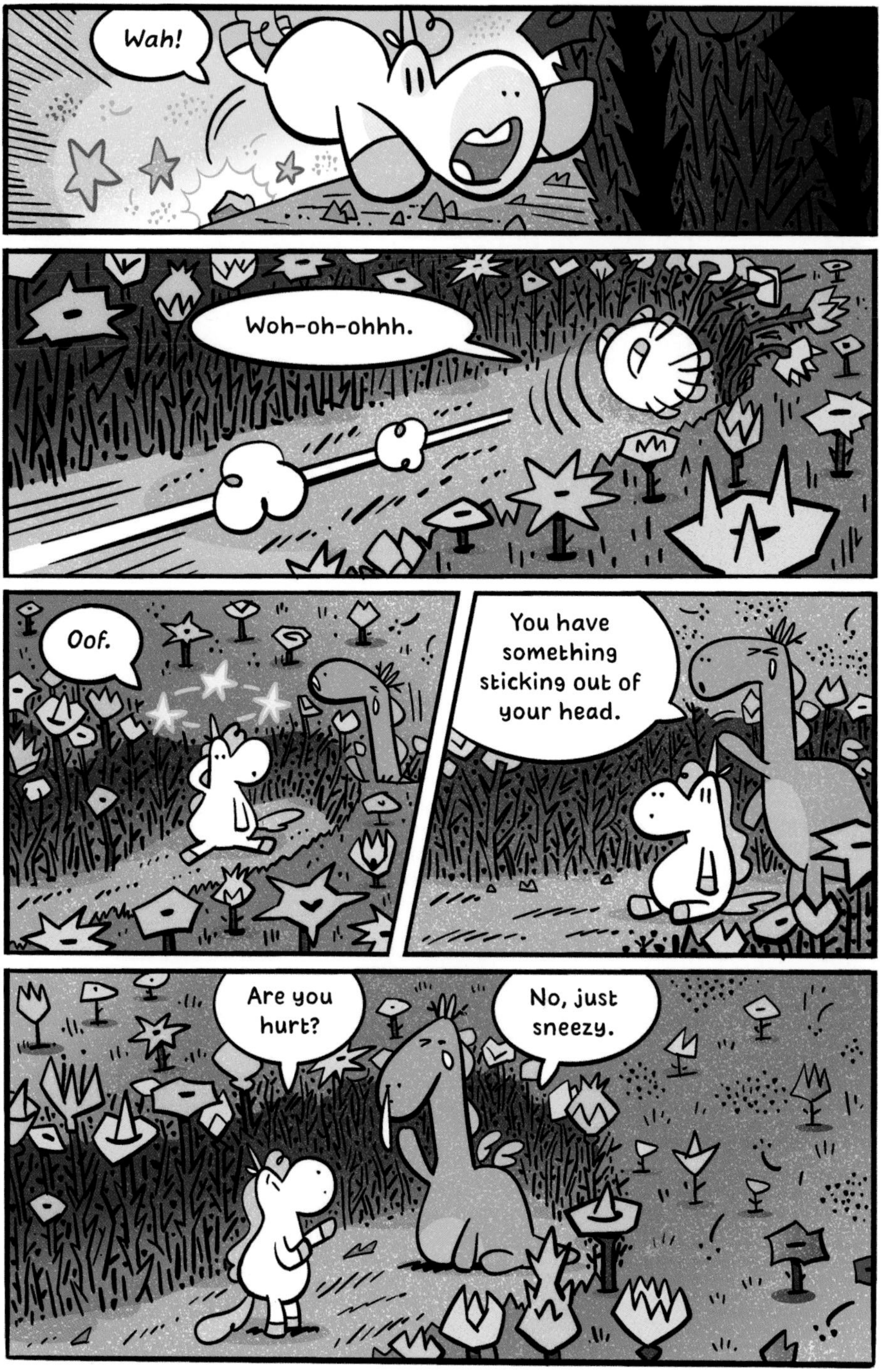
Wah!
Woh-oh-ohhh.
Oof.
You have something sticking out of your head.
Are you hurt?
No, just sneezy.

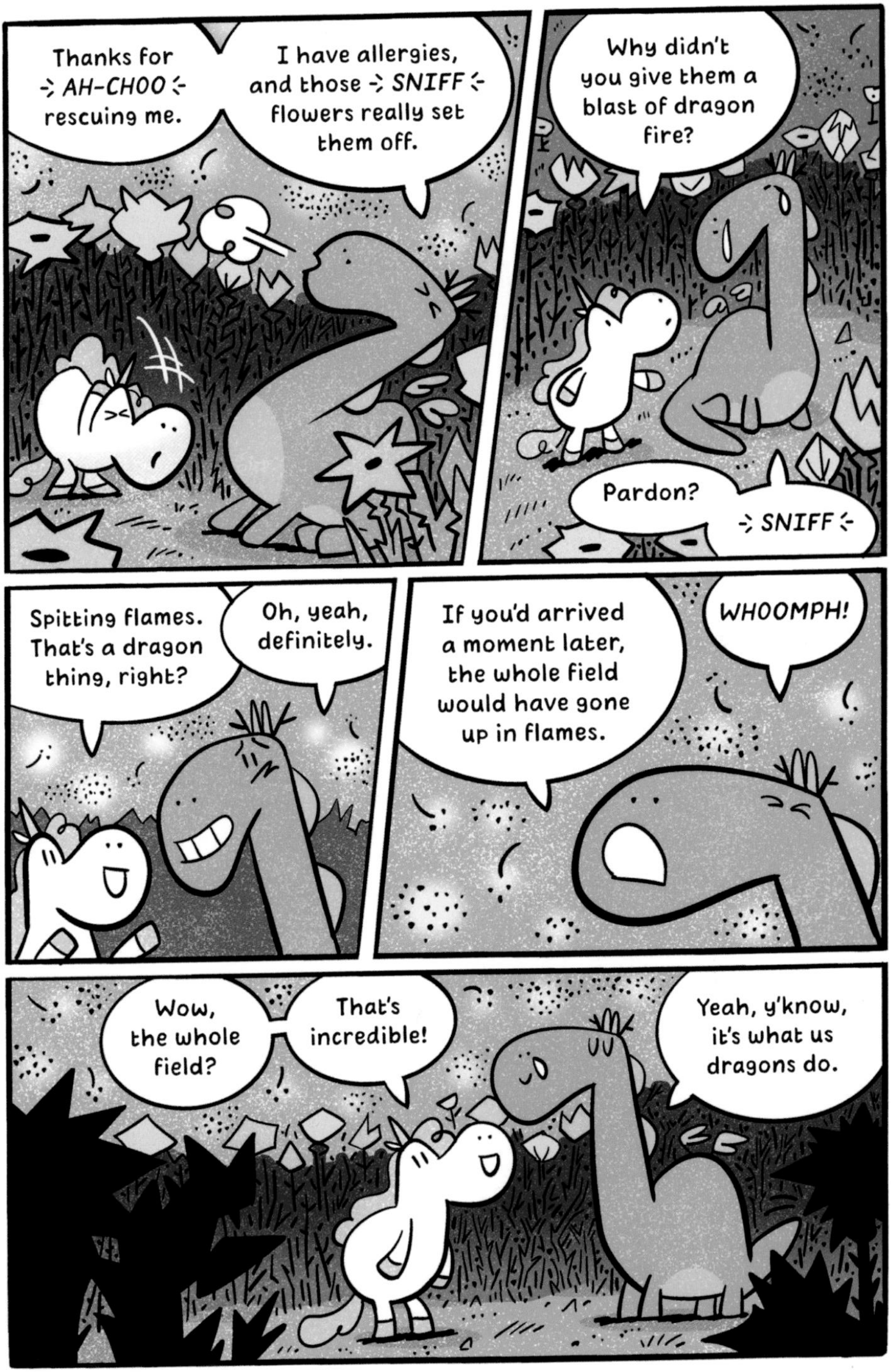
Thanks for -;- AH-CHOO -;- rescuing me.
I have allergies, and those -;- SNIFF -;- flowers really set them off.
Why didn't you give them a blast of dragon fire?
Pardon?
-;- SNIFF -;-
Spitting flames. That's a dragon thing, right?
Oh, yeah, definitely.
If you'd arrived a moment later, the whole field would have gone up in flames.
WHOOMPH!
Wow, the whole field?
That's incredible!
Yeah, y'know, it's what us dragons do.

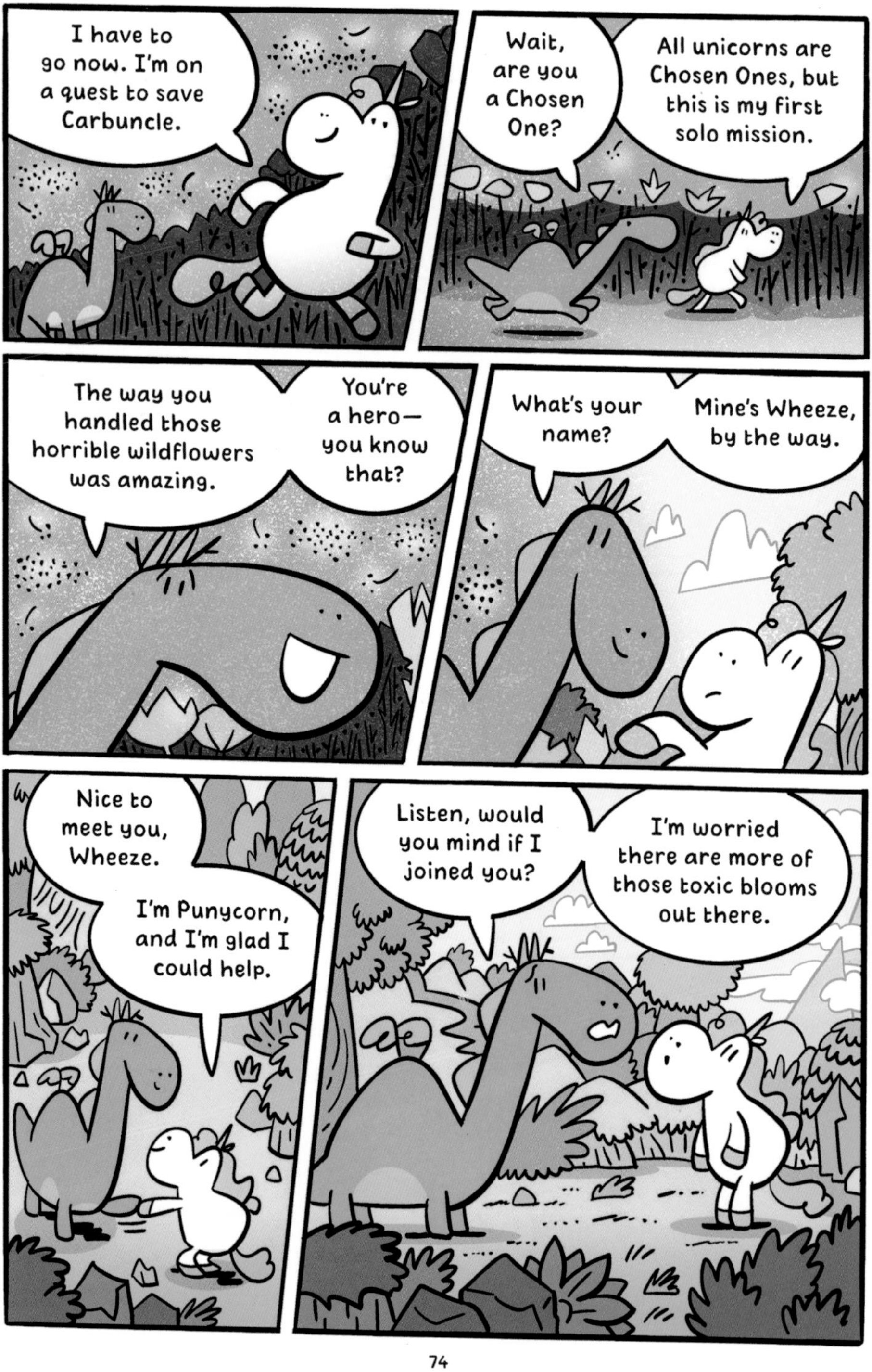
I have to go now. I'm on a quest to save Carbuncle.
Wait, are you a Chosen One?
All unicorns are Chosen Ones, but this is my first solo mission.
The way you handled those horrible wildflowers was amazing.
You're a hero—you know that?
What's your name?
Mine's Wheeze, by the way.
Nice to meet you, Wheeze.
I'm Punycorn, and I'm glad I could help.
Listen, would you mind if I joined you?
I'm worried there are more of those toxic blooms out there.

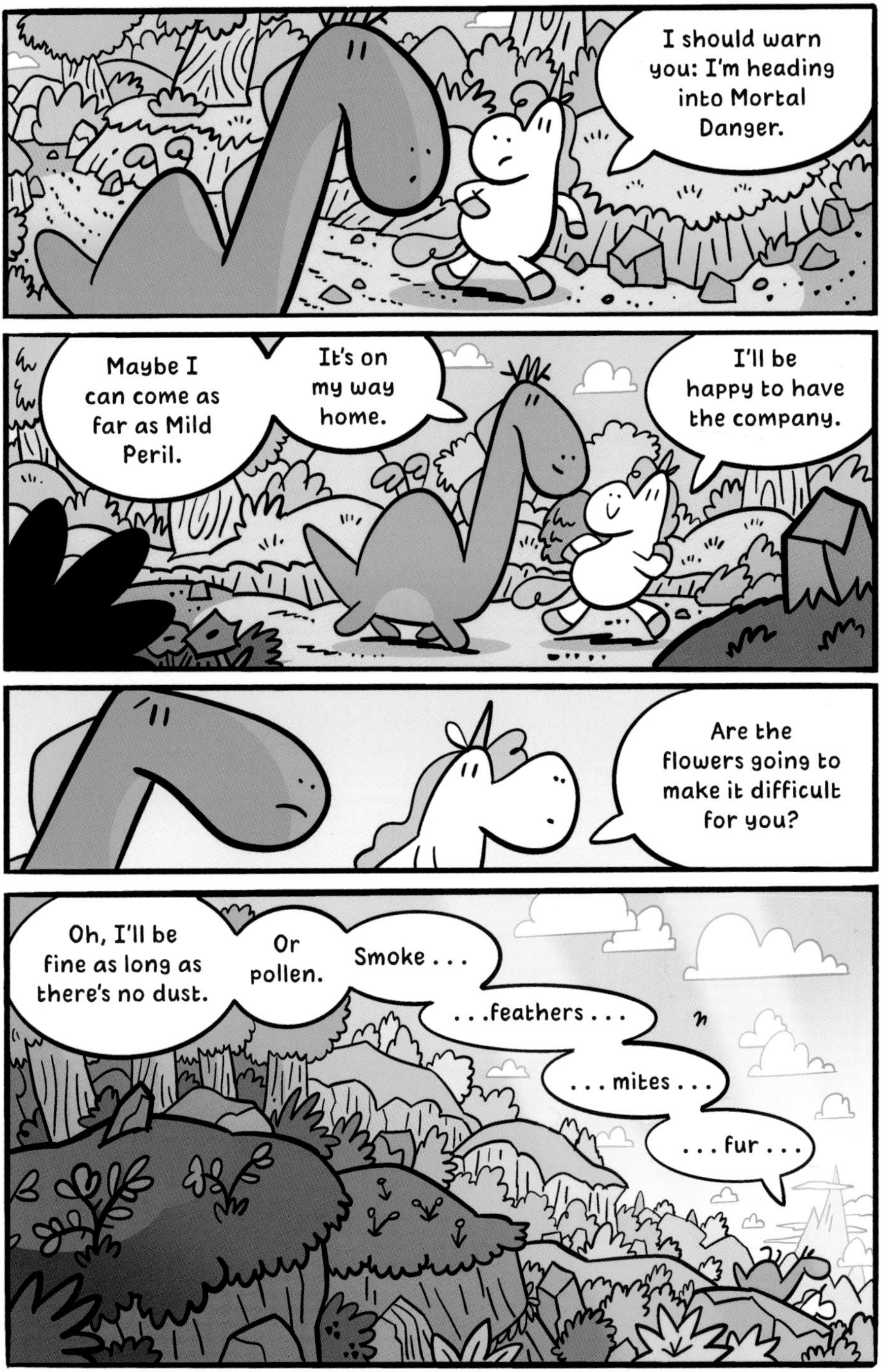
I should warn you: I'm heading into Mortal Danger.
Maybe I can come as far as Mild Peril.
It's on my way home.
I'll be happy to have the company.
Are the flowers going to make it difficult for you?
Oh, I'll be fine as long as there's no dust.
Or pollen.
Smoke . . .
. . .feathers . . .
. . . mites . . .
. . . fur . . .

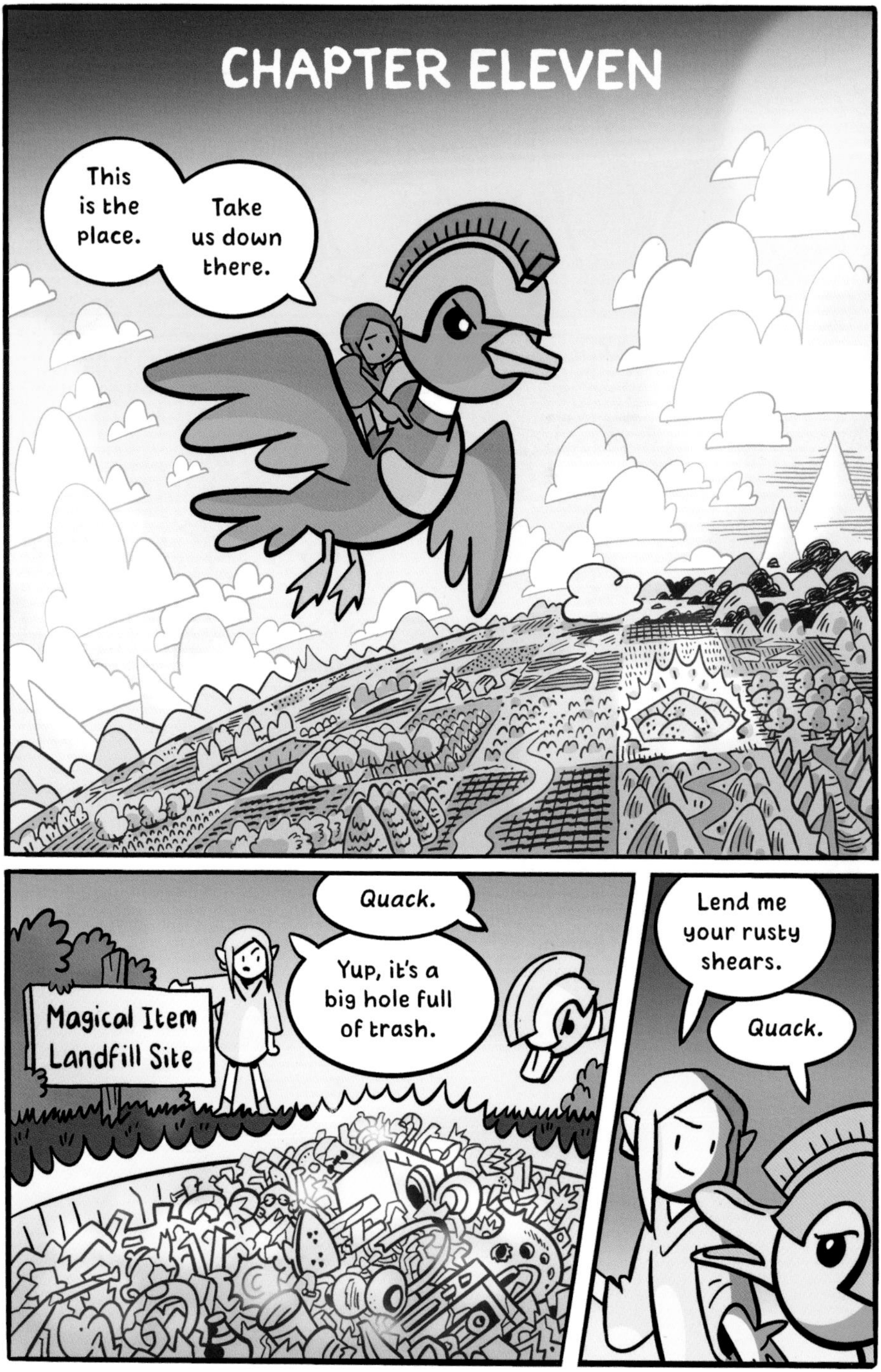
CHAPTER ELEVEN
This is the place.
Take us down there.
Quack.
Yup, it's a big hole full of trash.
Magical Item Landfill Site
Lend me your rusty shears.
Quack.

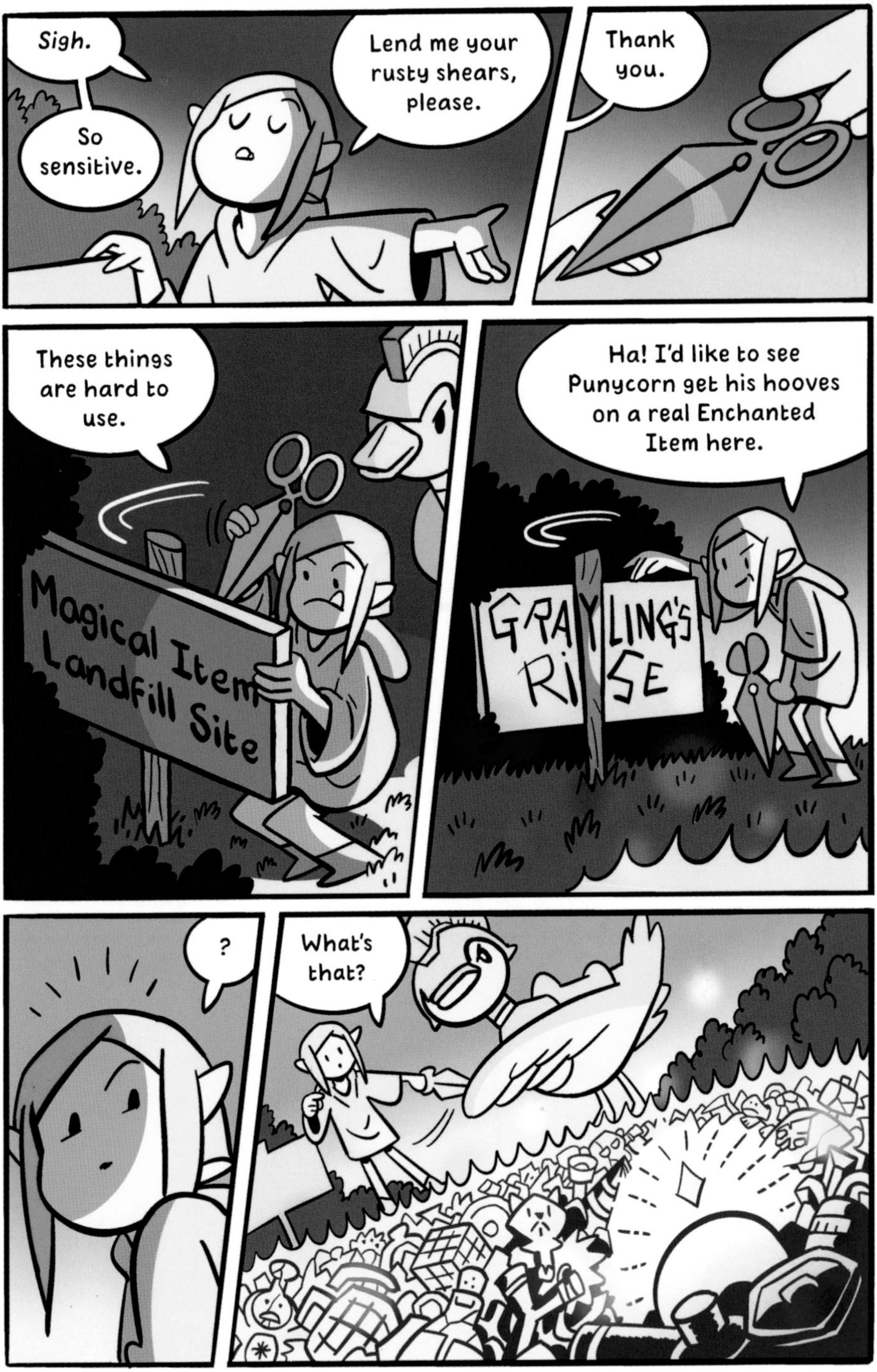
Sigh.
So sensitive.
Lend me your rusty shears, please.
Thank you.
These things are hard to use.
Magical Item Landfill Site
Ha! I'd like to see Punycorn get his hooves on a real Enchanted Item here.
GRAYLING'S RISE
?
What's that?

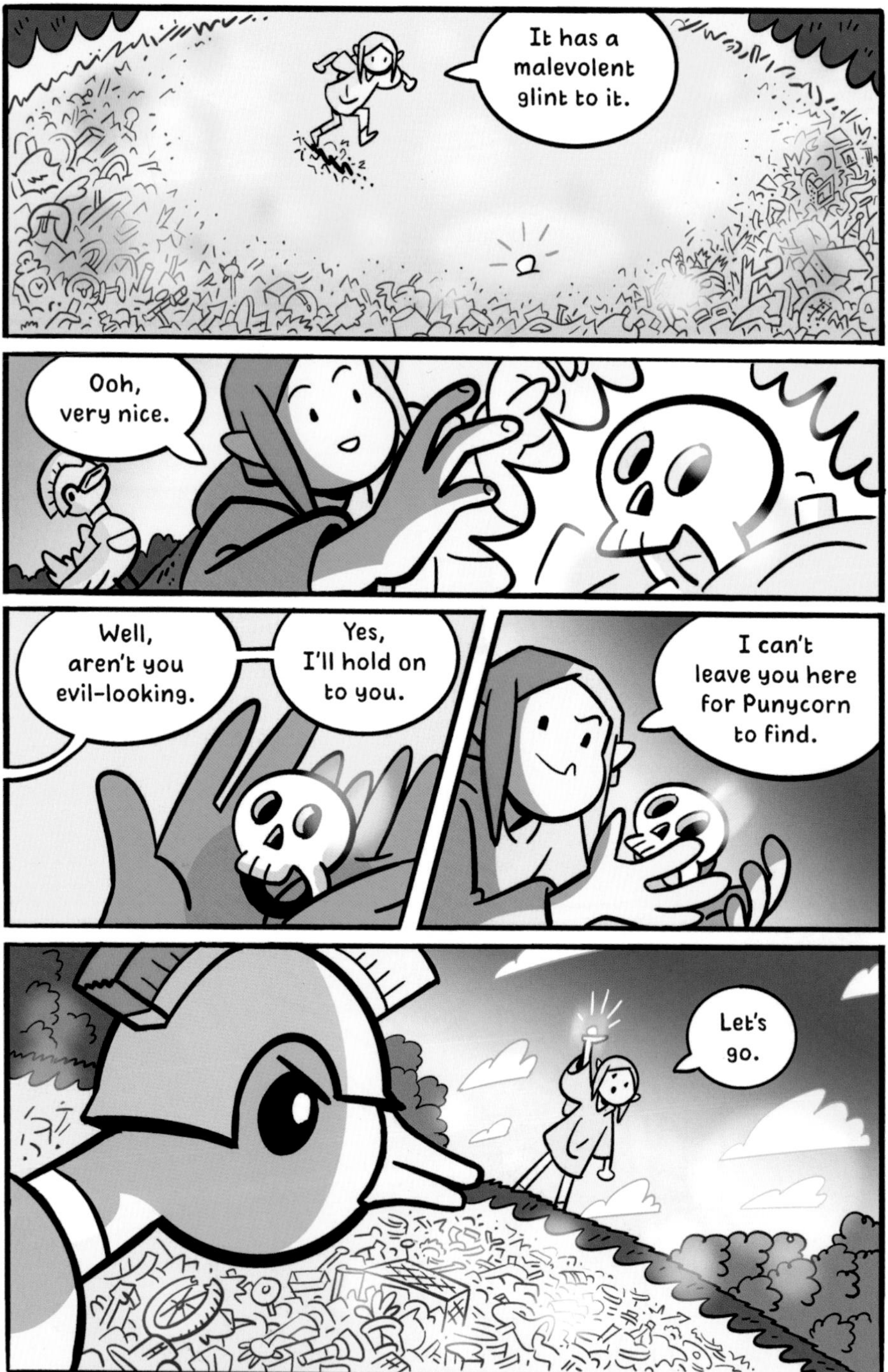
It has a malevolent glint to it.
Ooh, very nice.
Well, aren't you evil-looking.
Yes, I'll hold on to you.
I can't leave you here for Punycorn to find.
Let's go.

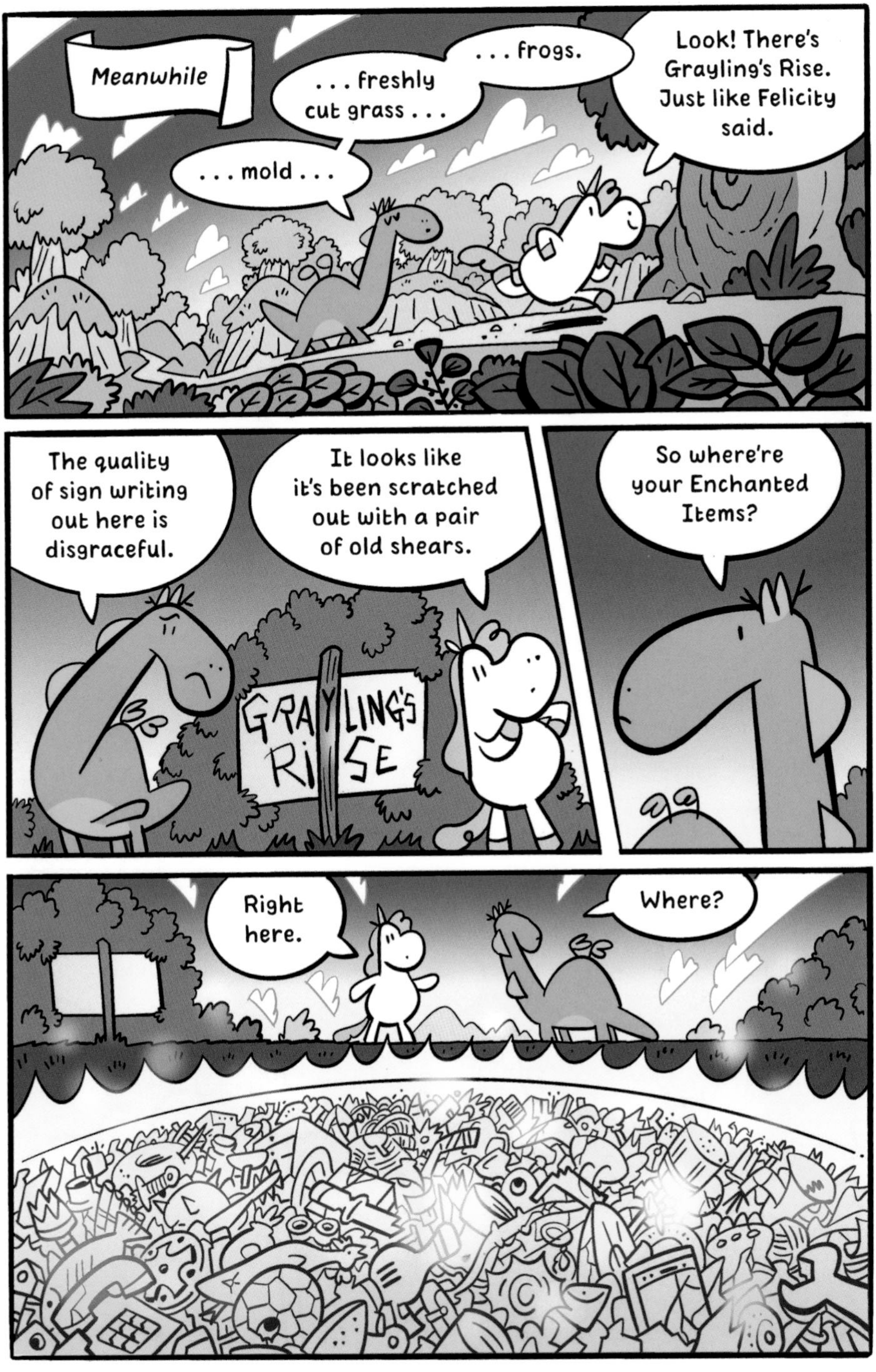

Meanwhile
. . . mold . . .
. . . freshly cut grass . . .
. . . frogs.
Look! There's Grayling's Rise. Just like Felicity said.
The quality of sign writing out here is disgraceful.
GRAYLING'S RISE
It looks like it's been scratched out with a pair of old shears.
So where're your Enchanted Items?
Right here.
Where?

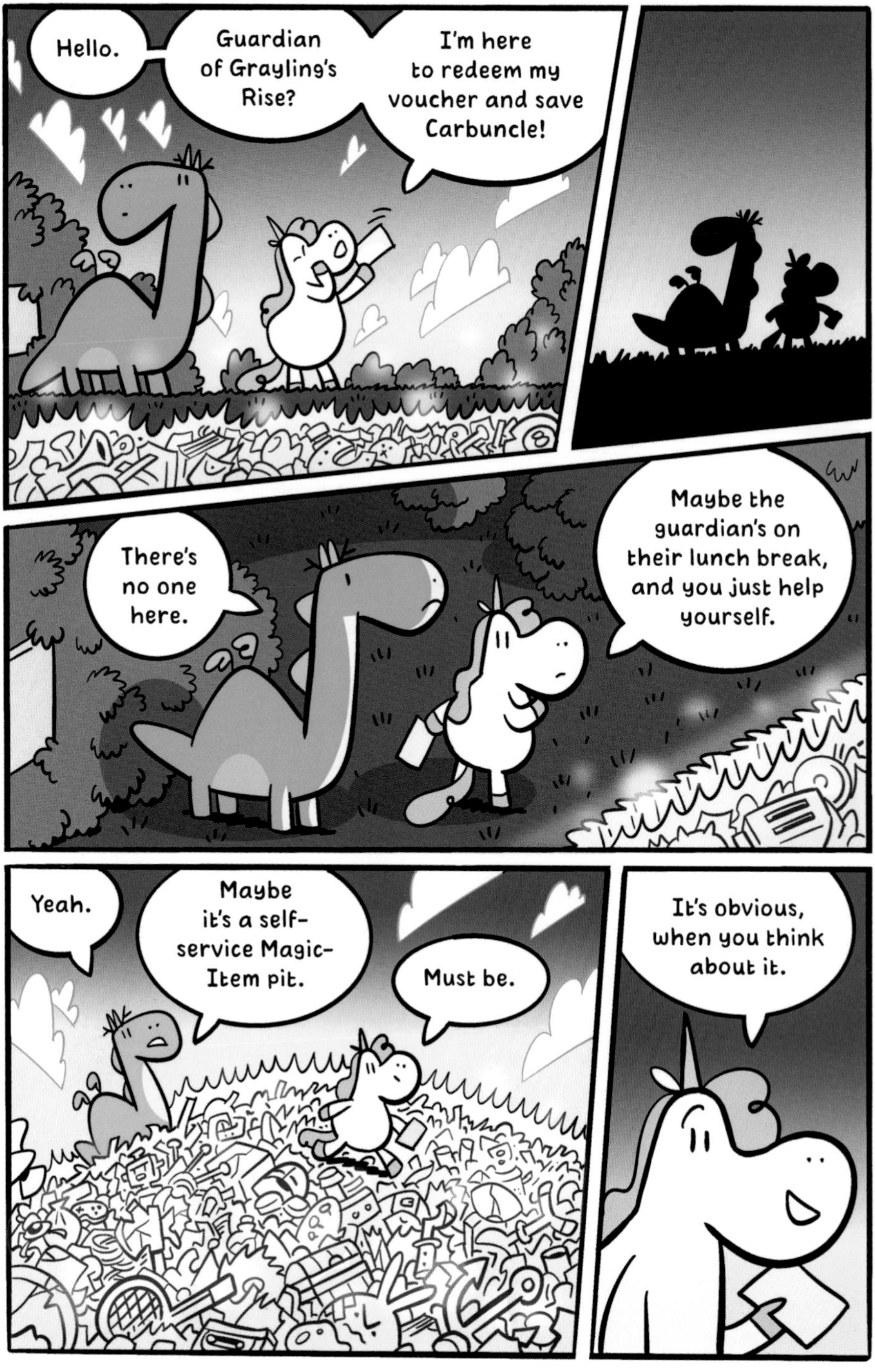

Hello.
Guardian of Grayling's Rise?
I'm here to redeem my voucher and save Carbuncle!
There's no one here.
Maybe the guardian's on their lunch break, and you just help yourself.
Yeah.
Maybe it's a self-service Magic-Item pit.
Must be.
It's obvious, when you think about it.

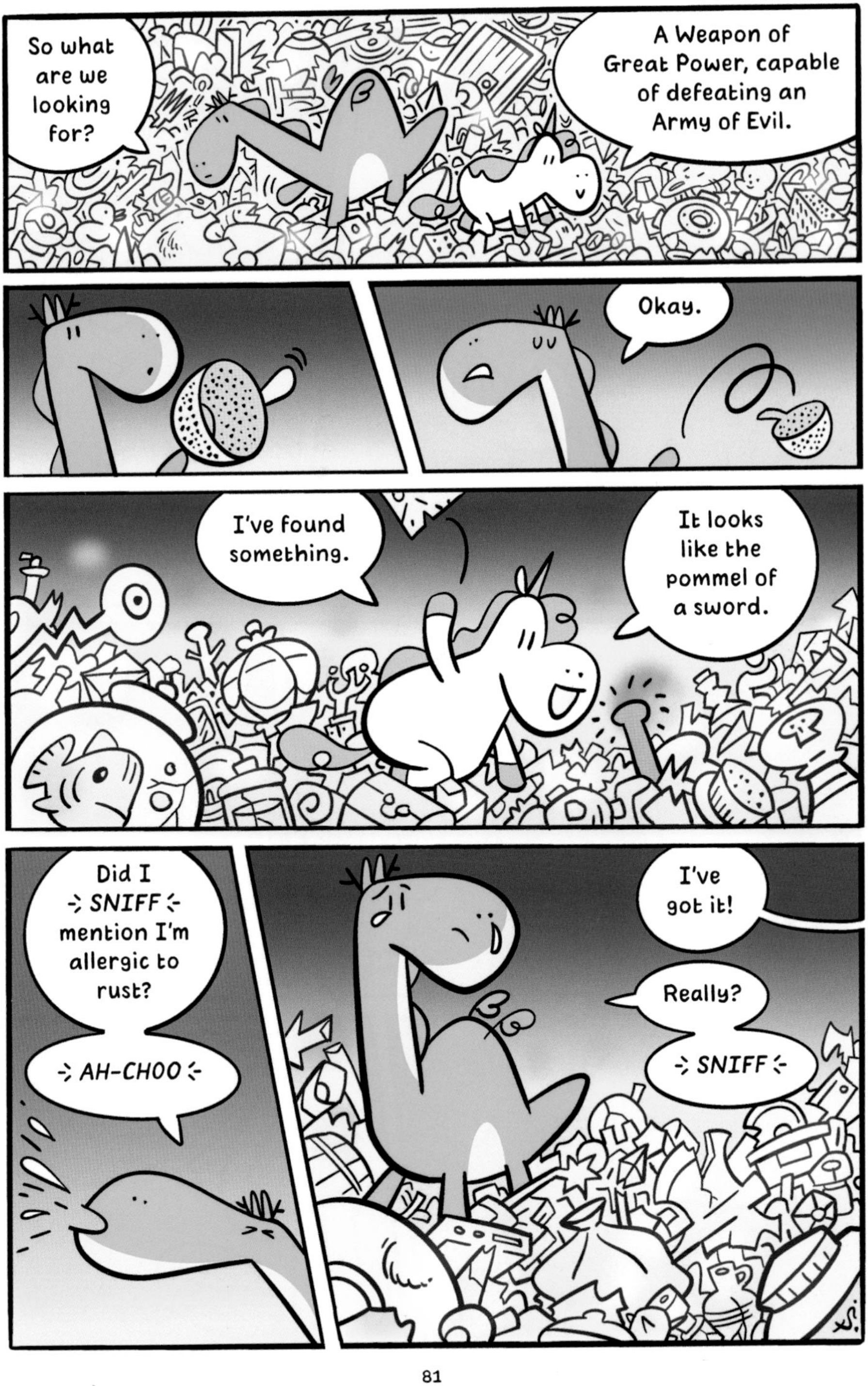
So what are we looking for?
A Weapon of Great Power, capable of defeating an Army of Evil.
Okay.
I've found something.
It looks like the pommel of a sword.
Did I -: SNIFF :- mention I'm allergic to rust?
-: AH-CHOO :-
I've got it!
Really?
-: SNIFF :-

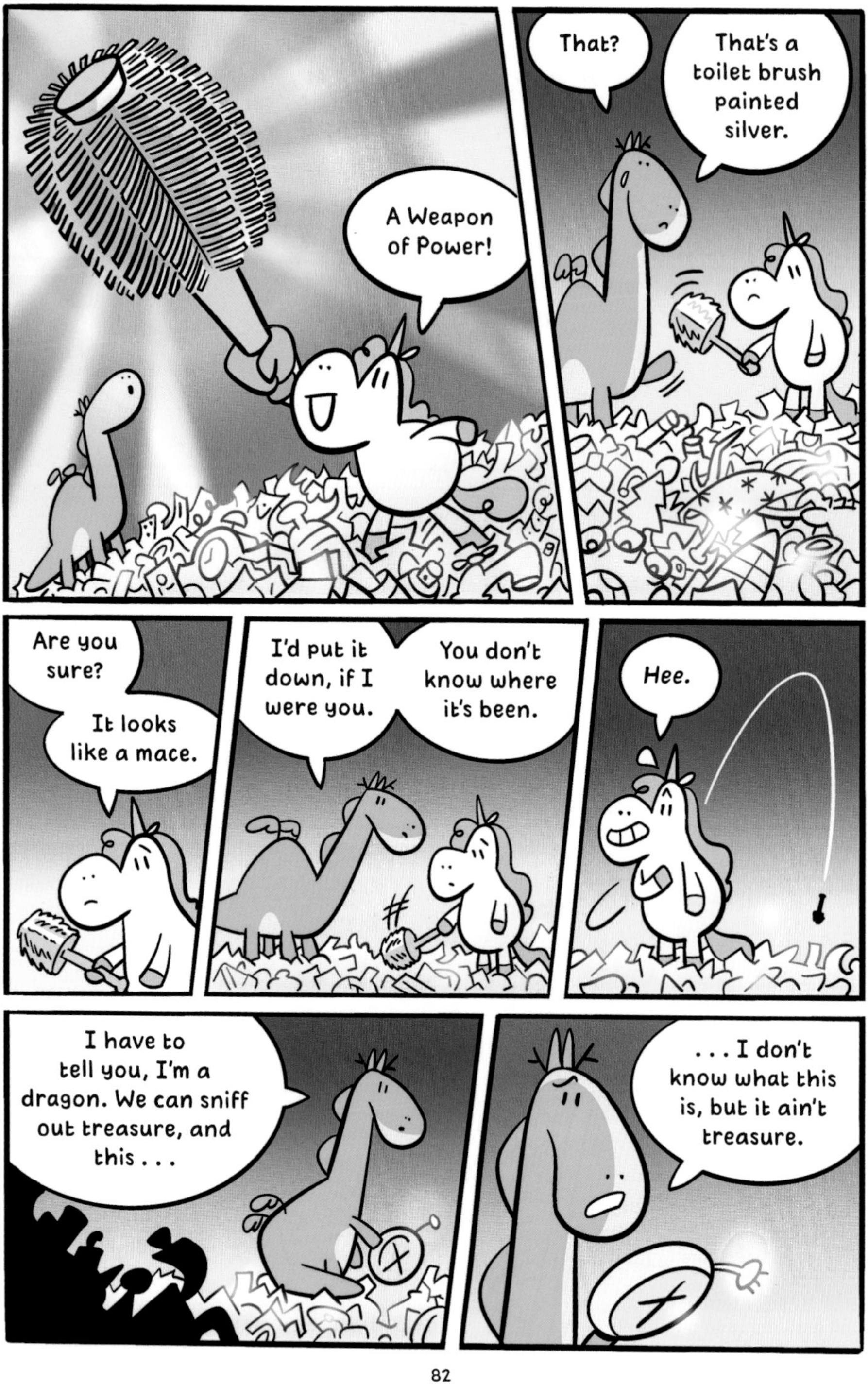
A Weapon of Power!
That?
That's a toilet brush painted silver.
Are you sure?
It looks like a mace.
I'd put it down, if I were you.
You don't know where it's been.
Hee.
I have to tell you, I'm a dragon. We can sniff out treasure, and this . . .
. . . I don't know what this is, but it ain't treasure.

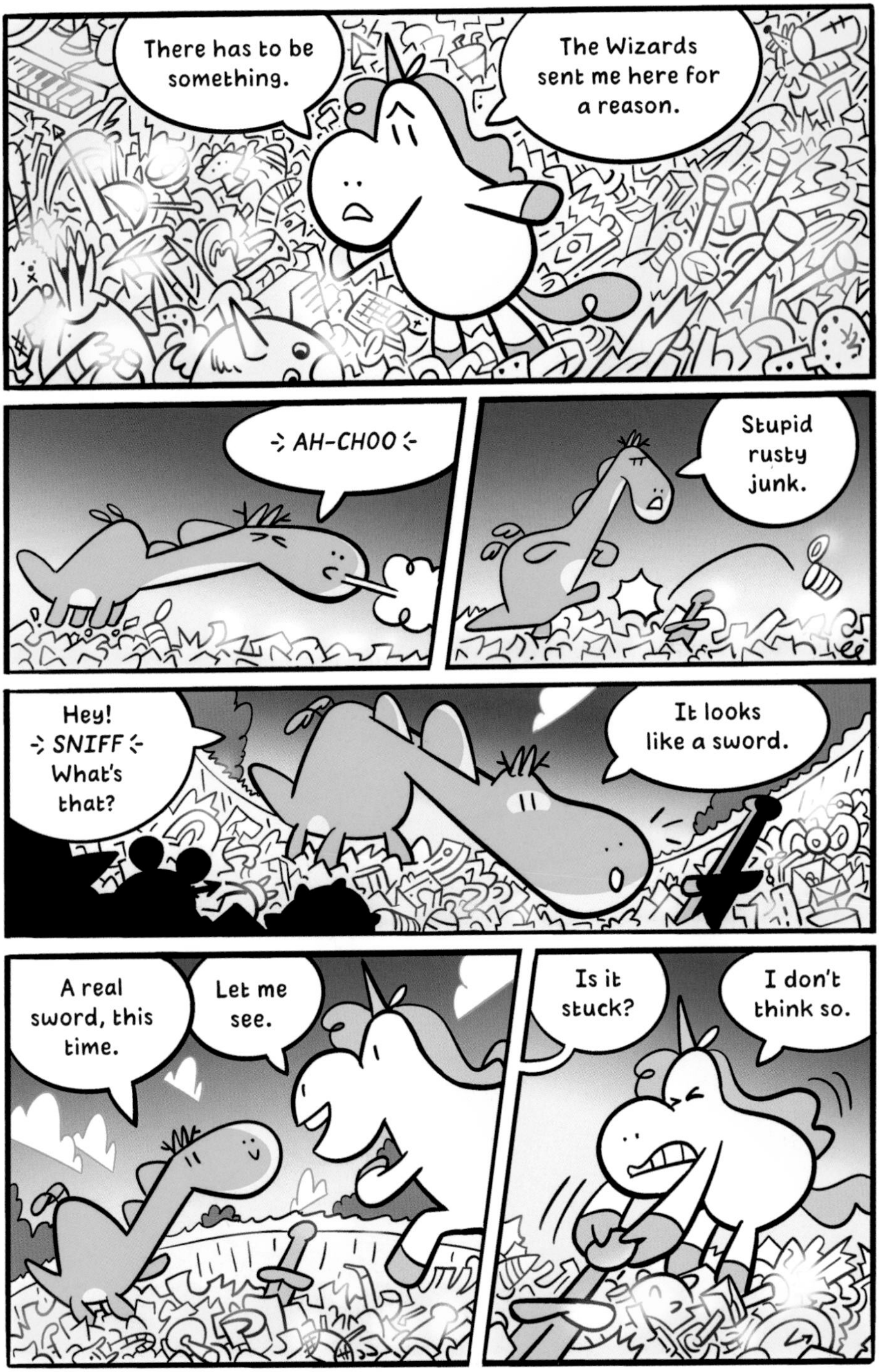
There has to be something.
The Wizards sent me here for a reason.
AH-CHOO
Stupid rusty junk.
Hey! SNIFF What's that?
It looks like a sword.
A real sword, this time.
Let me see.
Is it stuck?
I don't think so.

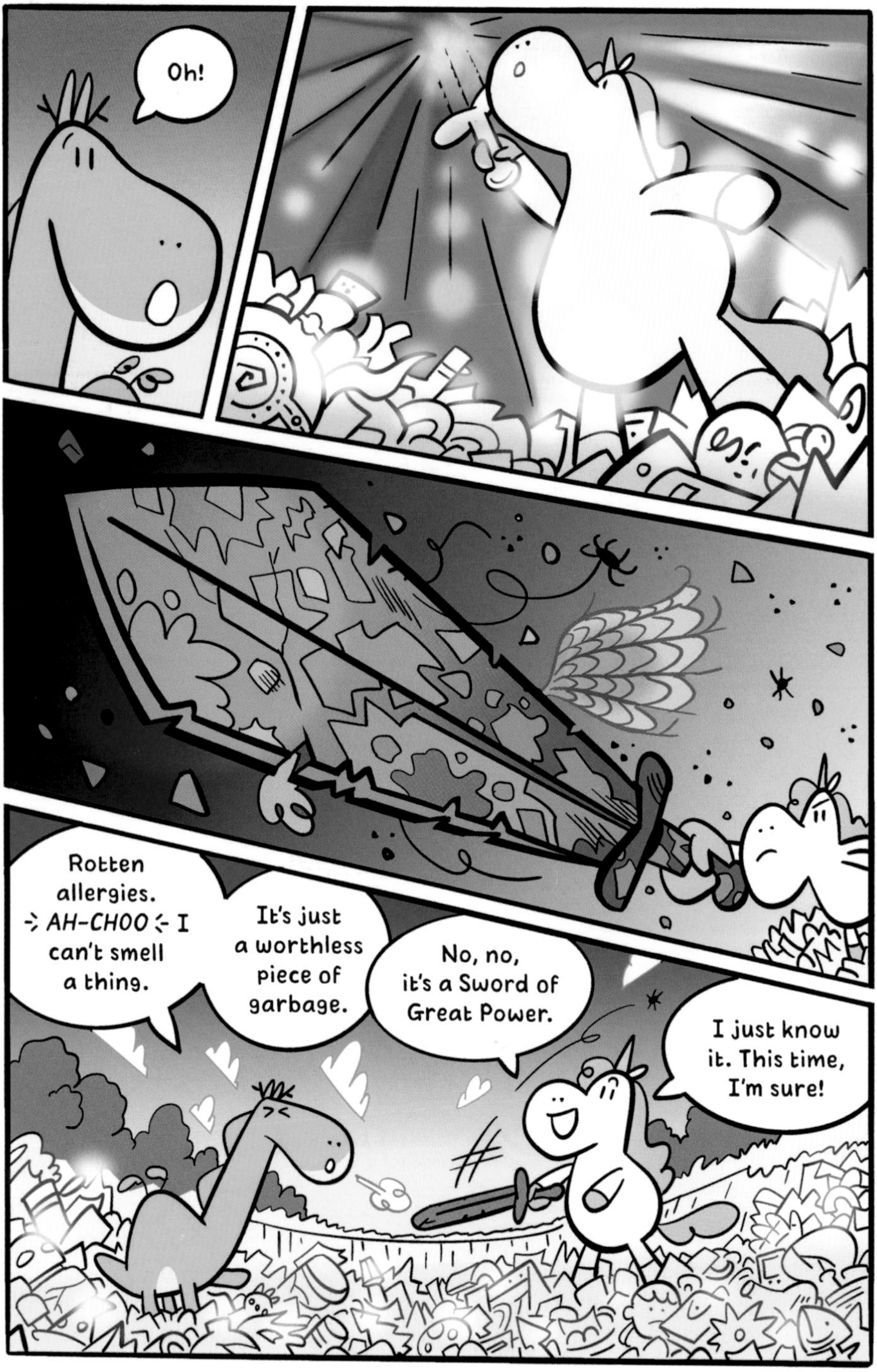
Oh!
Rotten allergies. AH-CHOO I can't smell a thing.
It's just a worthless piece of garbage.
No, no, it's a Sword of Great Power.
I just know it. This time, I'm sure!

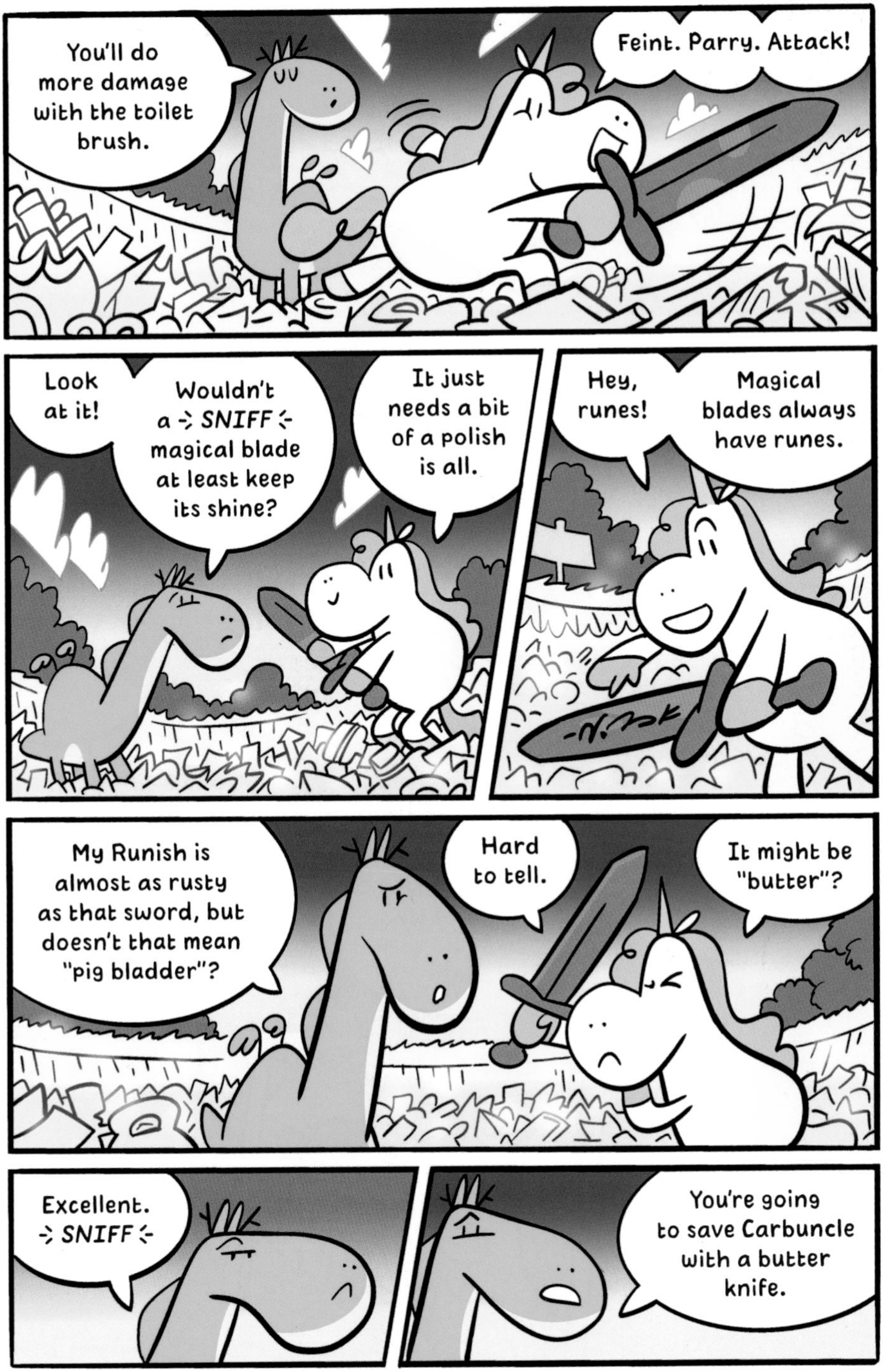
You'll do more damage with the toilet brush.
Feint. Parry. Attack!
Look at it!
Wouldn't a SNIFF magical blade at least keep its shine?
It just needs a bit of a polish is all.
Hey, runes!
Magical blades always have runes.
My Runish is almost as rusty as that sword, but doesn't that mean "pig bladder"?
Hard to tell.
It might be "butter"?
Excellent. SNIFF
You're going to save Carbuncle with a butter knife.

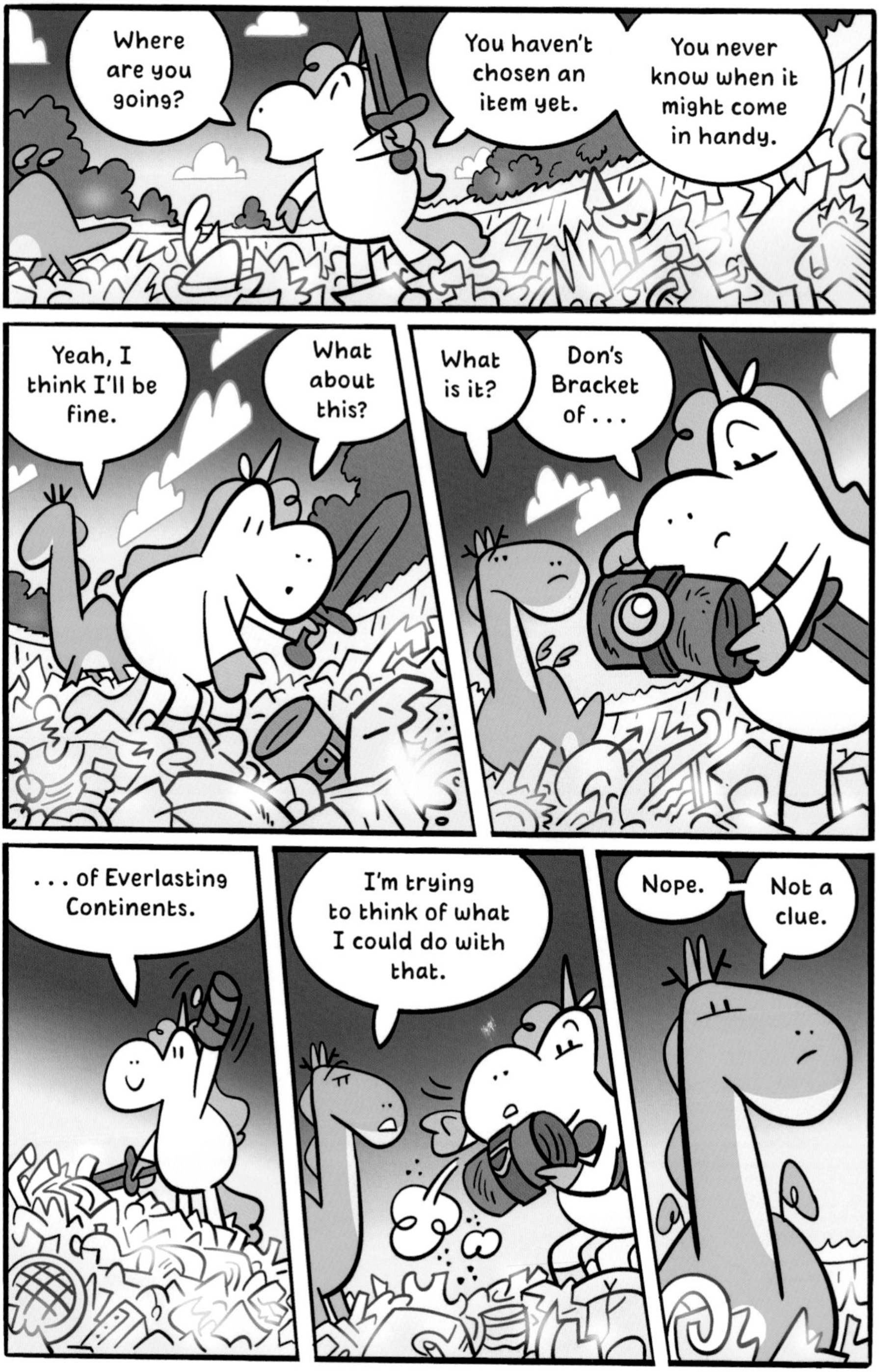
Where are you going?
You haven't chosen an item yet.
You never know when it might come in handy.
Yeah, I think I'll be fine.
What about this?
What is it?
Don's Bracket of . . .
. . . of Everlasting Continents.
I'm trying to think of what I could do with that.
Nope.
Not a clue.

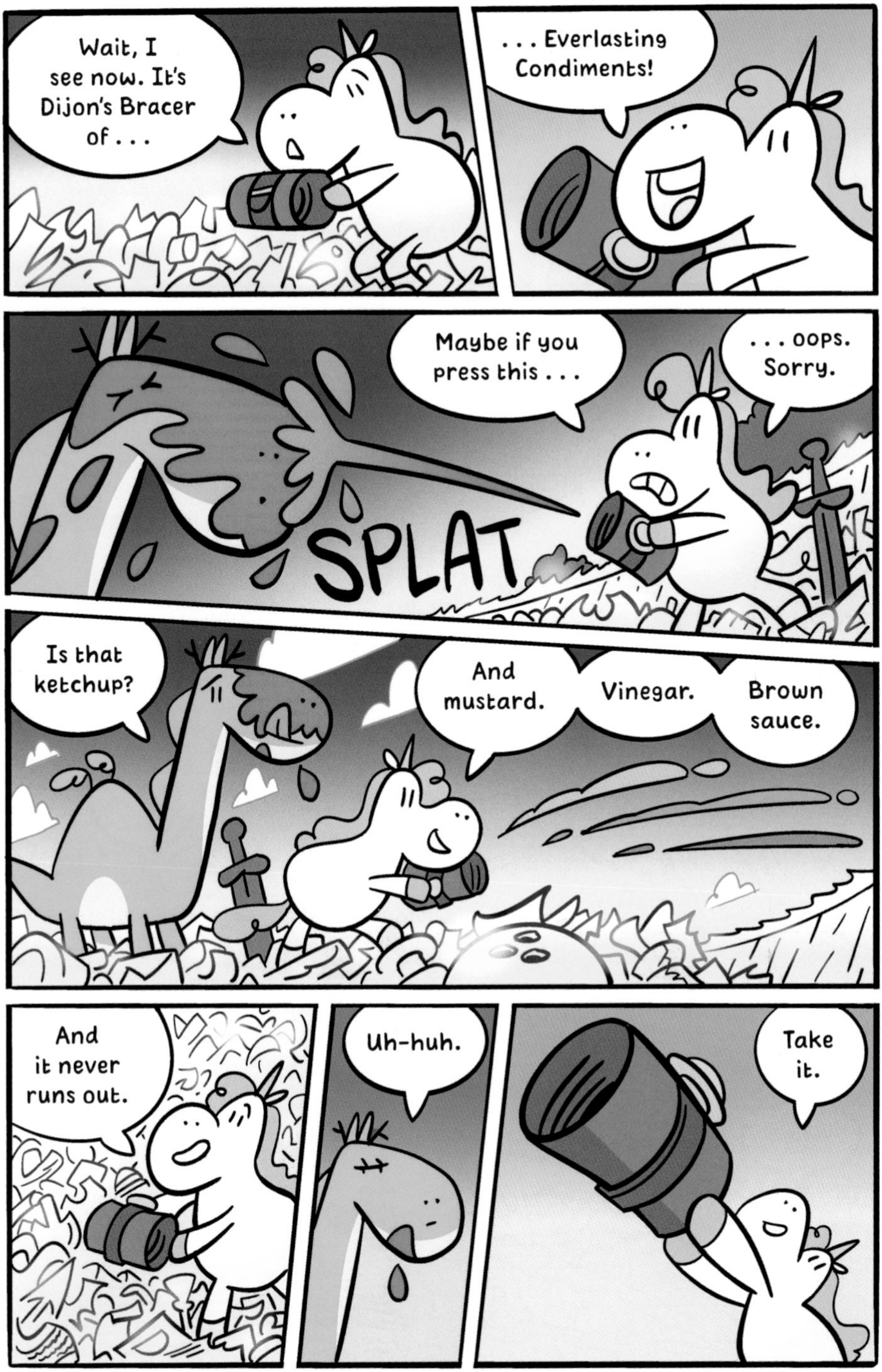
Wait, I see now. It's Dijon's Bracer of . . .
. . . Everlasting Condiments!
Maybe if you press this . . .
SPLAT
. . . oops. Sorry.
Is that ketchup?
And mustard.
Vinegar.
Brown sauce.
And it never runs out.
Uh-huh.
Take it.

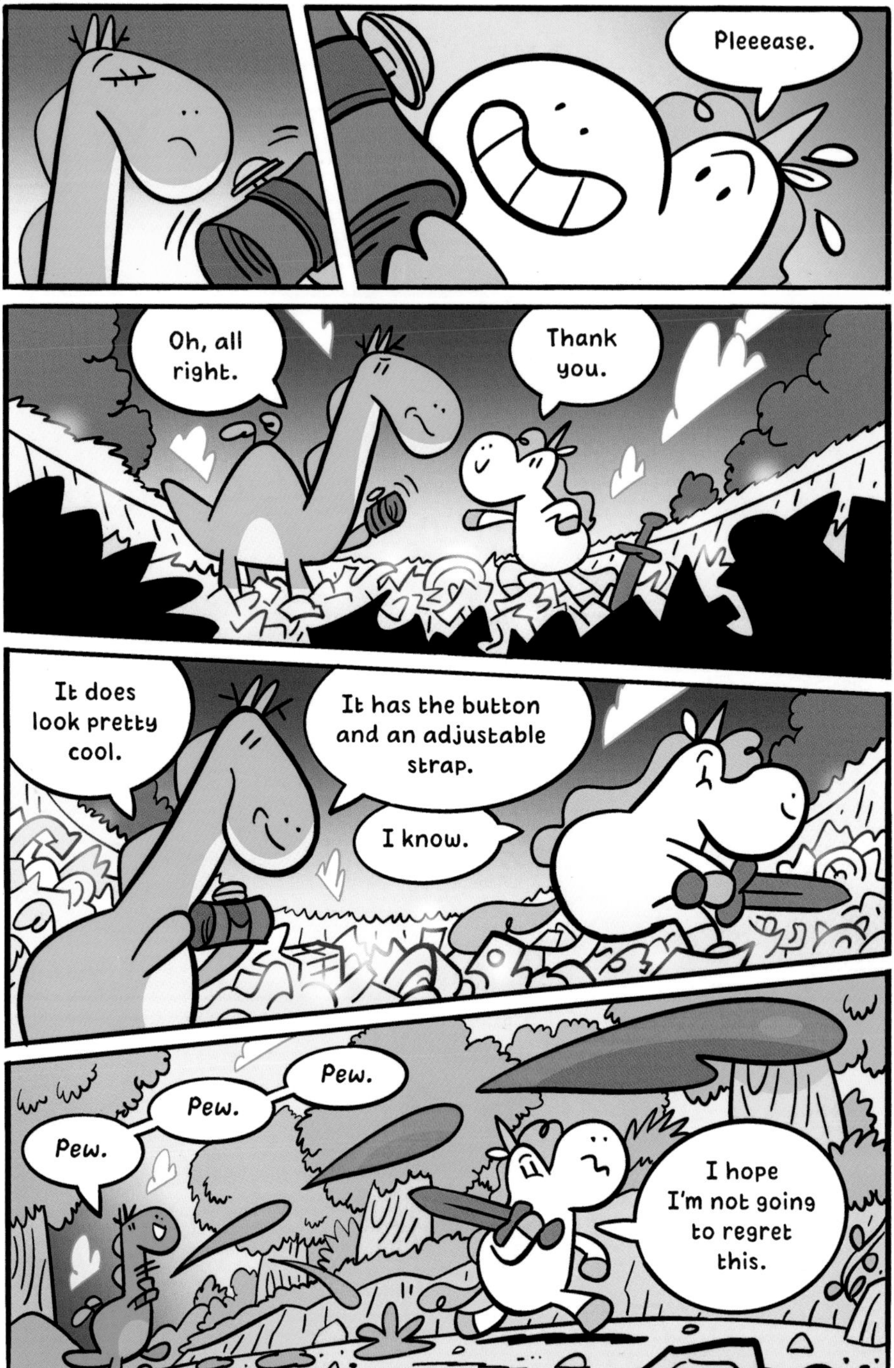
Pleeease.
Oh, all right.
Thank you.
It does look pretty cool.
It has the button and an adjustable strap.
I know.
Pew.
Pew.
Pew.
I hope I'm not going to regret this.

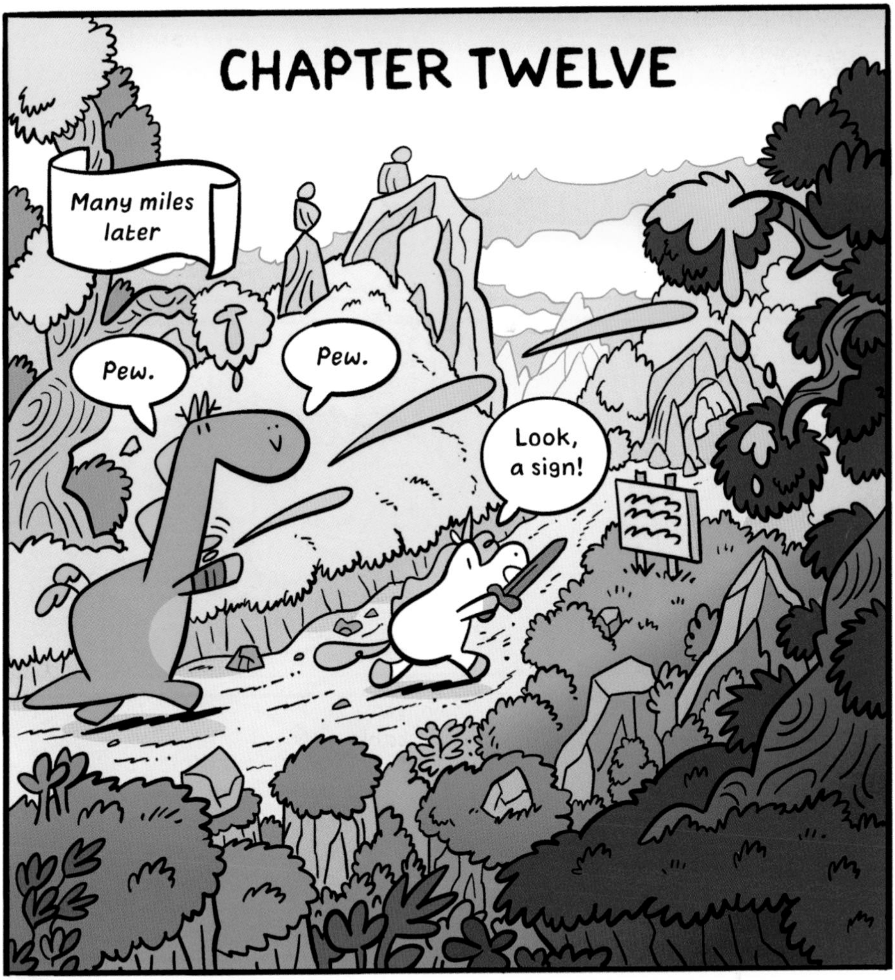
CHAPTER TWELVE
Many miles later
Pew.
Pew.
Look, a sign!

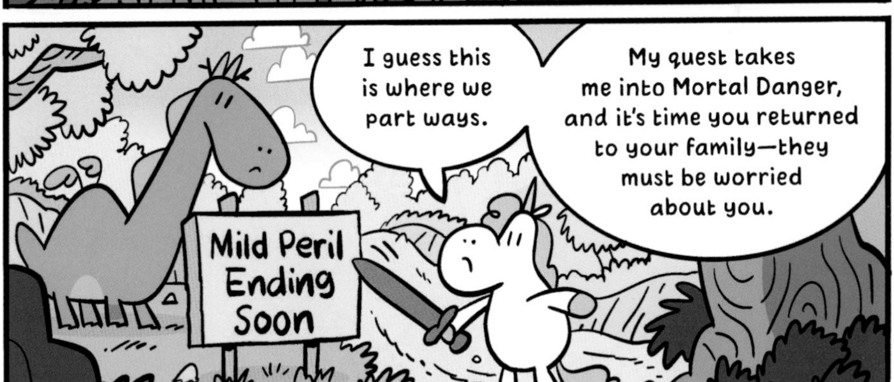
I guess this is where we part ways.
My quest takes me into Mortal Danger, and it's time you returned to your family—they must be worried about you.
Mild Peril Ending Soon

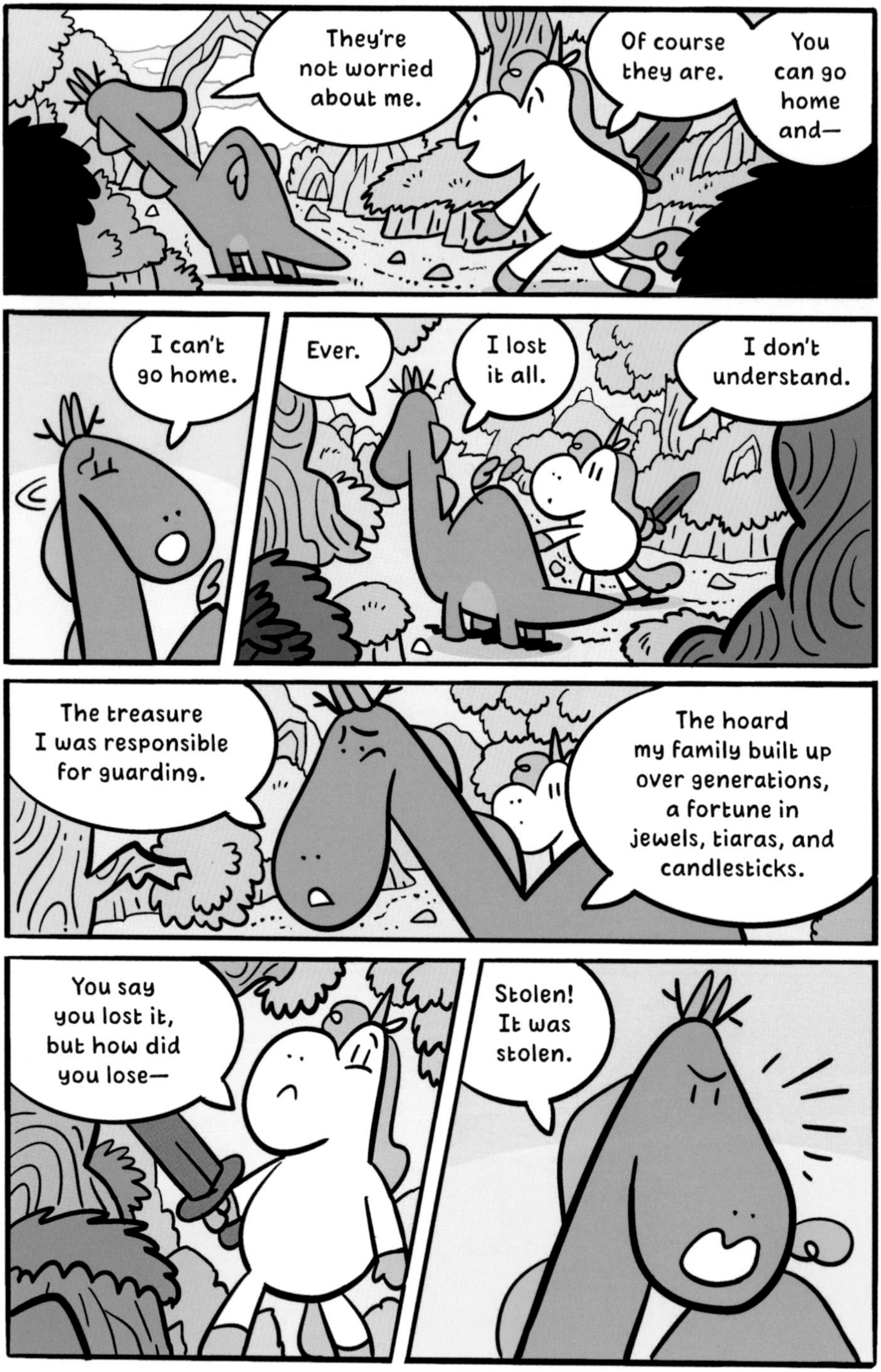
They're not worried about me.
Of course they are.
You can go home and—
I can't go home.
Ever.
I lost it all.
I don't understand.
The treasure I was responsible for guarding.
The hoard my family built up over generations, a fortune in jewels, tiaras, and candlesticks.
You say you lost it, but how did you lose—
Stolen! It was stolen.

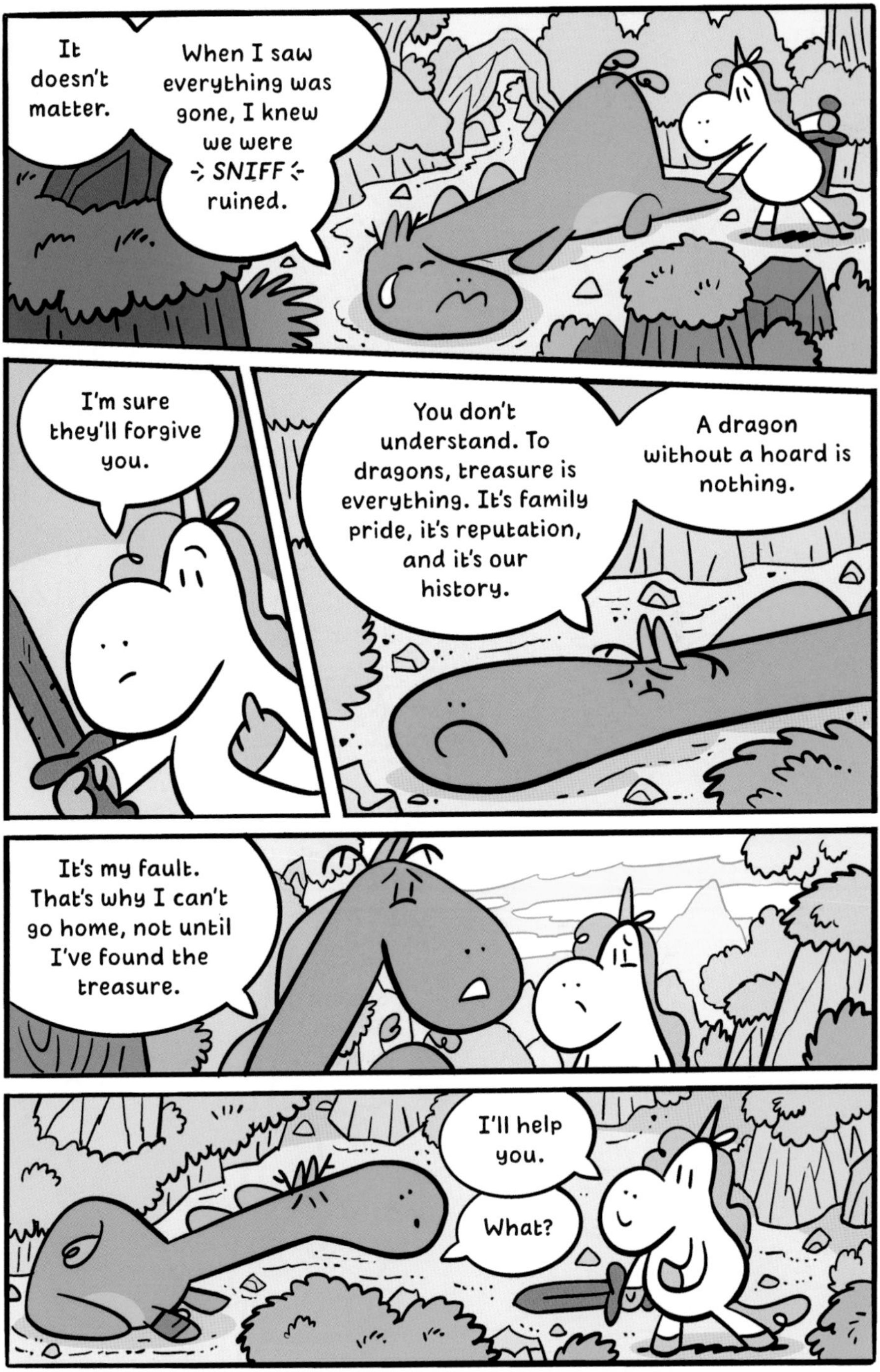
It doesn't matter.
When I saw everything was gone, I knew we were -SNIFF- ruined.
I'm sure they'll forgive you.
You don't understand. To dragons, treasure is everything. It's family pride, it's reputation, and it's our history.
A dragon without a hoard is nothing.
It's my fault. That's why I can't go home, not until I've found the treasure.
I'll help you.
What?

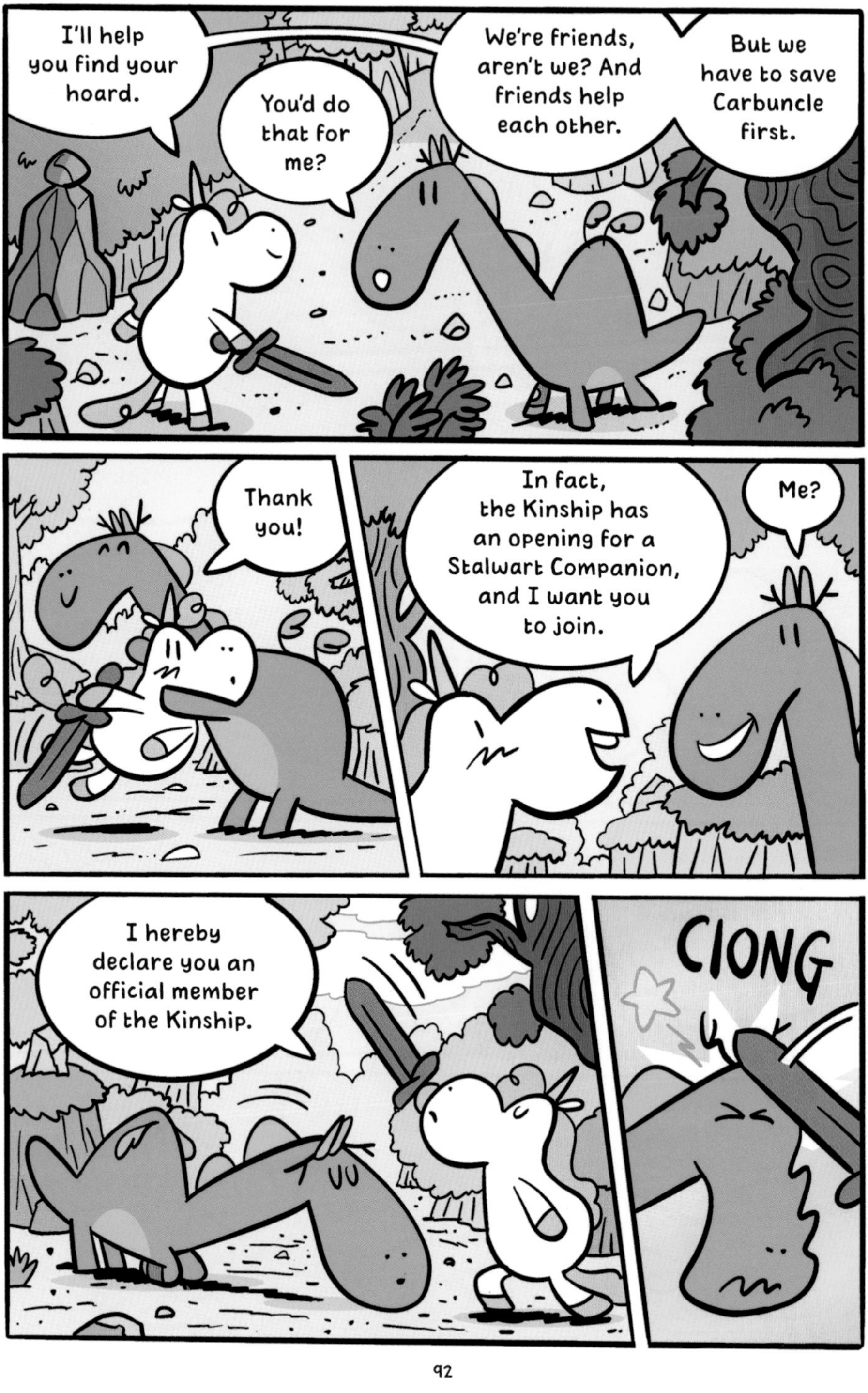
I'll help you find your hoard.
You'd do that for me?
We're friends, aren't we? And friends help each other.
But we have to save Carbuncle first.
Thank you!
In fact, the Kinship has an opening for a Stalwart Companion, and I want you to join.
Me?
I hereby declare you an official member of the Kinship.
CIONG

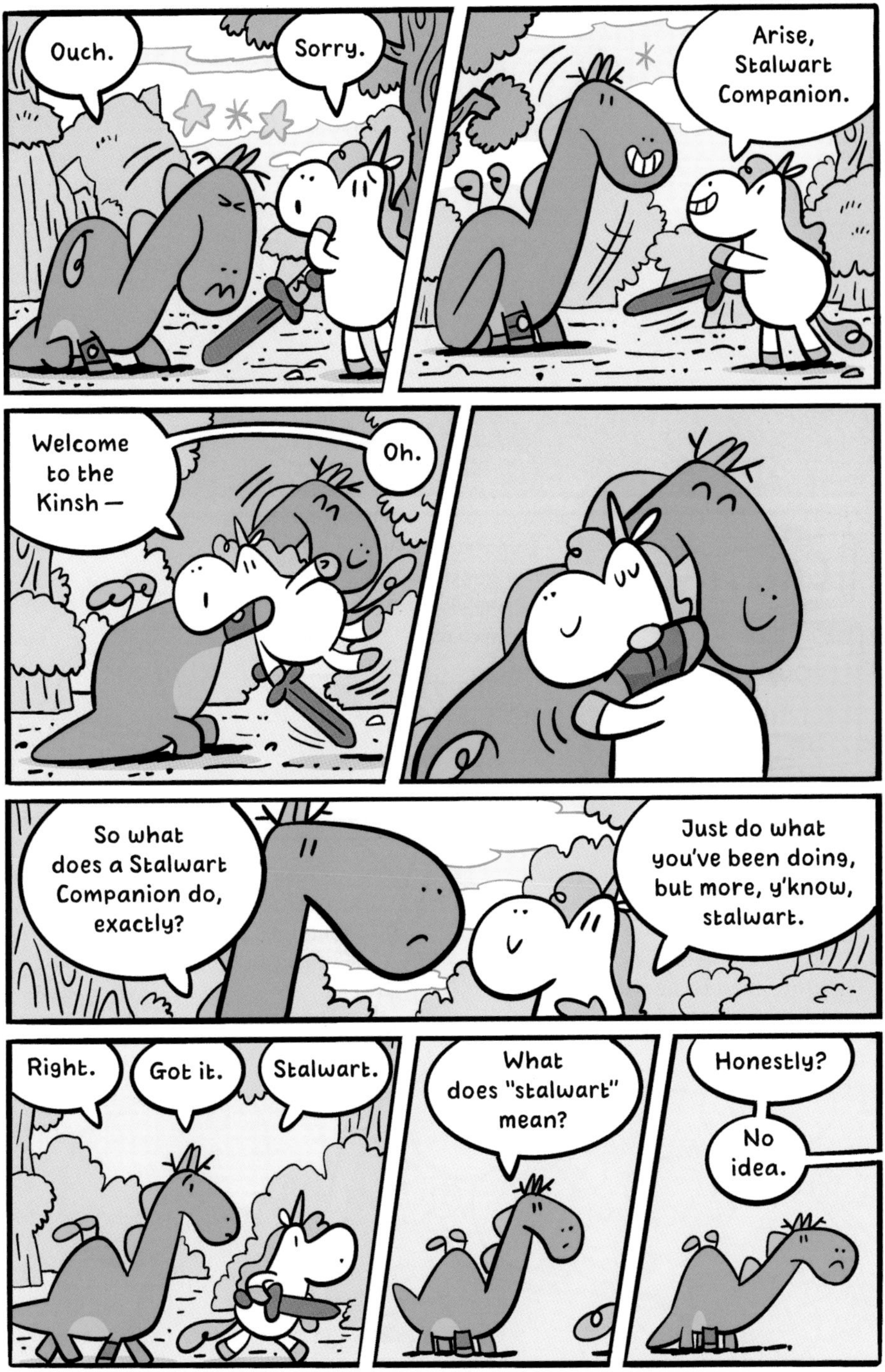
Ouch.
Sorry.
Arise, Stalwart Companion.
Welcome to the Kinsh—
Oh.
So what does a Stalwart Companion do, exactly?
Just do what you've been doing, but more, y'know, stalwart.
Right.
Got it.
Stalwart.
What does "stalwart" mean?
Honestly?
No idea.

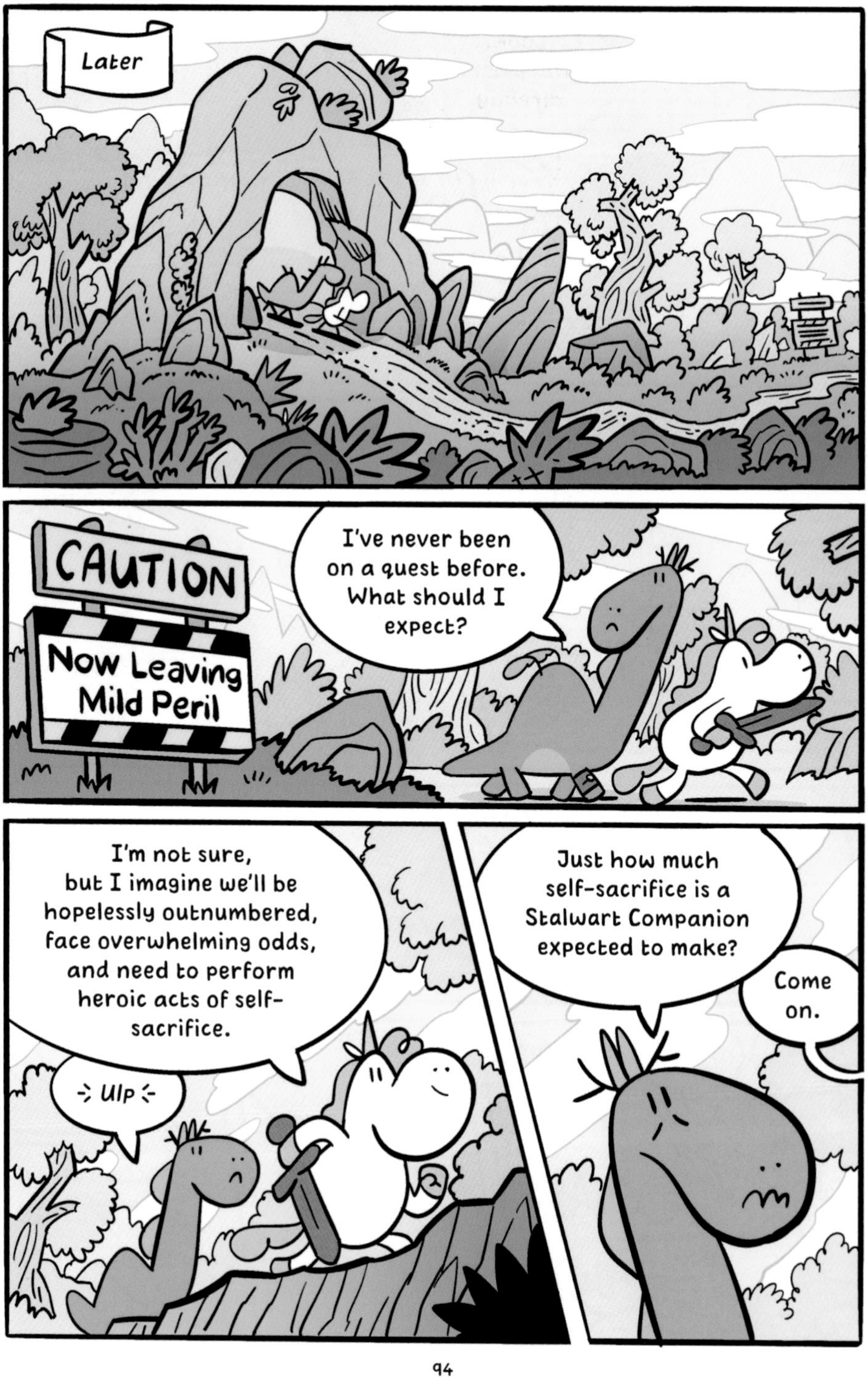

Later
CAUTION
Now Leaving Mild Peril
I've never been on a quest before. What should I expect?
I'm not sure, but I imagine we'll be hopelessly outnumbered, face overwhelming odds, and need to perform heroic acts of self-sacrifice.
Ulp
Just how much self-sacrifice is a Stalwart Companion expected to make?
Come on.

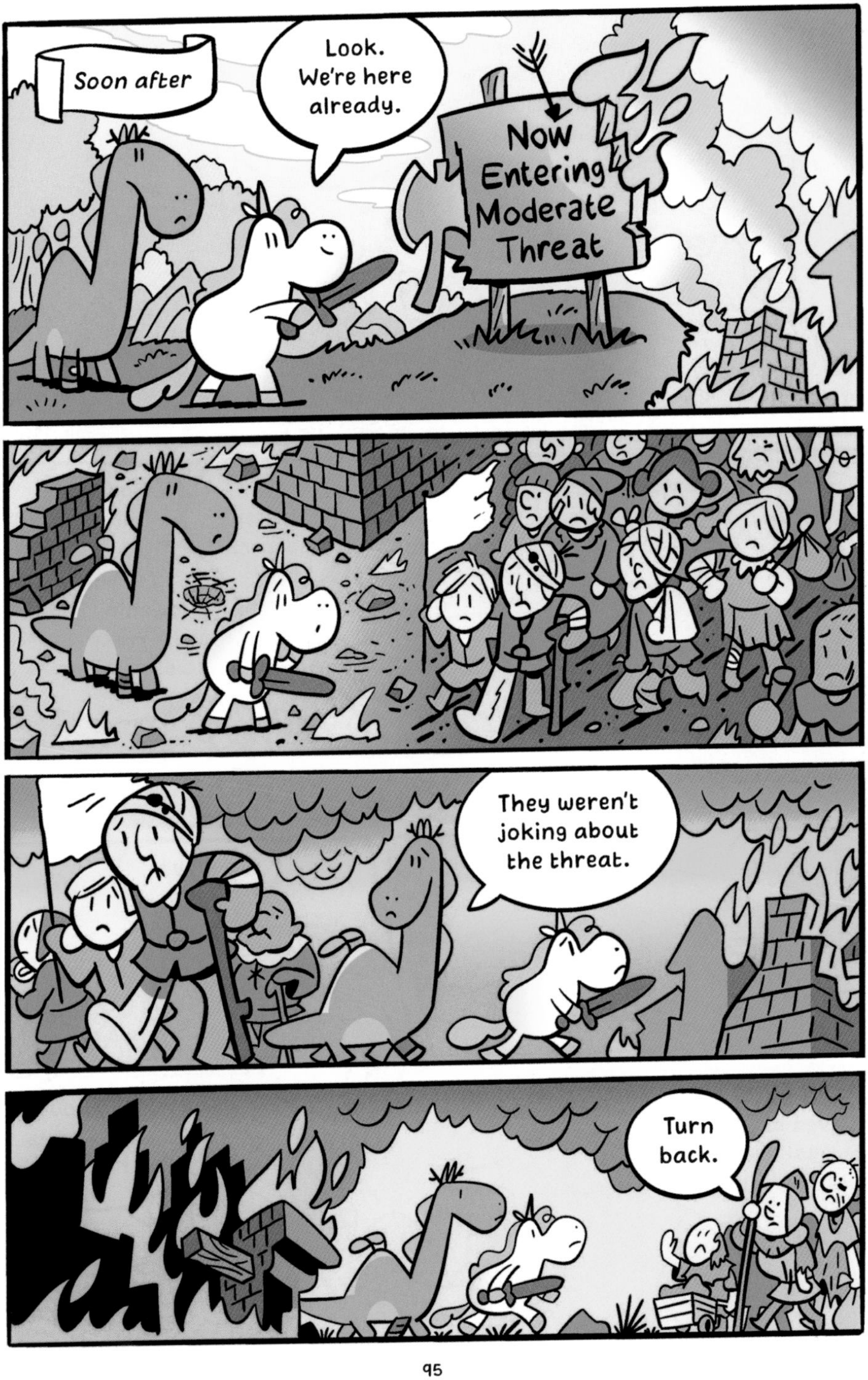
Soon after
Look. We're here already.
Now Entering Moderate Threat
They weren't joking about the threat.
Turn back.

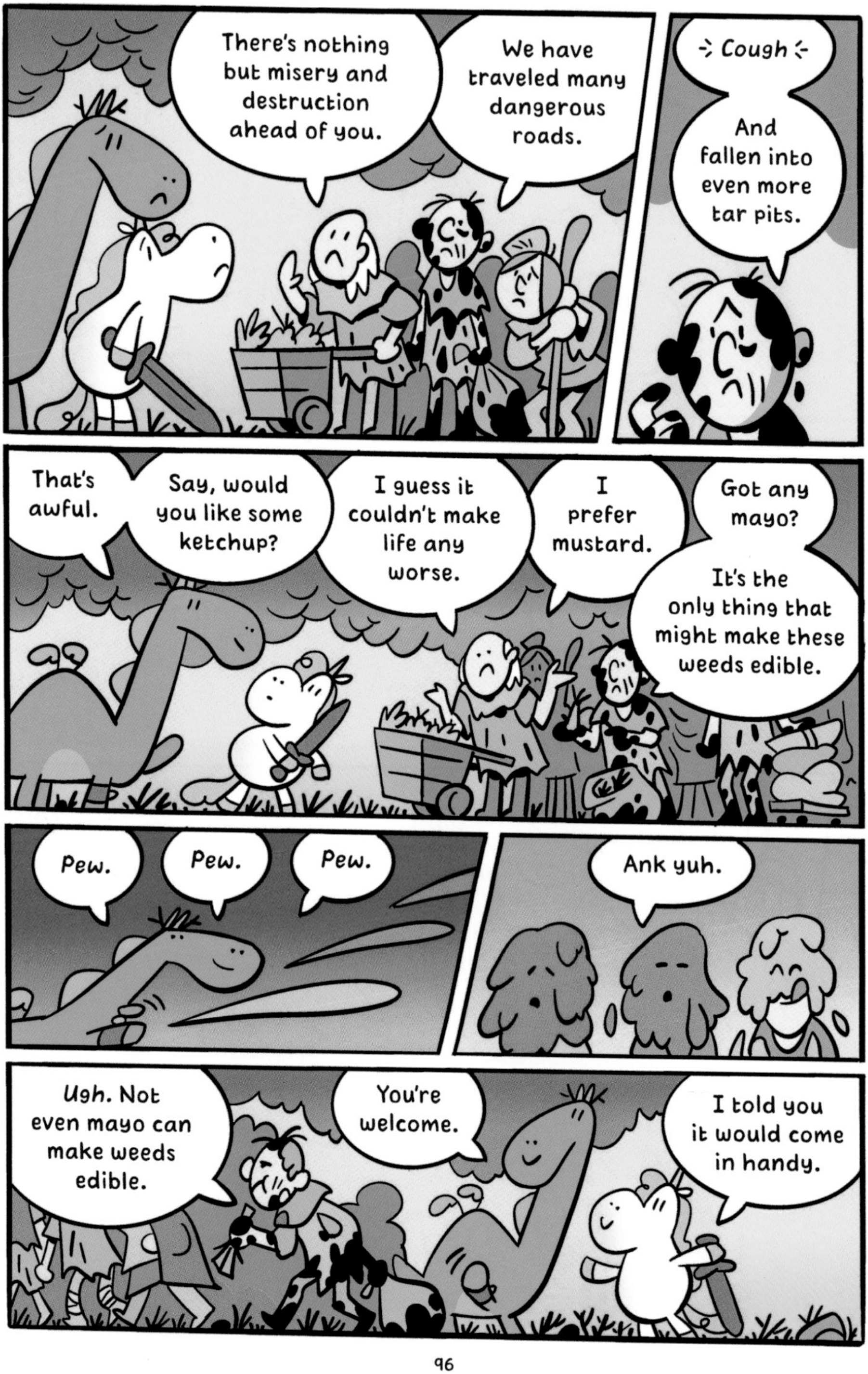
There's nothing but misery and destruction ahead of you.
We have traveled many dangerous roads.
Cough
And fallen into even more tar pits.
That's awful.
Say, would you like some ketchup?
I guess it couldn't make life any worse.
I prefer mustard.
Got any mayo?
It's the only thing that might make these weeds edible.
Pew.
Pew.
Pew.
Ank yuh.
Ugh. Not even mayo can make weeds edible.
You're welcome.
I told you it would come in handy.

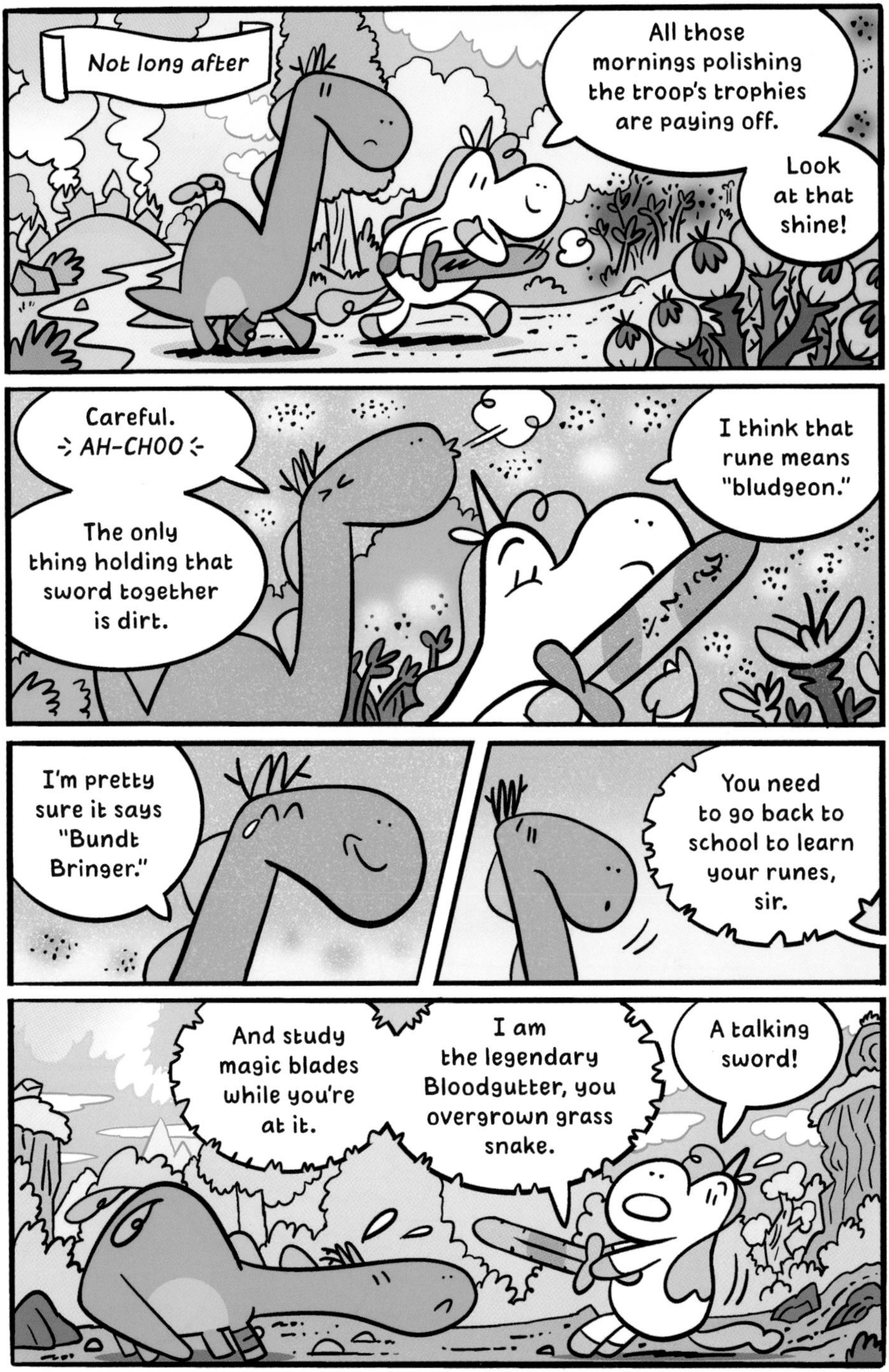
Not long after
All those mornings polishing the troop's trophies are paying off.
Look at that shine!
Careful.
AH-CHOO
The only thing holding that sword together is dirt.
I think that rune means "bludgeon."
I'm pretty sure it says "Bundt Bringer."
You need to go back to school to learn your runes, sir.
And study magic blades while you're at it.
I am the legendary Bloodgutter, you overgrown grass snake.
A talking sword!

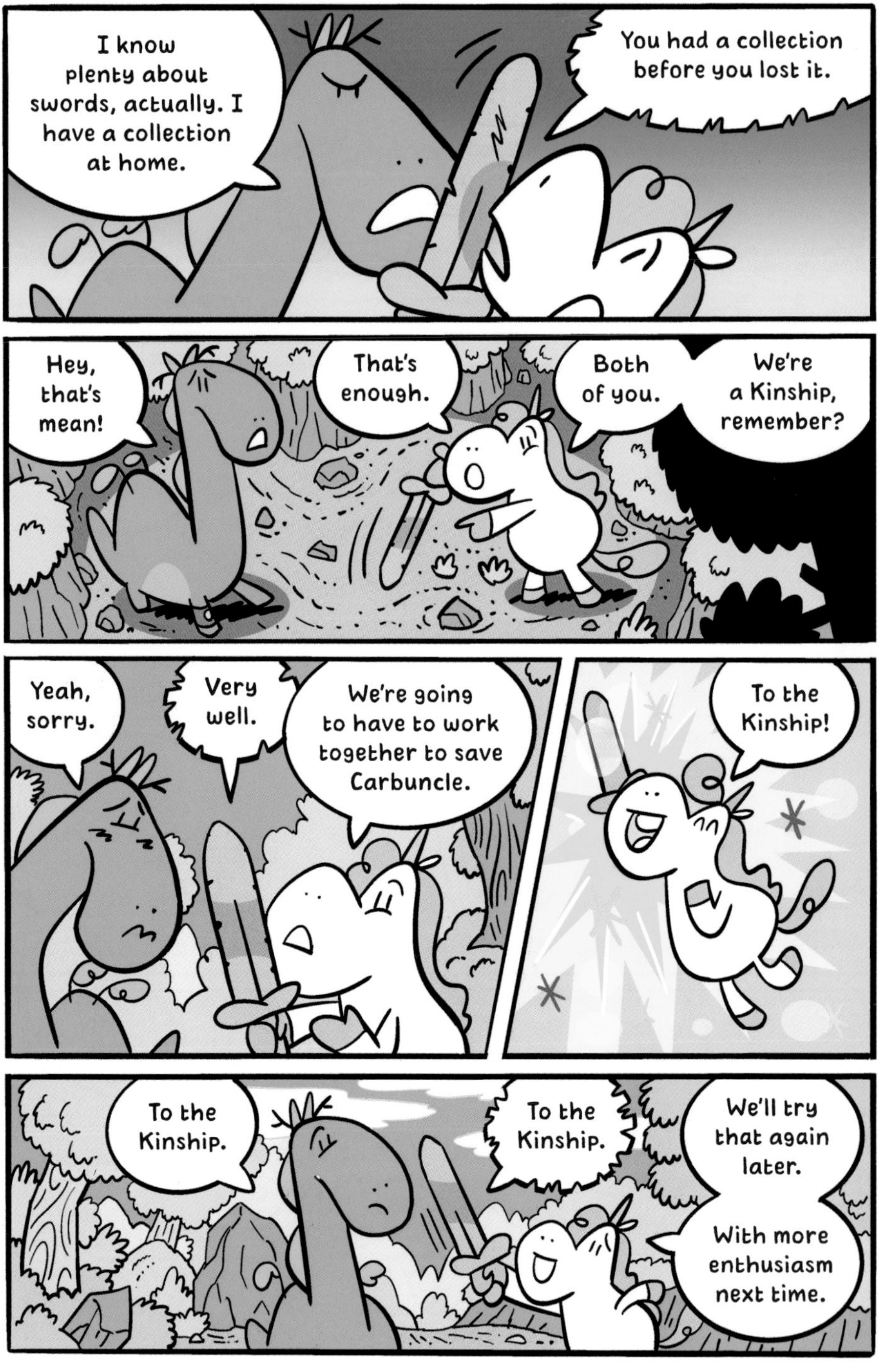
I know plenty about swords, actually. I have a collection at home.
You had a collection before you lost it.
Hey, that's mean!
That's enough.
Both of you.
We're a Kinship, remember?
Yeah, sorry.
Very well.
We're going to have to work together to save Carbuncle.
To the Kinship!
To the Kinship.
To the Kinship.
We'll try that again later.
With more enthusiasm next time.

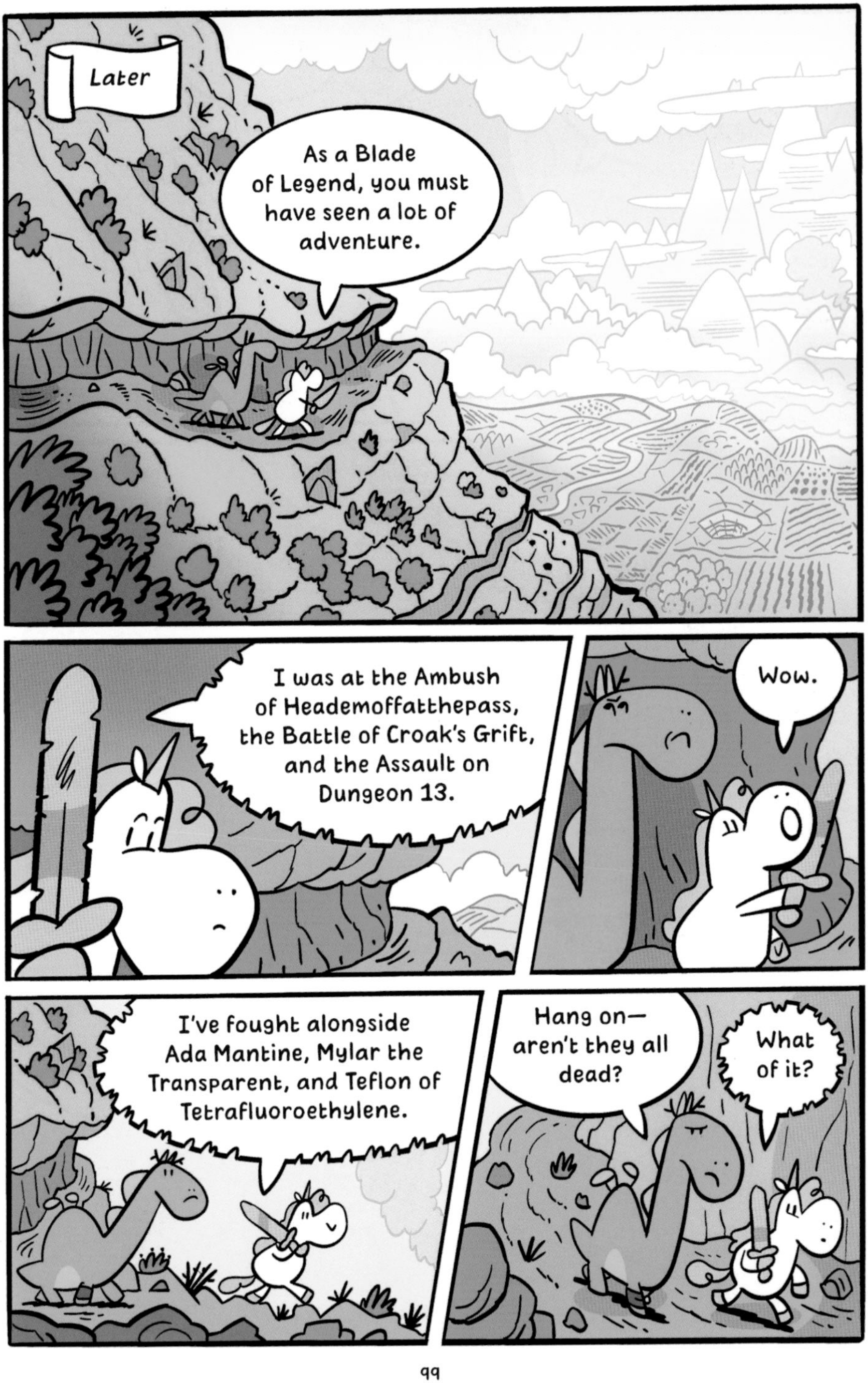
Later
As a Blade of Legend, you must have seen a lot of adventure.
I was at the Ambush of Heademoffatthepass, the Battle of Croak's Grift, and the Assault on Dungeon 13.
Wow.
I've fought alongside Ada Mantine, Mylar the Transparent, and Teflon of Tetrafluoroethylene.
Hang on— aren't they all dead?
What of it?

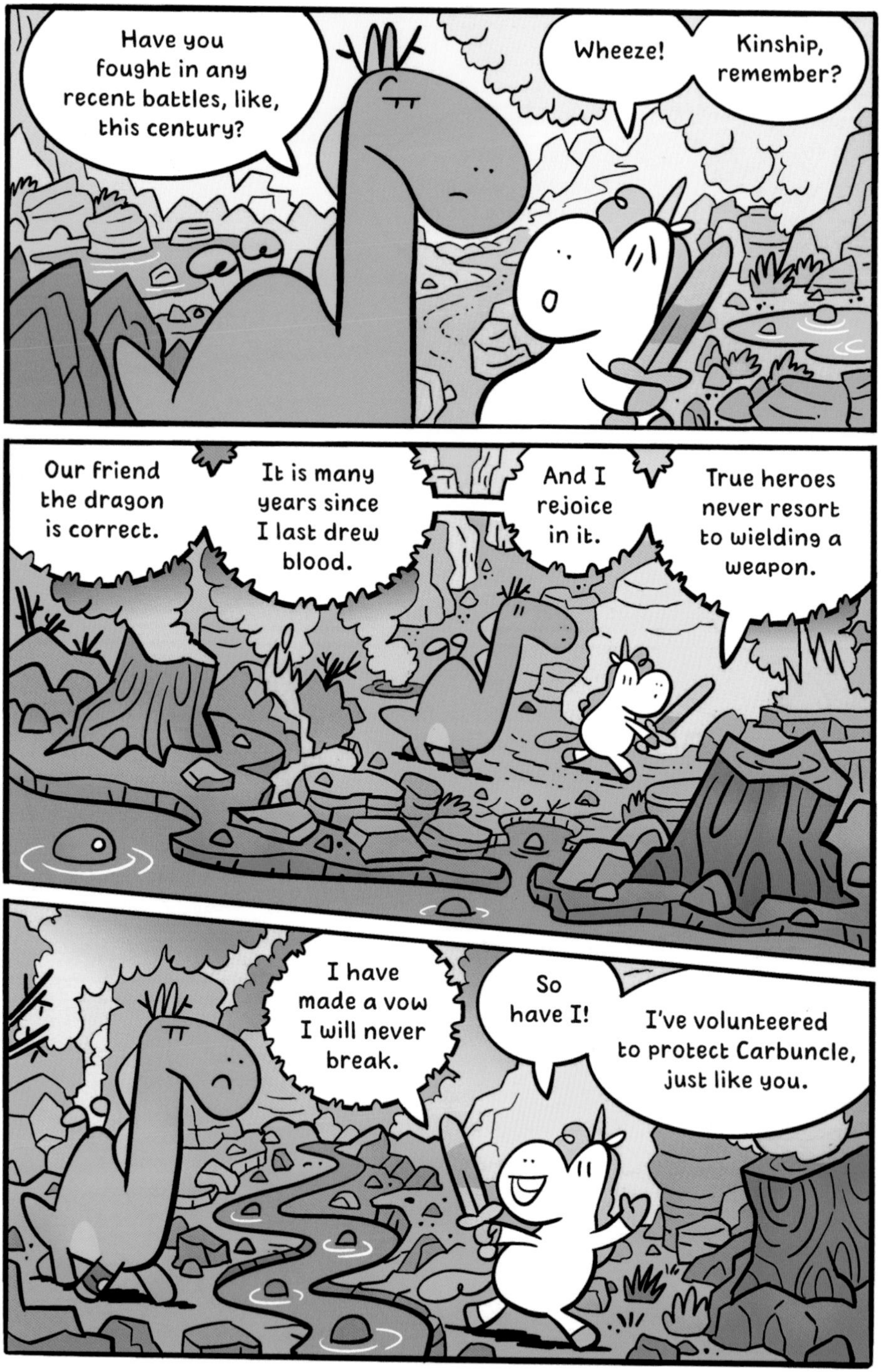
Have you fought in any recent battles, like, this century?
Wheeze!
Kinship, remember?
Our friend the dragon is correct.
It is many years since I last drew blood.
And I rejoice in it.
True heroes never resort to wielding a weapon.
I have made a vow I will never break.
So have I!
I've volunteered to protect Carbuncle, just like you.

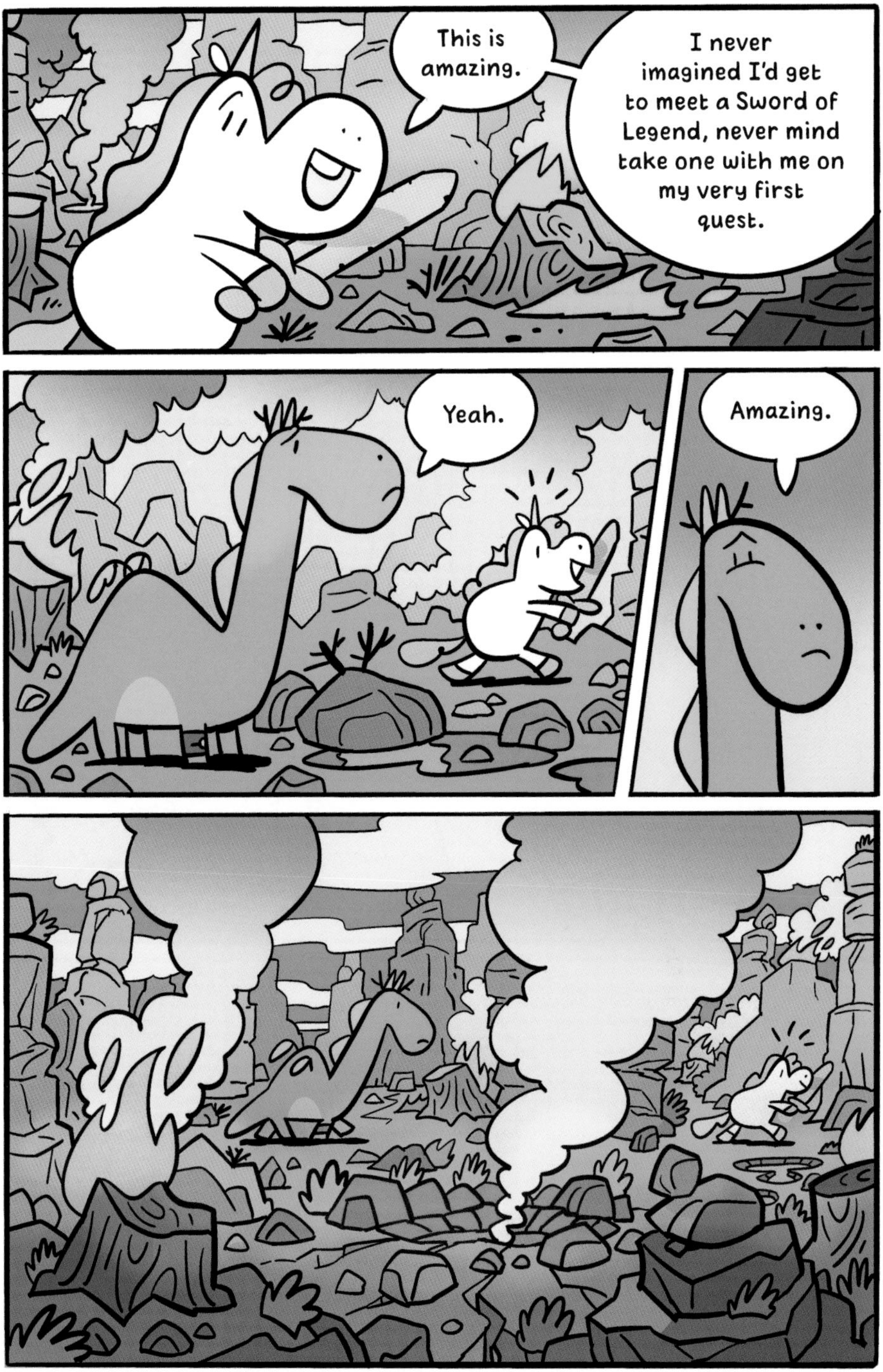
This is amazing.
I never imagined I'd get to meet a Sword of Legend, never mind take one with me on my very first quest.
Yeah.
Amazing.

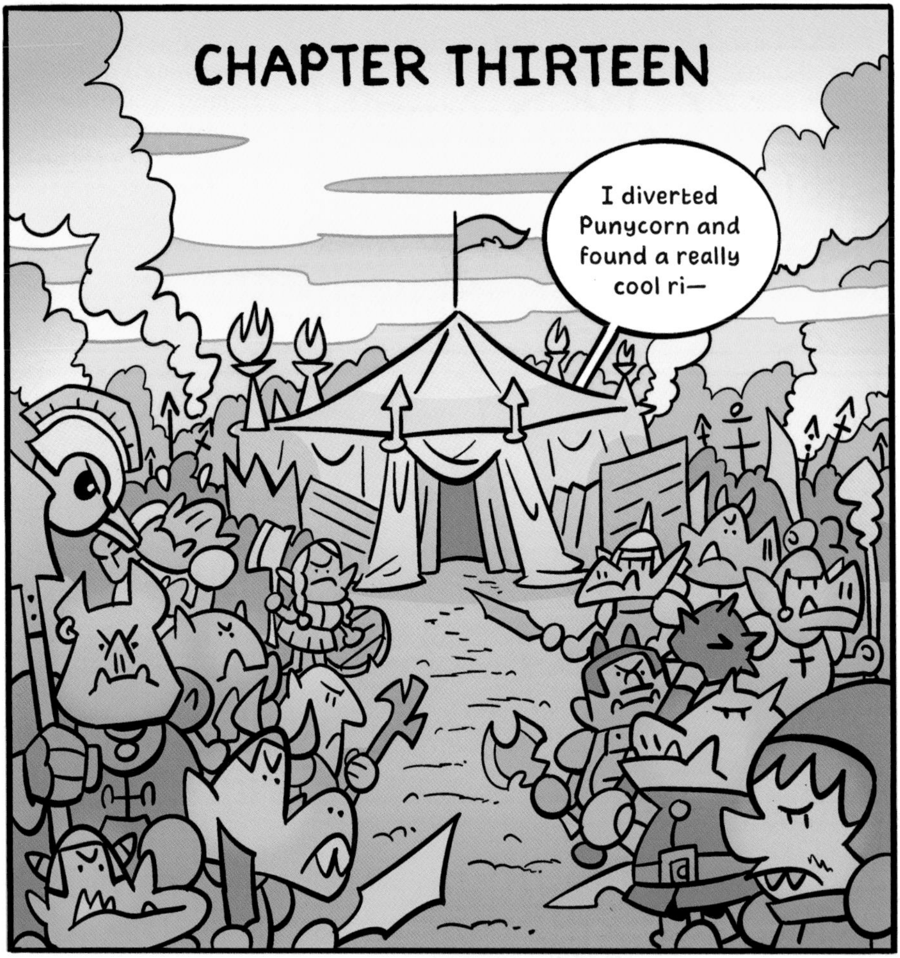
CHAPTER THIRTEEN
I diverted Punycorn and found a really cool ri—

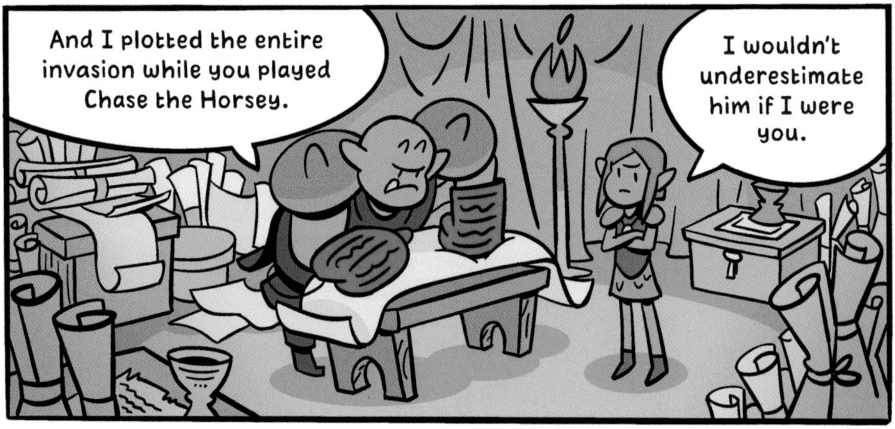
And I plotted the entire invasion while you played Chase the Horsey.
I wouldn't underestimate him if I were you.

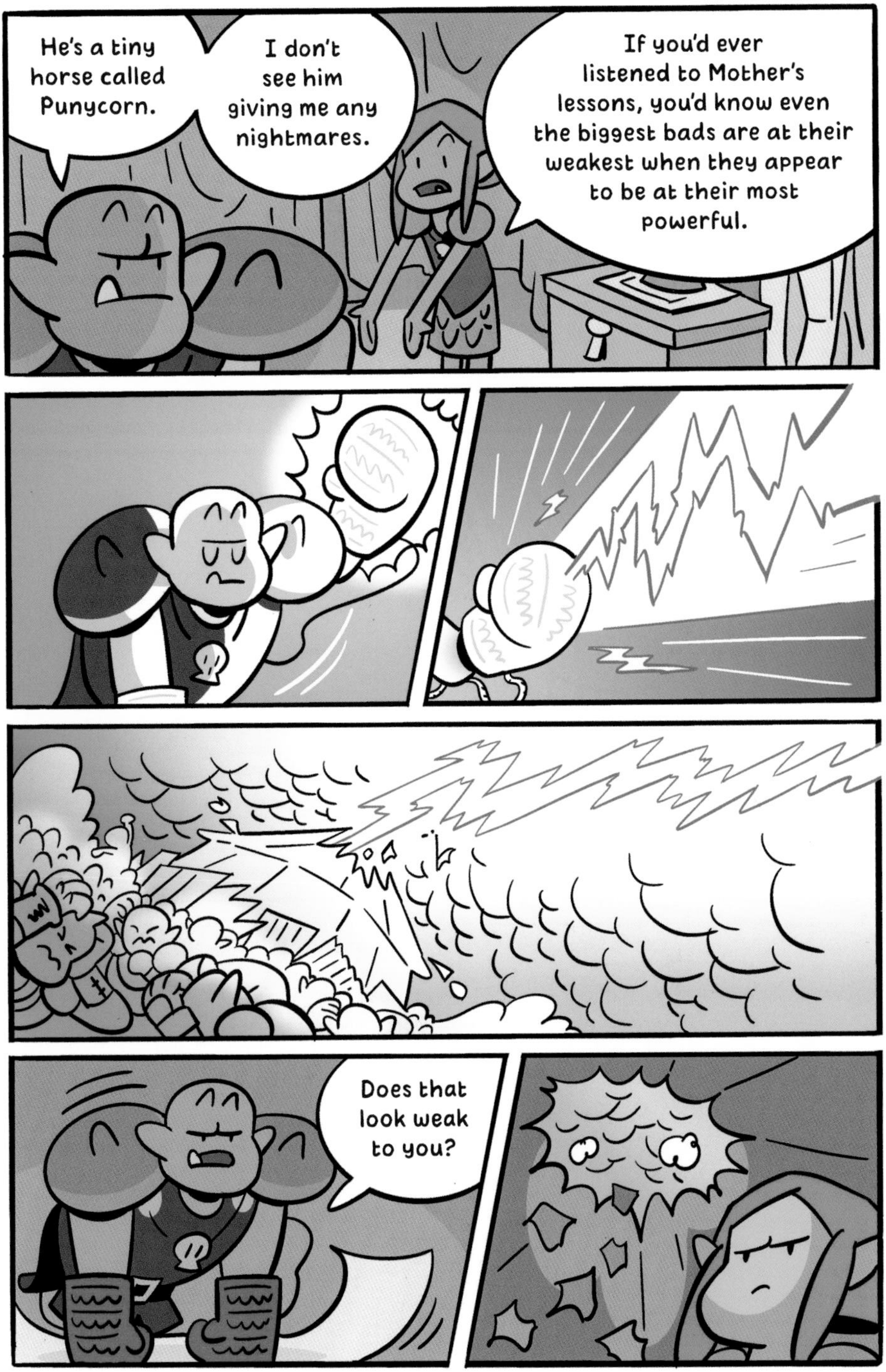
He's a tiny horse called Punycorn.
I don't see him giving me any nightmares.
If you'd ever listened to Mother's lessons, you'd know even the biggest bads are at their weakest when they appear to be at their most powerful.
Does that look weak to you?

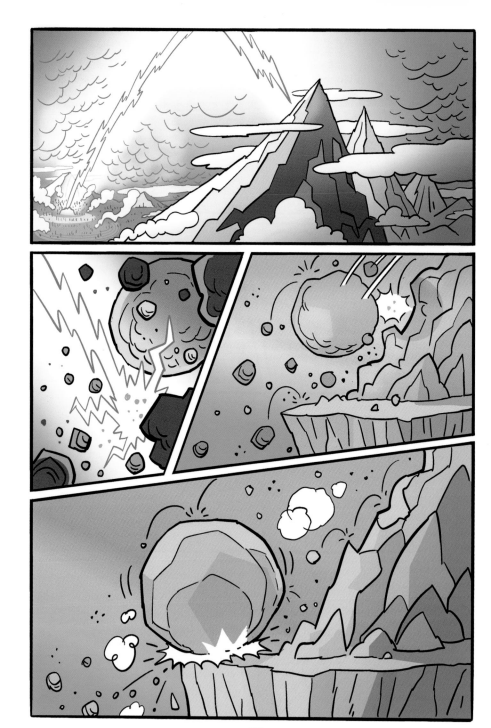

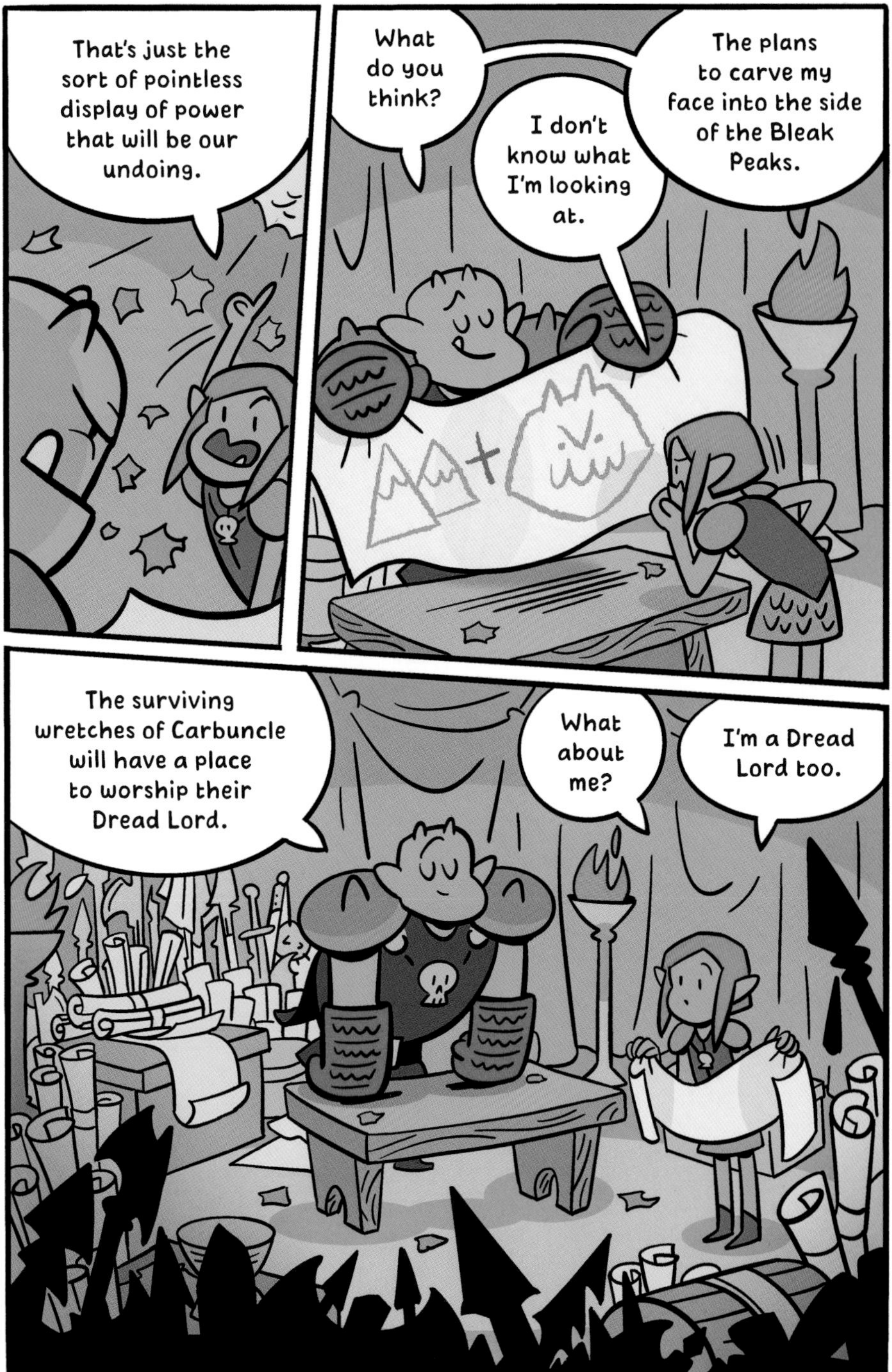
That's just the sort of pointless display of power that will be our undoing.
What do you think?
The plans to carve my face into the side of the Bleak Peaks.
I don't know what I'm looking at.
The surviving wretches of Carbuncle will have a place to worship their Dread Lord.
What about me?
I'm a Dread Lord too.

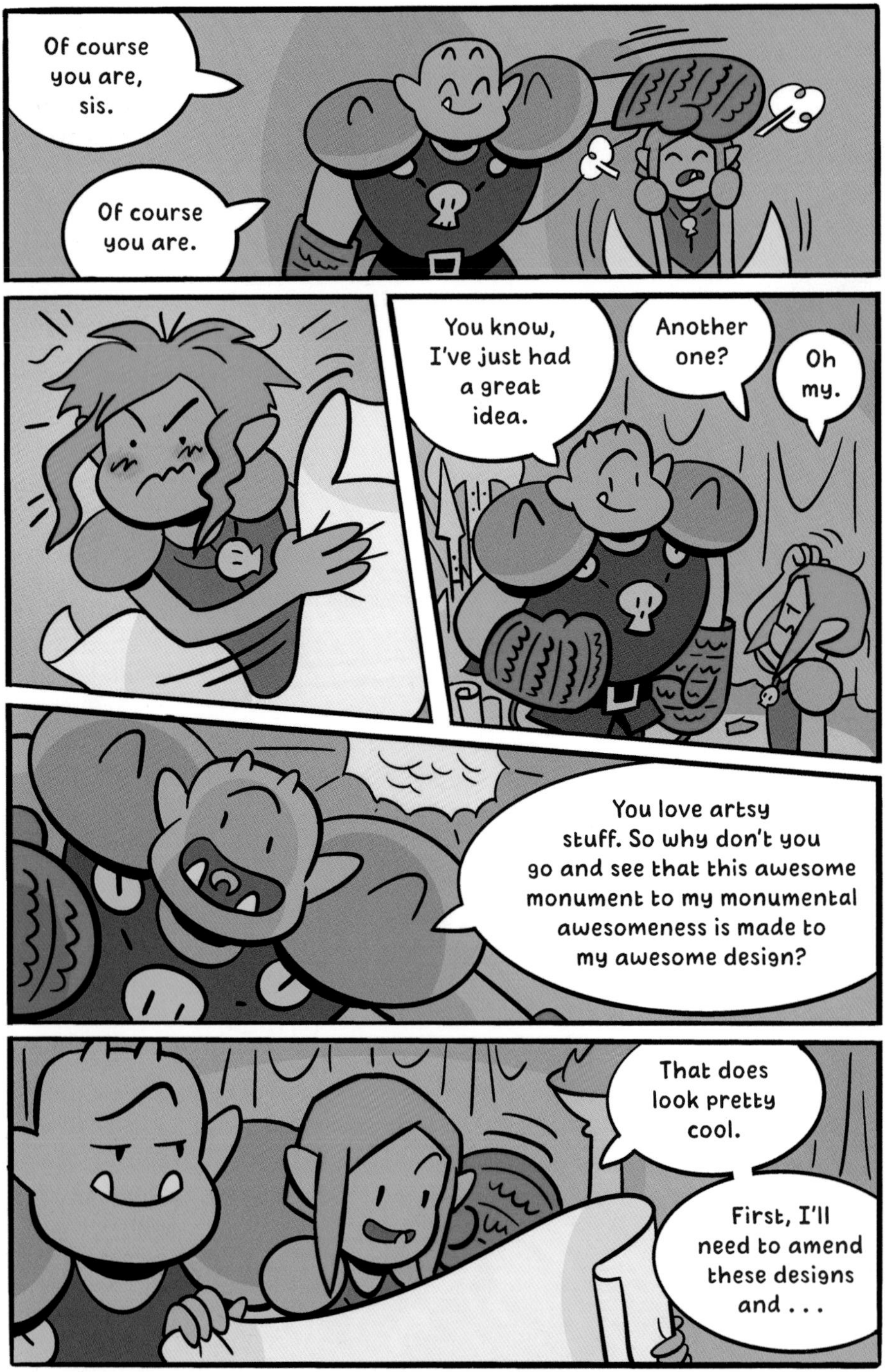
Of course
you are,
sis.
Of course
you are.
You know,
I've just had
a great
idea.
Another
one?
Oh
my.
You love artsy
stuff. So why don't you
go and see that this awesome
monument to my monumental
awesomeness is made to
my awesome design?
That does
look pretty
cool.
First, I'll
need to amend
these designs
and . . .

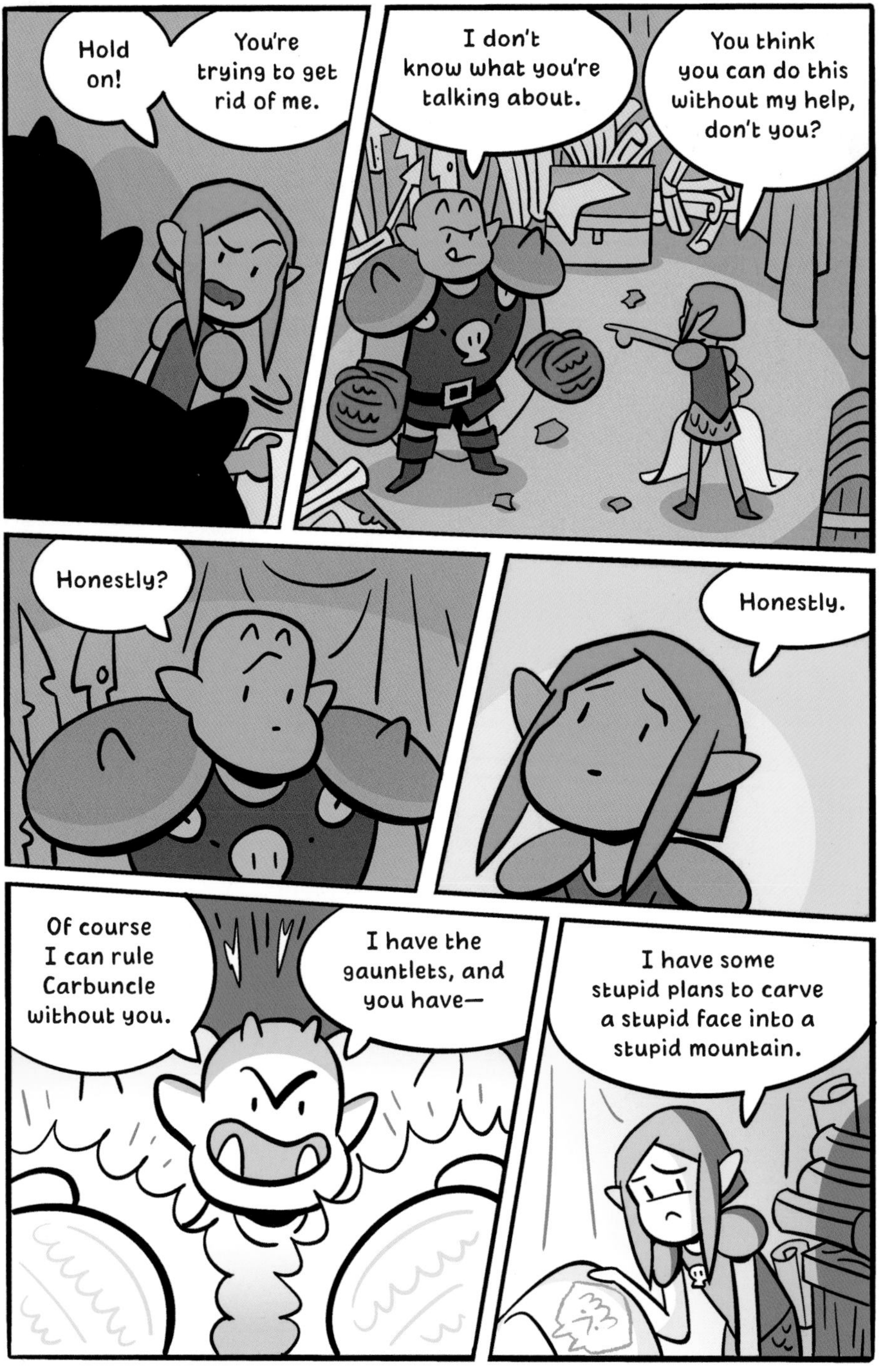
Hold on!
You're trying to get rid of me.
I don't know what you're talking about.
You think you can do this without my help, don't you?
Honestly?
Honestly.
Of course I can rule Carbuncle without you.
I have the gauntlets, and you have—
I have some stupid plans to carve a stupid face into a stupid mountain.

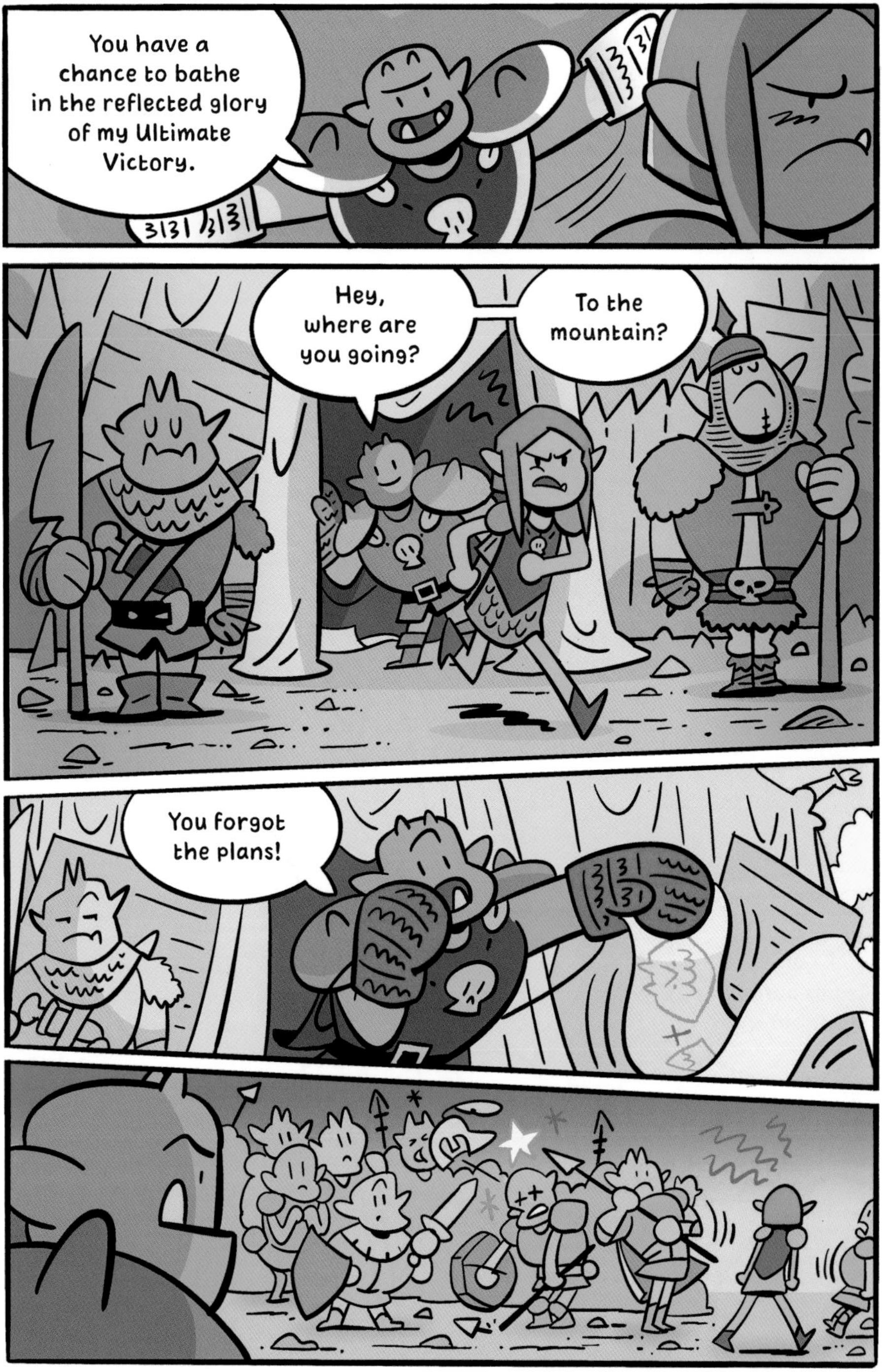
You have a chance to bathe in the reflected glory of my Ultimate Victory.
Hey, where are you going?
To the mountain?
You forgot the plans!

CHAPTER FOURTEEN

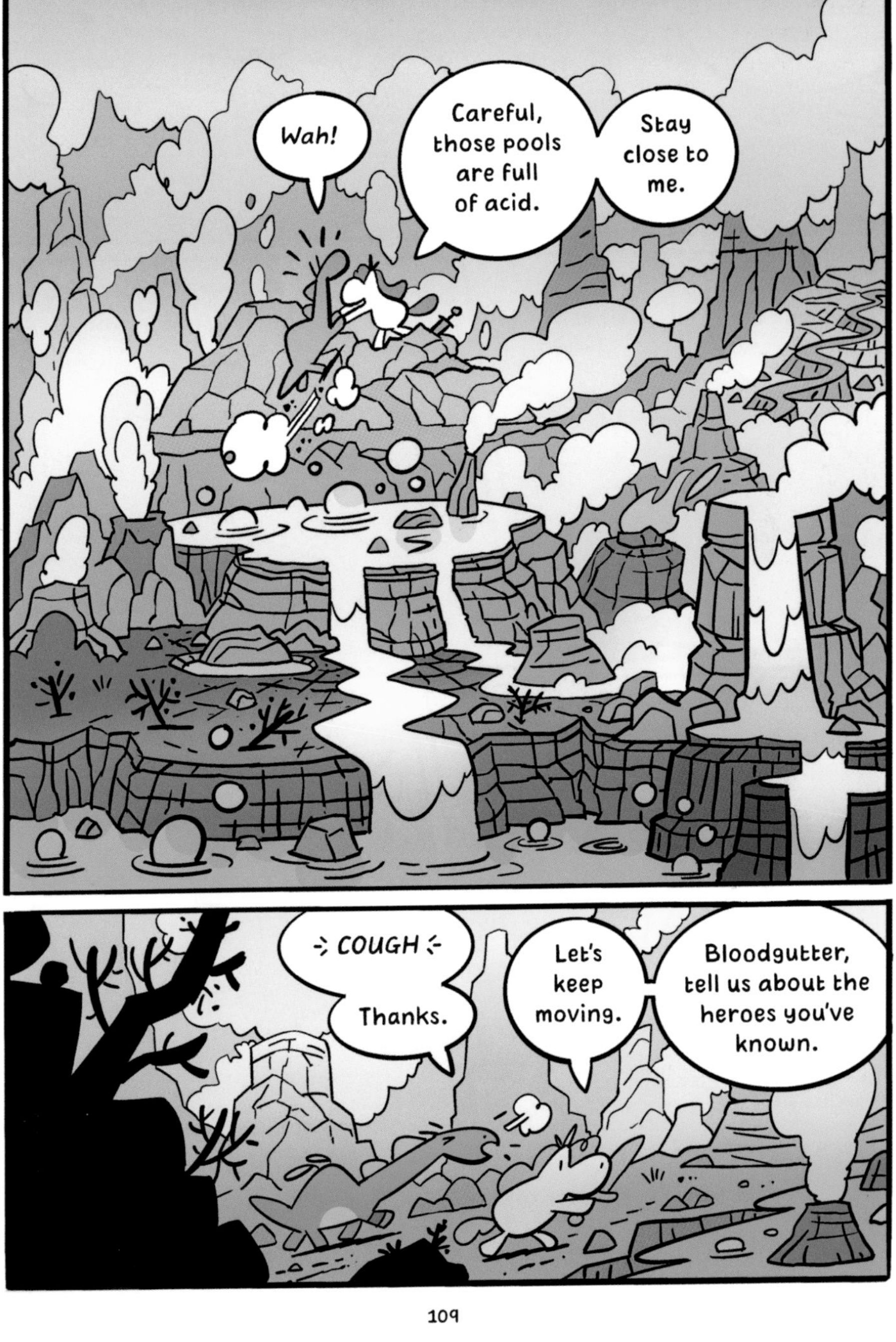
Wah!
Careful, those pools are full of acid.
Stay close to me.
COUGH
Thanks.
Let's keep moving.
Bloodgutter, tell us about the heroes you've known.

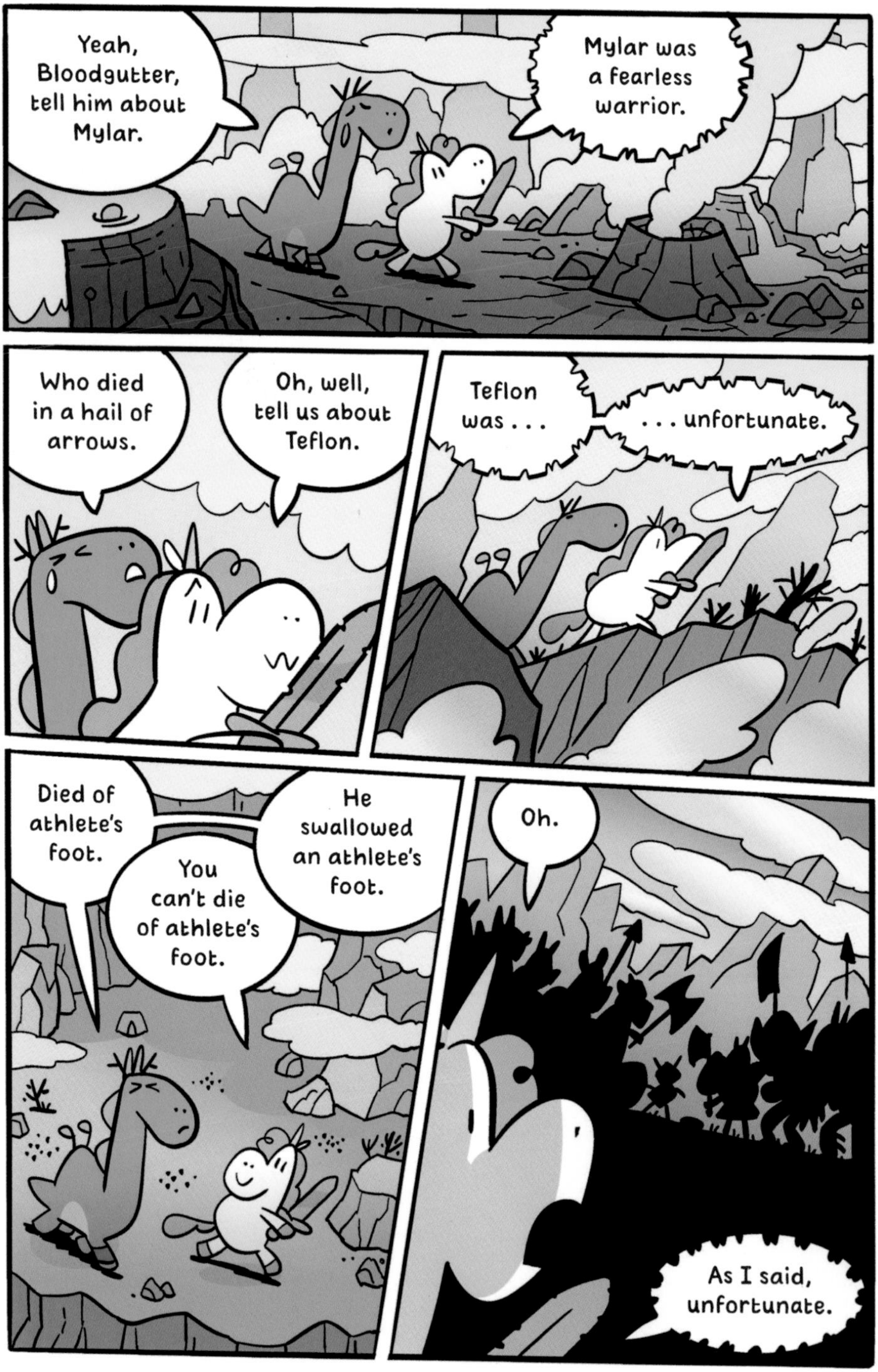
Yeah, Bloodgutter, tell him about Mylar.
Mylar was a fearless warrior.
Who died in a hail of arrows.
Oh, well, tell us about Teflon.
Teflon was . . .
. . . unfortunate.
Died of athlete's foot.
You can't die of athlete's foot.
He swallowed an athlete's foot.
Oh.
As I said, unfortunate.

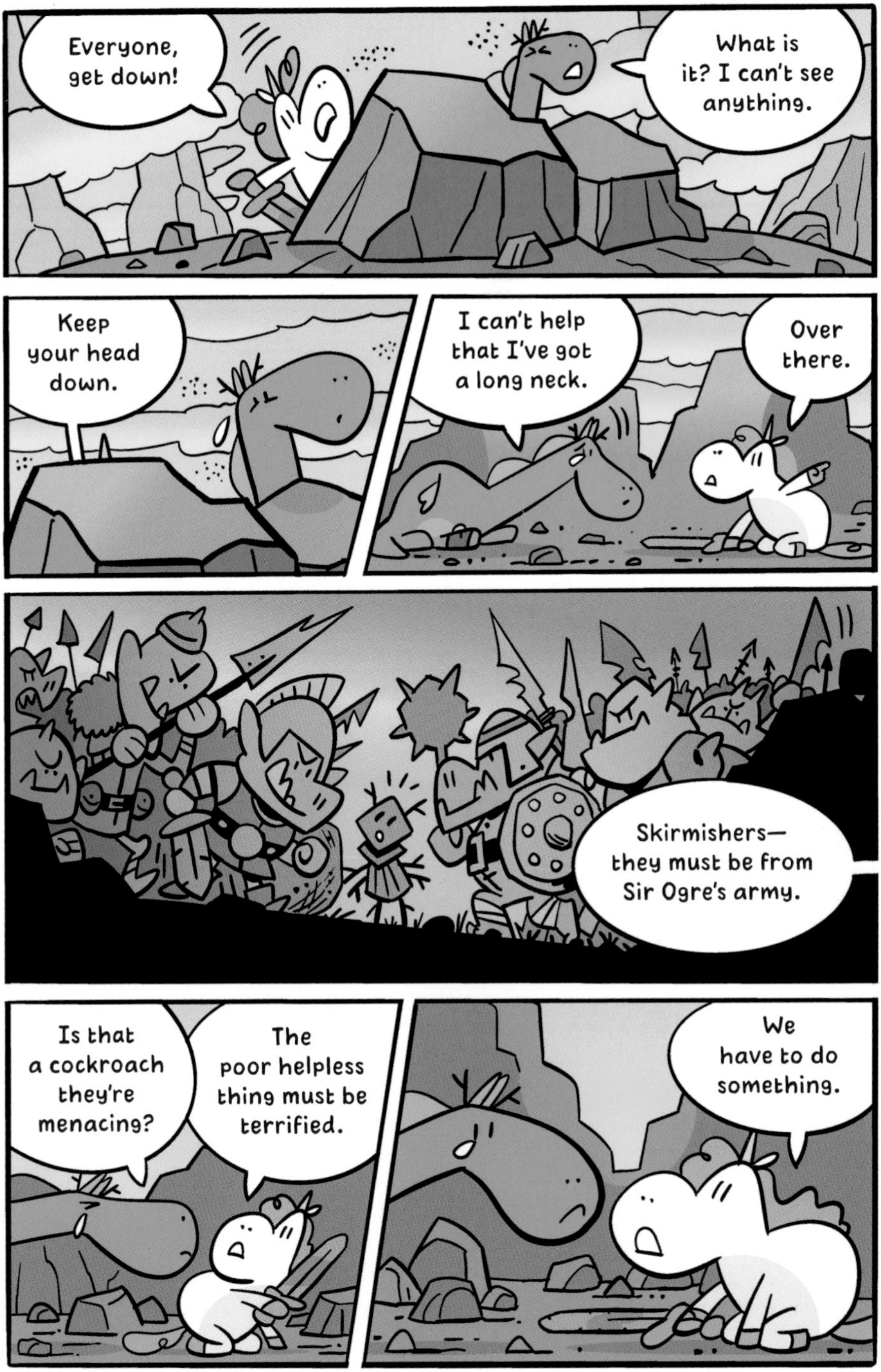
Everyone, get down!
What is it? I can't see anything.
Keep your head down.
I can't help that I've got a long neck.
Over there.
Skirmishers— they must be from Sir Ogre's army.
Is that a cockroach they're menacing?
The poor helpless thing must be terrified.
We have to do something.

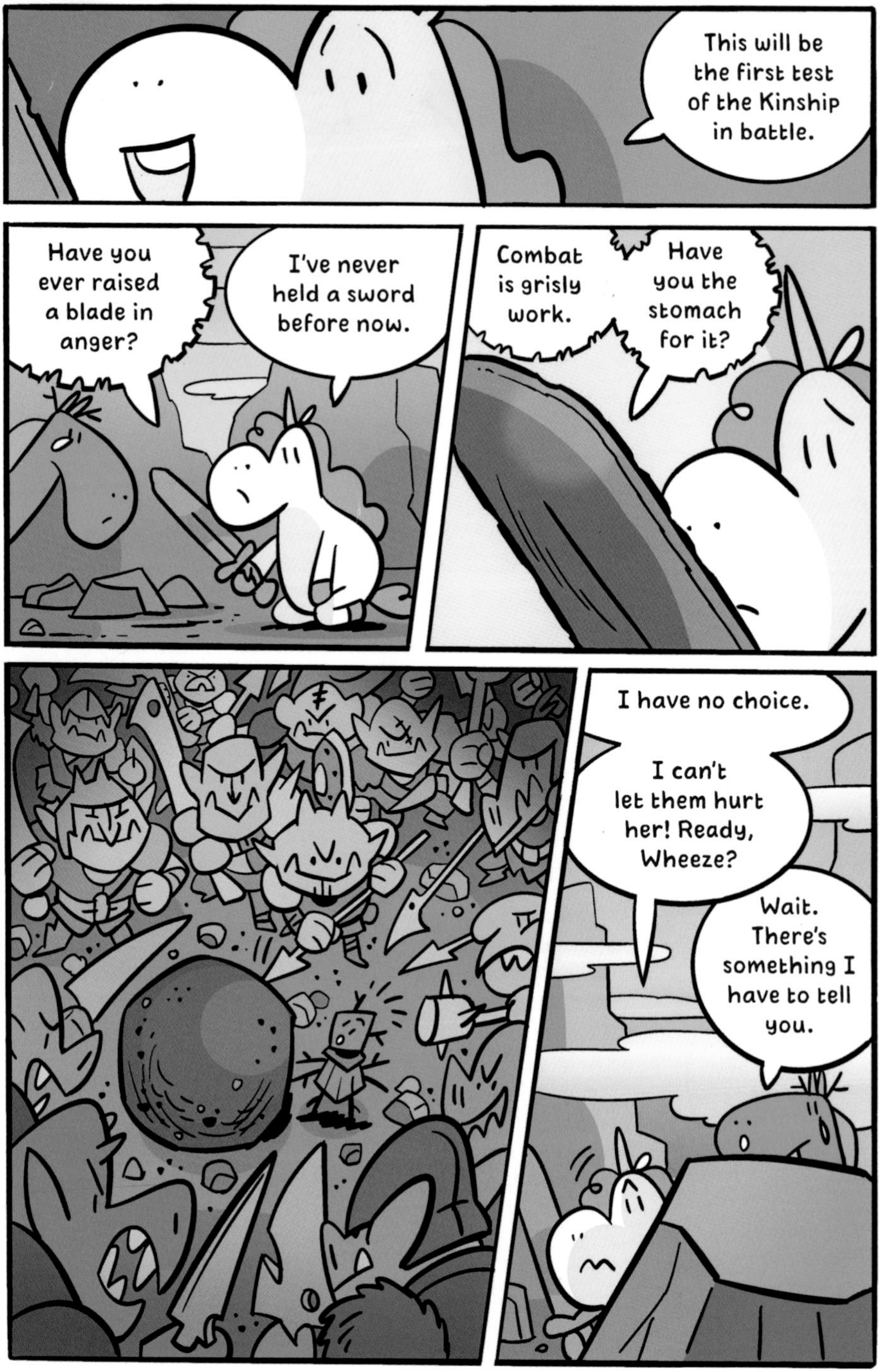
This will be the first test of the Kinship in battle.
Have you ever raised a blade in anger?
I've never held a sword before now.
Combat is grisly work.
Have you the stomach for it?
I have no choice.
I can't let them hurt her! Ready, Wheeze?
Wait. There's something I have to tell you.

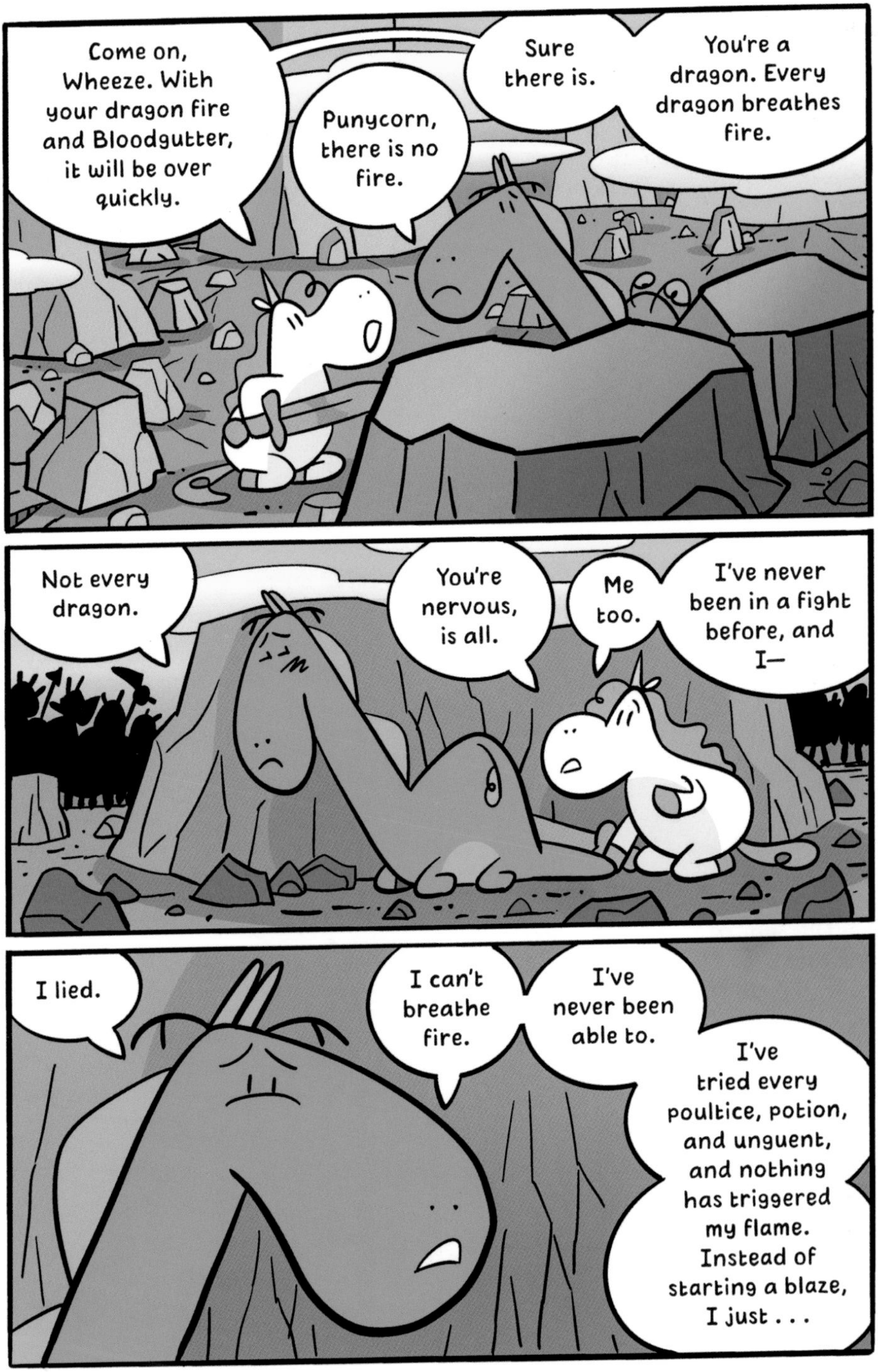

Come on, Wheeze. With your dragon fire and Bloodgutter, it will be over quickly.
Punycorn, there is no fire.
Sure there is.
You're a dragon. Every dragon breathes fire.
Not every dragon.
You're nervous, is all.
Me too.
I've never been in a fight before, and I—
I lied.
I can't breathe fire.
I've never been able to.
I've tried every poultice, potion, and unguent, and nothing has triggered my flame. Instead of starting a blaze, I just . . .

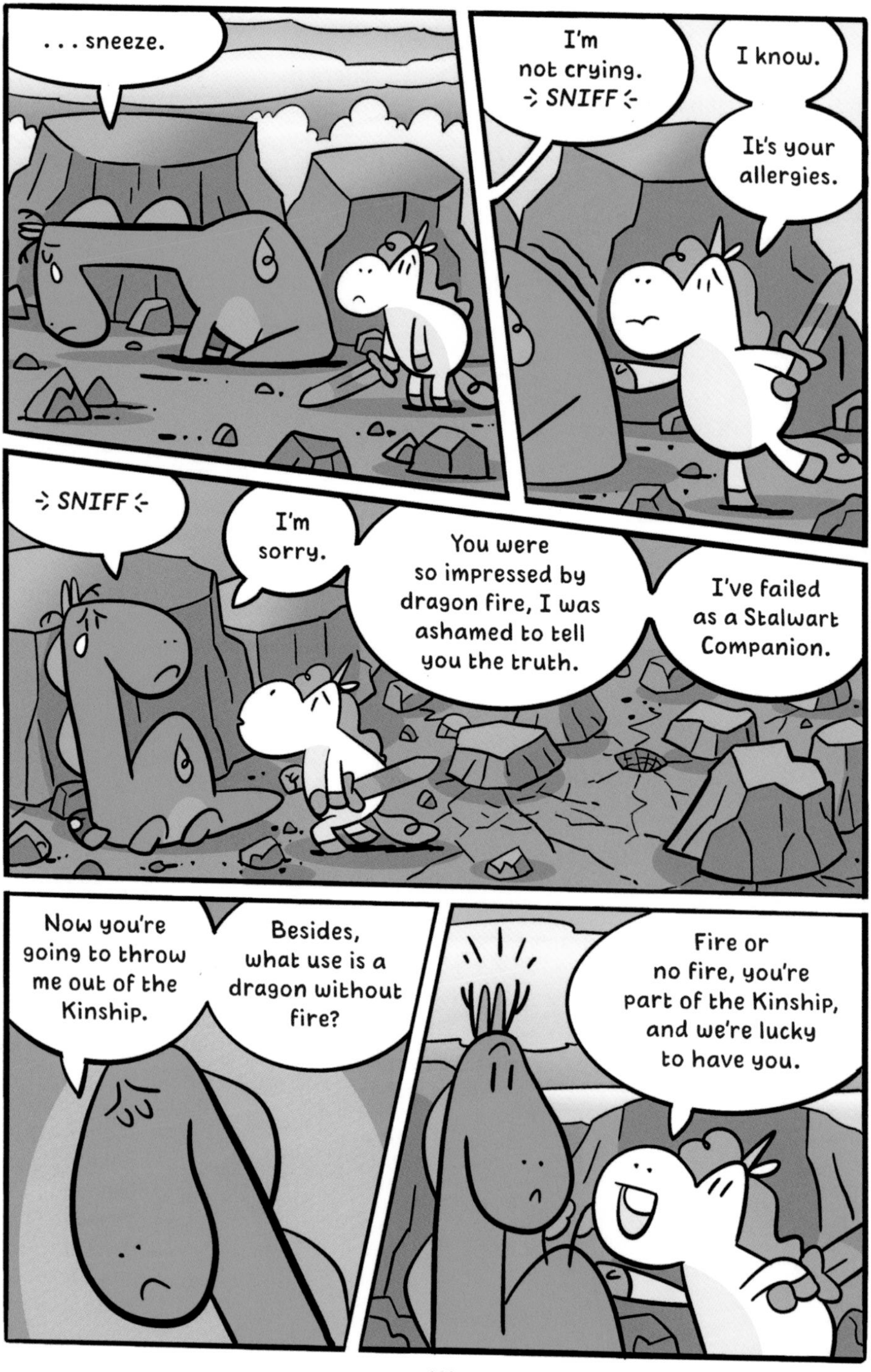
. . . sneeze.
I'm not crying. SNIFF
I know.
It's your allergies.
SNIFF
I'm sorry.
You were so impressed by dragon fire, I was ashamed to tell you the truth.
I've failed as a Stalwart Companion.
Now you're going to throw me out of the Kinship.
Besides, what use is a dragon without fire?
Fire or no fire, you're part of the Kinship, and we're lucky to have you.

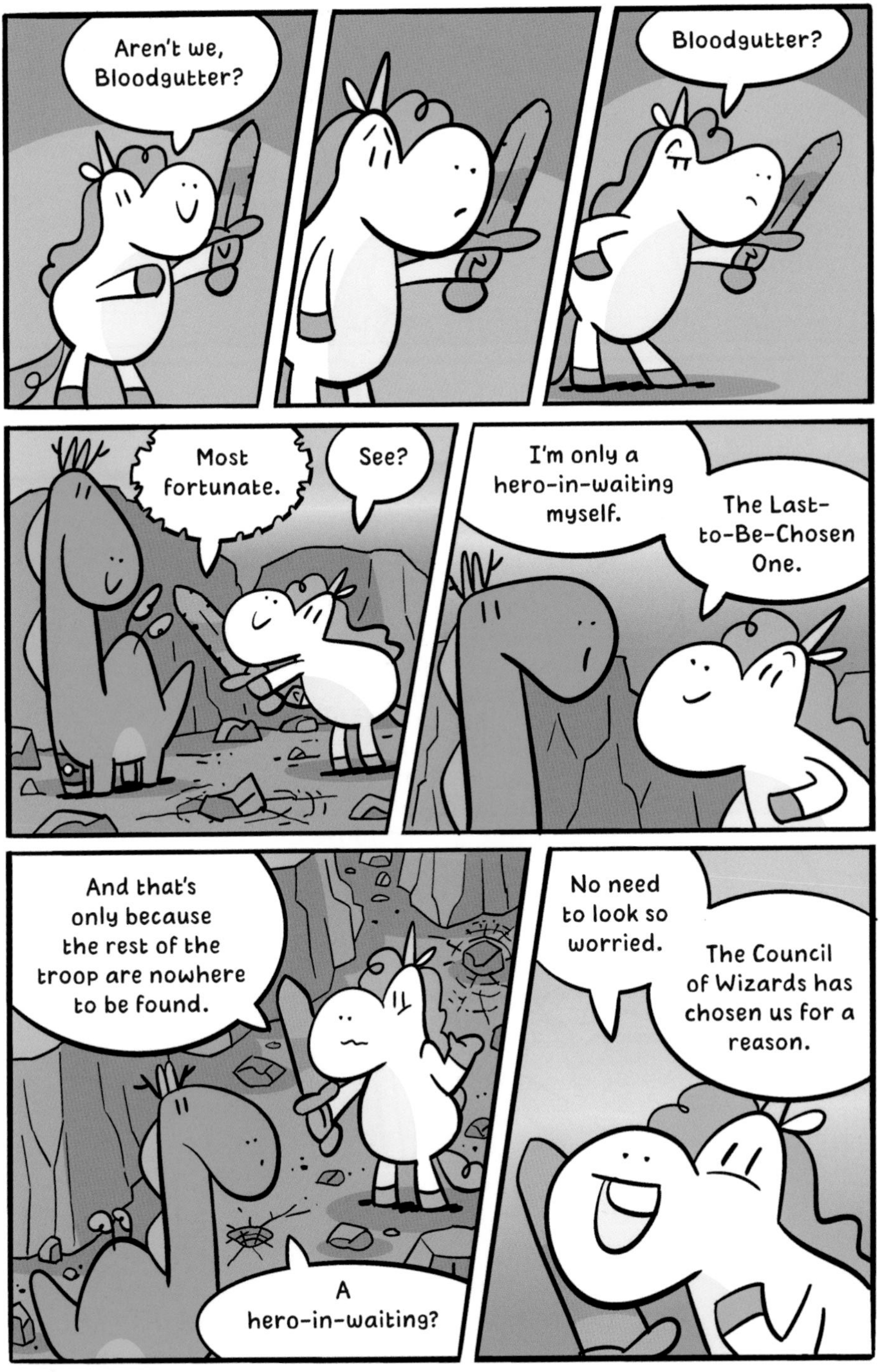
Aren't we, Bloodgutter?
Bloodgutter?
Most fortunate.
See?
I'm only a hero-in-waiting myself.
The Last-to-Be-Chosen One.
And that's only because the rest of the troop are nowhere to be found.
A hero-in-waiting?
No need to look so worried.
The Council of Wizards has chosen us for a reason.

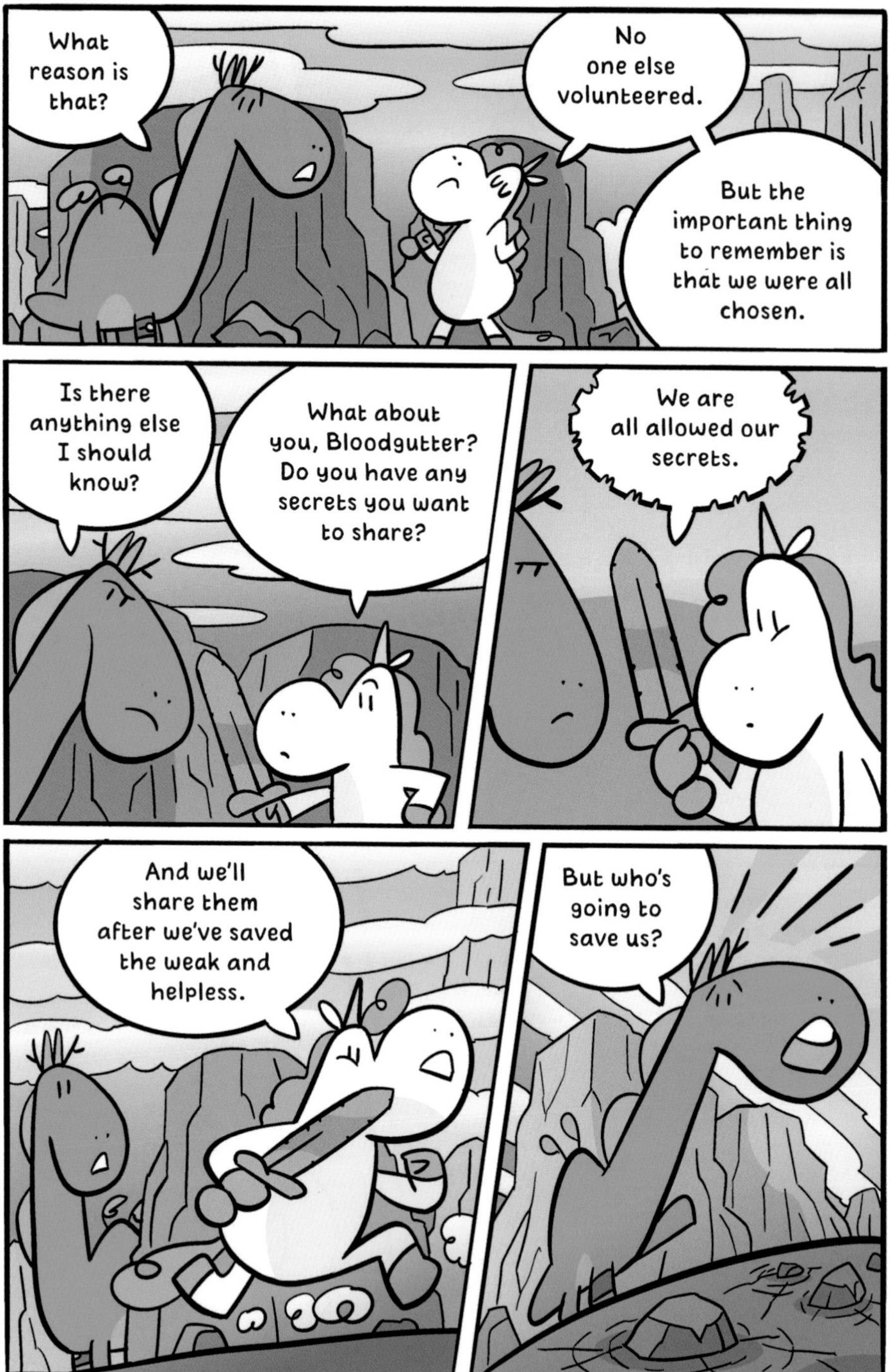
What reason is that?
No one else volunteered.
But the important thing to remember is that we were all chosen.
Is there anything else I should know?
What about you, Bloodgutter? Do you have any secrets you want to share?
We are all allowed our secrets.
And we'll share them after we've saved the weak and helpless.
But who's going to save us?

CHAPTER FIFTEEN

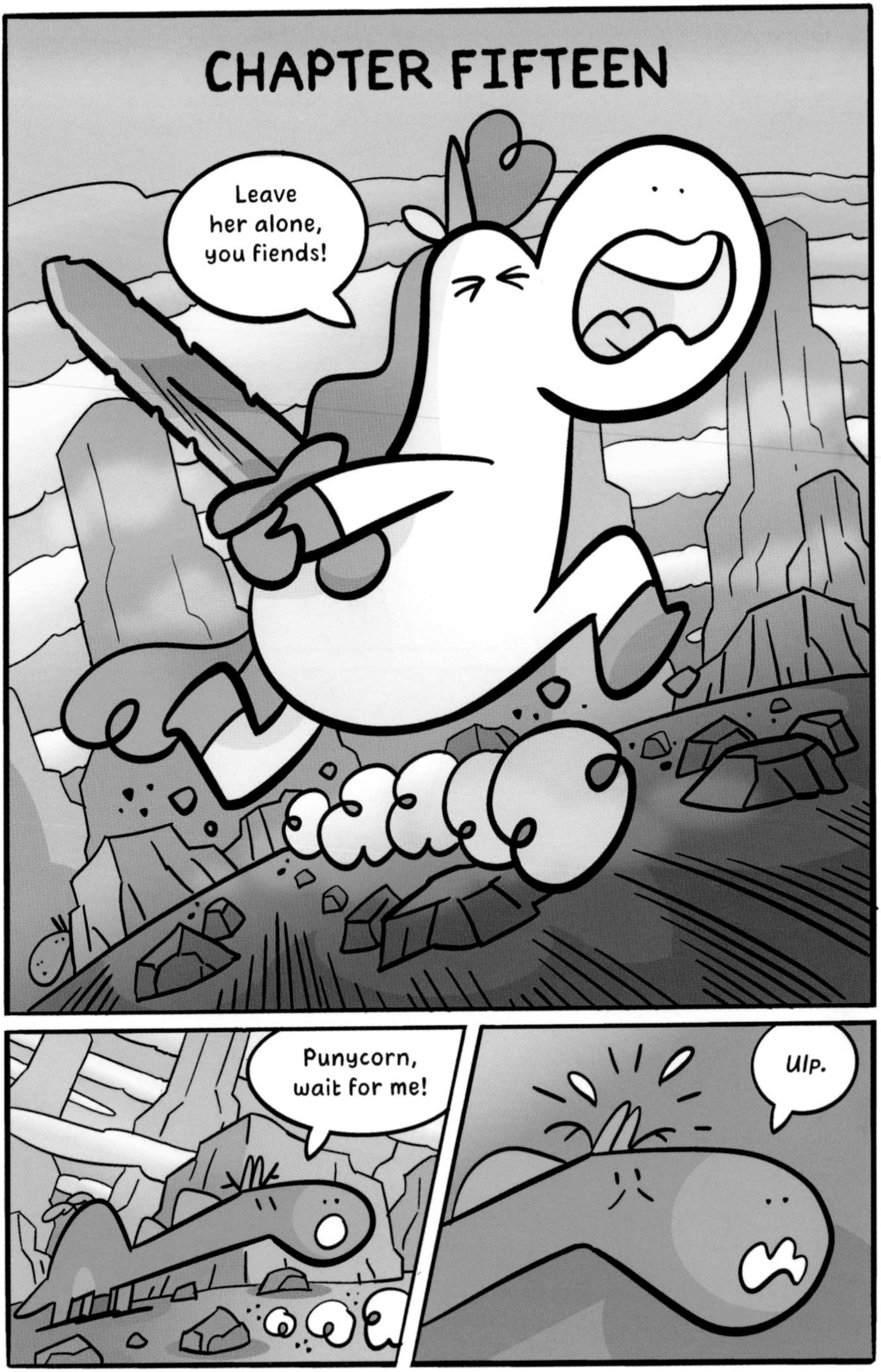
Leave her alone, you fiends!
Punycorn, wait for me!
Ulp.

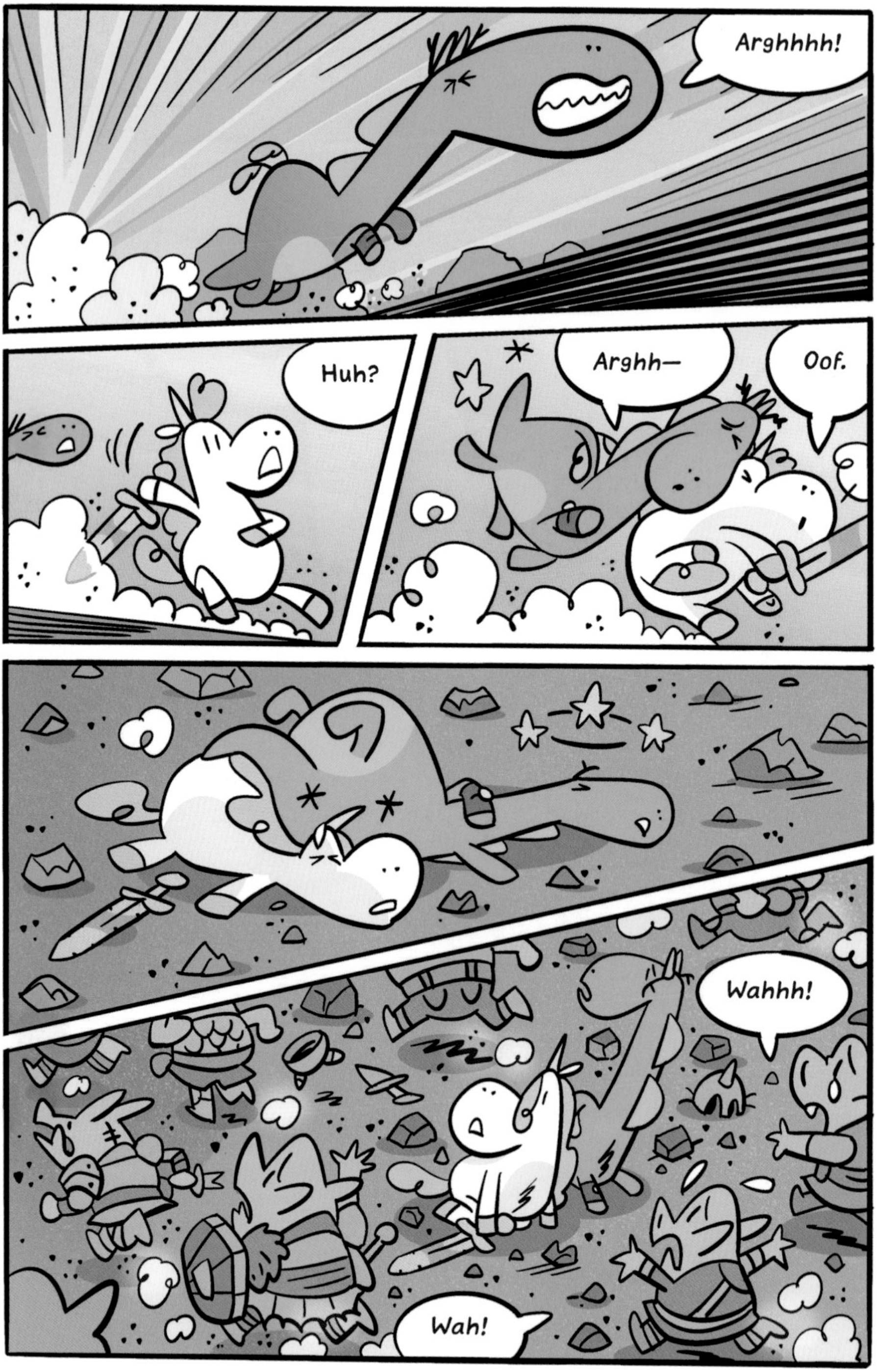
Arghhhh!
Huh?
Arghh—
Oof.
Wahhh!
Wah!

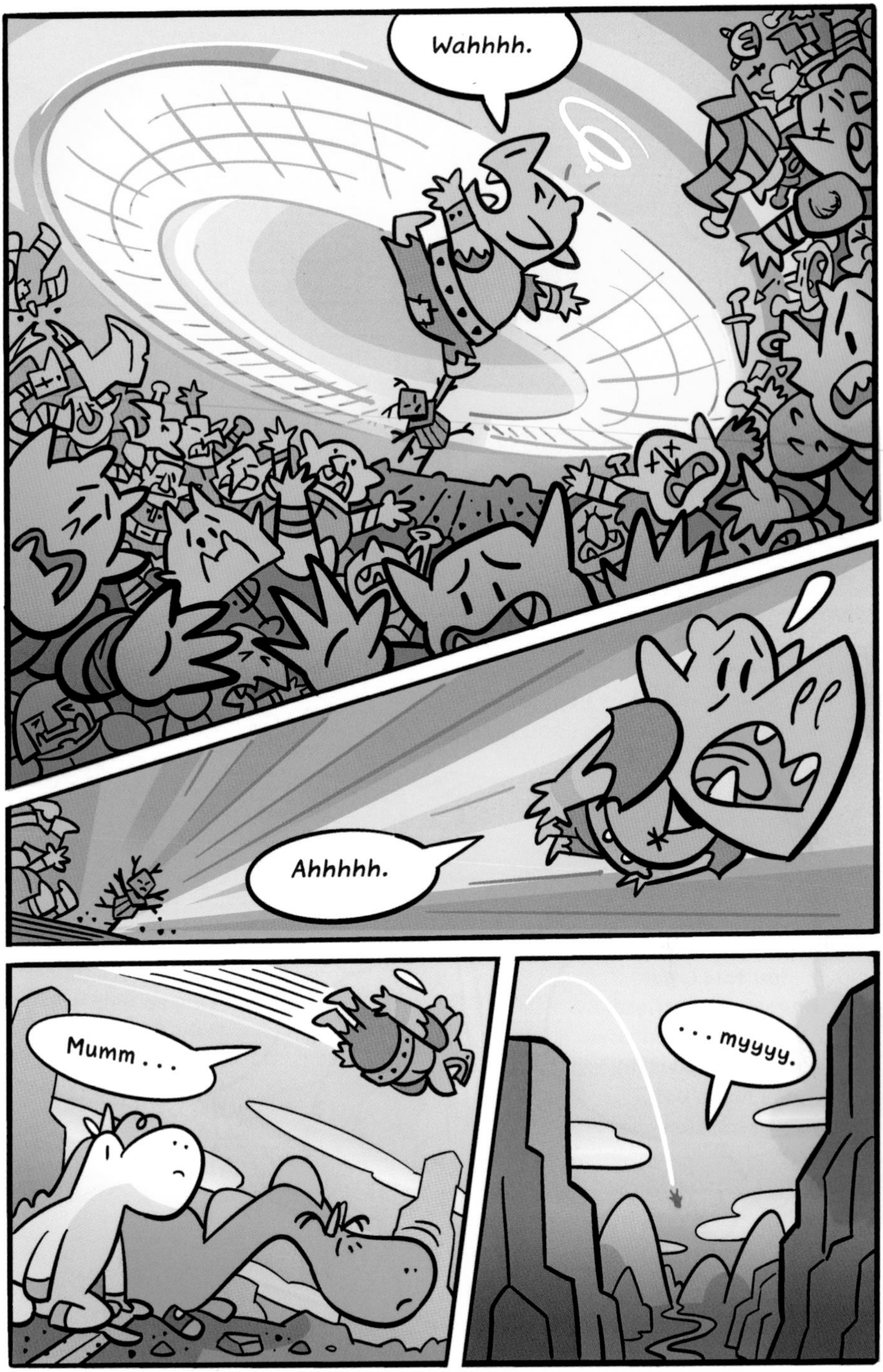
Wahhhh.
Ahhhhh.
Mumm . . .
. . . myyyy.

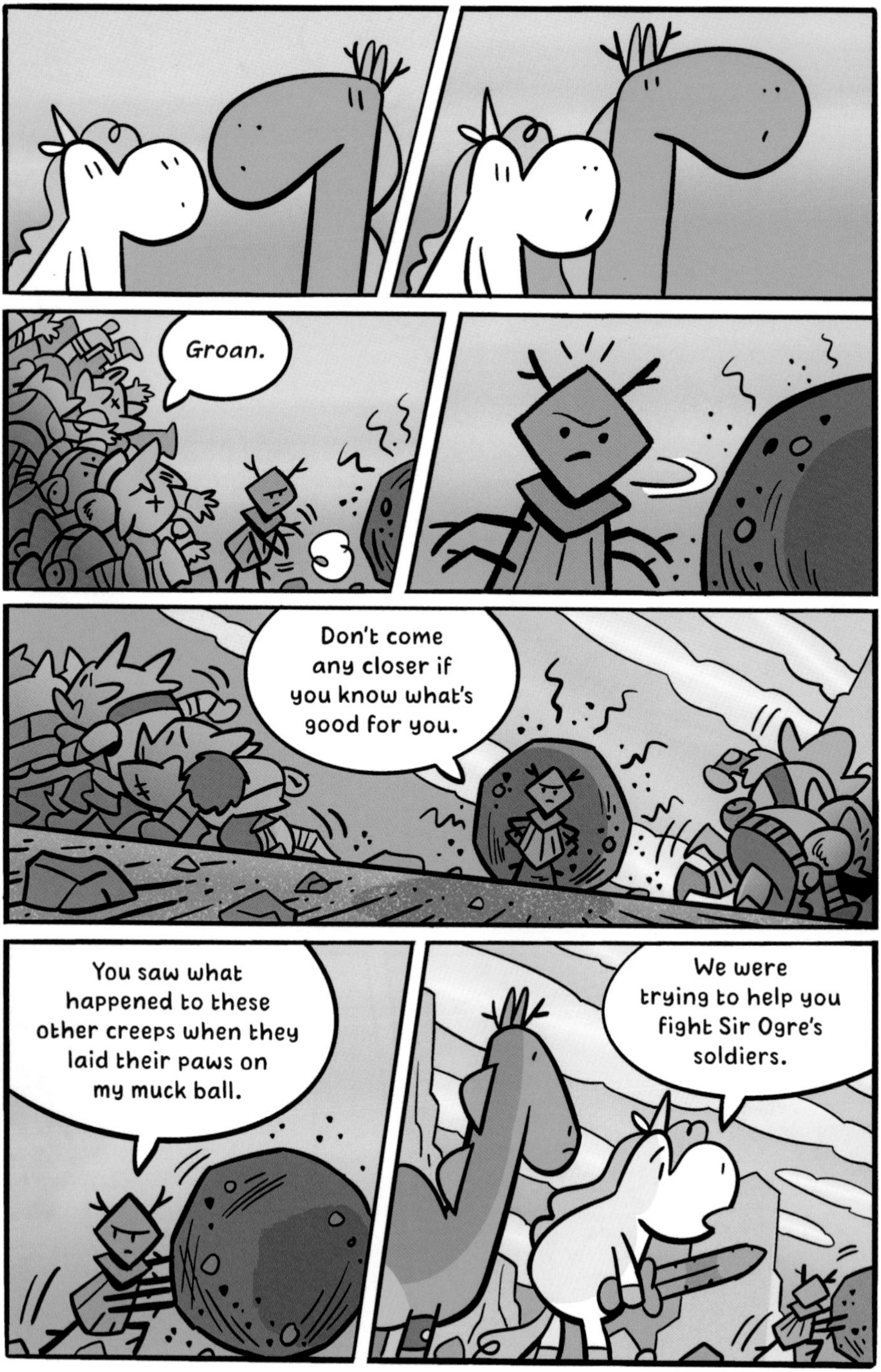

Groan.
Don't come any closer if you know what's good for you.
You saw what happened to these other creeps when they laid their paws on my muck ball.
We were trying to help you fight Sir Ogre's soldiers.

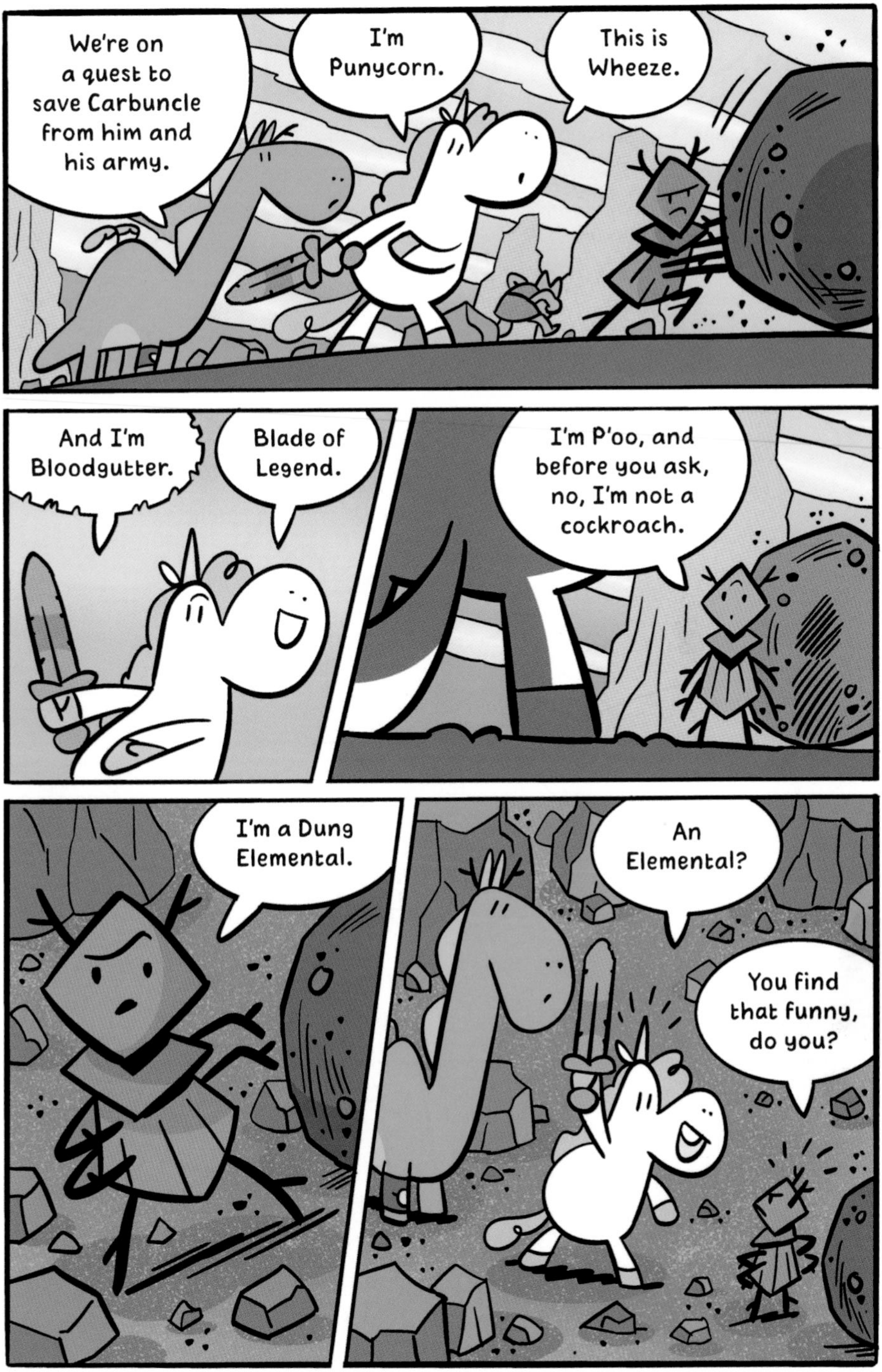
We're on a quest to save Carbuncle from him and his army.
I'm Punycorn.
This is Wheeze.
And I'm Bloodgutter.
Blade of Legend.
I'm P'oo, and before you ask, no, I'm not a cockroach.
I'm a Dung Elemental.
An Elemental?
You find that funny, do you?

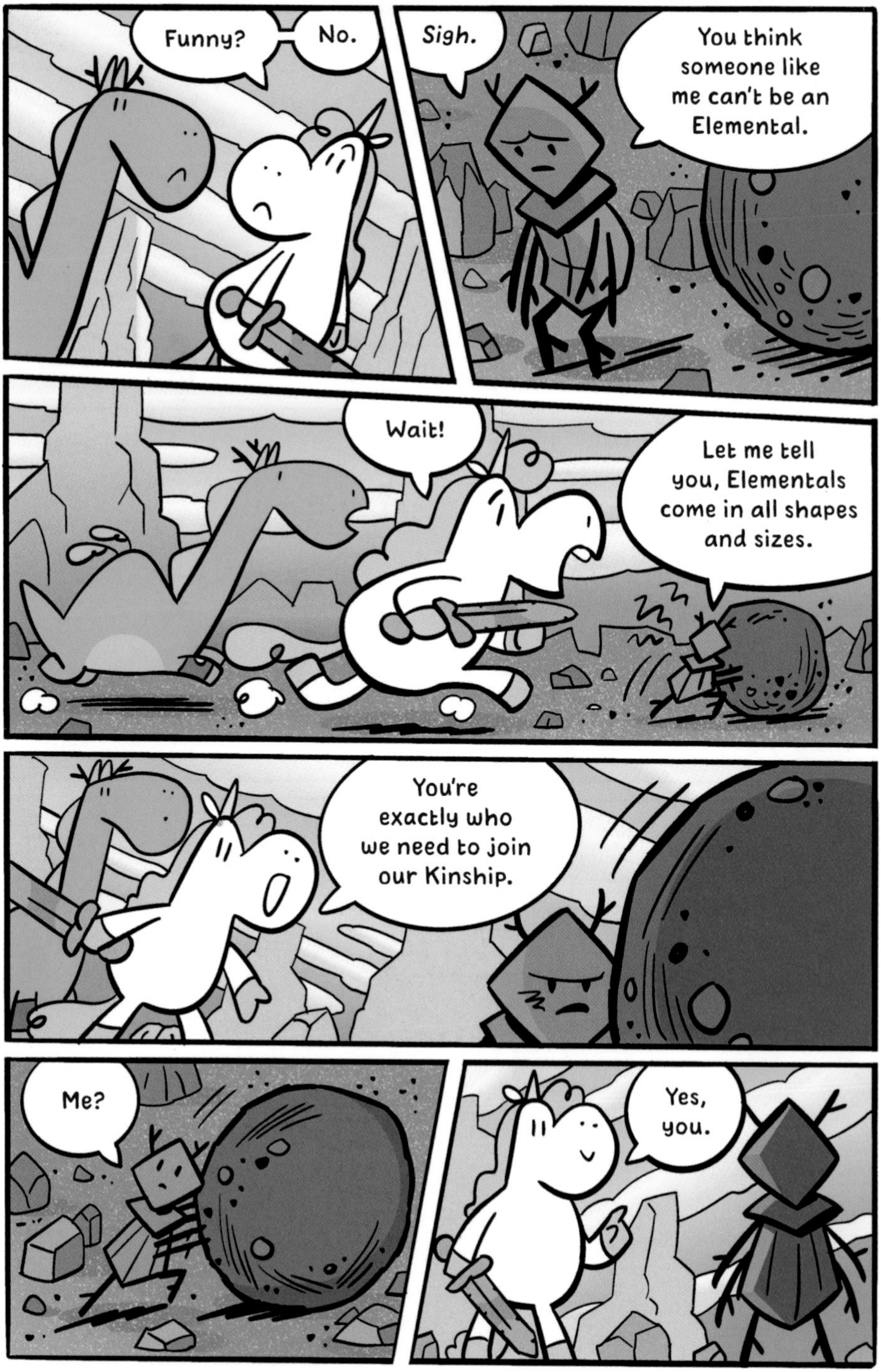
Funny?
No.
Sigh.
You think someone like me can't be an Elemental.
Wait!
Let me tell you, Elementals come in all shapes and sizes.
You're exactly who we need to join our Kinship.
Me?
Yes, you.

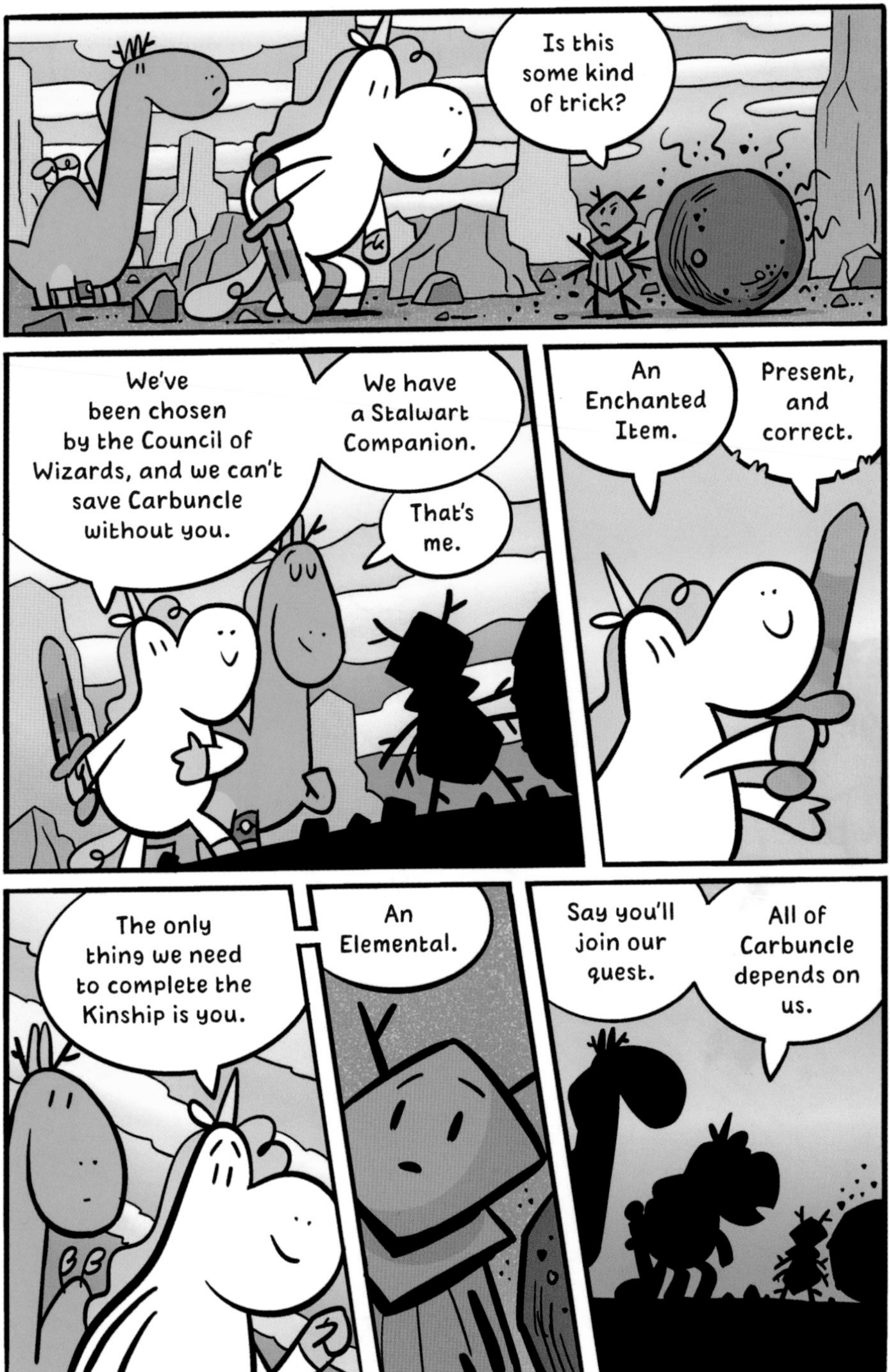
Is this some kind of trick?
We've been chosen by the Council of Wizards, and we can't save Carbuncle without you.
We have a Stalwart Companion.
That's me.
An Enchanted Item.
Present, and correct.
The only thing we need to complete the Kinship is you.
An Elemental.
Say you'll join our quest.
All of Carbuncle depends on us.

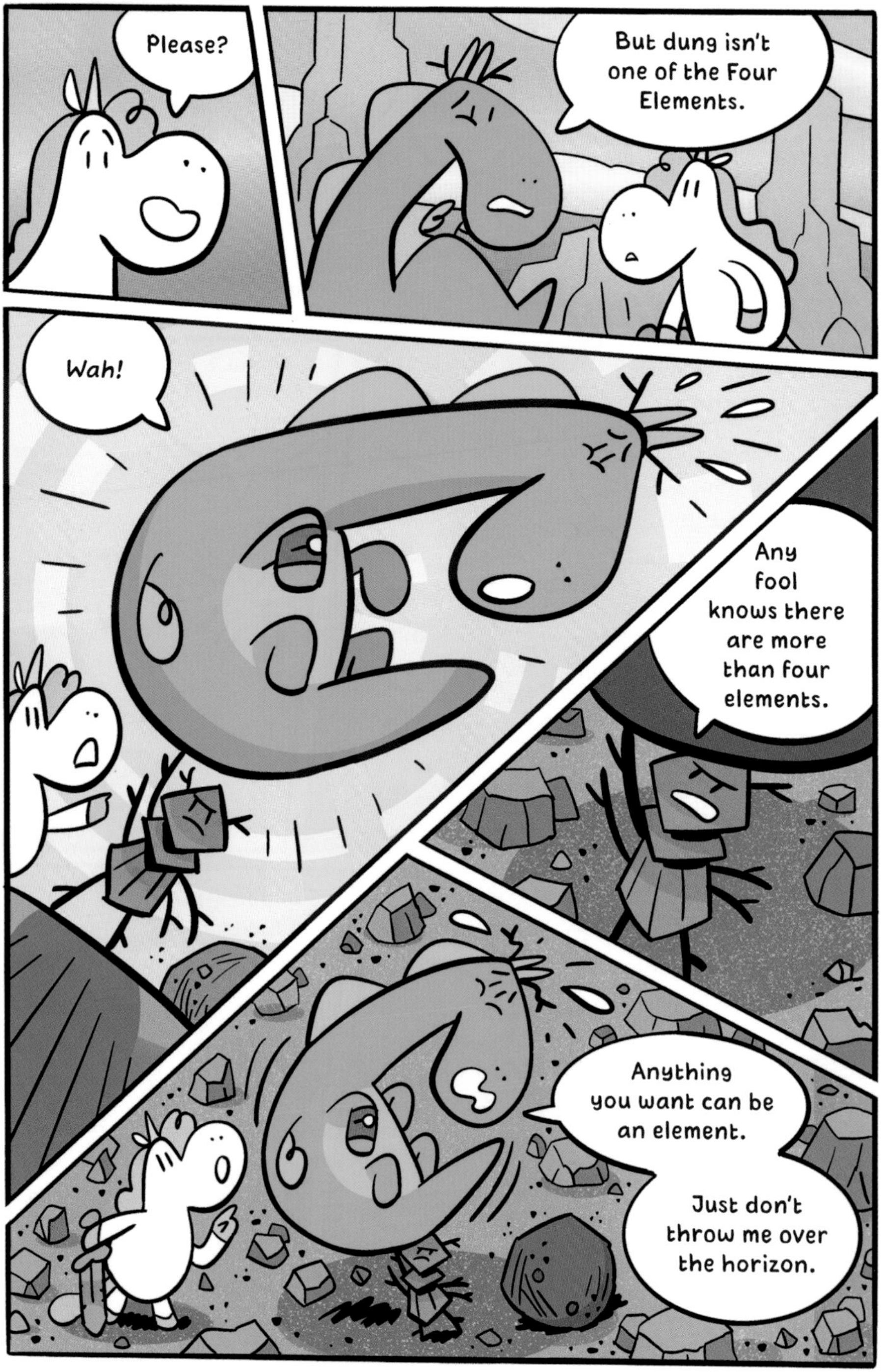
Please?
But dung isn't one of the Four Elements.
Wah!
Any fool knows there are more than four elements.
Anything you want can be an element.
Just don't throw me over the horizon.

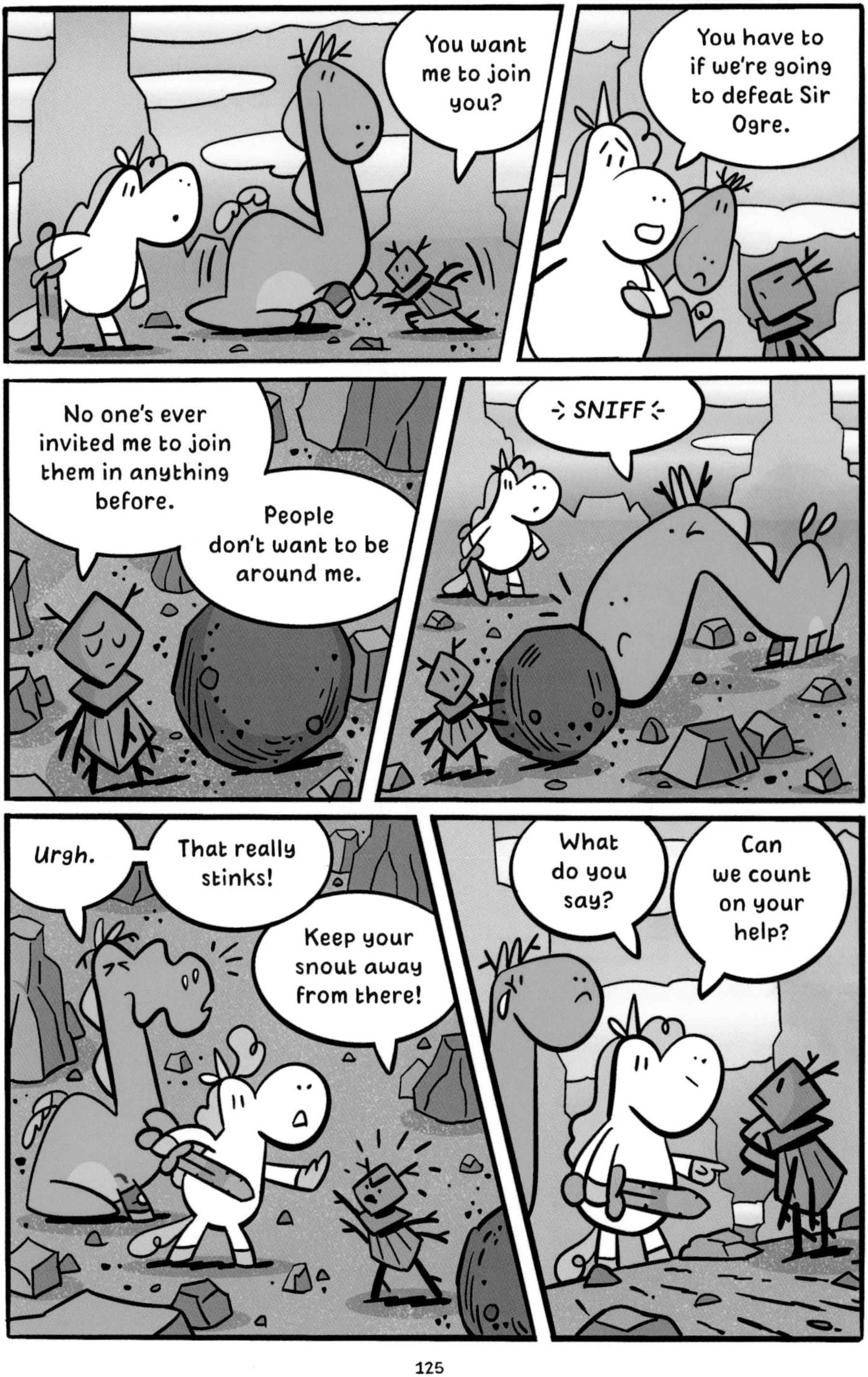
You want me to join you?
You have to if we're going to defeat Sir Ogre.
No one's ever invited me to join them in anything before.
People don't want to be around me.
SNIFF
Urgh.
That really stinks!
Keep your snout away from there!
What do you say?
Can we count on your help?

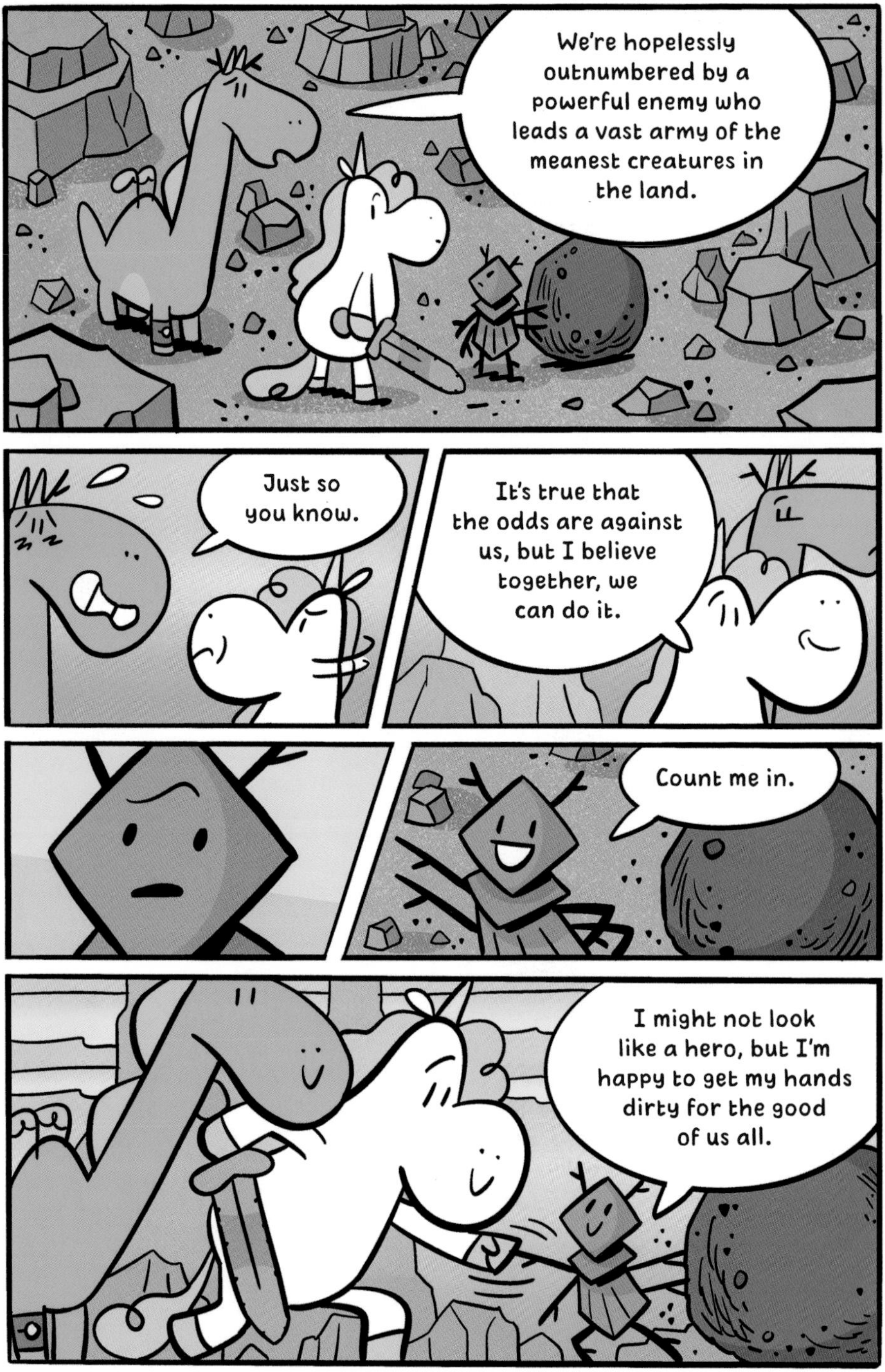
We're hopelessly outnumbered by a powerful enemy who leads a vast army of the meanest creatures in the land.
Just so you know.
It's true that the odds are against us, but I believe together, we can do it.
Count me in.
I might not look like a hero, but I'm happy to get my hands dirty for the good of us all.

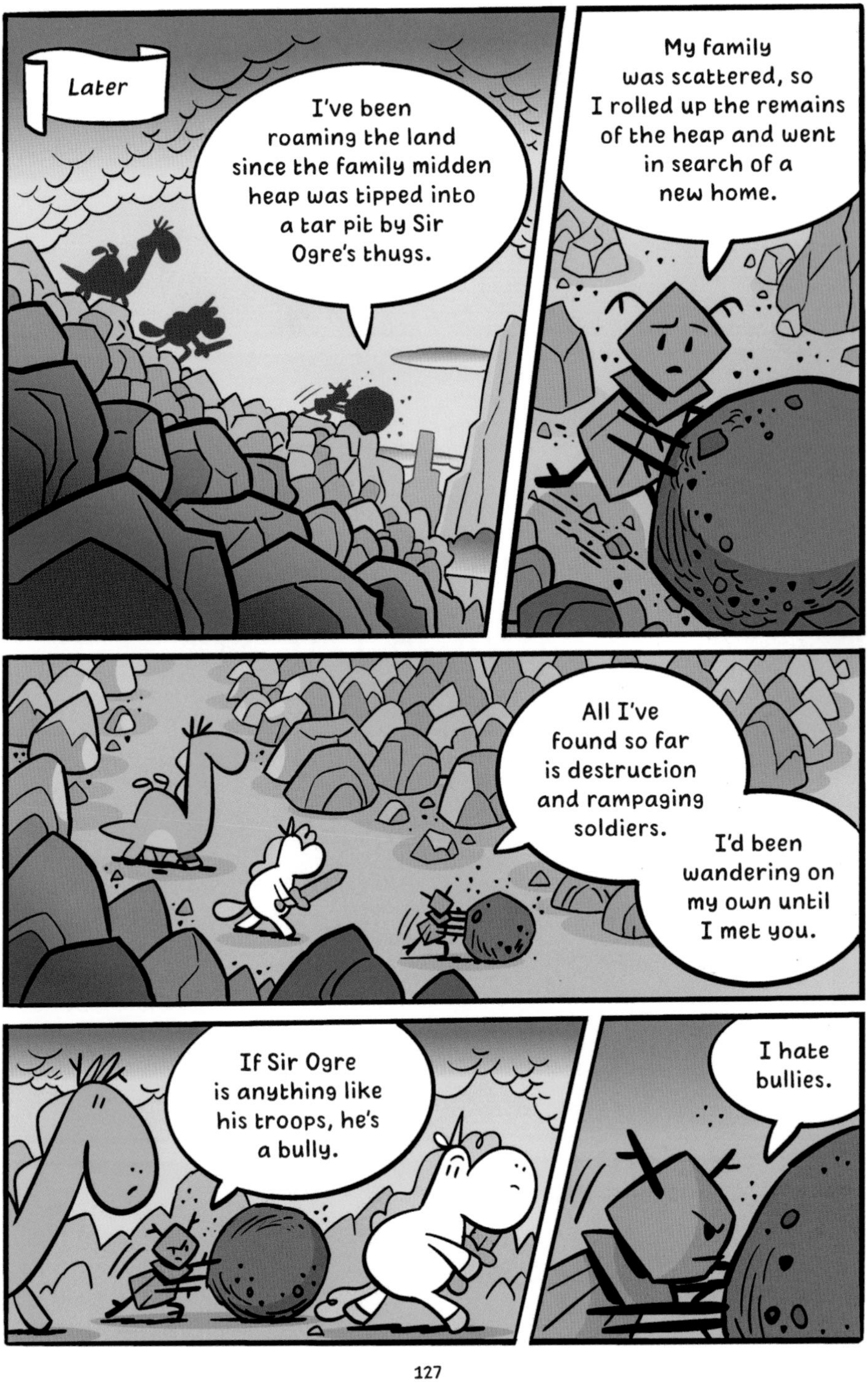
Later
I've been roaming the land since the family midden heap was tipped into a tar pit by Sir Ogre's thugs.
My family was scattered, so I rolled up the remains of the heap and went in search of a new home.
All I've found so far is destruction and rampaging soldiers.
I'd been wandering on my own until I met you.
If Sir Ogre is anything like his troops, he's a bully.
I hate bullies.

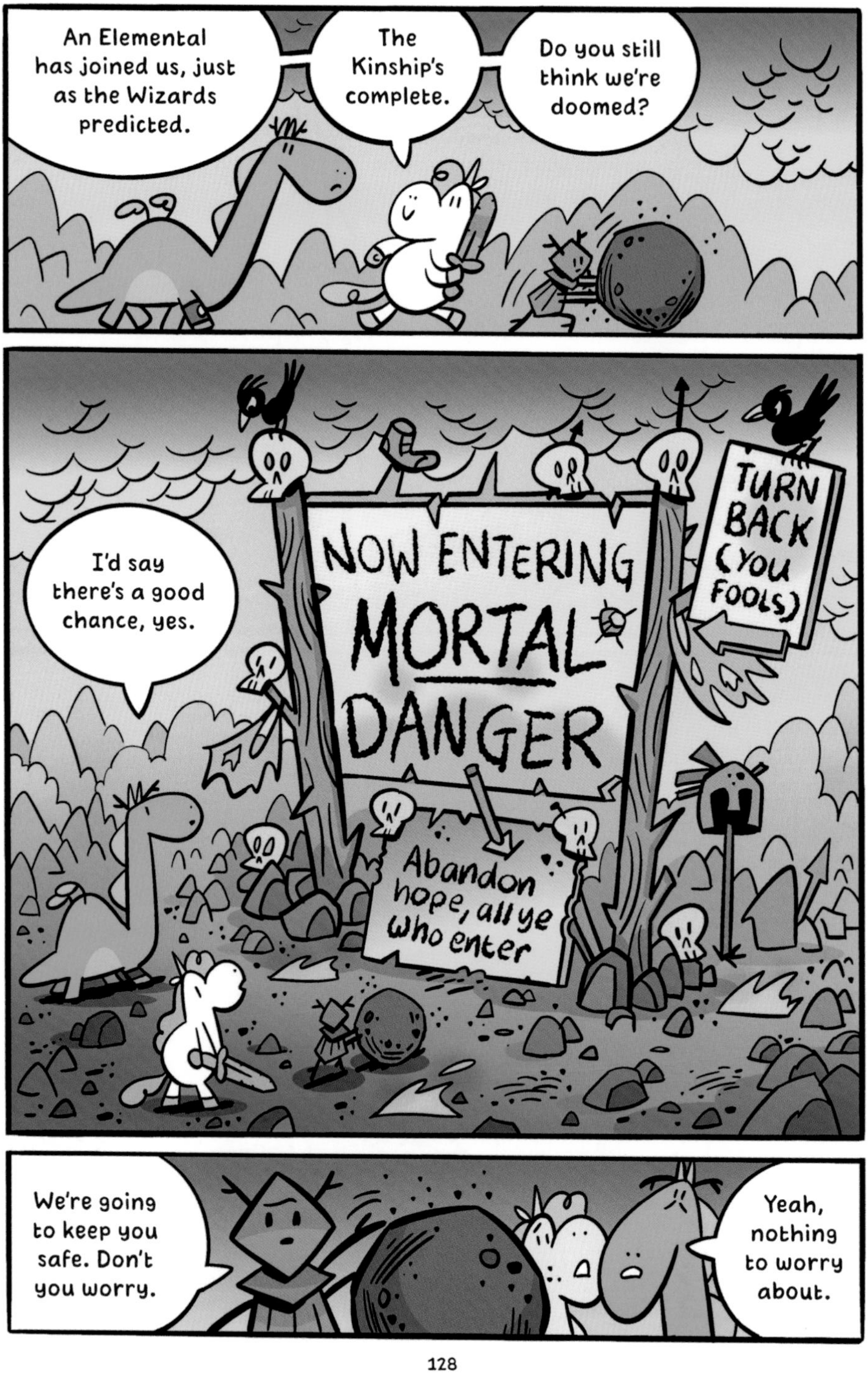
An Elemental has joined us, just as the Wizards predicted.
The Kinship's complete.
Do you still think we're doomed?
I'd say there's a good chance, yes.
NOW ENTERING MORTAL DANGER
TURN BACK (YOU FOOLS)
Abandon hope, all ye who enter
We're going to keep you safe. Don't you worry.
Yeah, nothing to worry about.

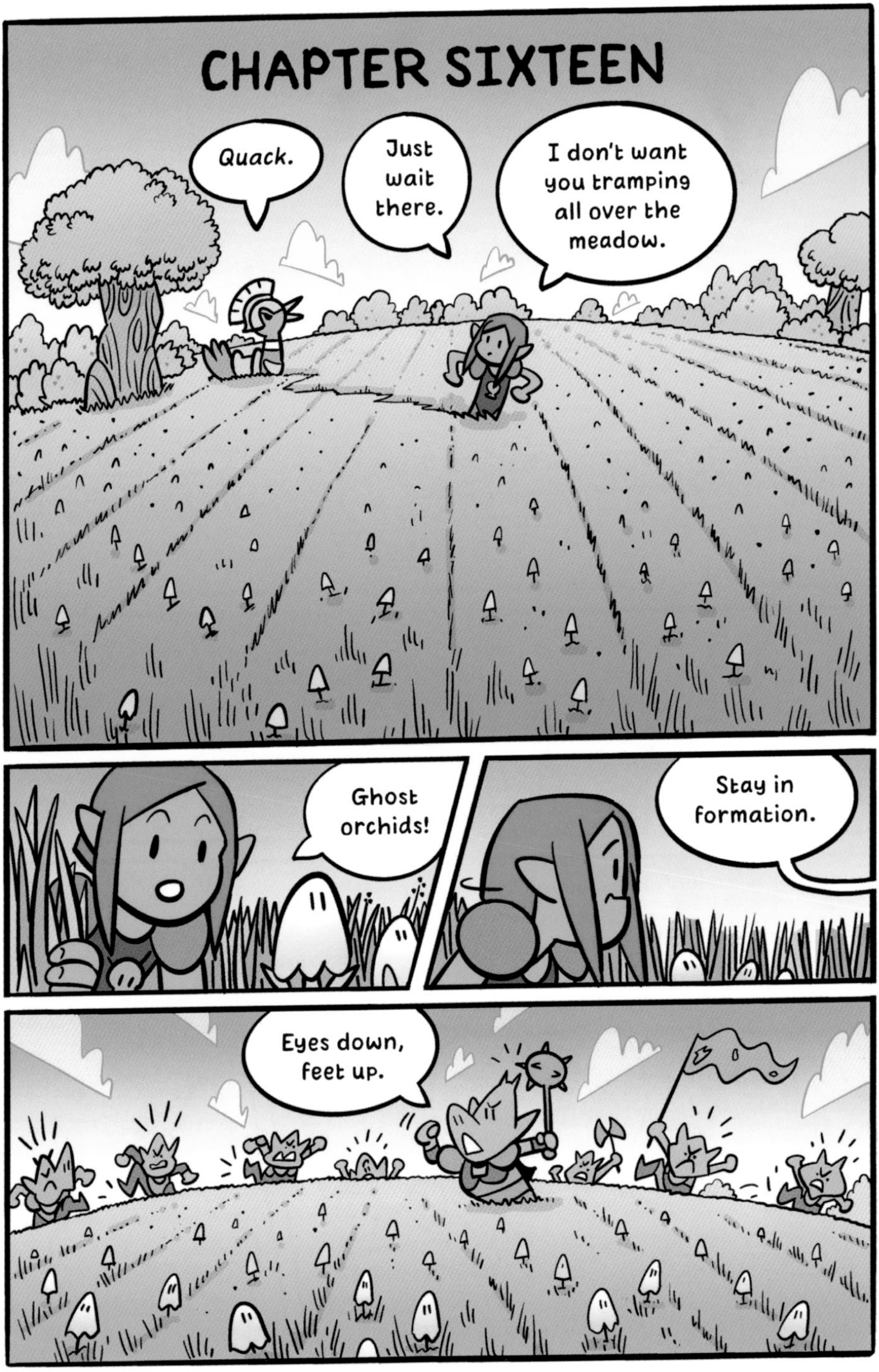
CHAPTER SIXTEEN
Quack.
Just wait there.
I don't want you tramping all over the meadow.
Ghost orchids!
Stay in formation.
Eyes down, feet up.

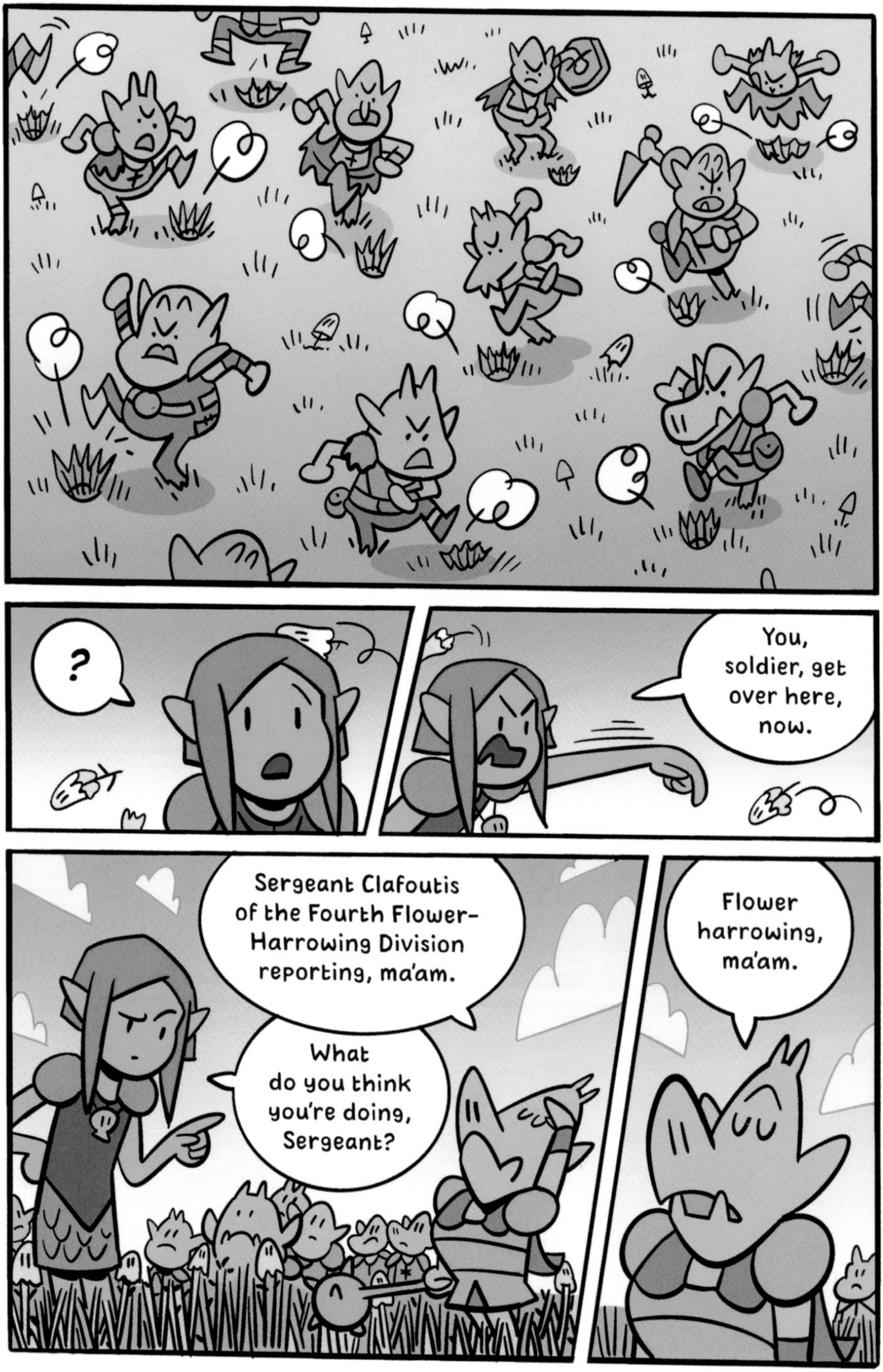
?
You, soldier, get over here, now.
Sergeant Clafoutis of the Fourth Flower-Harrowing Division reporting, ma'am.
What do you think you're doing, Sergeant?
Flower harrowing, ma'am.

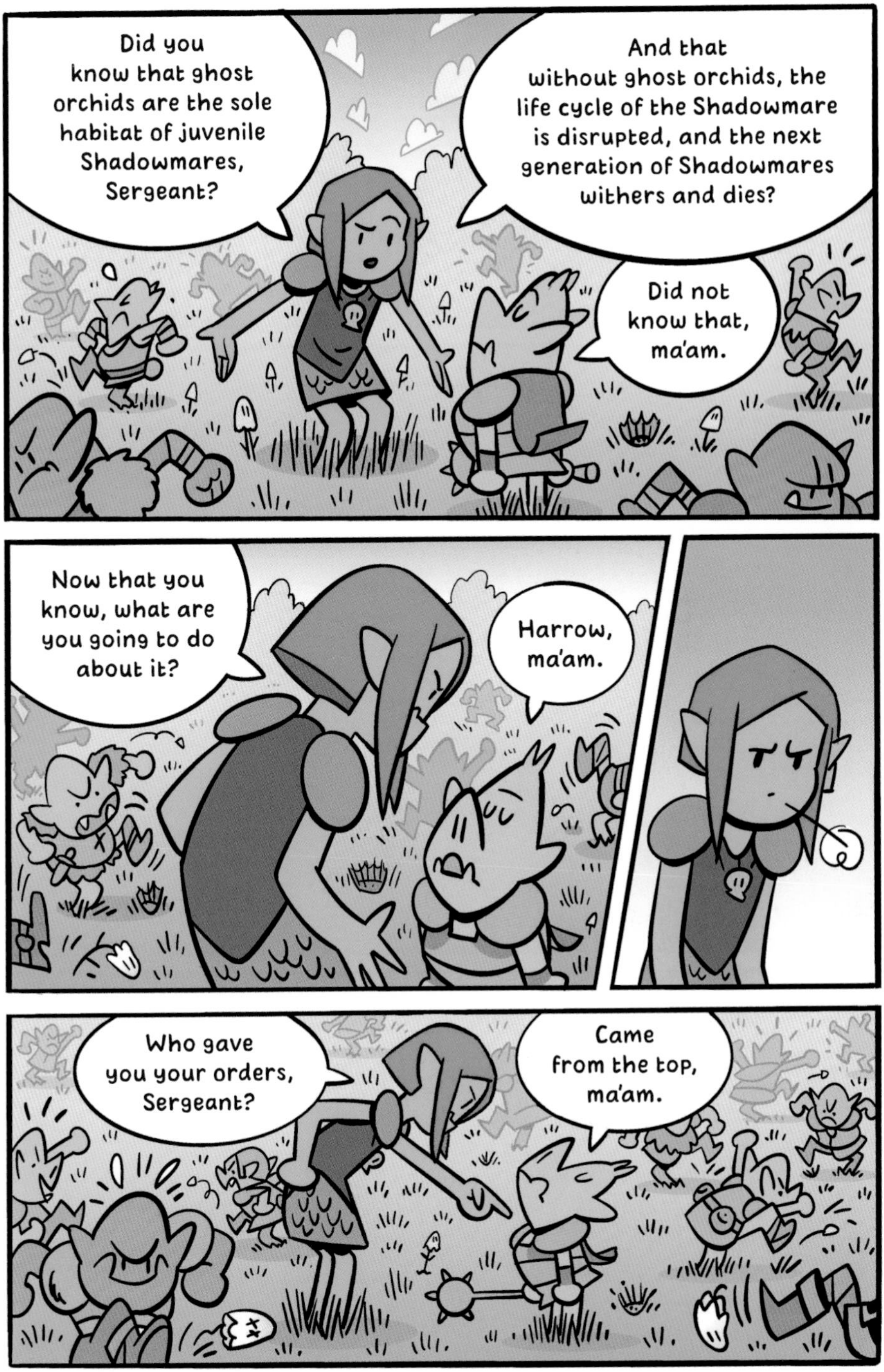
Did you know that ghost orchids are the sole habitat of juvenile Shadowmares, Sergeant?
And that without ghost orchids, the life cycle of the Shadowmare is disrupted, and the next generation of Shadowmares withers and dies?
Did not know that, ma'am.
Now that you know, what are you going to do about it?
Harrow, ma'am.
Who gave you your orders, Sergeant?
Came from the top, ma'am.

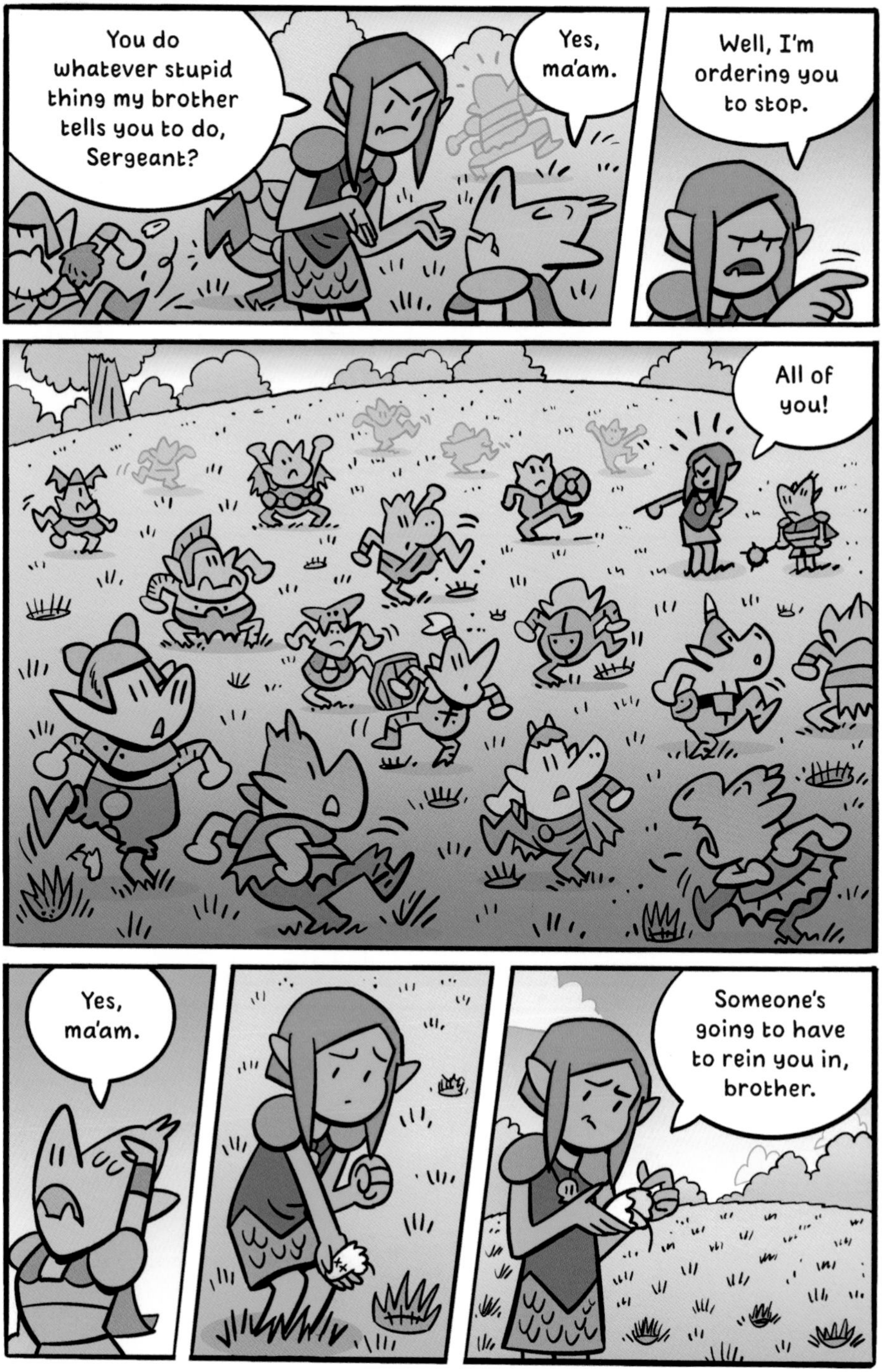
You do whatever stupid thing my brother tells you to do, Sergeant?
Yes, ma'am.
Well, I'm ordering you to stop.
All of you!
Yes, ma'am.
Someone's going to have to rein you in, brother.

CHAPTER SEVENTEEN

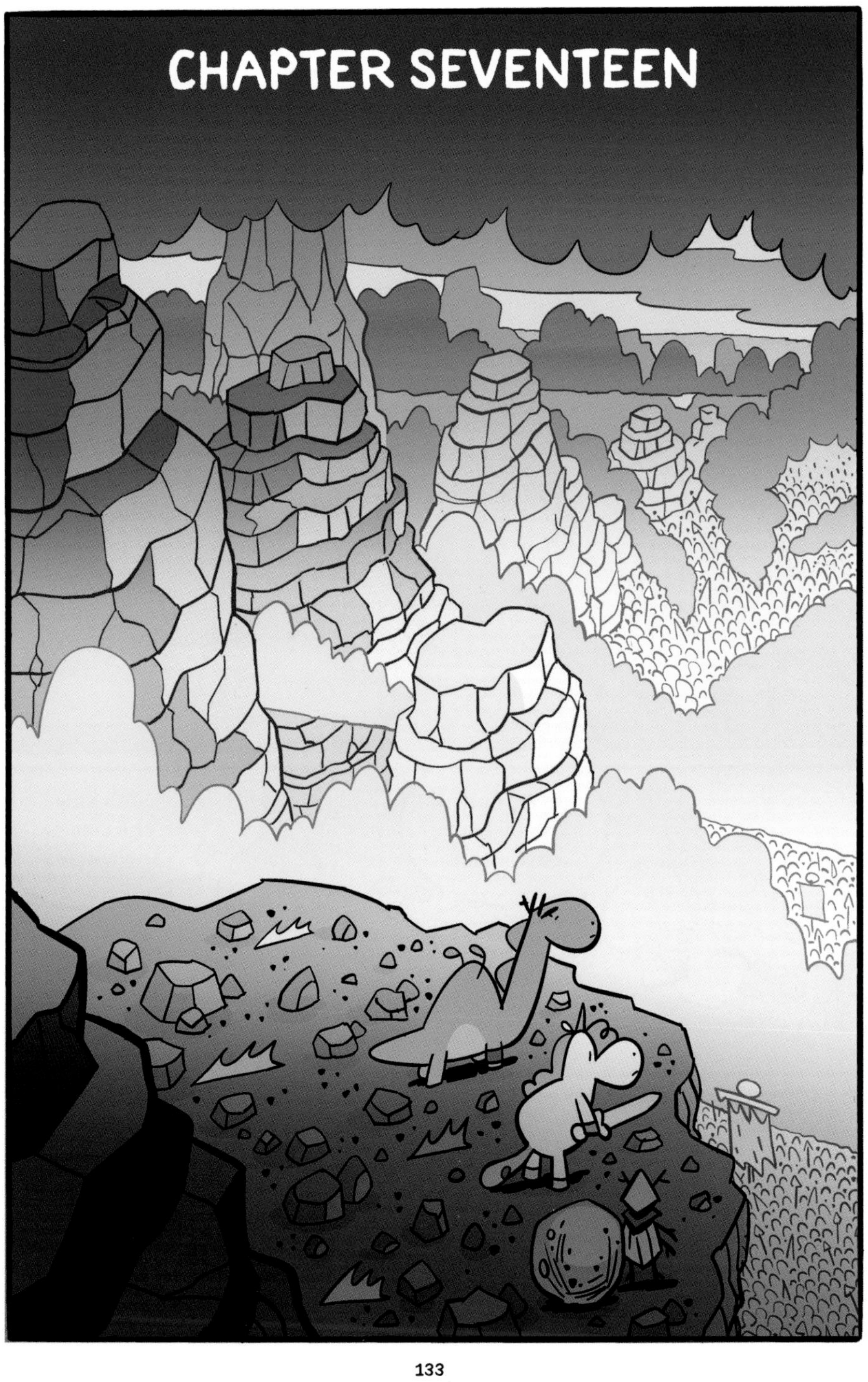

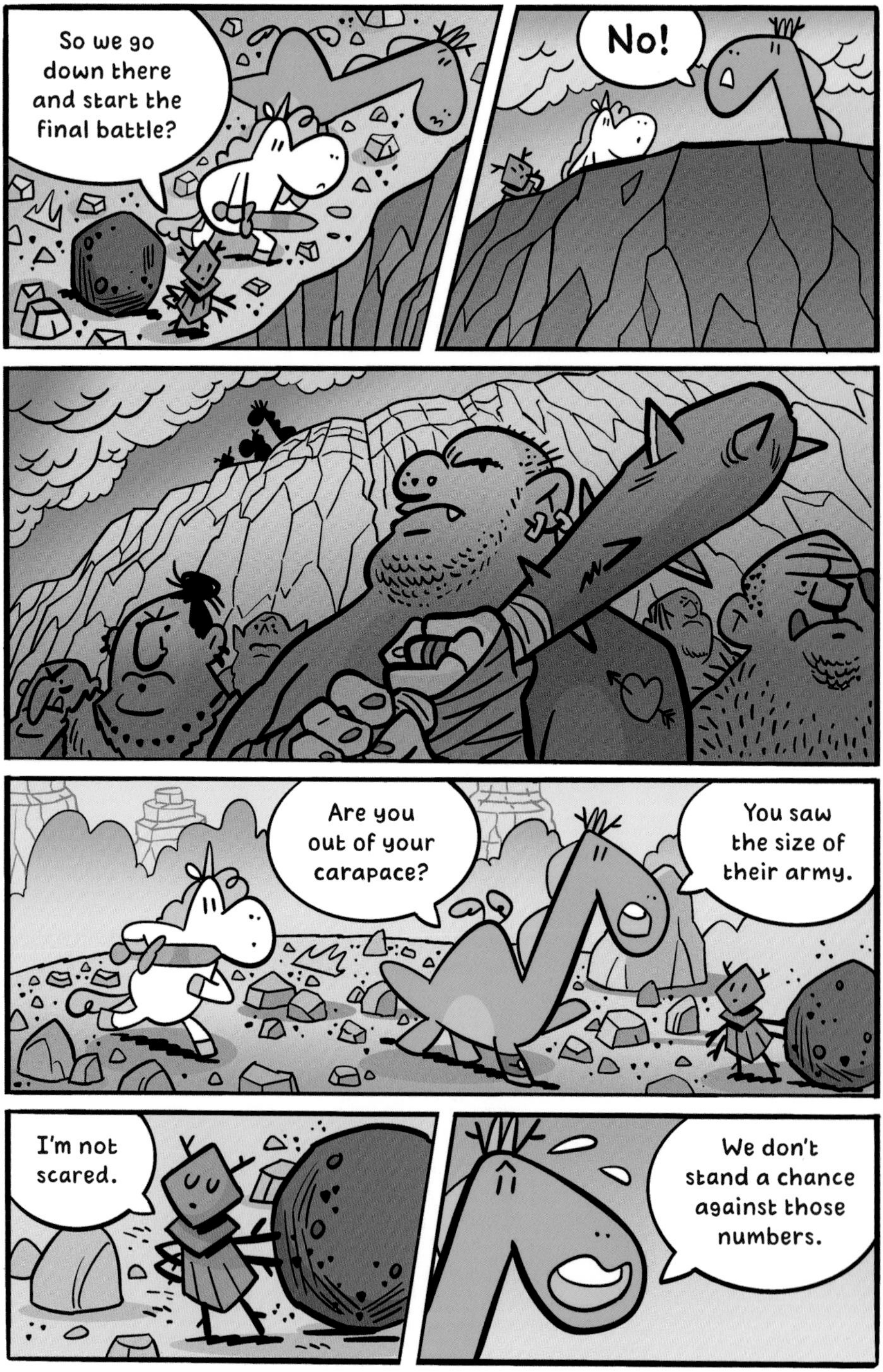
So we go down there and start the final battle?
No!
Are you out of your carapace?
You saw the size of their army.
I'm not scared.
We don't stand a chance against those numbers.

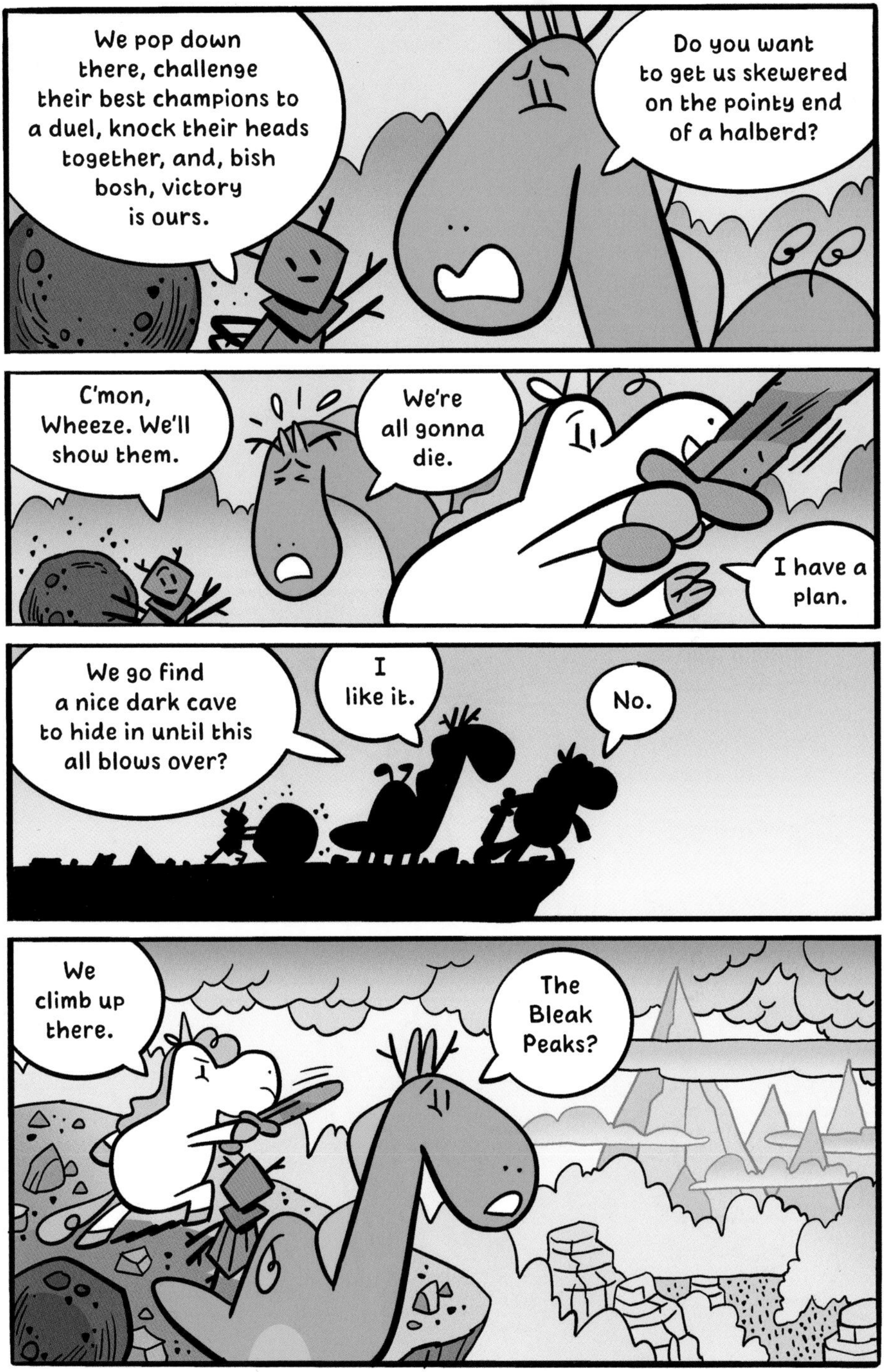
We pop down there, challenge their best champions to a duel, knock their heads together, and, bish bosh, victory is ours.
Do you want to get us skewered on the pointy end of a halberd?
C'mon, Wheeze. We'll show them.
We're all gonna die.
I have a plan.
We go find a nice dark cave to hide in until this all blows over?
I like it.
No.
We climb up there.
The Bleak Peaks?

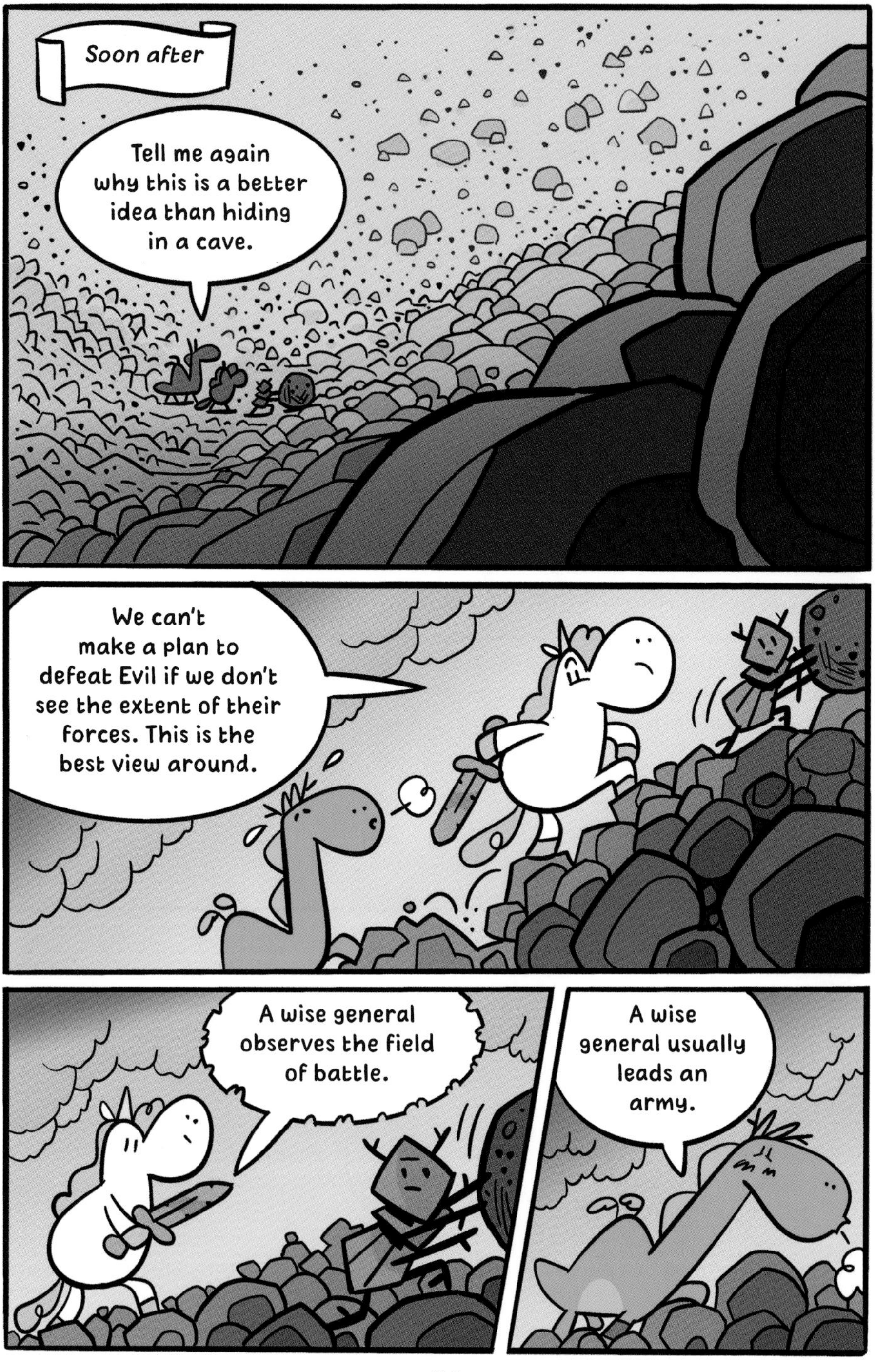
Soon after
Tell me again why this is a better idea than hiding in a cave.
We can't make a plan to defeat Evil if we don't see the extent of their forces. This is the best view around.
A wise general observes the field of battle.
A wise general usually leads an army.

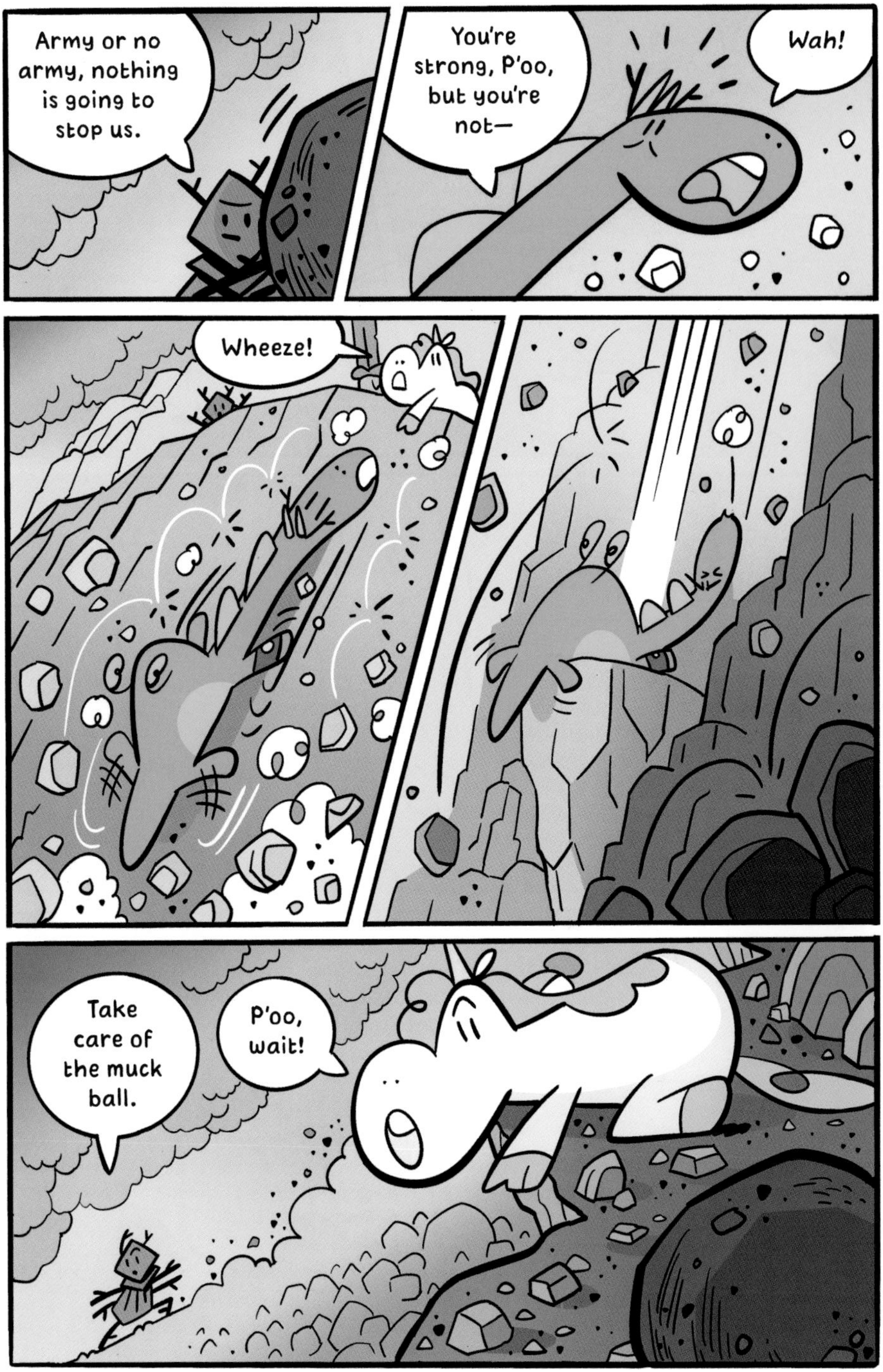
Army or no army, nothing is going to stop us.
You're strong, P'oo, but you're not—
Wah!
Wheeze!
Take care of the muck ball.
P'oo, wait!

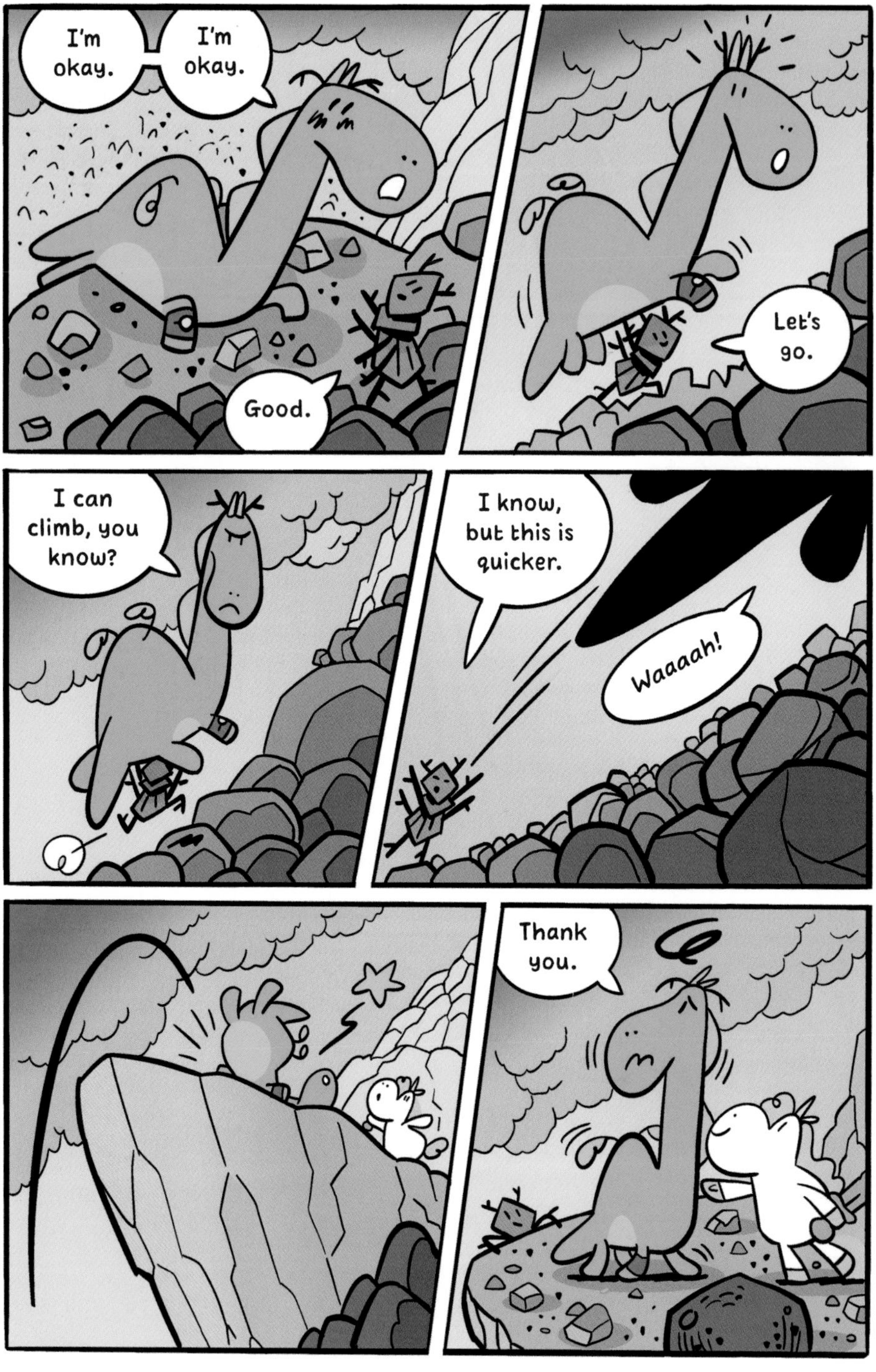
I'm okay.
I'm okay.
Good.
Let's go.
I can climb, you know?
I know, but this is quicker.
Waaaah!
Thank you.

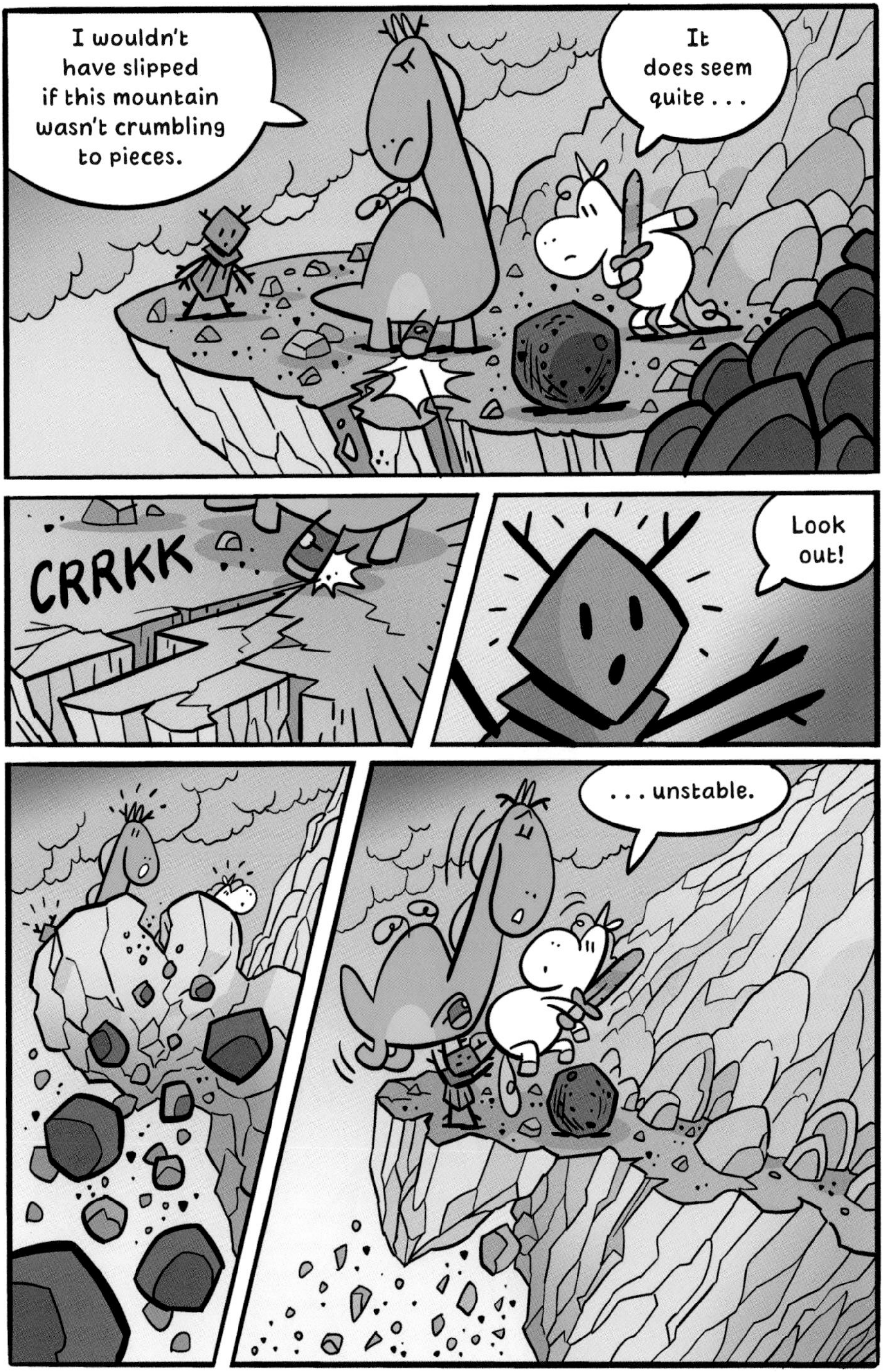
I wouldn't have slipped if this mountain wasn't crumbling to pieces.
It does seem quite . . .
CRRKK
Look out!
. . . unstable.

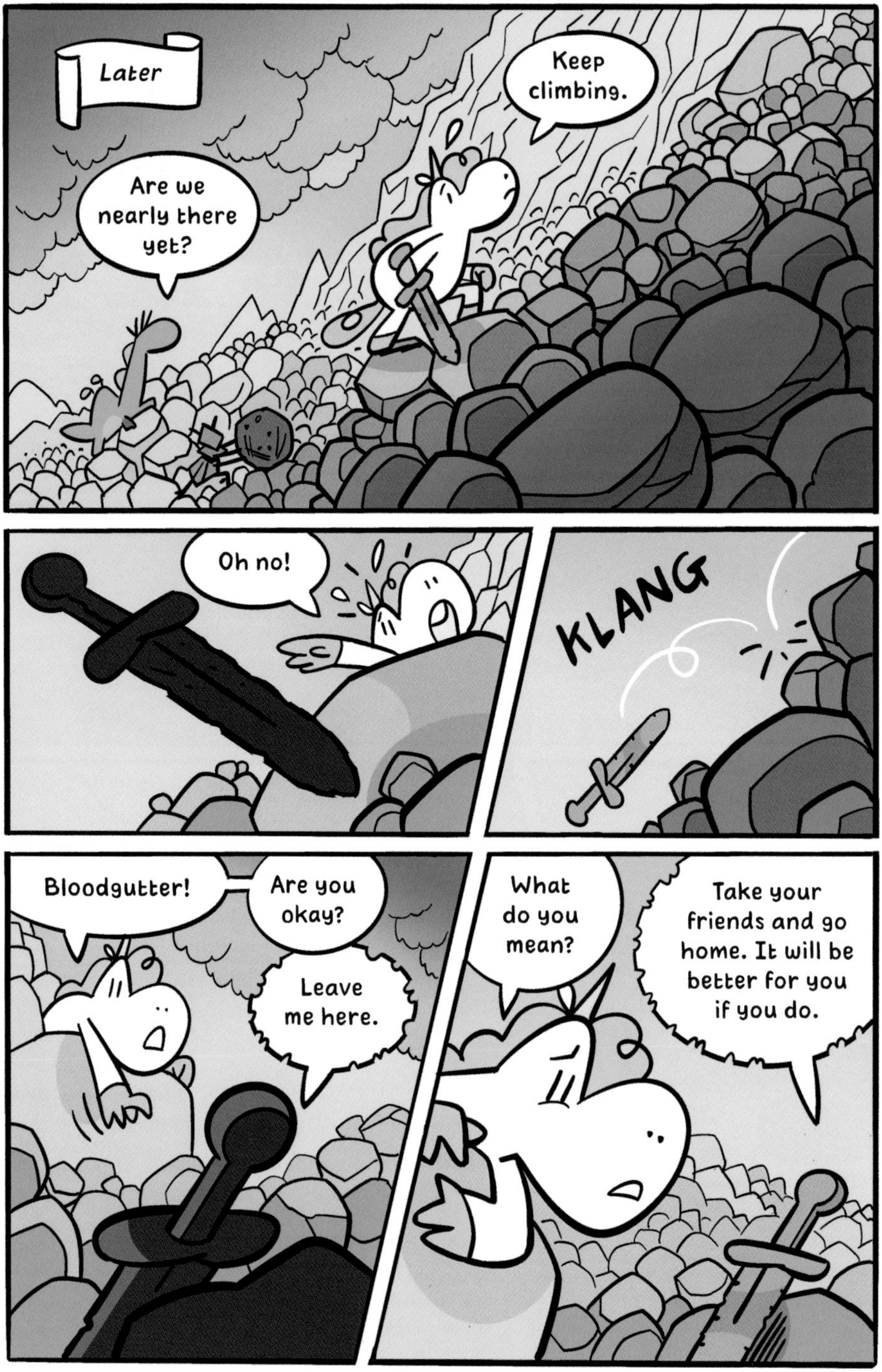
Later
Are we nearly there yet?
Keep climbing.
Oh no!
KLANG
Bloodgutter!
Are you okay?
Leave me here.
What do you mean?
Take your friends and go home. It will be better for you if you do.

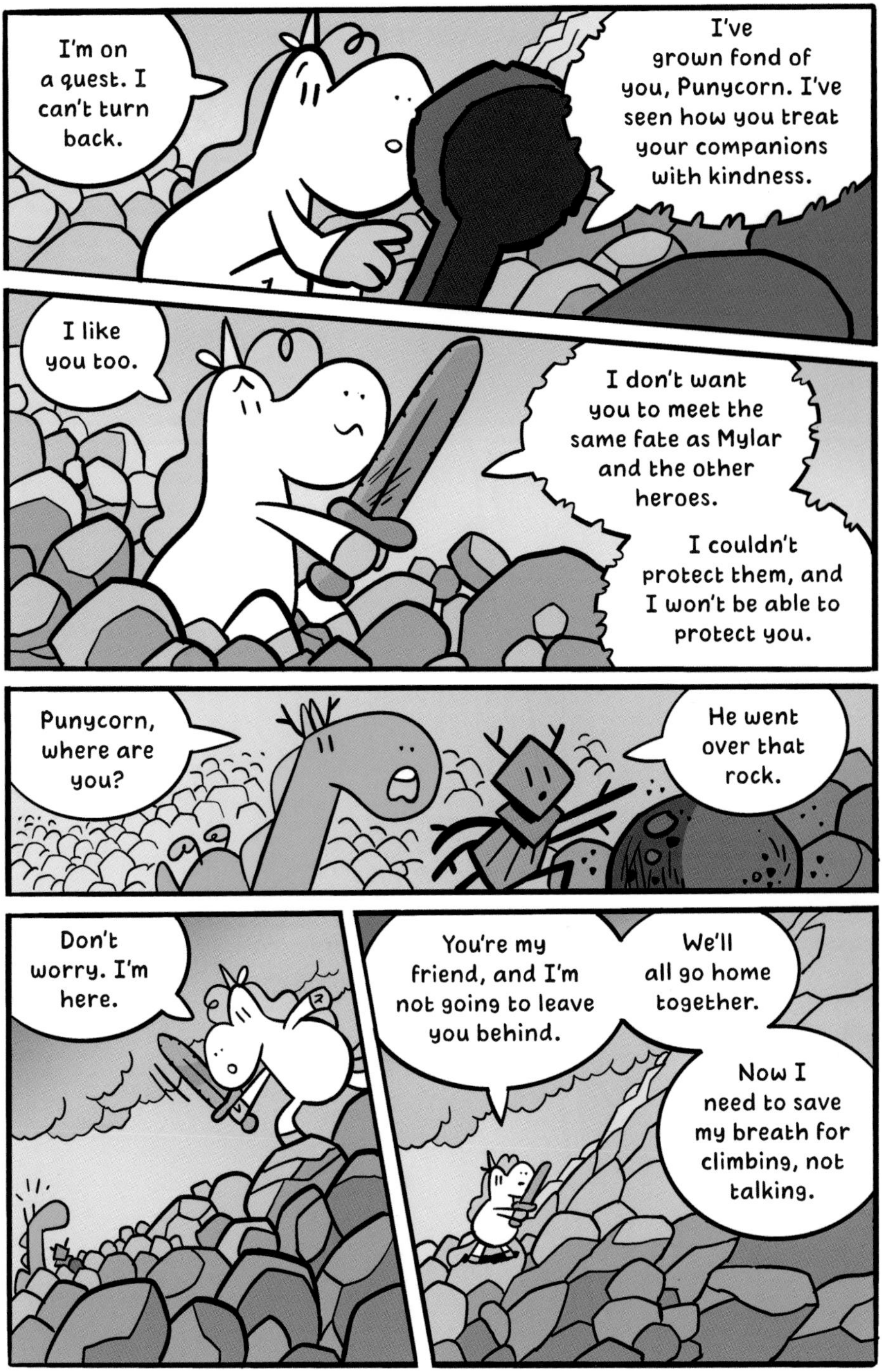
I'm on a quest. I can't turn back.
I've grown fond of you, Punycorn. I've seen how you treat your companions with kindness.
I like you too.
I don't want you to meet the same fate as Mylar and the other heroes.
I couldn't protect them, and I won't be able to protect you.
Punycorn, where are you?
He went over that rock.
Don't worry. I'm here.
You're my friend, and I'm not going to leave you behind.
We'll all go home together.
Now I need to save my breath for climbing, not talking.

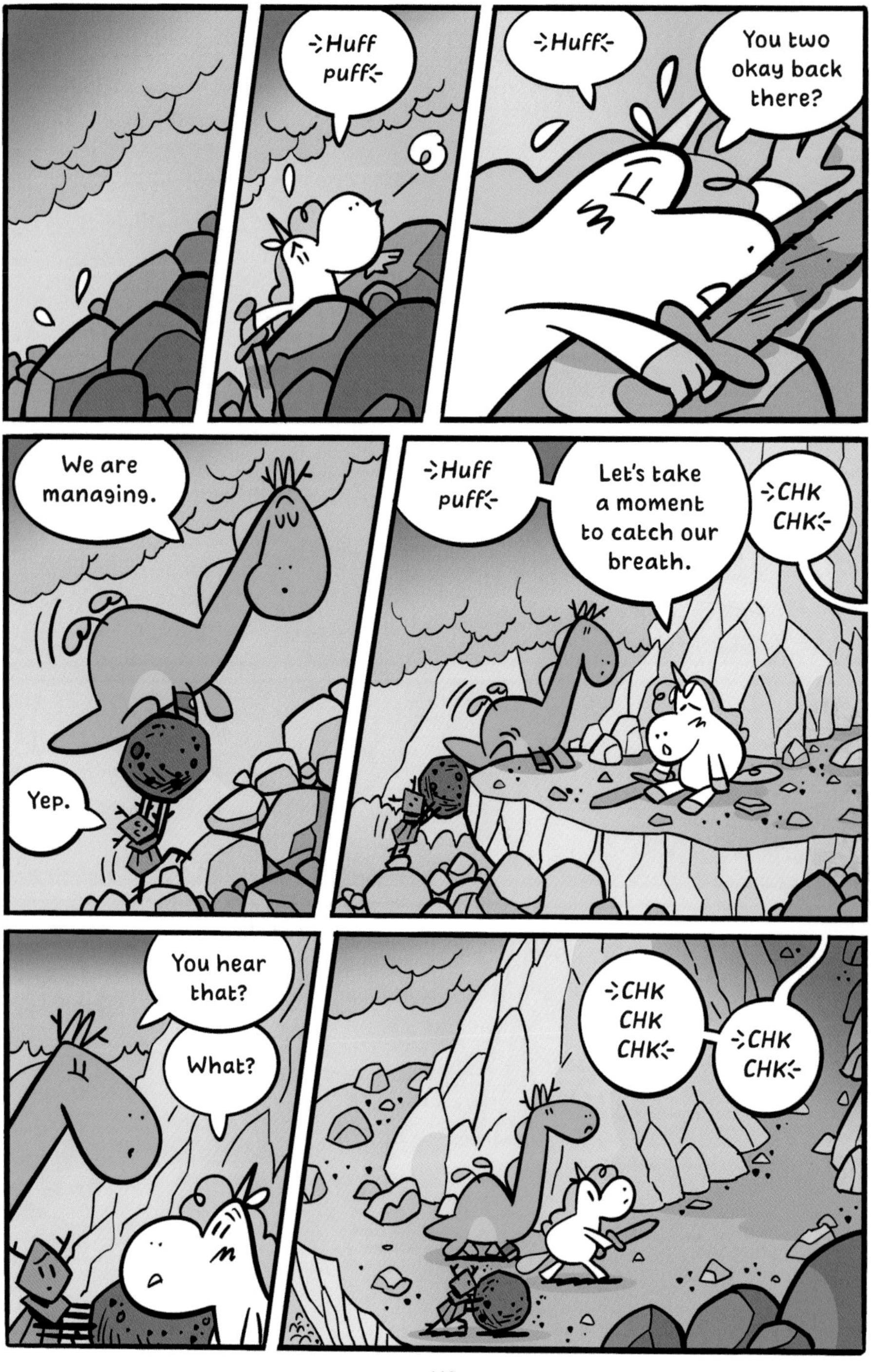
Huff puff
Huff
You two okay back there?
We are managing.
Yep.
Huff puff
Let's take a moment to catch our breath.
CHK CHK
You hear that?
What?
CHK CHK CHK
CHK CHK

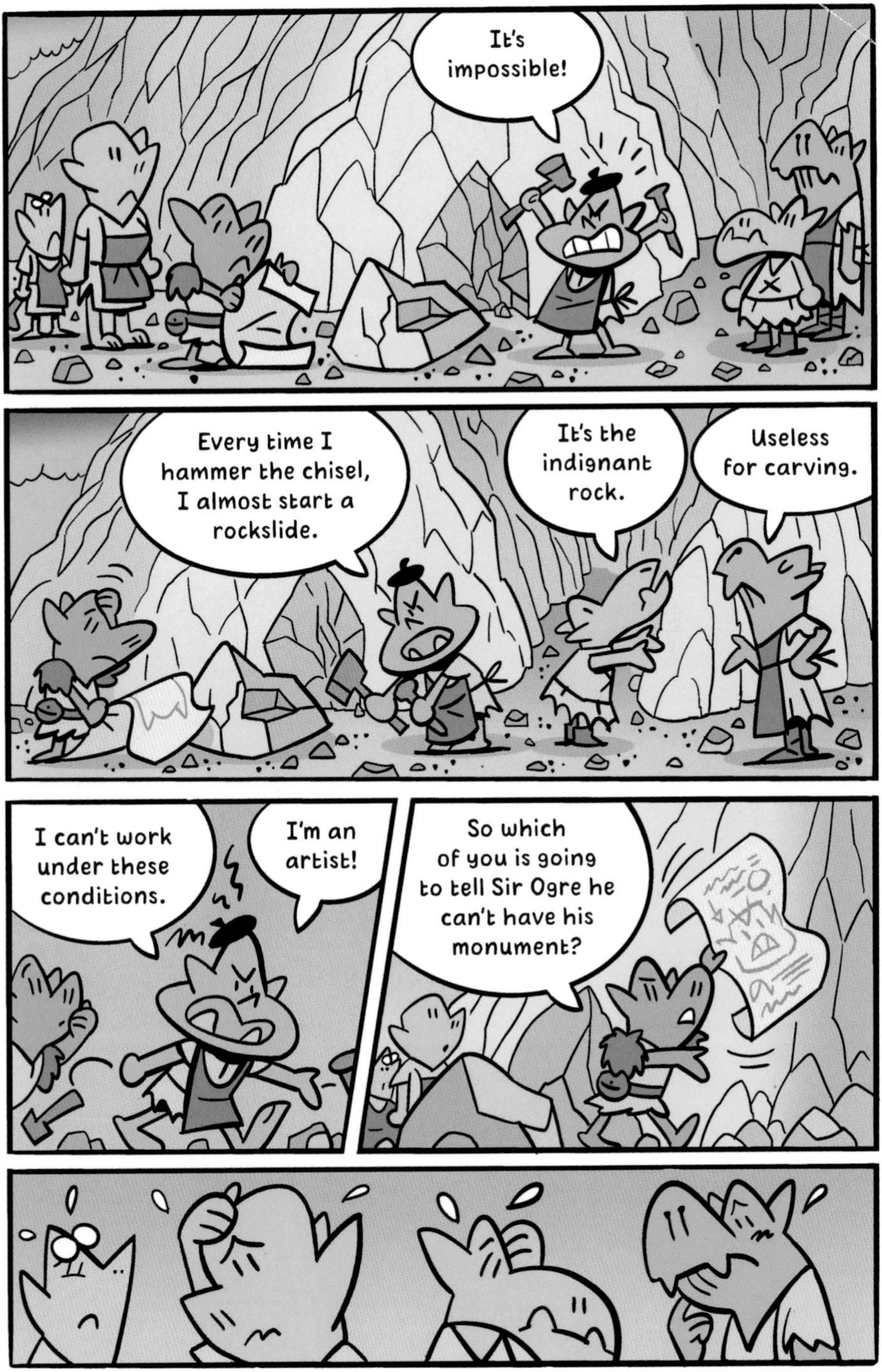
It's impossible!
Every time I hammer the chisel, I almost start a rockslide.
It's the indignant rock.
Useless for carving.
I can't work under these conditions.
I'm an artist!
So which of you is going to tell Sir Ogre he can't have his monument?

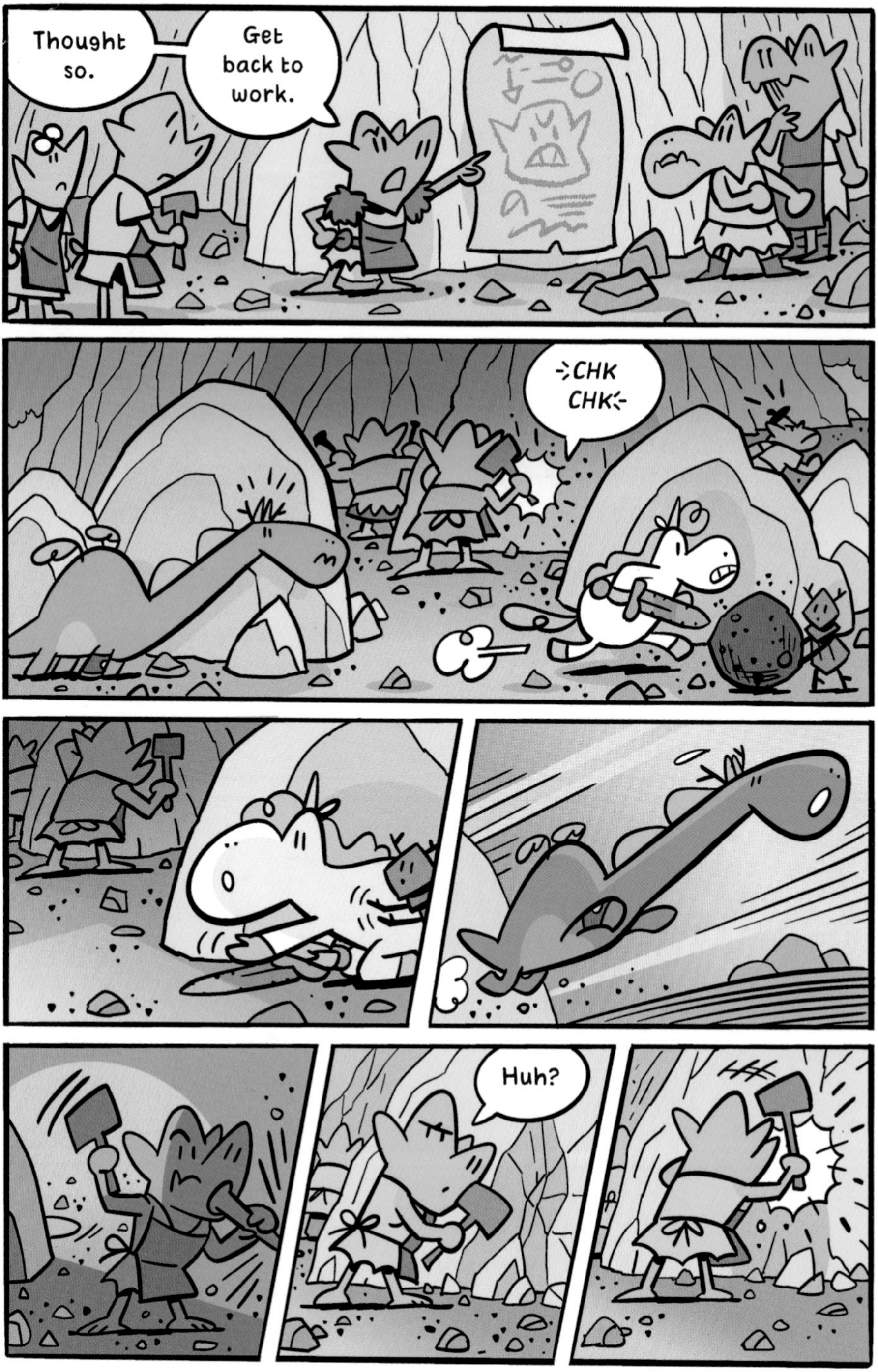
Thought so.
Get back to work.
CHK CHK
Huh?

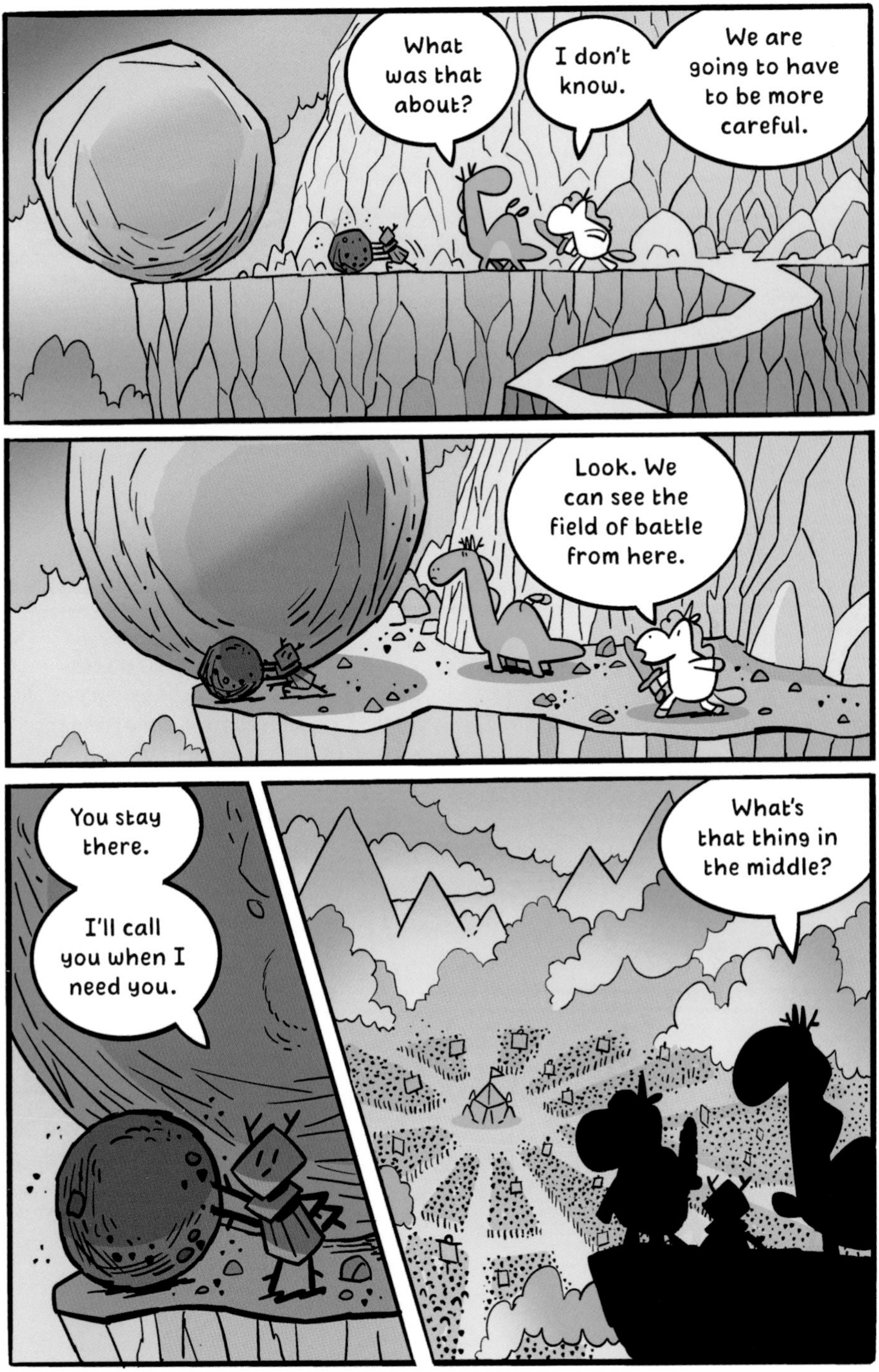
What was that about?
I don't know.
We are going to have to be more careful.
Look. We can see the field of battle from here.
You stay there.
I'll call you when I need you.
What's that thing in the middle?

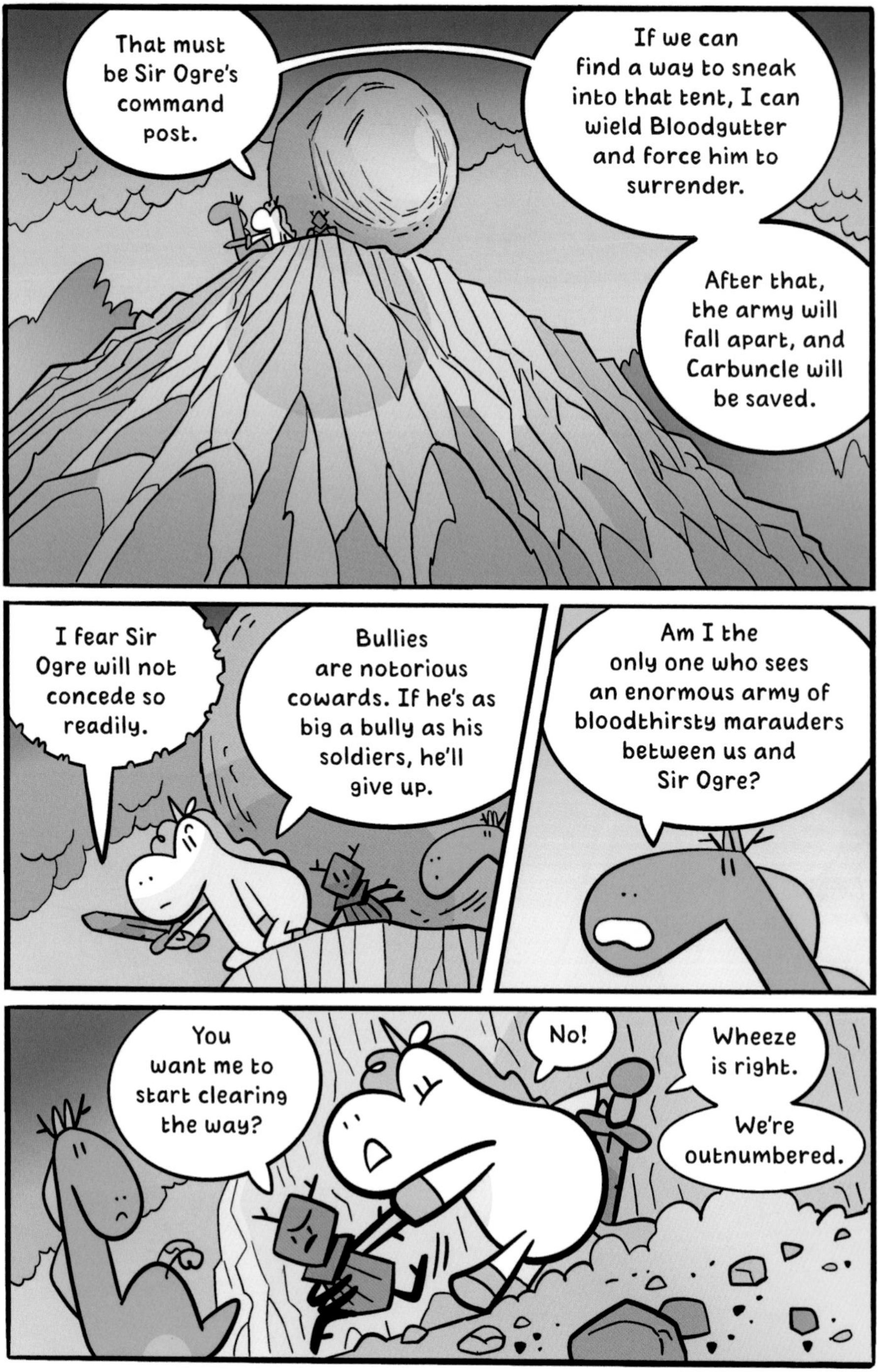

That must be Sir Ogre's command post.
If we can find a way to sneak into that tent, I can wield Bloodgutter and force him to surrender.
After that, the army will fall apart, and Carbuncle will be saved.
I fear Sir Ogre will not concede so readily.
Bullies are notorious cowards. If he's as big a bully as his soldiers, he'll give up.
Am I the only one who sees an enormous army of bloodthirsty marauders between us and Sir Ogre?
You want me to start clearing the way?
No!
Wheeze is right.
We're outnumbered.

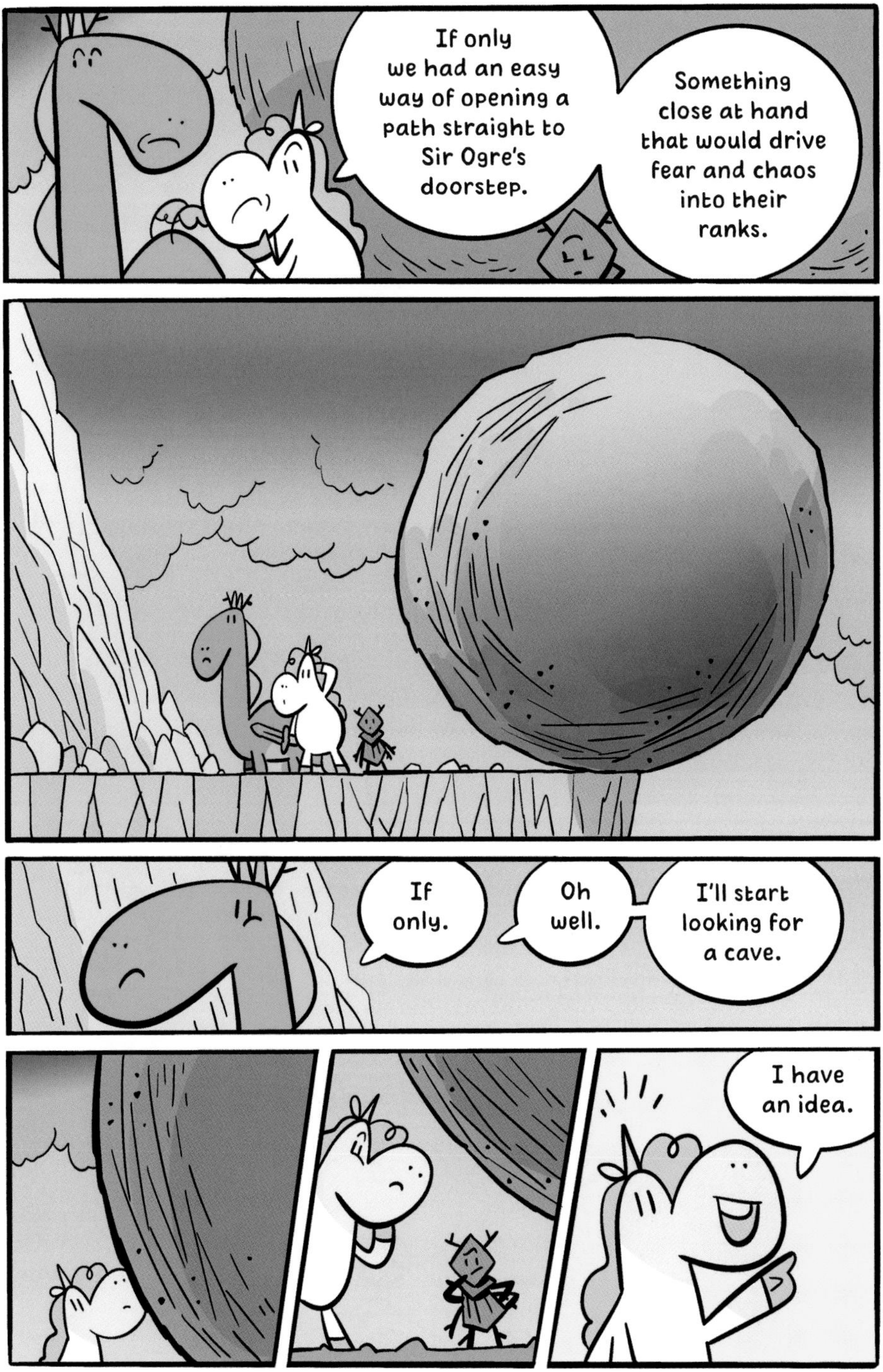
If only we had an easy way of opening a path straight to Sir Ogre's doorstep.
Something close at hand that would drive fear and chaos into their ranks.
If only.
Oh well.
I'll start looking for a cave.
I have an idea.

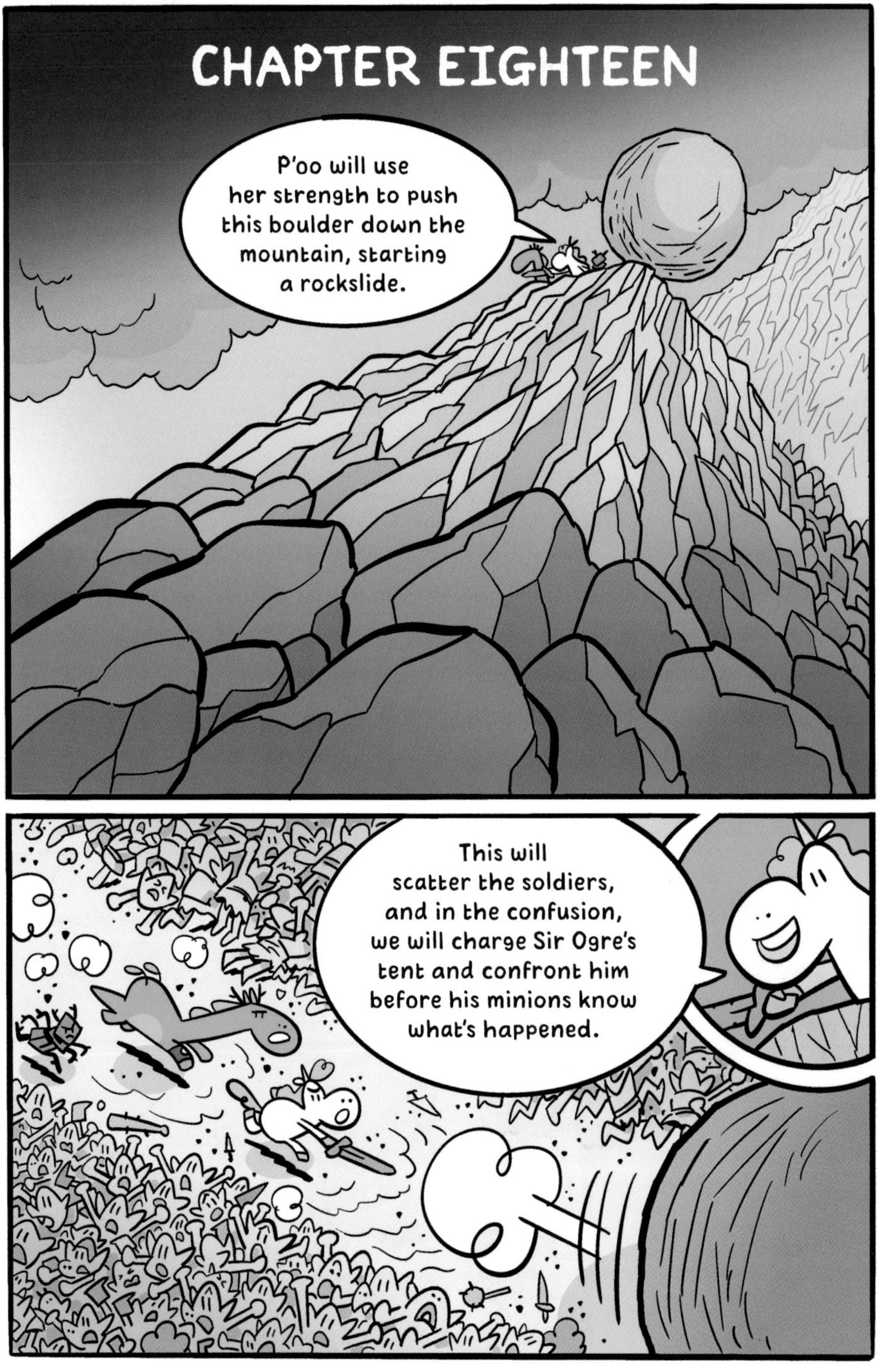
CHAPTER EIGHTEEN
P'oo will use her strength to push this boulder down the mountain, starting a rockslide.
This will scatter the soldiers, and in the confusion, we will charge Sir Ogre's tent and confront him before his minions know what's happened.

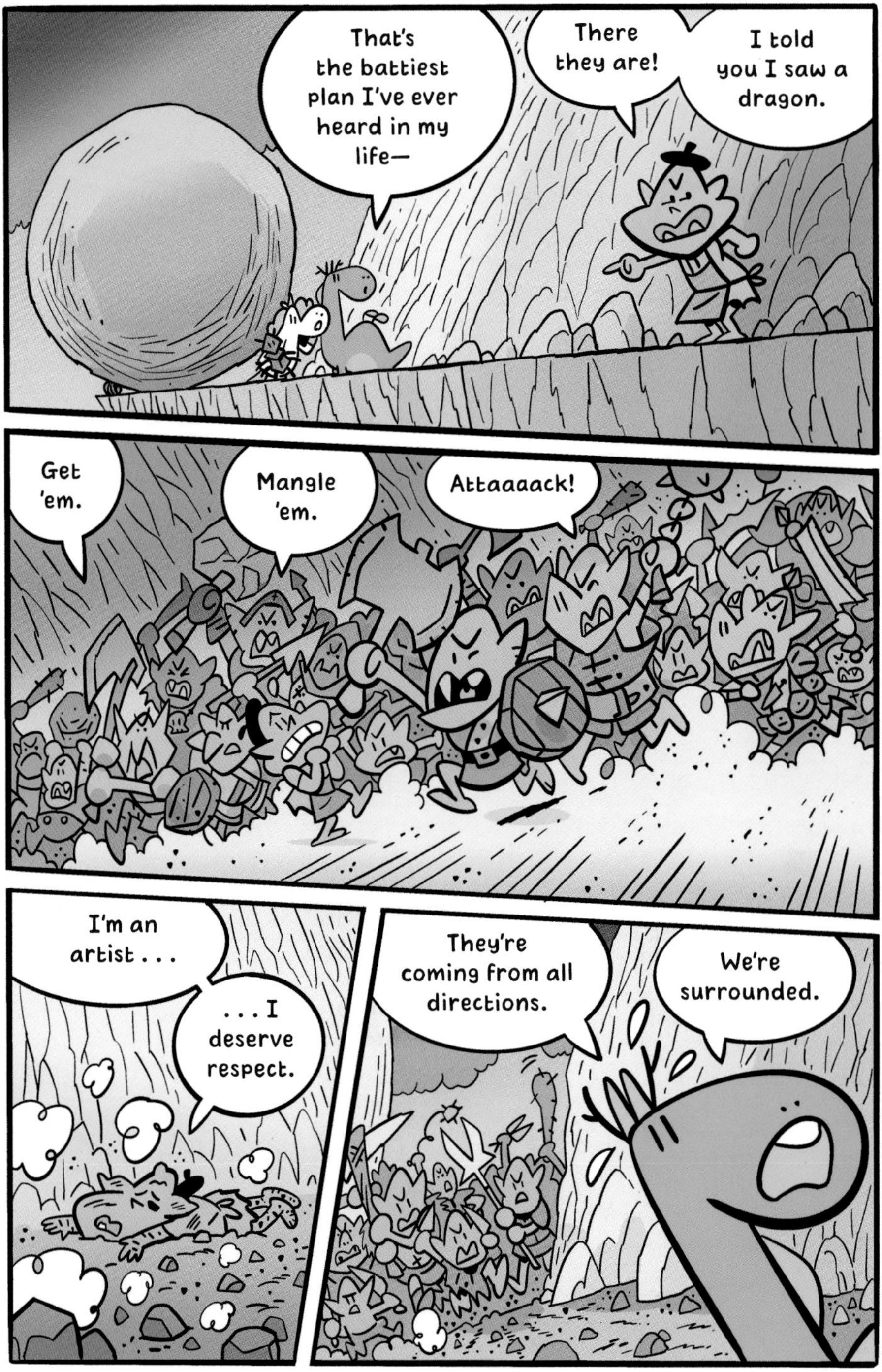
That's the battiest plan I've ever heard in my life—
There they are!
I told you I saw a dragon.
Get 'em.
Mangle 'em.
Attaaaack!
I'm an artist . . .
. . . I deserve respect.
They're coming from all directions.
We're surrounded.

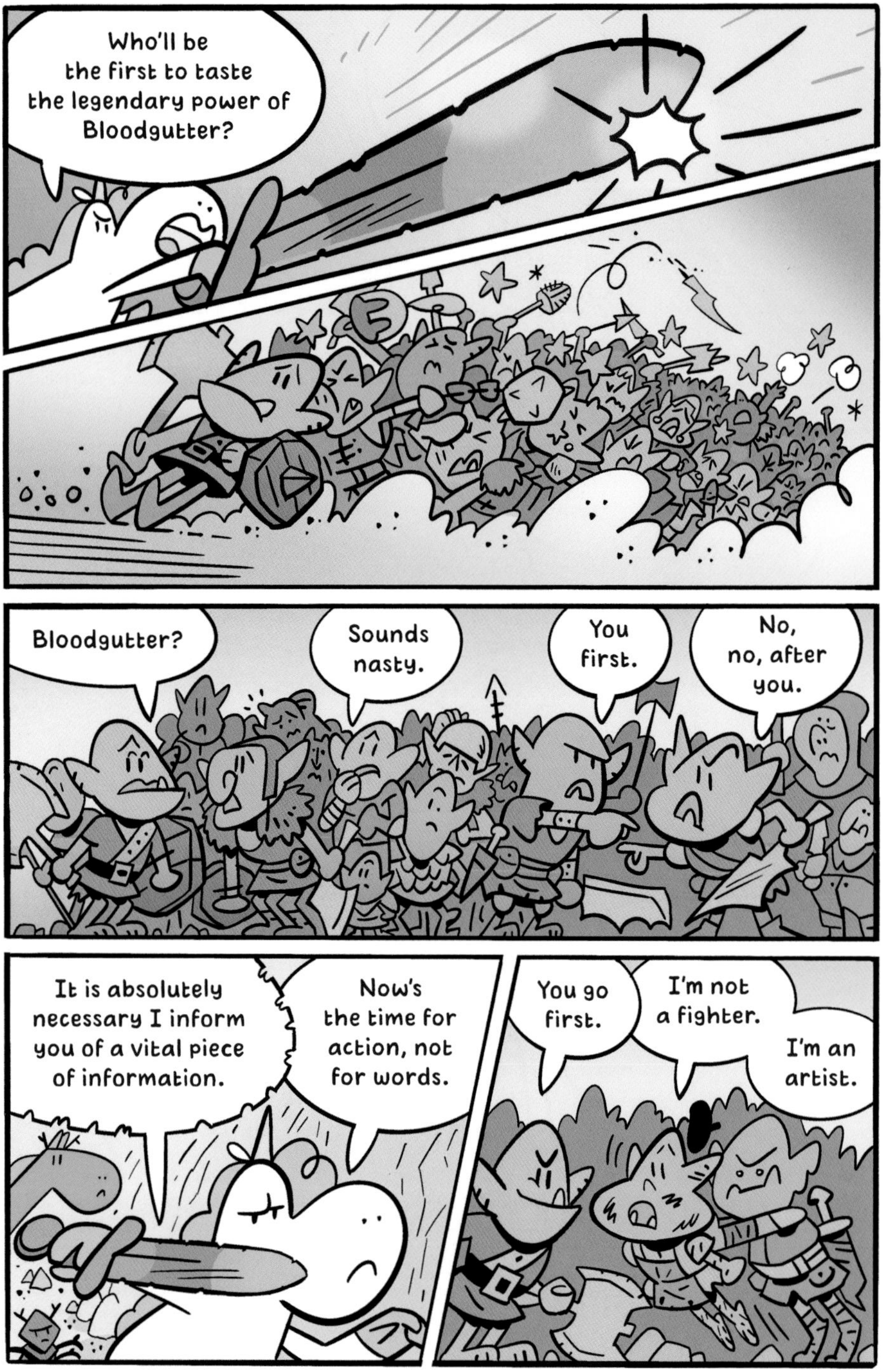
Who'll be the first to taste the legendary power of Bloodgutter?
Bloodgutter?
Sounds nasty.
You first.
No, no, after you.
It is absolutely necessary I inform you of a vital piece of information.
Now's the time for action, not for words.
You go first.
I'm not a fighter.
I'm an artist.

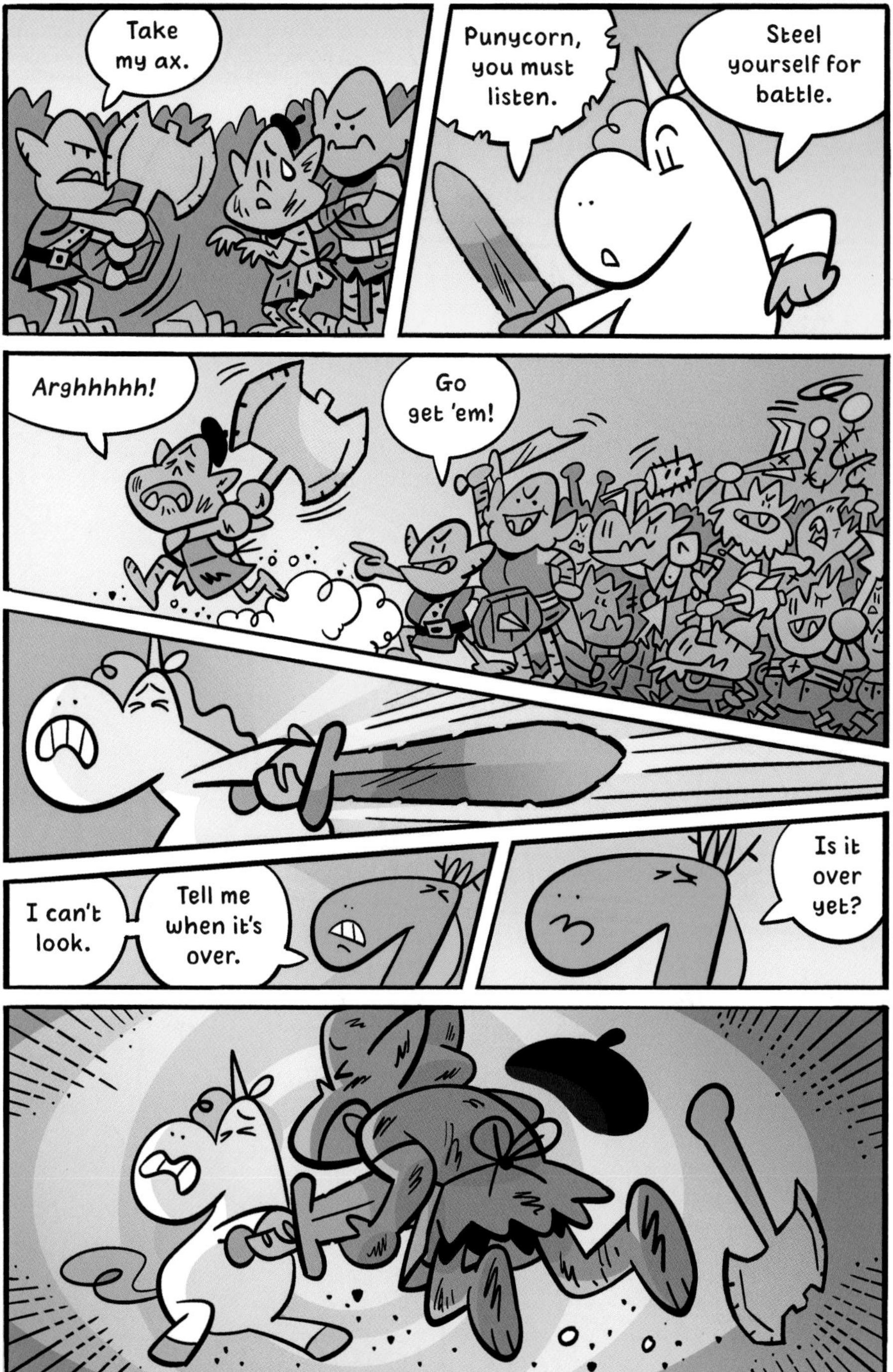
Take my ax.
Punycorn, you must listen.
Steel yourself for battle.
Arghhhhh!
Go get 'em!
I can't look.
Tell me when it's over.
Is it over yet?

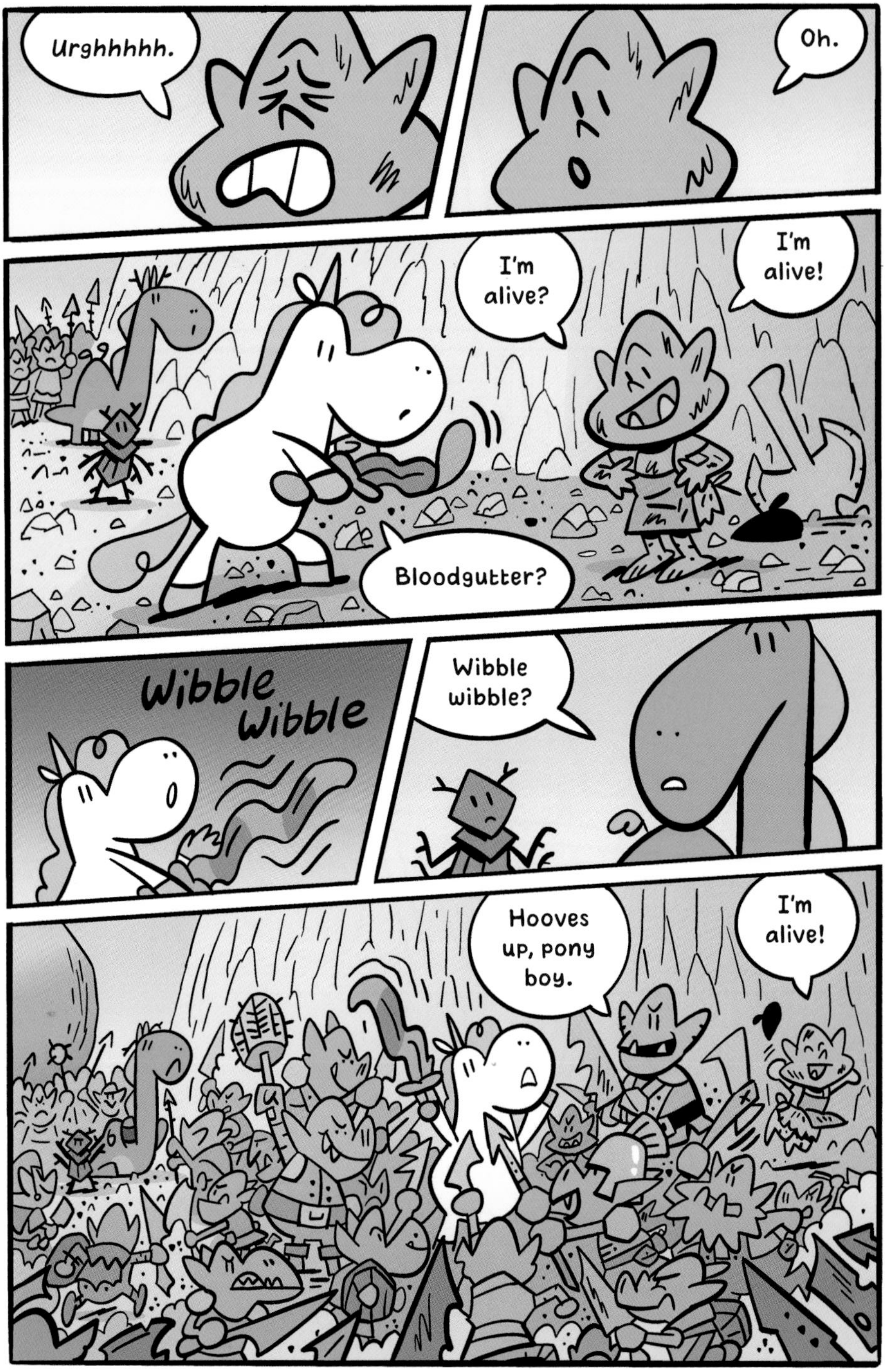
Urghhhhh.
Oh.
I'm alive?
I'm alive!
Bloodgutter?
Wibble Wibble
Wibble wibble?
Hooves up, pony boy.
I'm alive!

CHAPTER NINETEEN

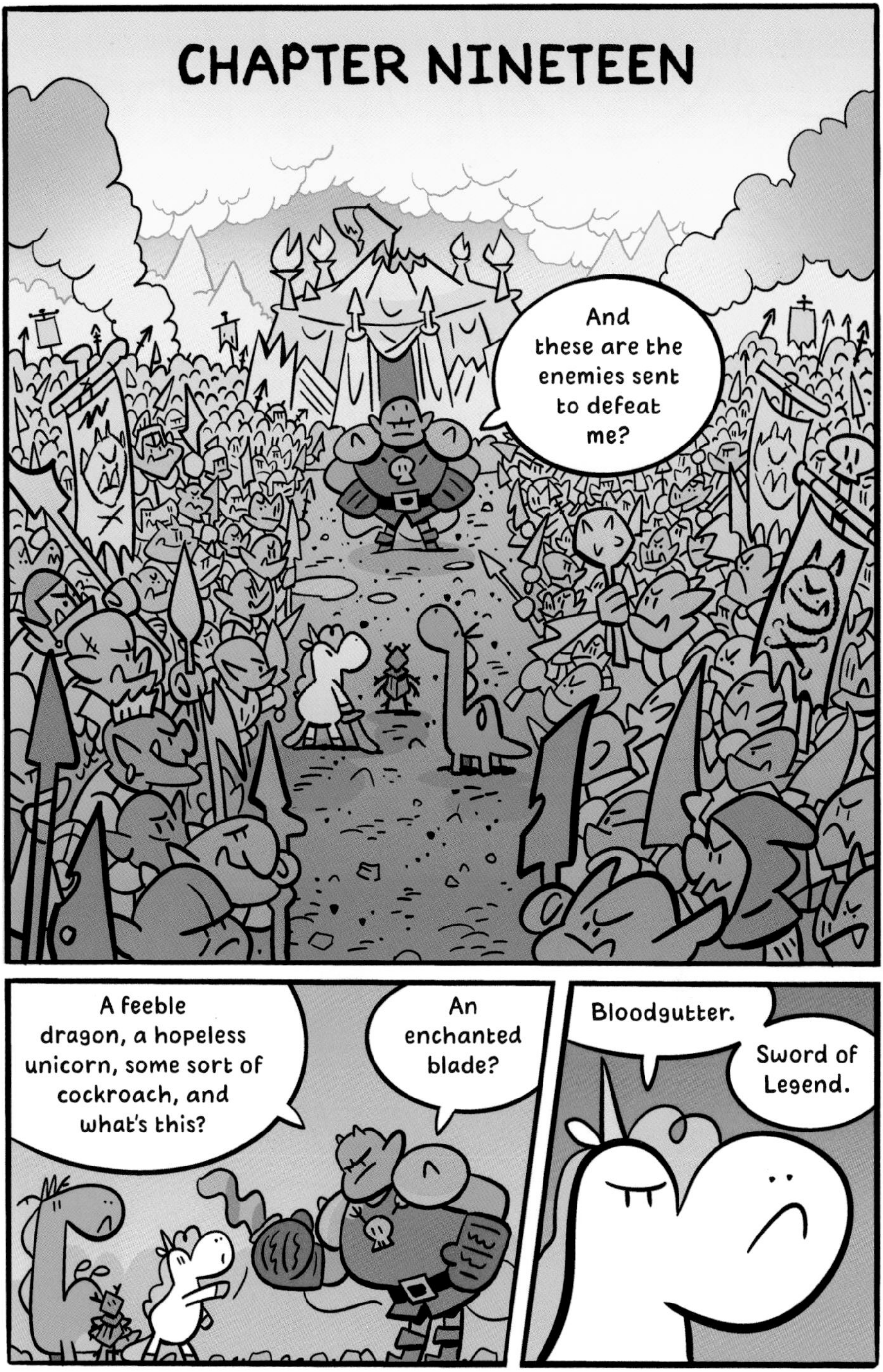
And these are the enemies sent to defeat me?
A feeble dragon, a hopeless unicorn, some sort of cockroach, and what's this?
An enchanted blade?
Bloodgutter.
Sword of Legend.

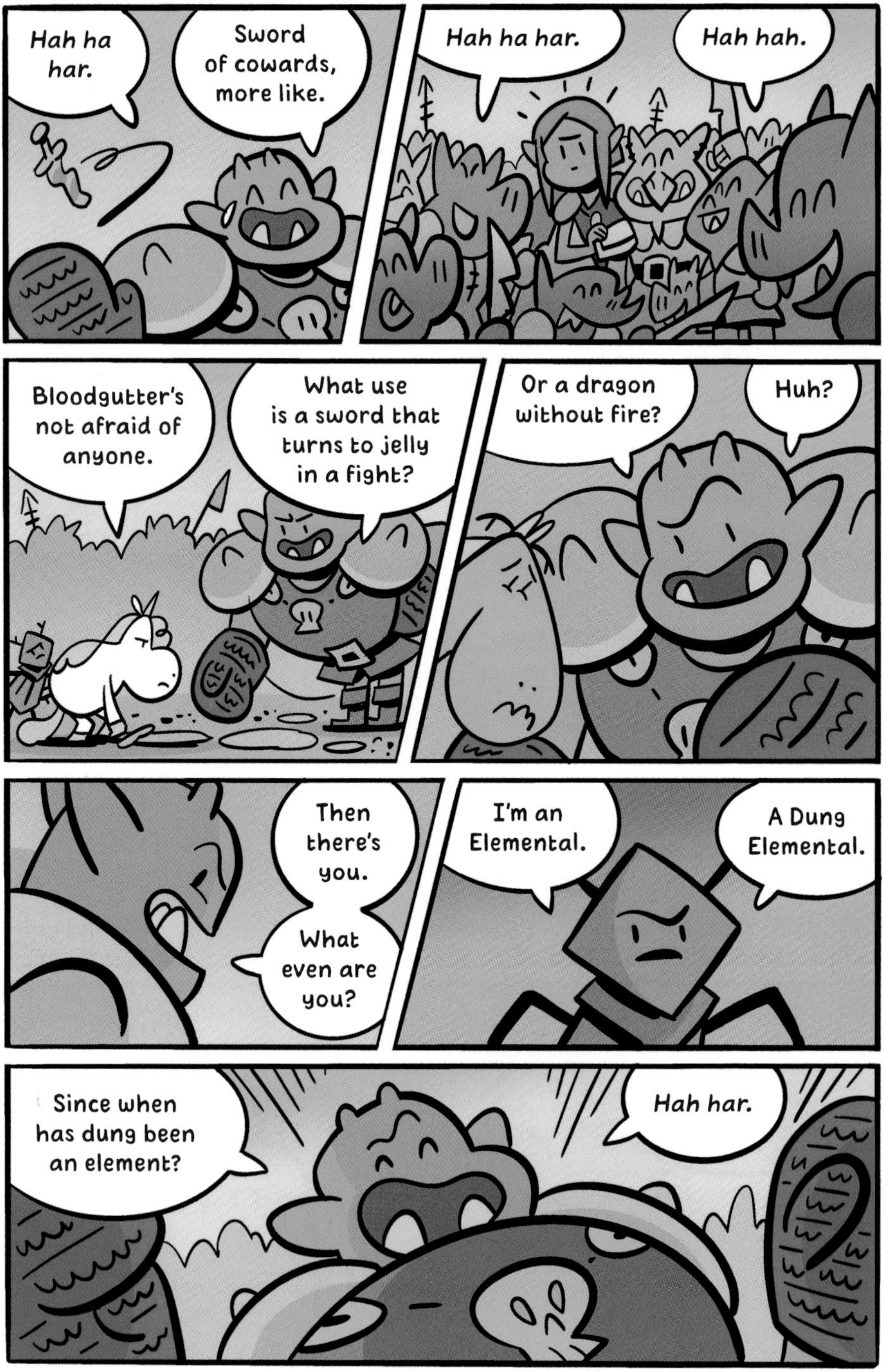
Hah ha har.
Sword of cowards, more like.
Hah ha har.
Hah hah.
Bloodgutter's not afraid of anyone.
What use is a sword that turns to jelly in a fight?
Or a dragon without fire?
Huh?
Then there's you.
What even are you?
I'm an Elemental.
A Dung Elemental.
Since when has dung been an element?
Hah har.

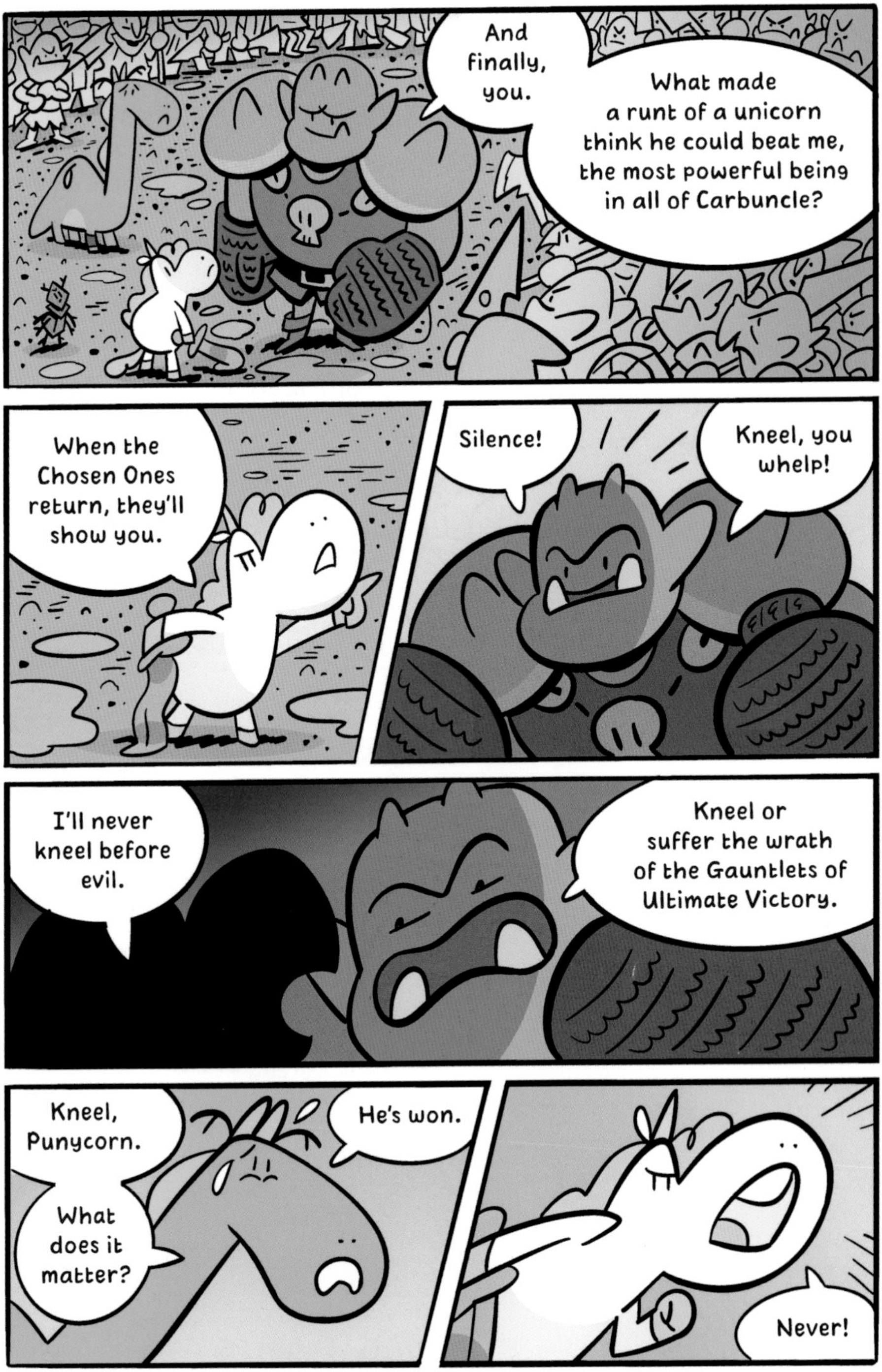
And finally, you.
What made a runt of a unicorn think he could beat me, the most powerful being in all of Carbuncle?
When the Chosen Ones return, they'll show you.
Silence!
Kneel, you whelp!
I'll never kneel before evil.
Kneel or suffer the wrath of the Gauntlets of Ultimate Victory.
Kneel, Punycorn.
What does it matter?
He's won.
Never!

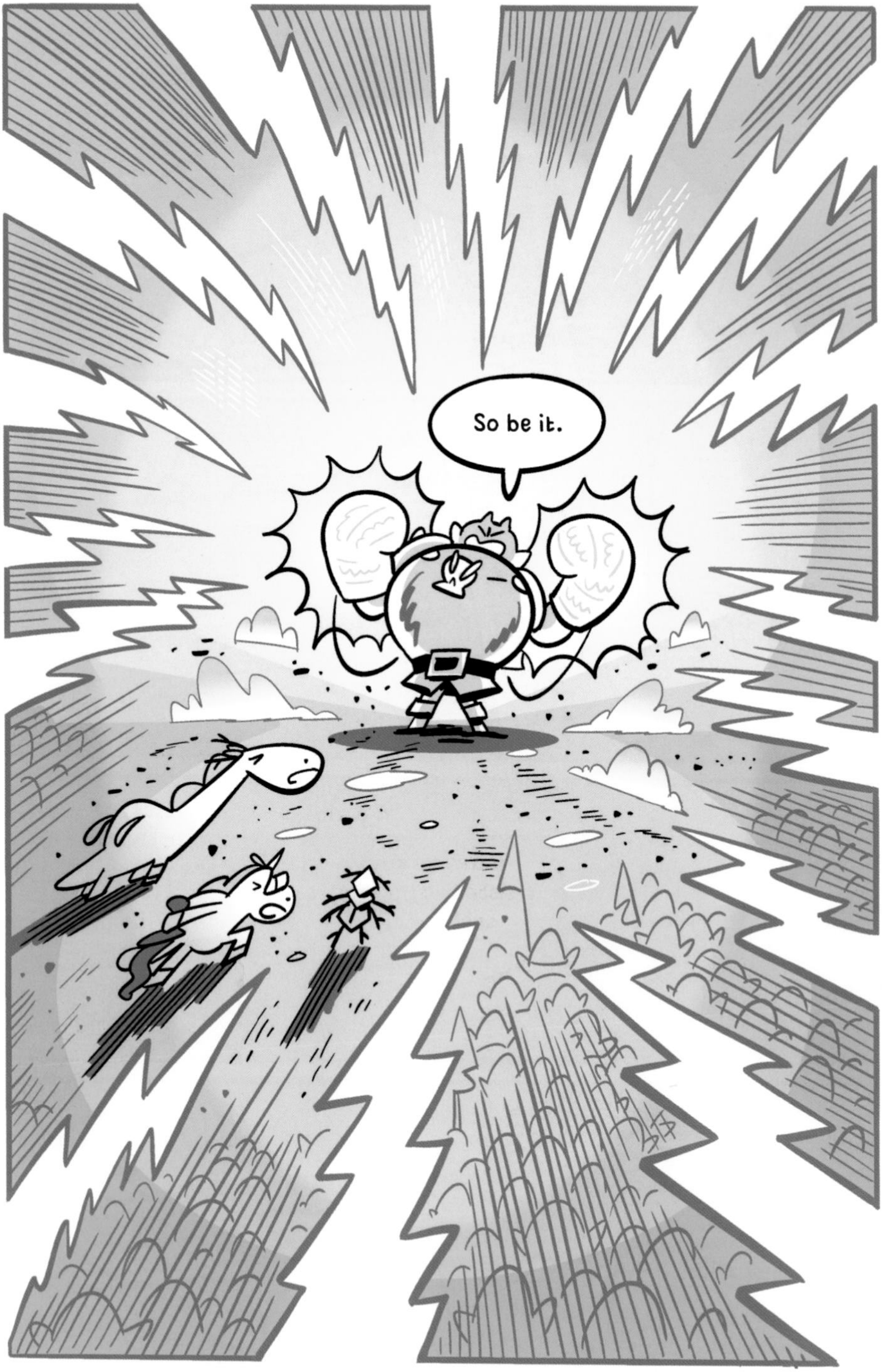
So be it.

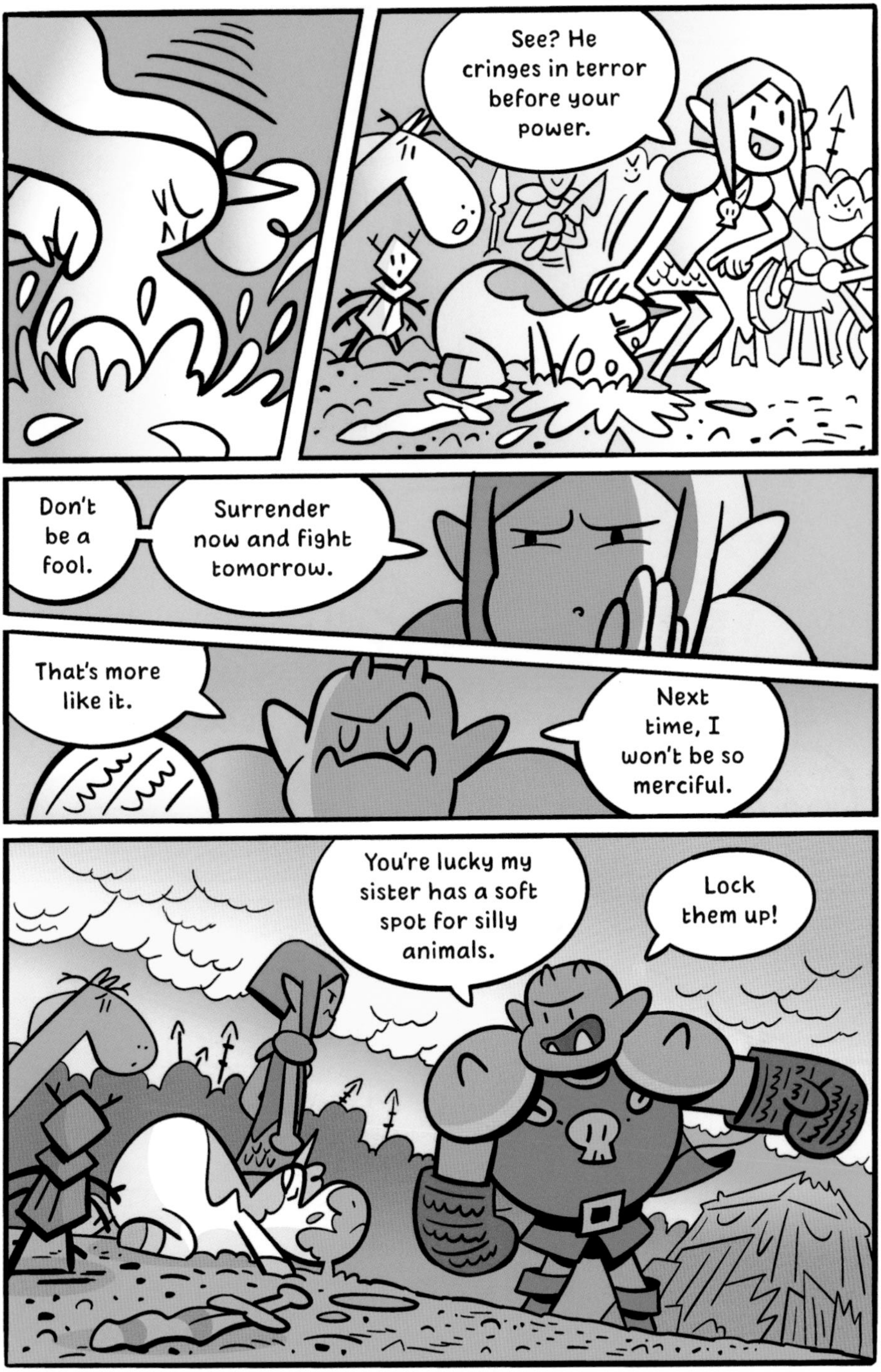
See? He cringes in terror before your power.
Don't be a fool.
Surrender now and fight tomorrow.
That's more like it.
Next time, I won't be so merciful.
You're lucky my sister has a soft spot for silly animals.
Lock them up!

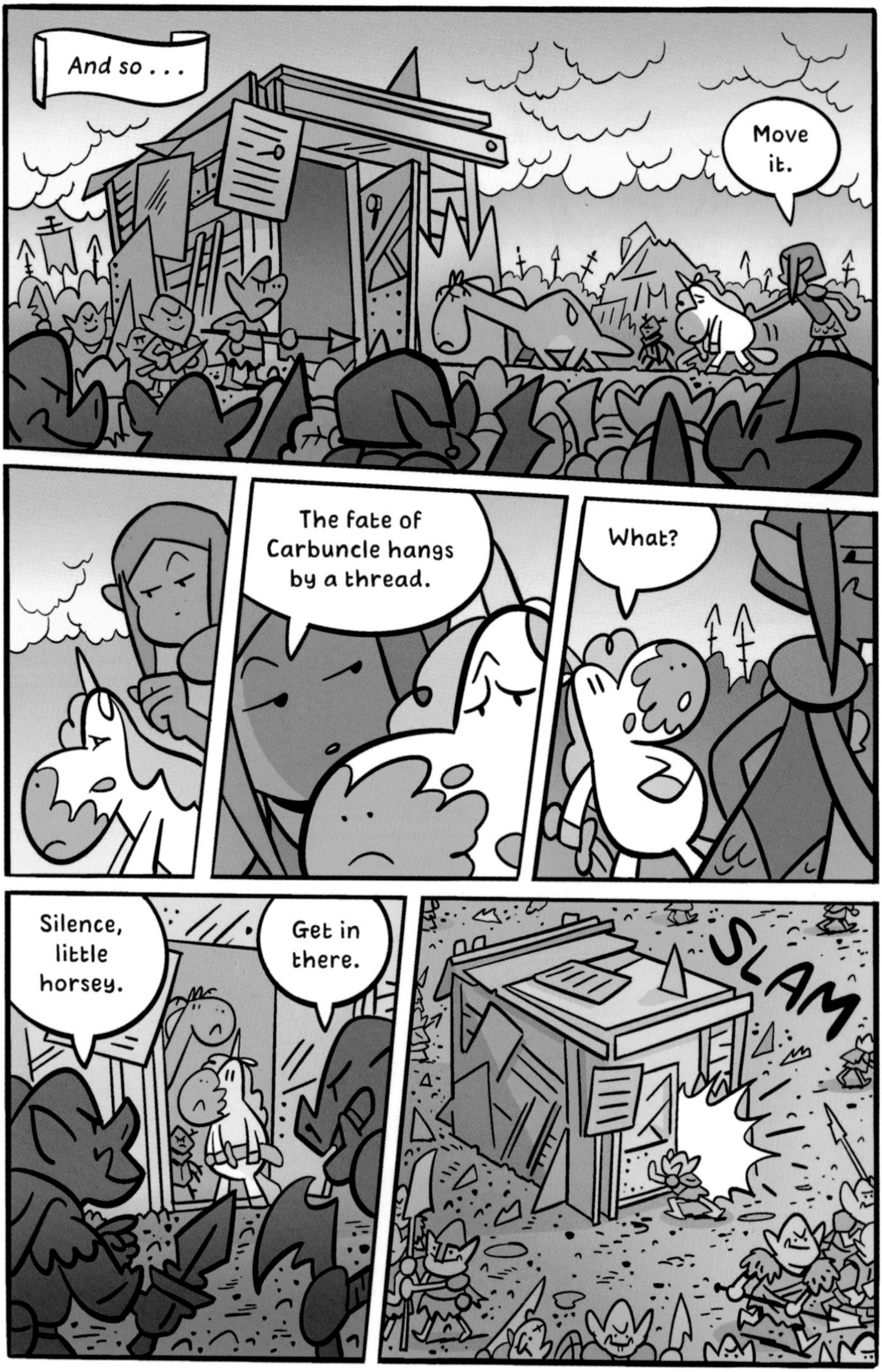
And so . . .
Move it.
The fate of Carbuncle hangs by a thread.
What?
Silence, little horsey.
Get in there.
SLAM

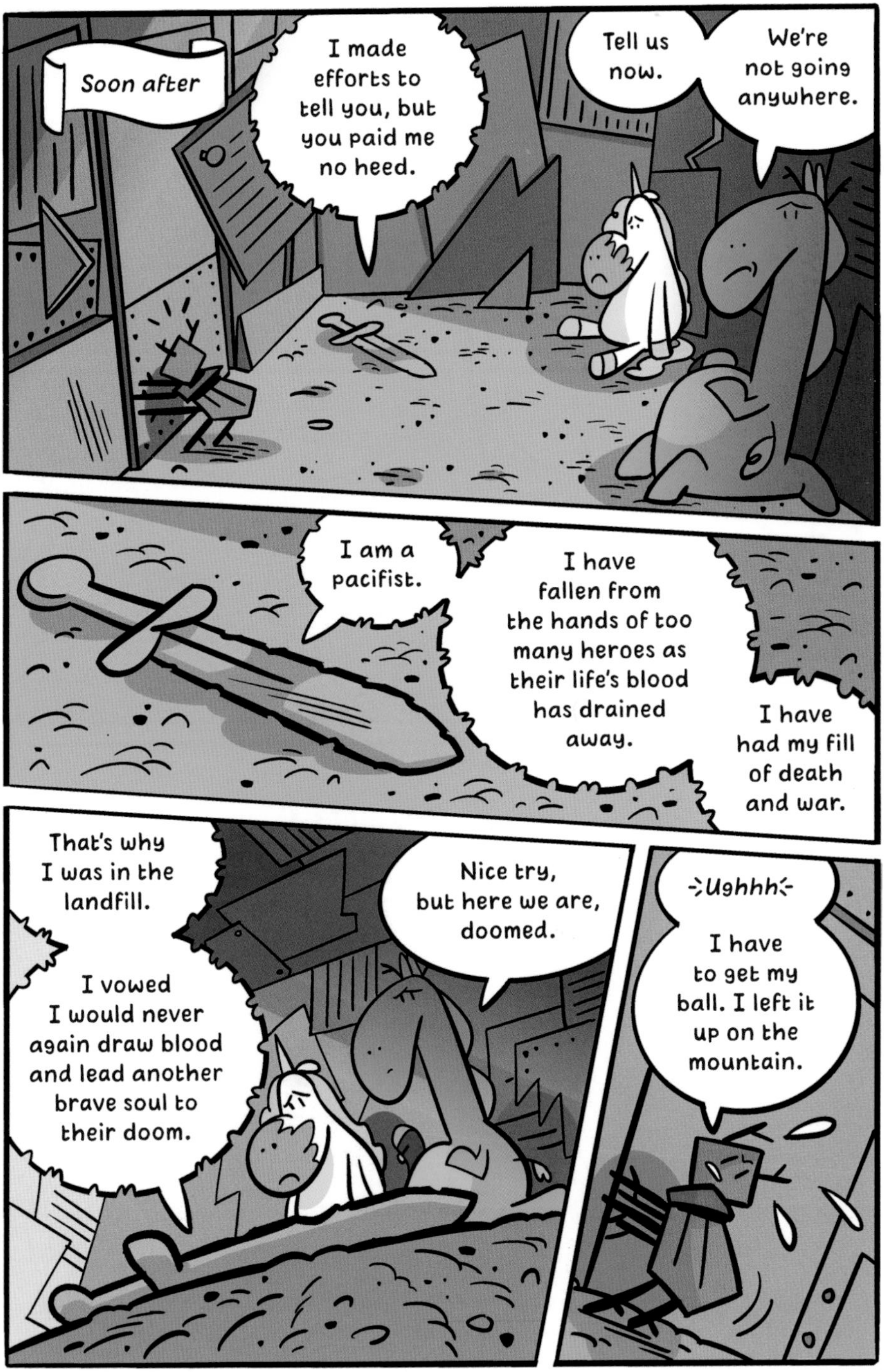

Soon after
I made efforts to tell you, but you paid me no heed.
Tell us now.
We're not going anywhere.
I am a pacifist.
I have fallen from the hands of too many heroes as their life's blood has drained away.
I have had my fill of death and war.
That's why I was in the landfill.
I vowed I would never again draw blood and lead another brave soul to their doom.
Nice try, but here we are, doomed.
Ughhh
I have to get my ball. I left it up on the mountain.

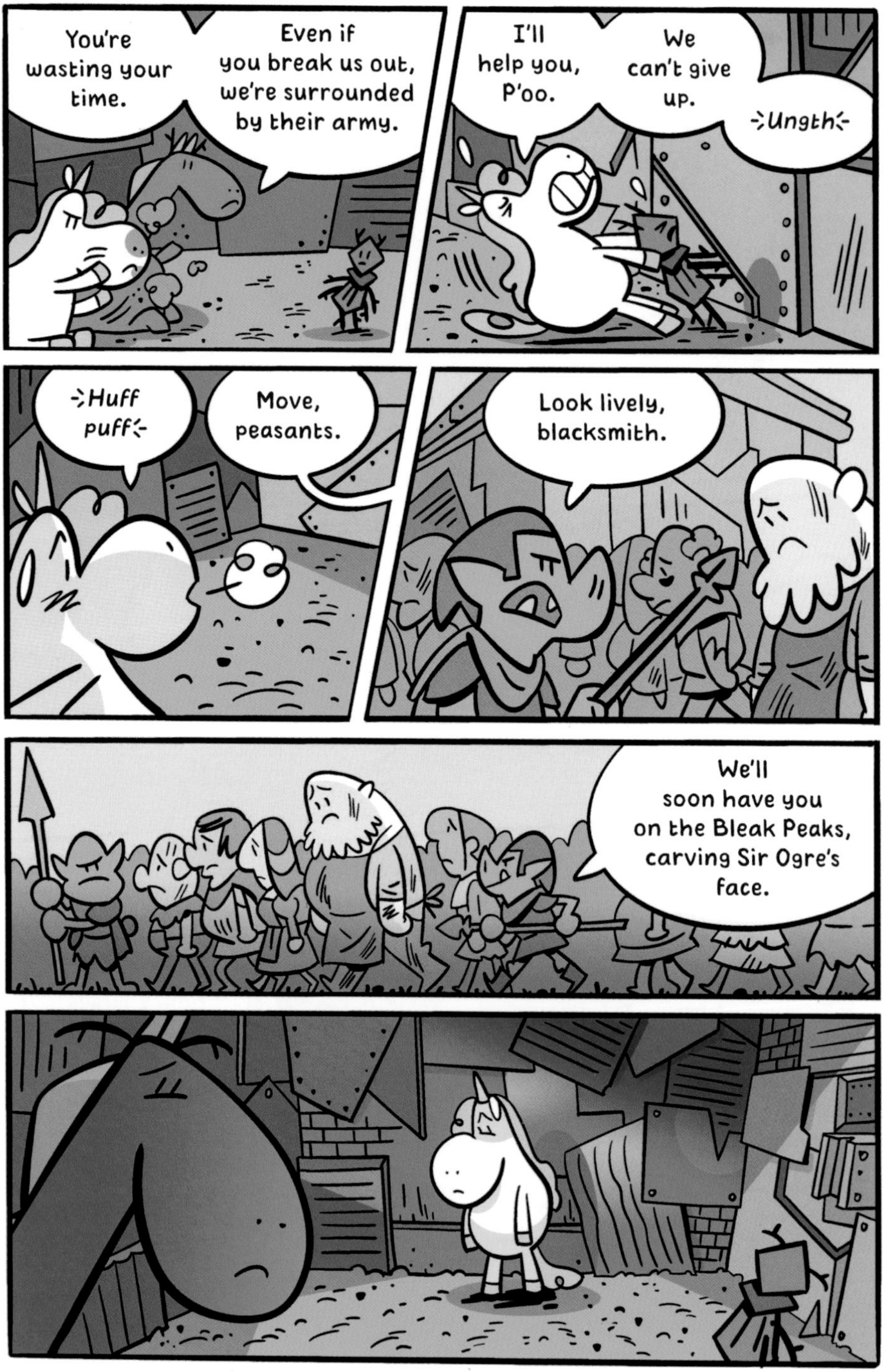
You're wasting your time.
Even if you break us out, we're surrounded by their army.
I'll help you, P'oo.
We can't give up.
-Ungth-
-Huff puff-
Move, peasants.
Look lively, blacksmith.
We'll soon have you on the Bleak Peaks, carving Sir Ogre's face.

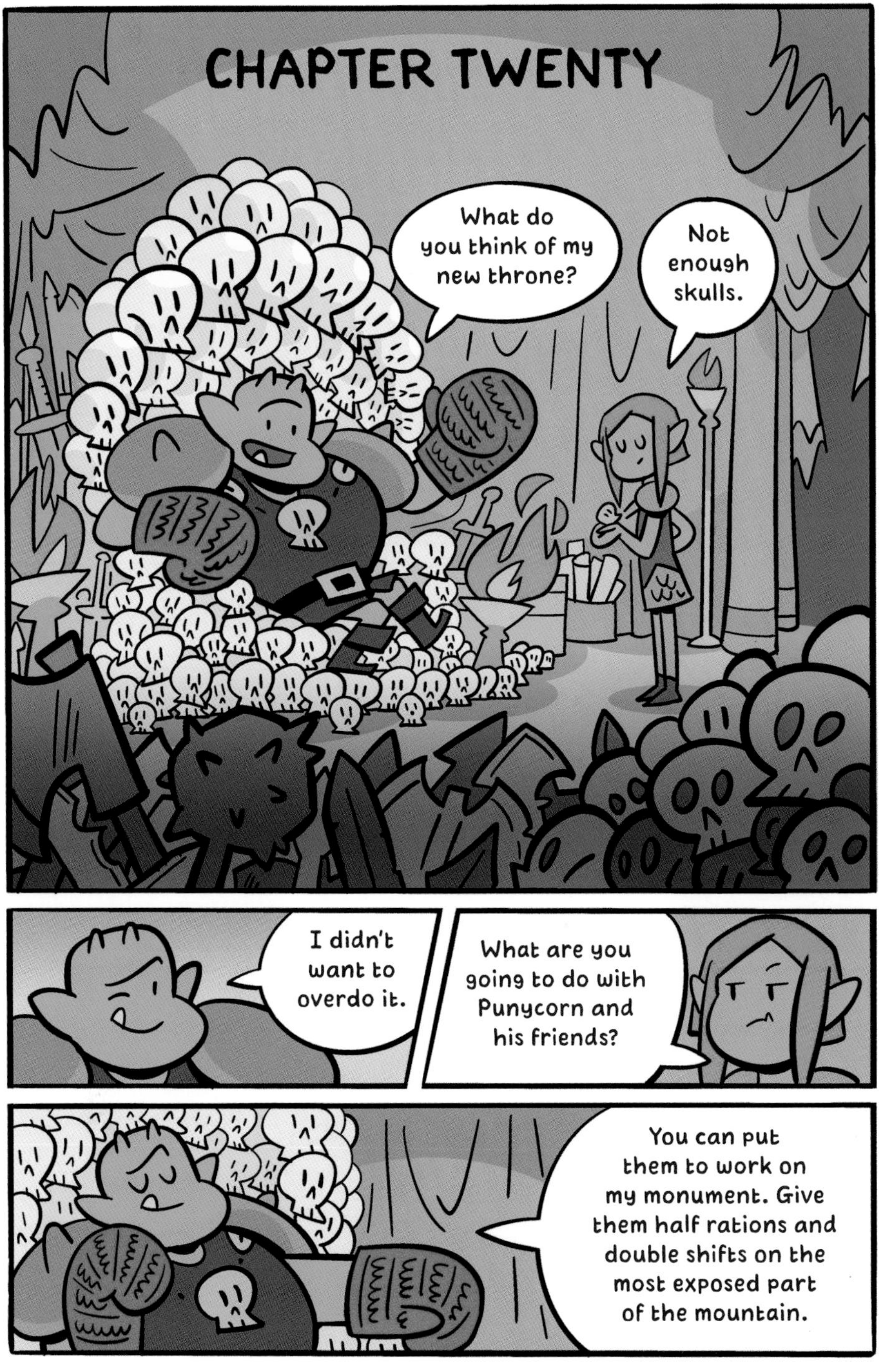
CHAPTER TWENTY
What do you think of my new throne?
Not enough skulls.
I didn't want to overdo it.
What are you going to do with Punycorn and his friends?
You can put them to work on my monument. Give them half rations and double shifts on the most exposed part of the mountain.

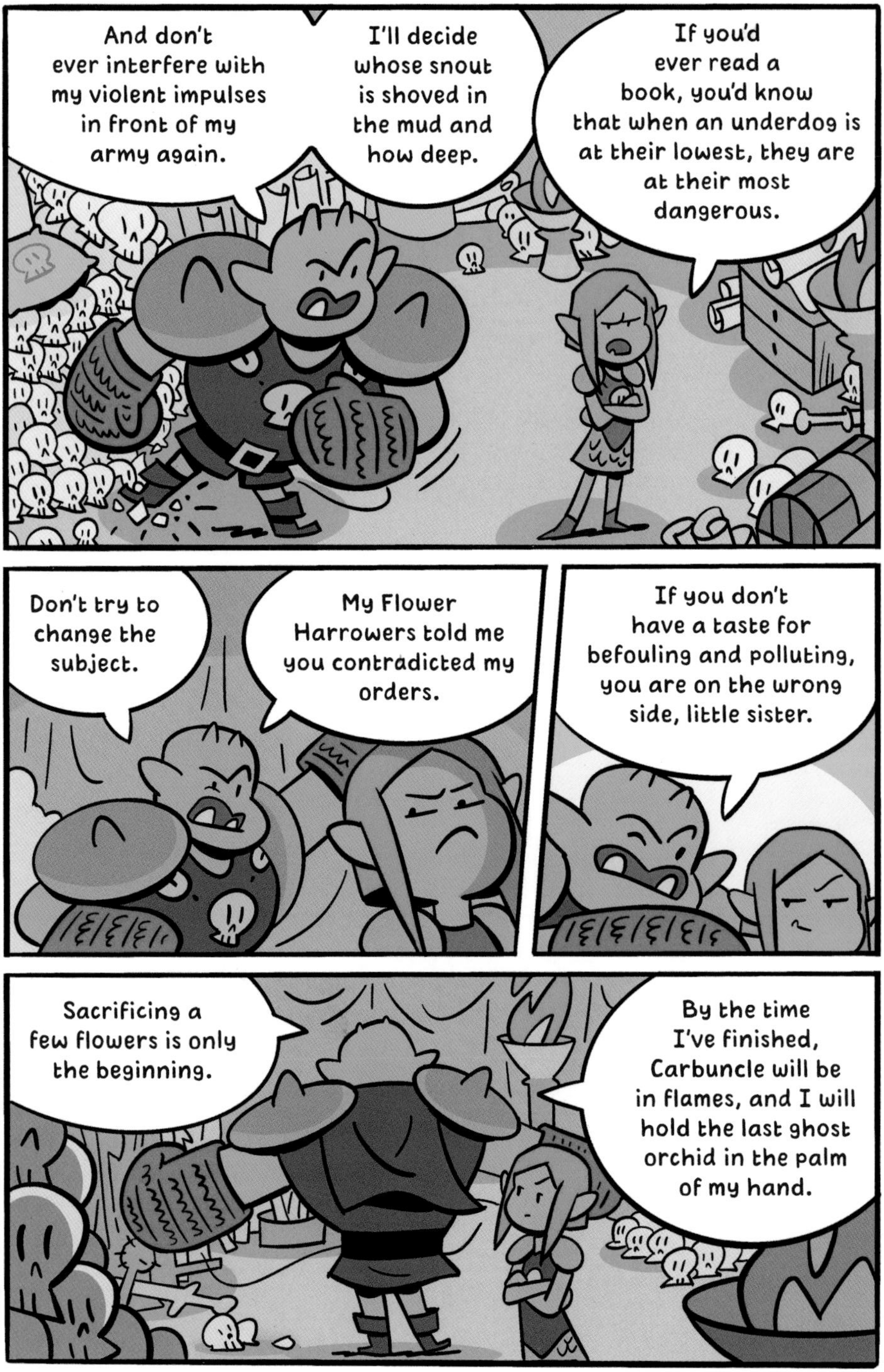
And don't ever interfere with my violent impulses in front of my army again.
I'll decide whose snout is shoved in the mud and how deep.
If you'd ever read a book, you'd know that when an underdog is at their lowest, they are at their most dangerous.
Don't try to change the subject.
My Flower Harrowers told me you contradicted my orders.
If you don't have a taste for befouling and polluting, you are on the wrong side, little sister.
Sacrificing a few flowers is only the beginning.
By the time I've finished, Carbuncle will be in flames, and I will hold the last ghost orchid in the palm of my hand.

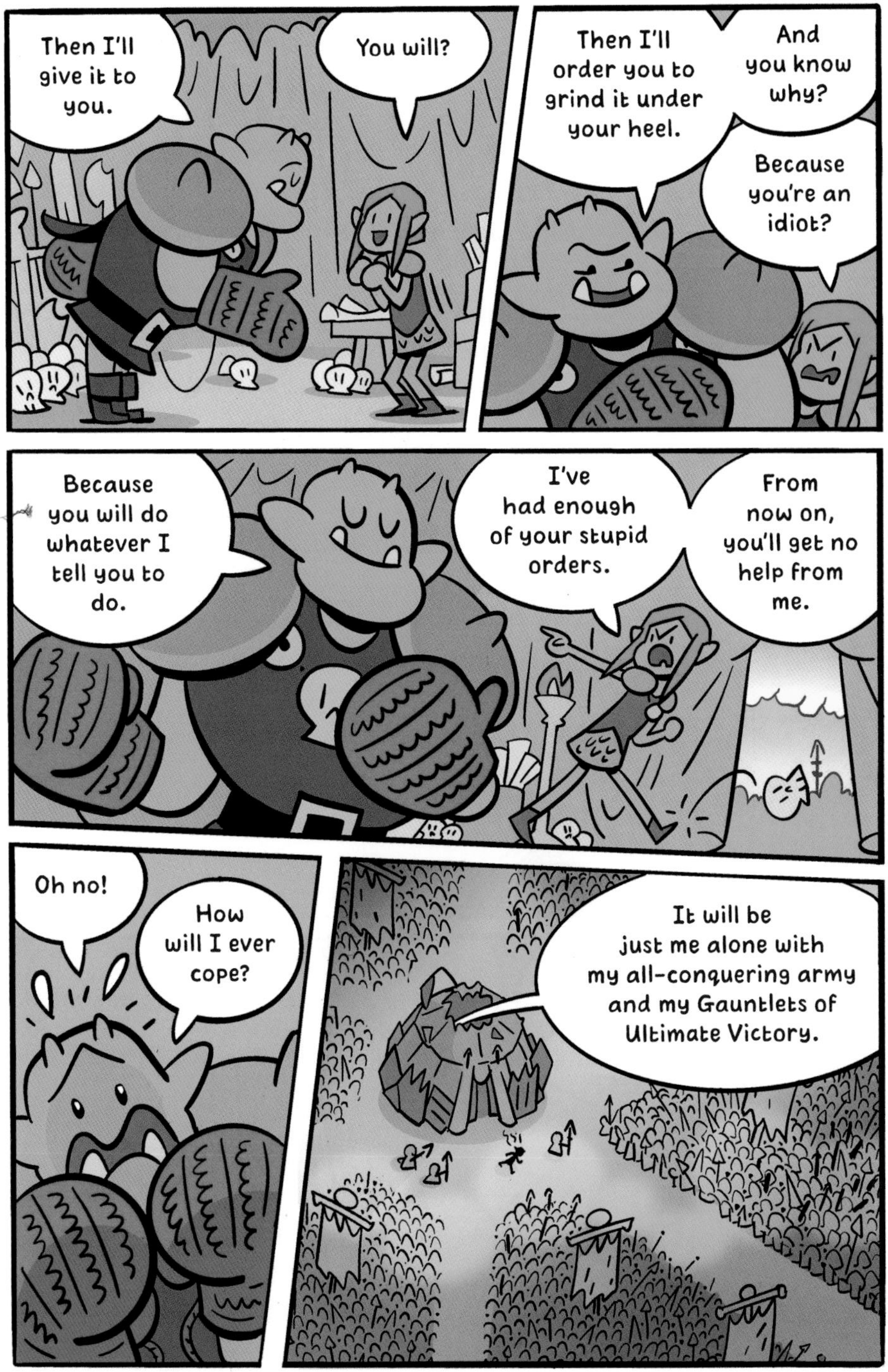
Then I'll give it to you.
You will?
Then I'll order you to grind it under your heel.
And you know why?
Because you're an idiot?
Because you will do whatever I tell you to do.
I've had enough of your stupid orders.
From now on, you'll get no help from me.
Oh no!
How will I ever cope?
It will be just me alone with my all-conquering army and my Gauntlets of Ultimate Victory.

CHAPTER TWENTY-ONE

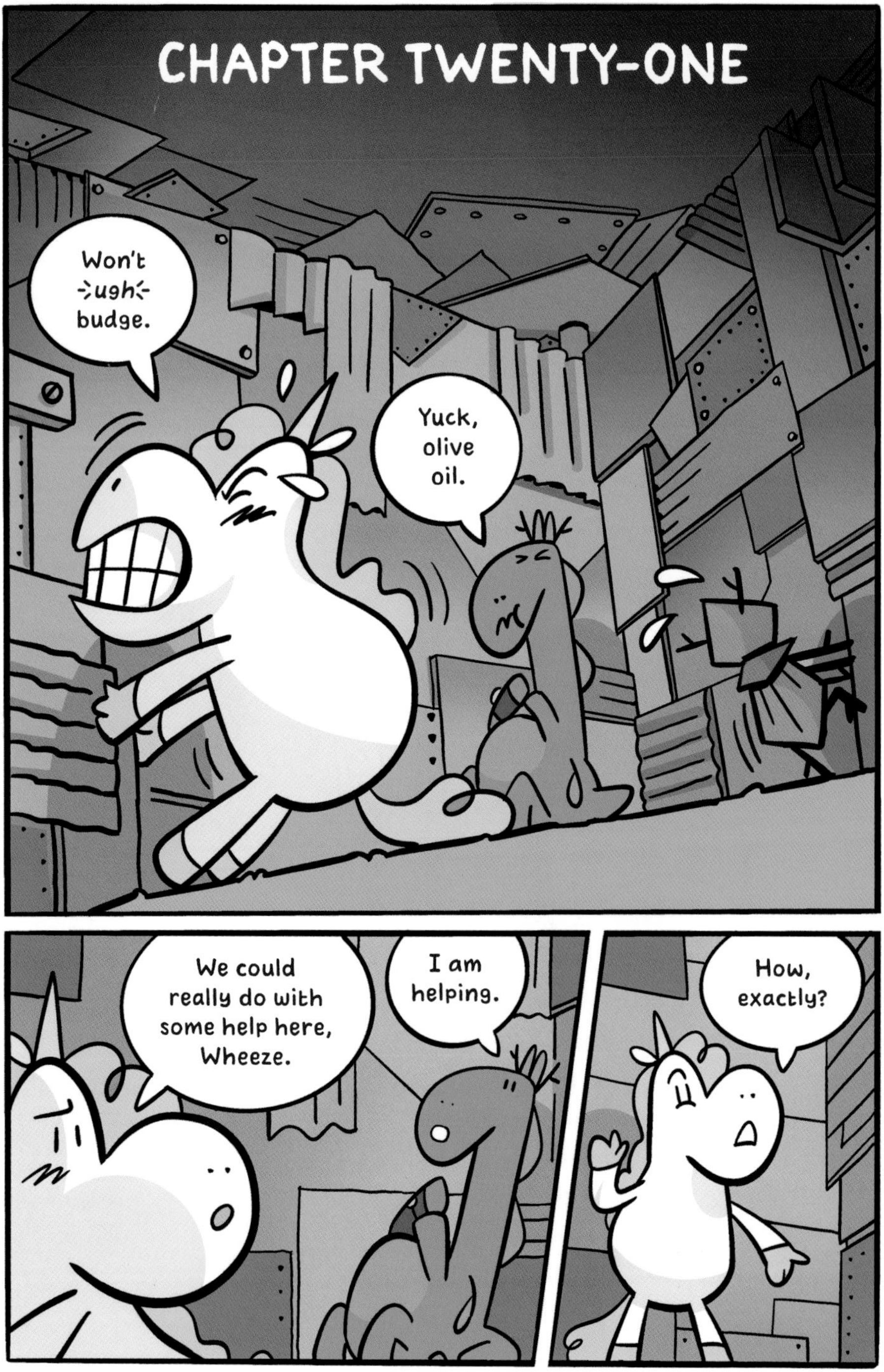

Won't -ugh- budge.
Yuck, olive oil.
We could really do with some help here, Wheeze.
I am helping.
How, exactly?

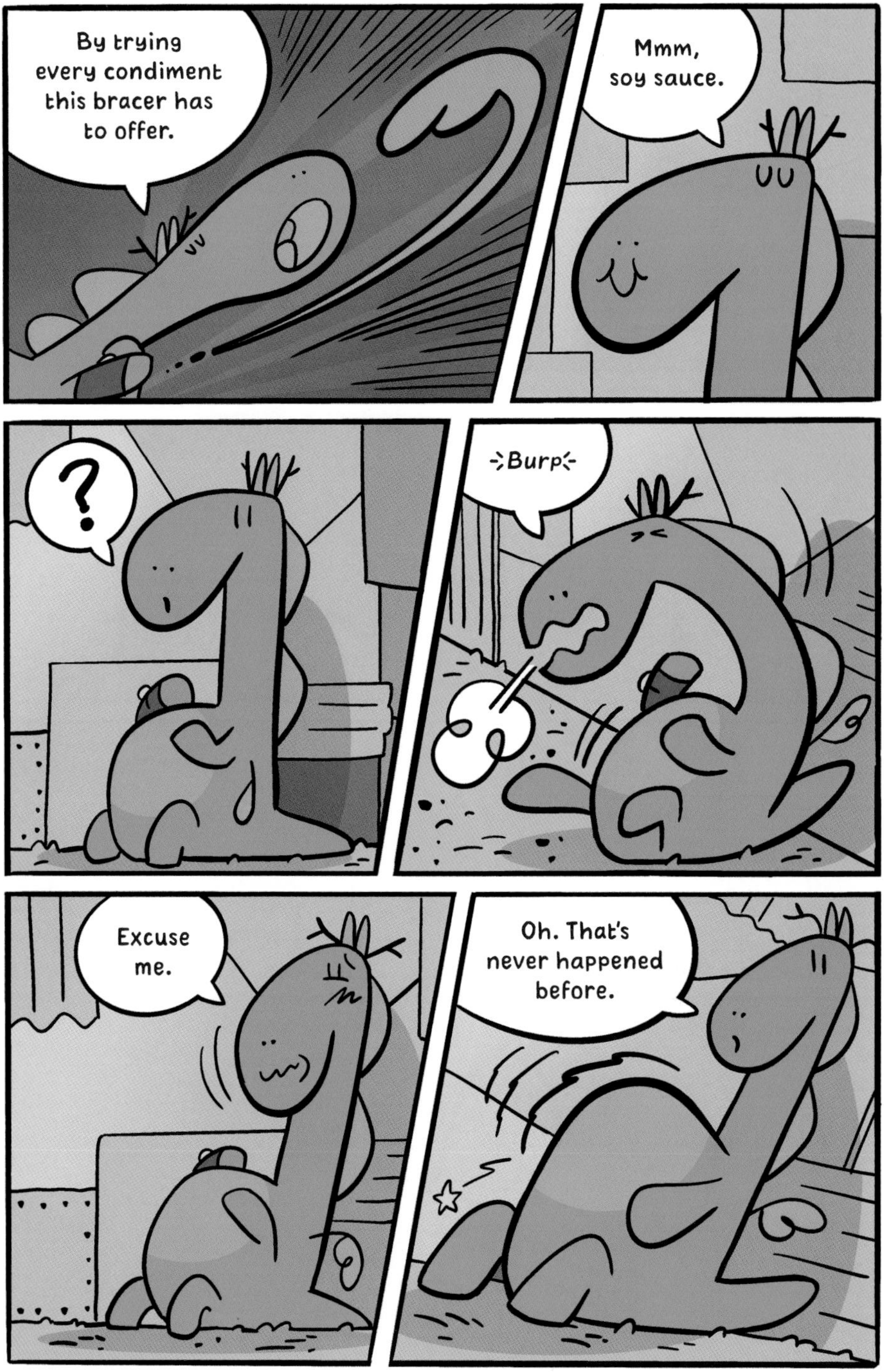
By trying every condiment this bracer has to offer.
Mmm, soy sauce.
?
Burp
Excuse me.
Oh. That's never happened before.

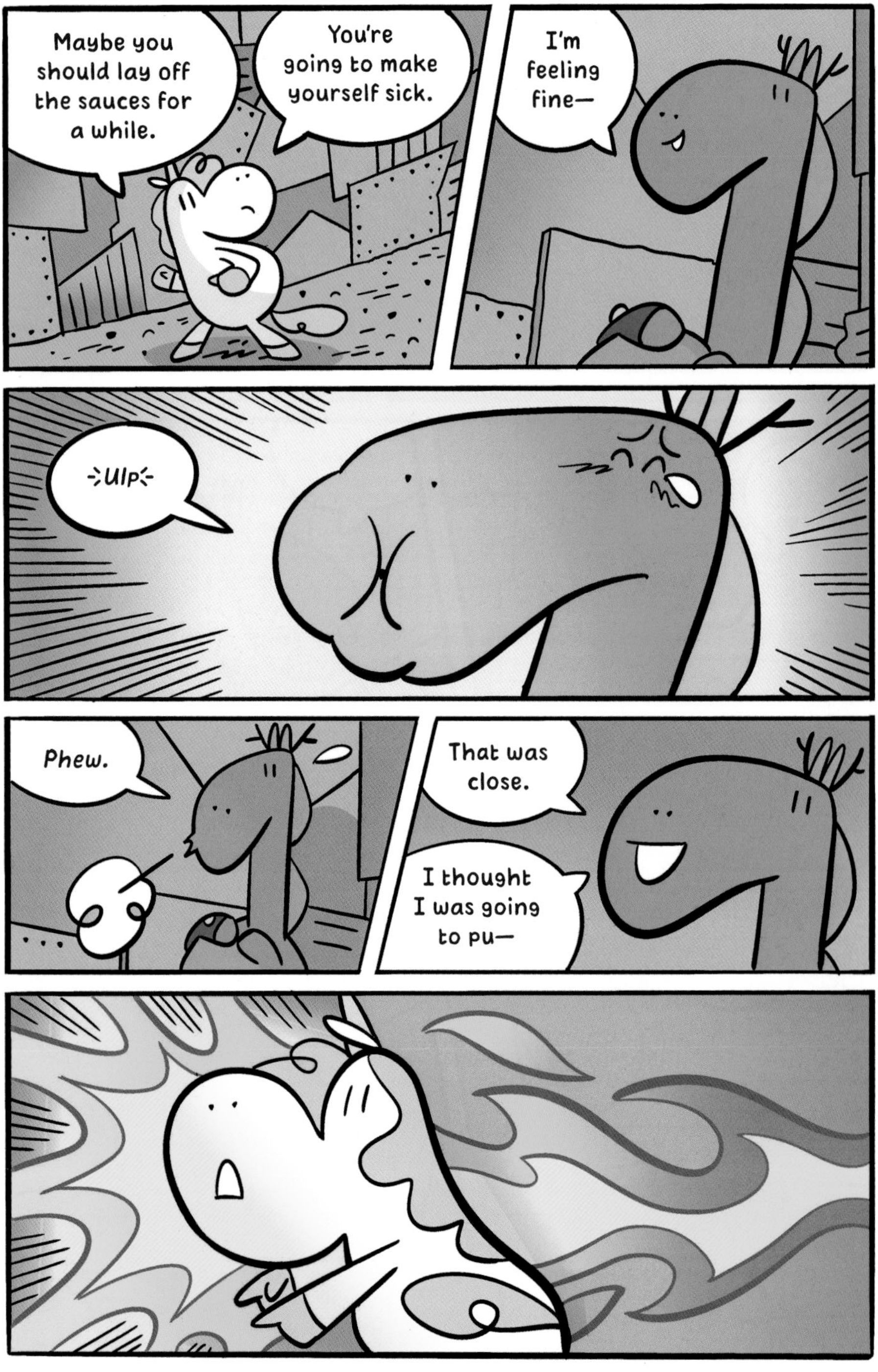
Maybe you should lay off the sauces for a while.
You're going to make yourself sick.
I'm feeling fine—
Ulp
Phew.
That was close.
I thought I was going to pu—

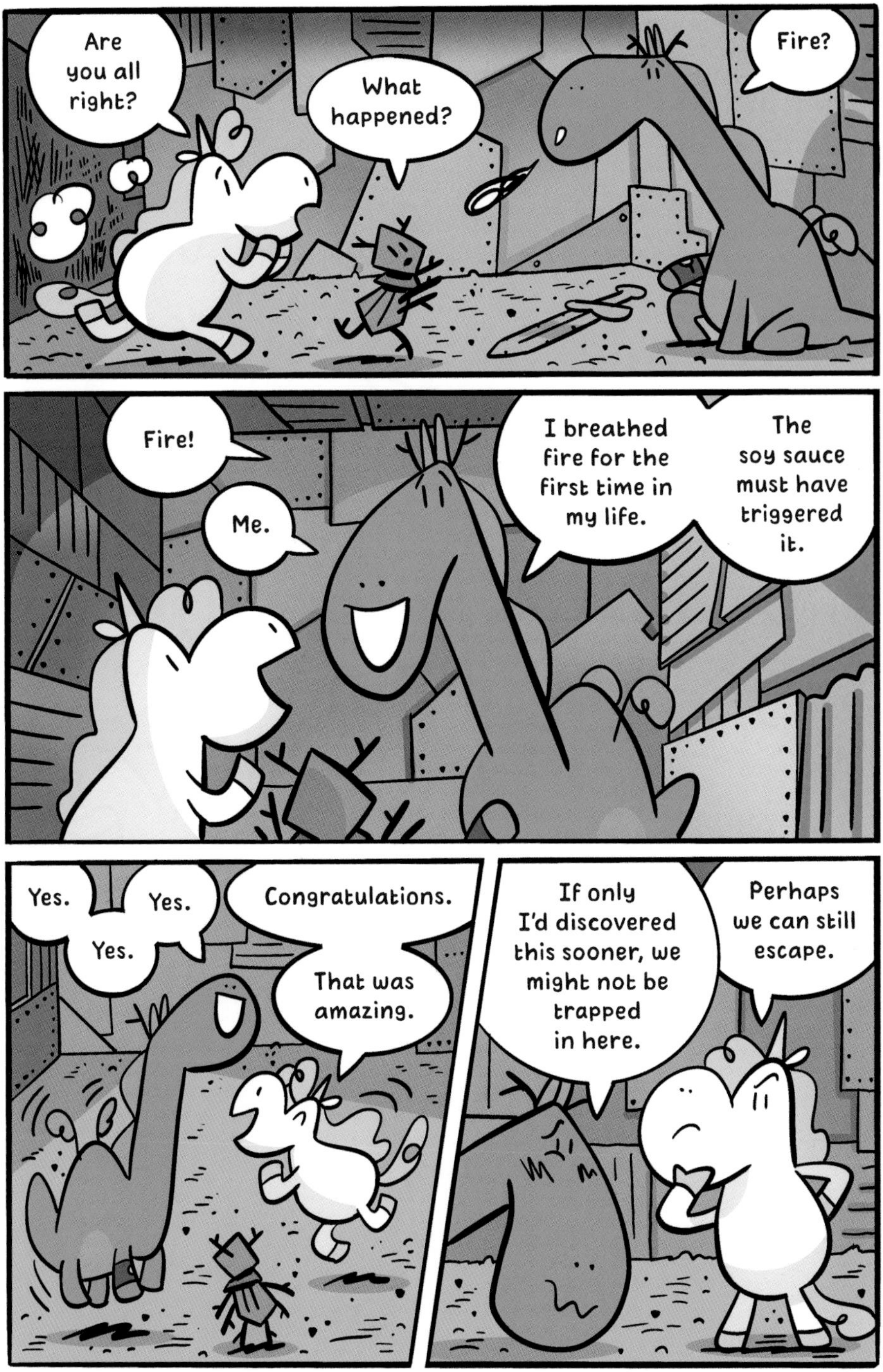
Are you all right?
What happened?
Fire?
Fire!
Me.
I breathed fire for the first time in my life.
The soy sauce must have triggered it.
Yes.
Yes.
Yes.
Congratulations.
That was amazing.
If only I'd discovered this sooner, we might not be trapped in here.
Perhaps we can still escape.

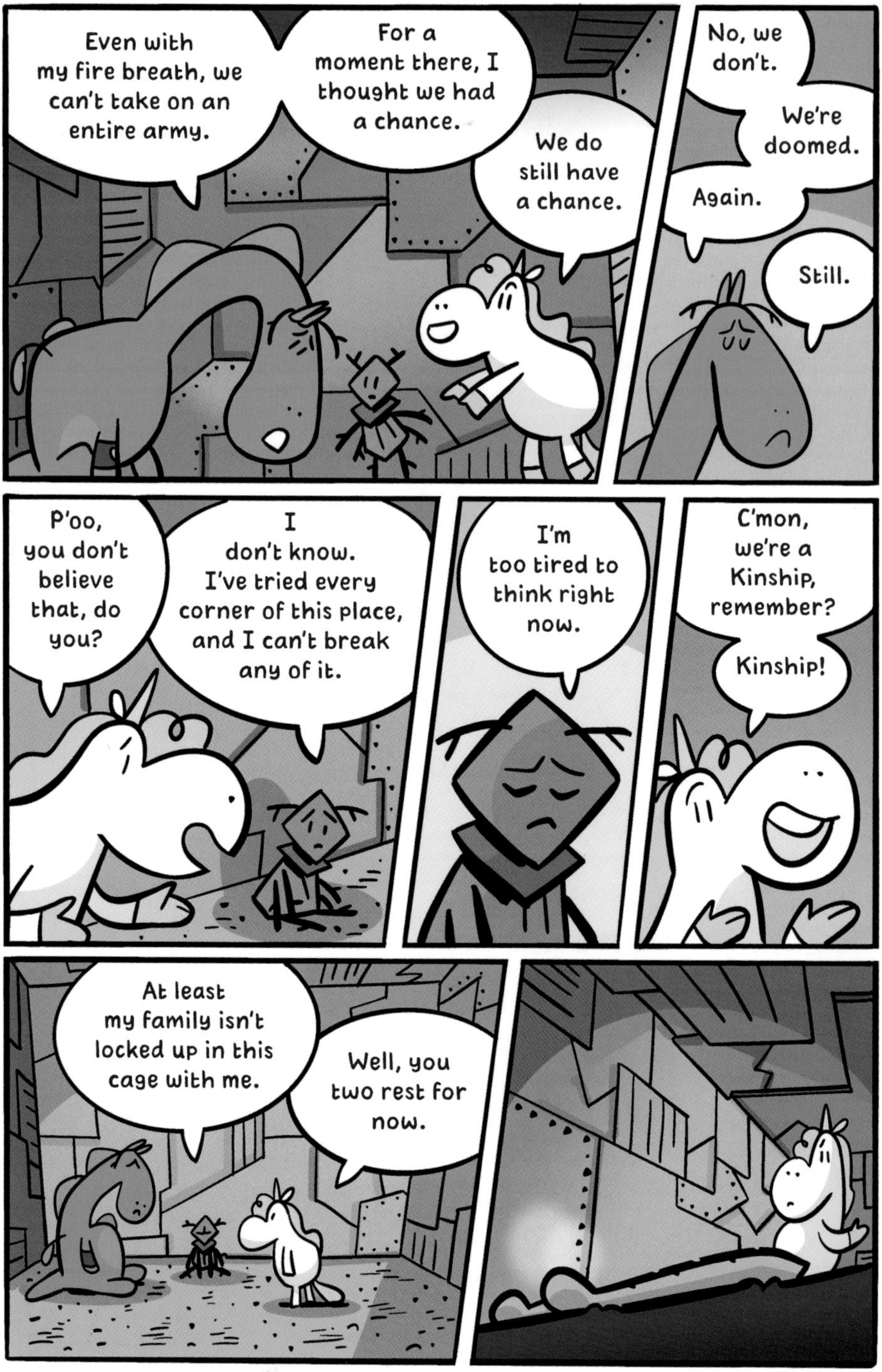
Even with my fire breath, we can't take on an entire army.
For a moment there, I thought we had a chance.
We do still have a chance.
No, we don't.
We're doomed.
Again.
Still.
P'oo, you don't believe that, do you?
I don't know. I've tried every corner of this place, and I can't break any of it.
I'm too tired to think right now.
C'mon, we're a Kinship, remember?
Kinship!
At least my family isn't locked up in this cage with me.
Well, you two rest for now.

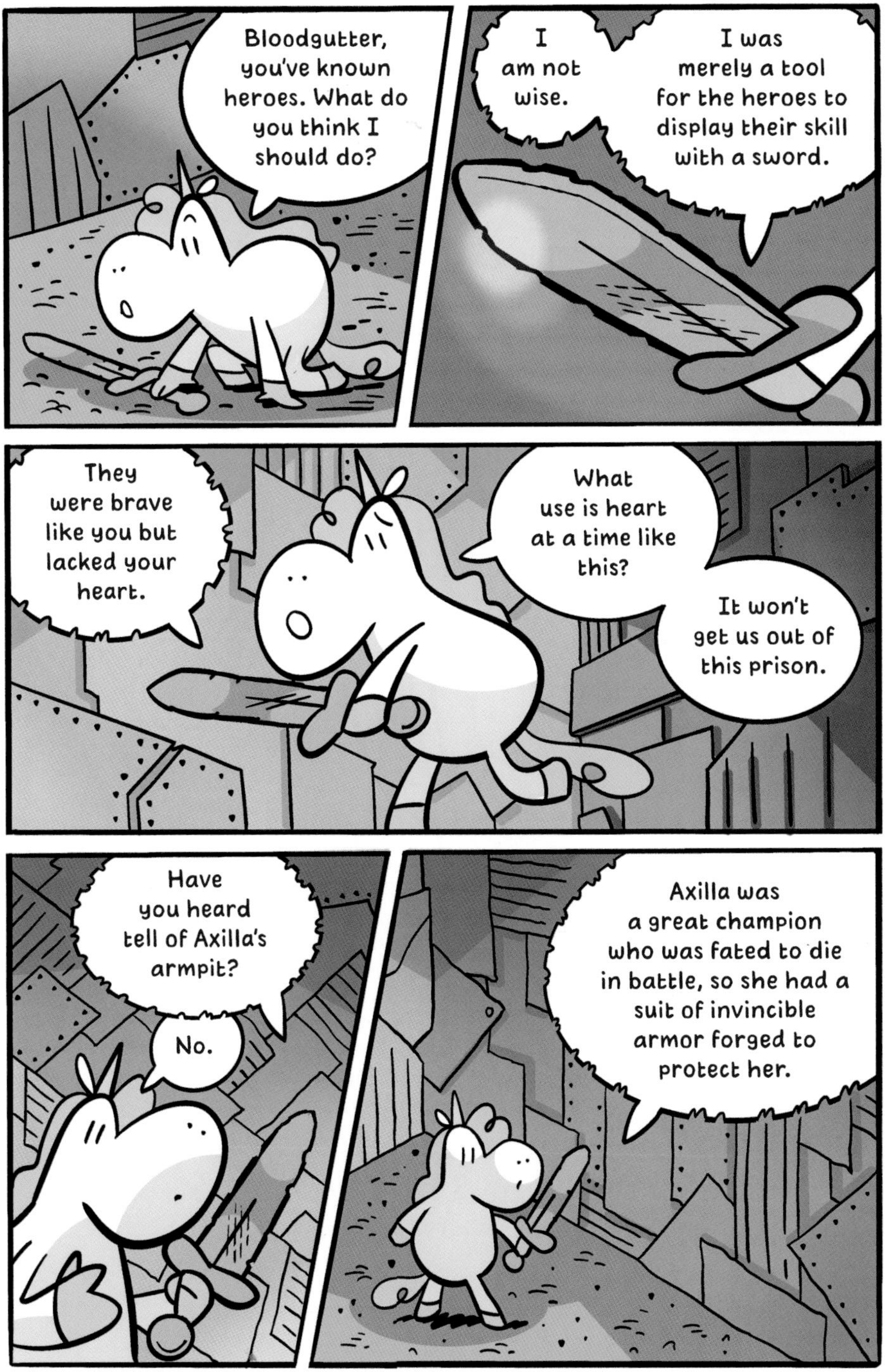
Bloodgutter, you've known heroes. What do you think I should do?
I am not wise.
I was merely a tool for the heroes to display their skill with a sword.
They were brave like you but lacked your heart.
What use is heart at a time like this?
It won't get us out of this prison.
Have you heard tell of Axilla's armpit?
No.
Axilla was a great champion who was fated to die in battle, so she had a suit of invincible armor forged to protect her.

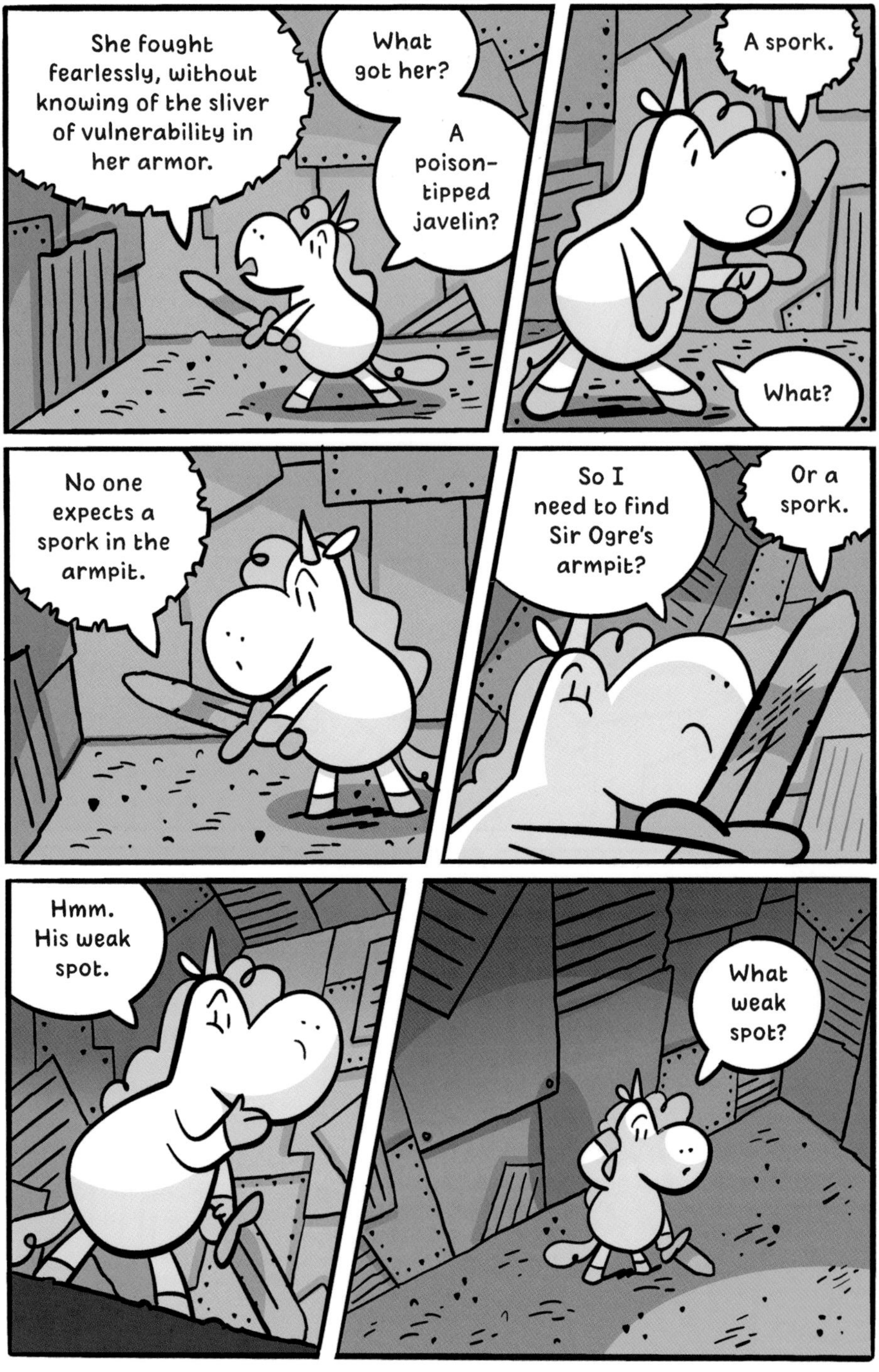
She fought fearlessly, without knowing of the sliver of vulnerability in her armor.
What got her?
A poison-tipped javelin?
A spork.
What?
No one expects a spork in the armpit.
So I need to find Sir Ogre's armpit?
Or a spork.
Hmm. His weak spot.
What weak spot?

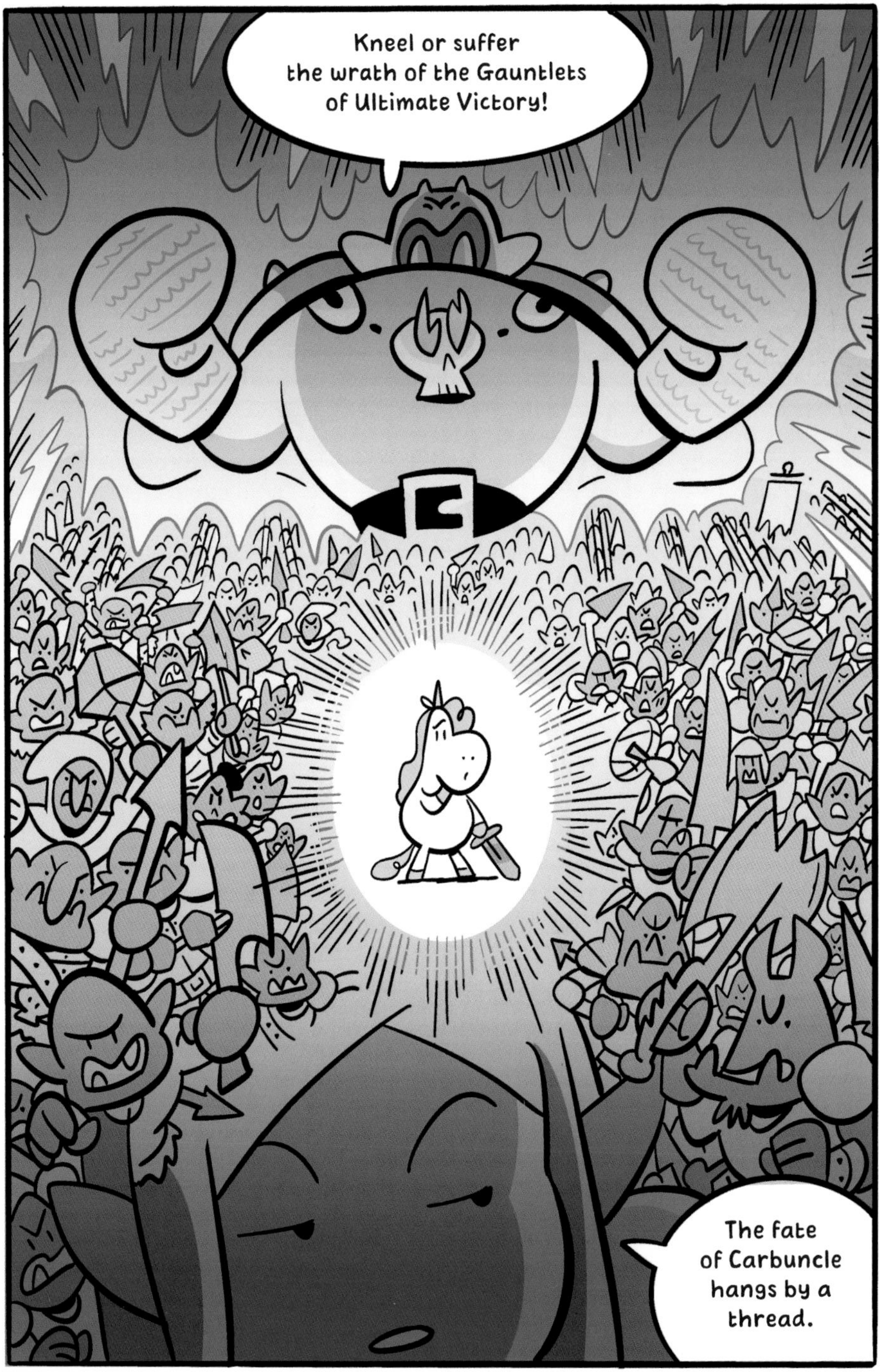
Kneel or suffer
the wrath of the Gauntlets
of Ultimate Victory!
The fate
of Carbuncle
hangs by a
thread.

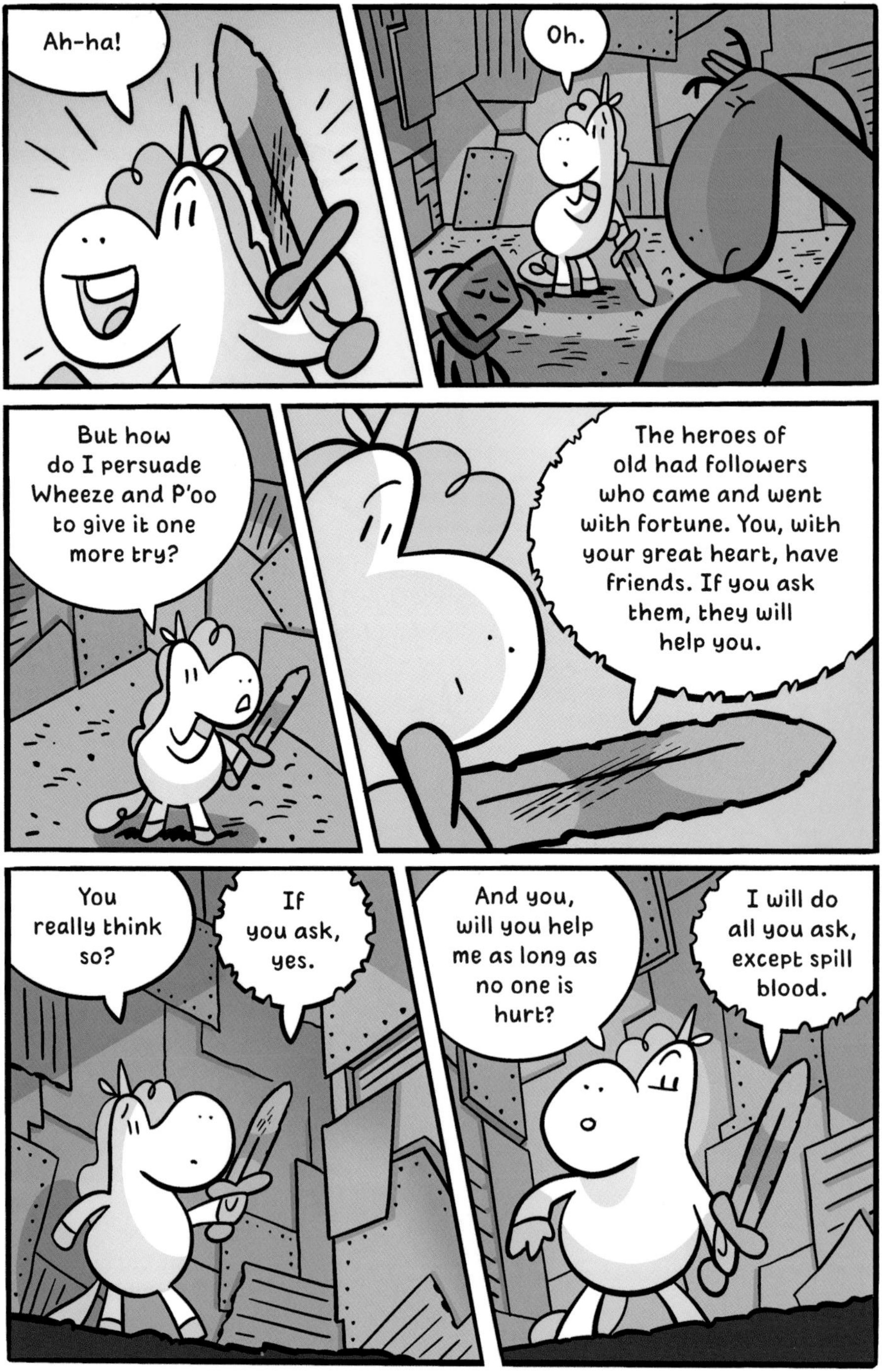

Ah-ha!
Oh.
But how do I persuade Wheeze and P'oo to give it one more try?
The heroes of old had followers who came and went with fortune. You, with your great heart, have friends. If you ask them, they will help you.
You really think so?
If you ask, yes.
And you, will you help me as long as no one is hurt?
I will do all you ask, except spill blood.

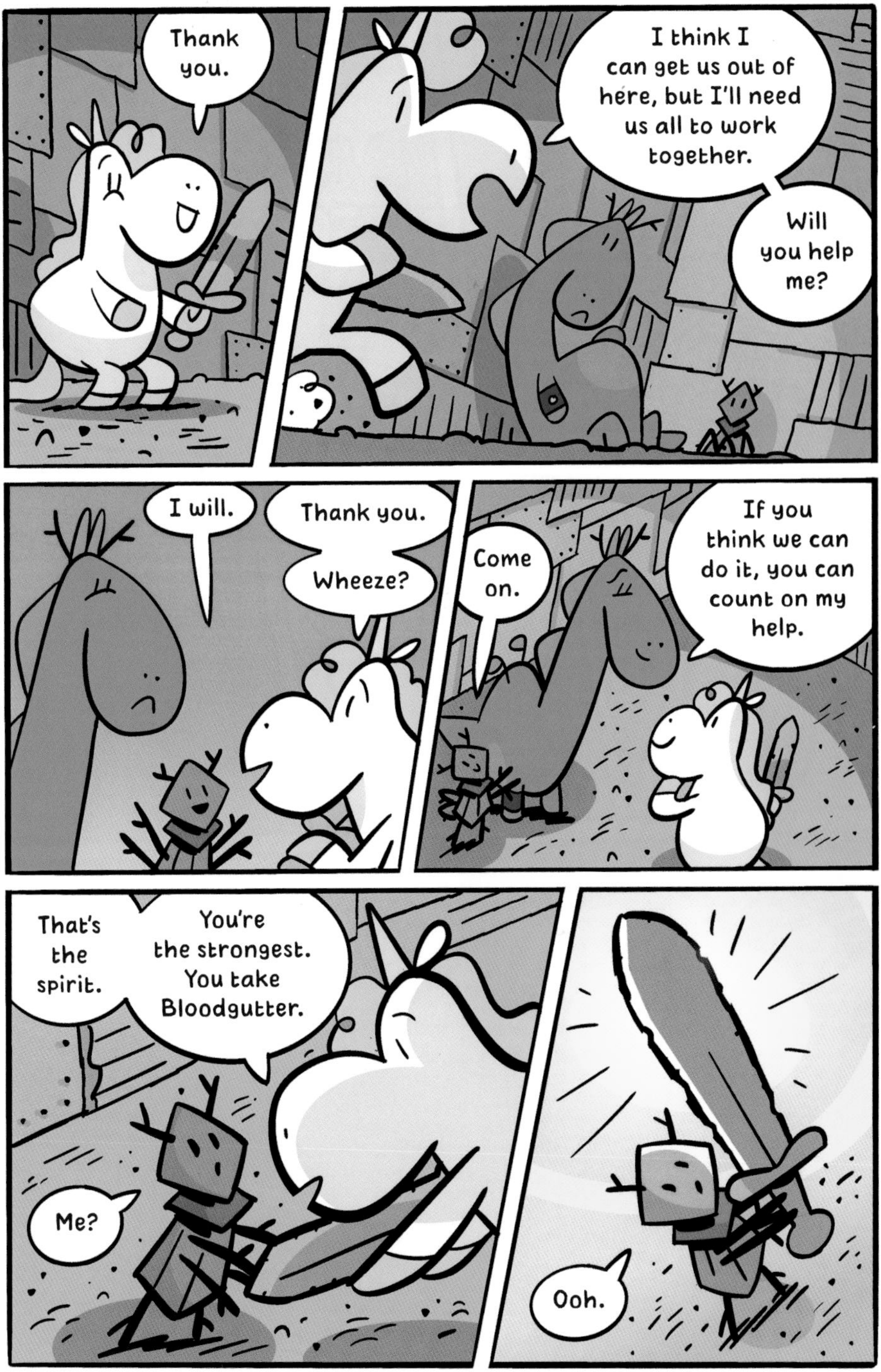
Thank you.
I think I can get us out of here, but I'll need us all to work together.
Will you help me?
I will.
Thank you.
Wheeze?
Come on.
If you think we can do it, you can count on my help.
That's the spirit.
You're the strongest. You take Bloodgutter.
Me?
Ooh.

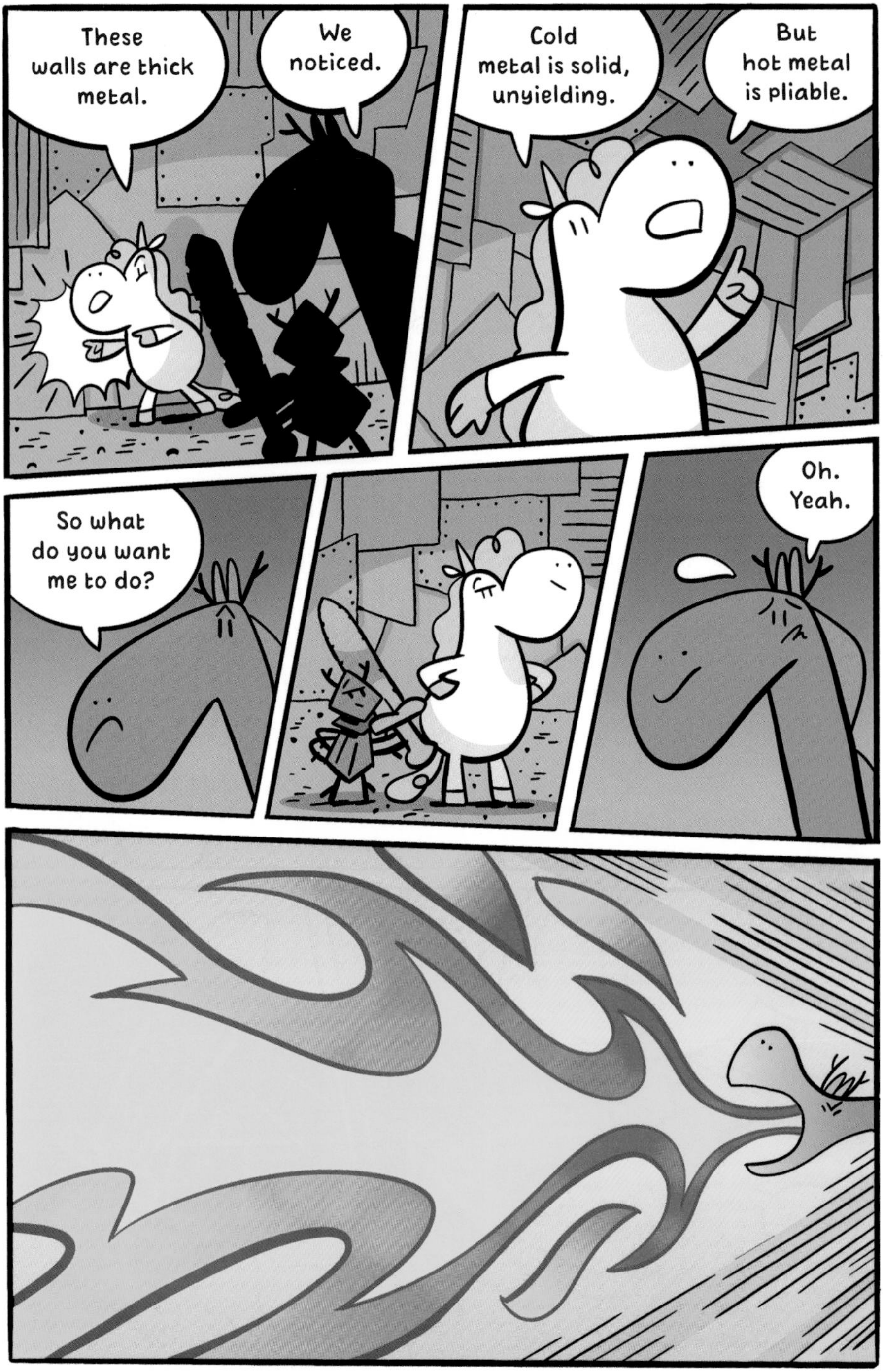

These walls are thick metal.
We noticed.
Cold metal is solid, unyielding.
But hot metal is pliable.
So what do you want me to do?
Oh. Yeah.

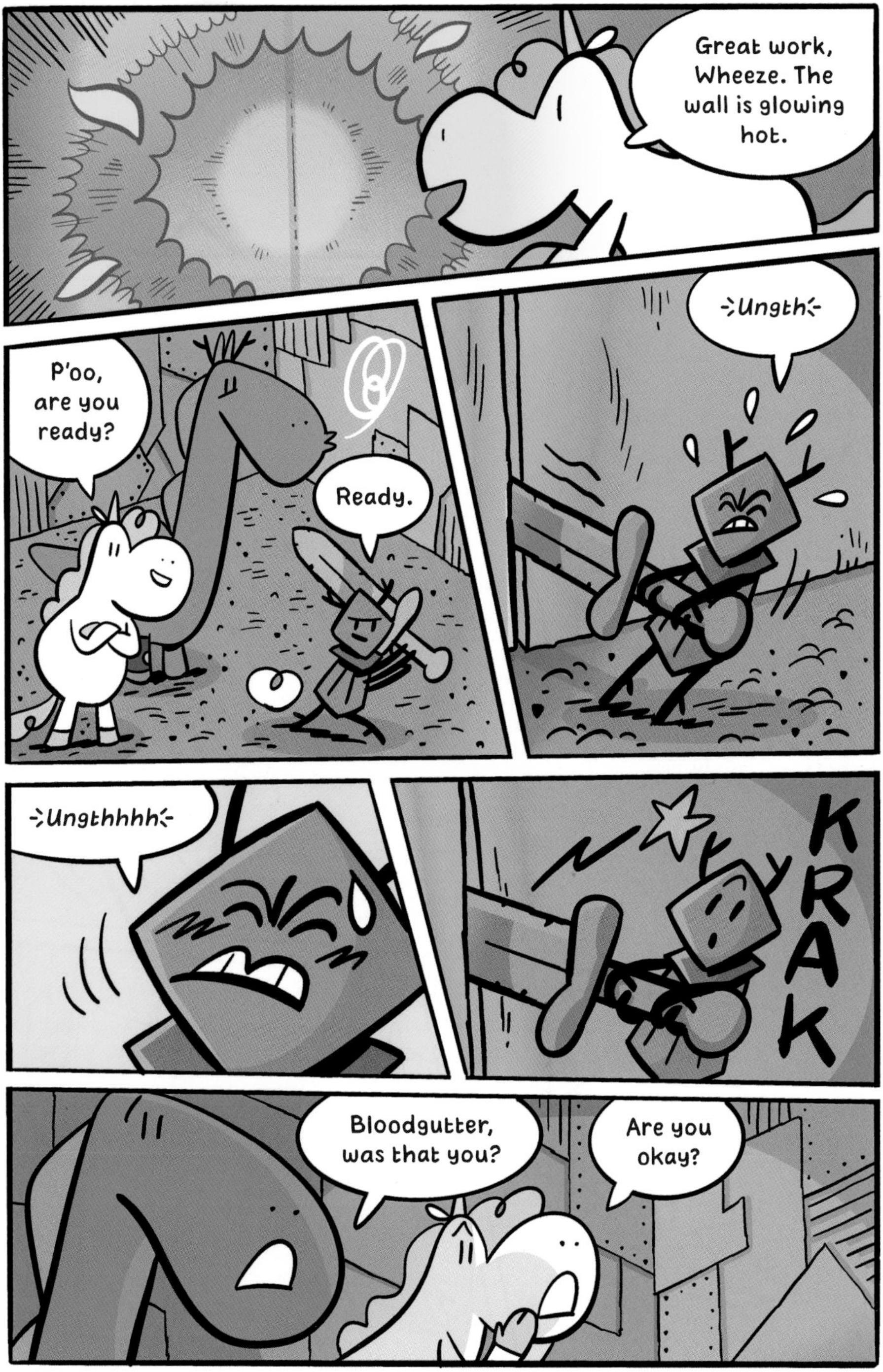
Great work, Wheeze. The wall is glowing hot.
P'oo, are you ready?
Ready.
Ungth
Ungthhhh
KRAK
Bloodgutter, was that you?
Are you okay?

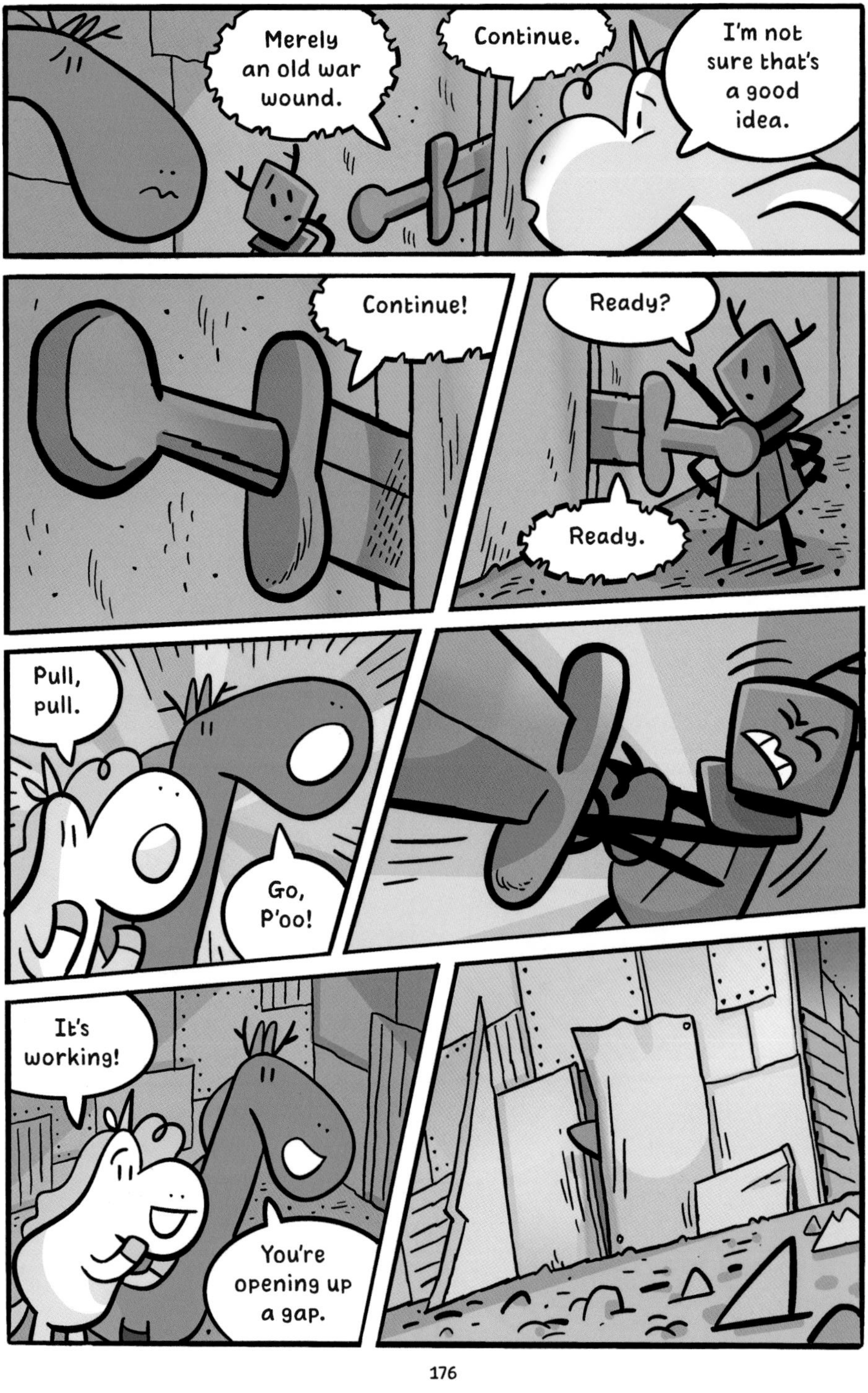
Merely an old war wound.
Continue.
I'm not sure that's a good idea.
Continue!
Ready?
Ready.
Pull, pull.
Go, P'oo!
It's working!
You're opening up a gap.

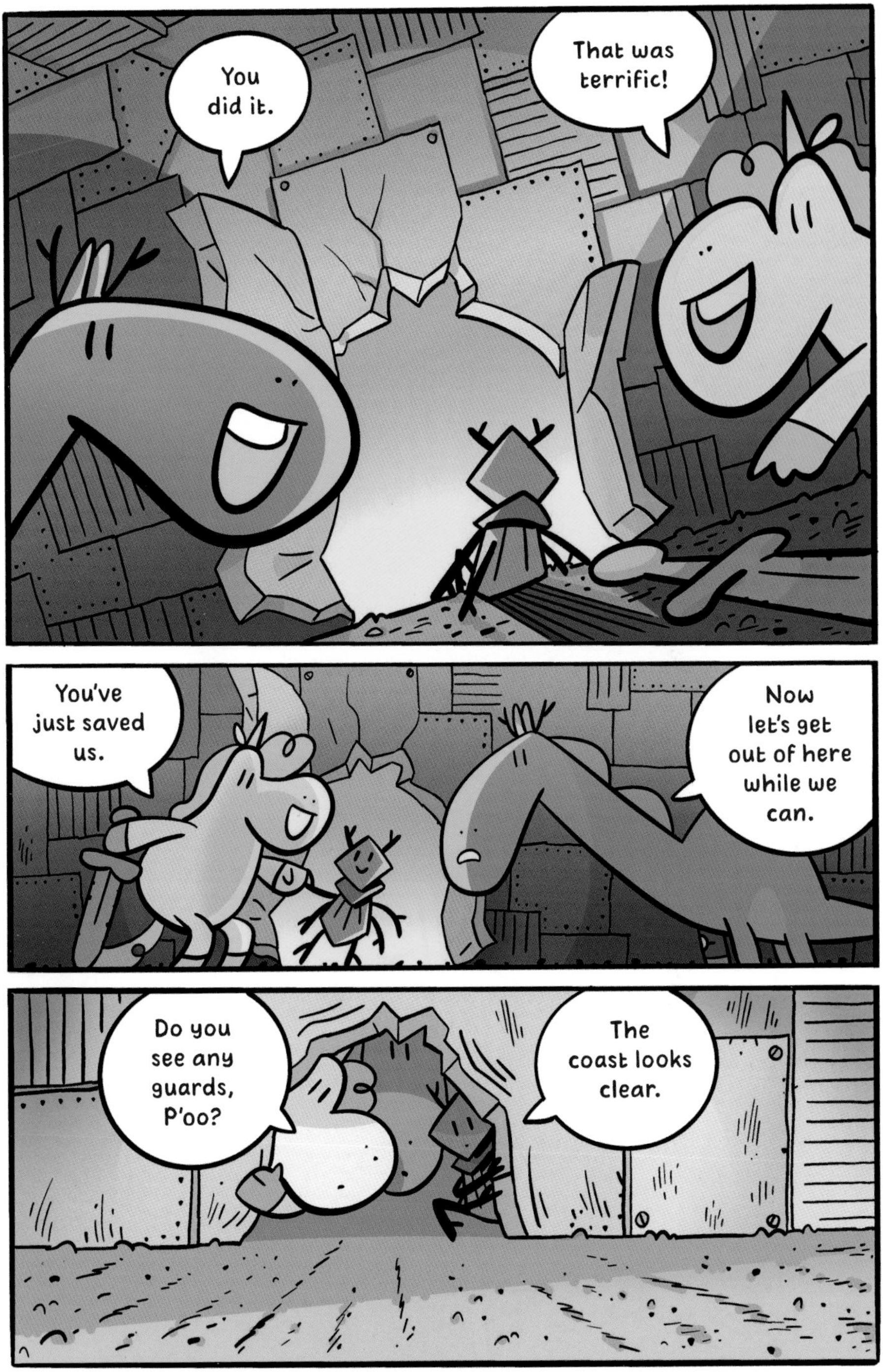
You did it.
That was terrific!
You've just saved us.
Now let's get out of here while we can.
Do you see any guards, P'oo?
The coast looks clear.

CHAPTER TWENTY-TWO

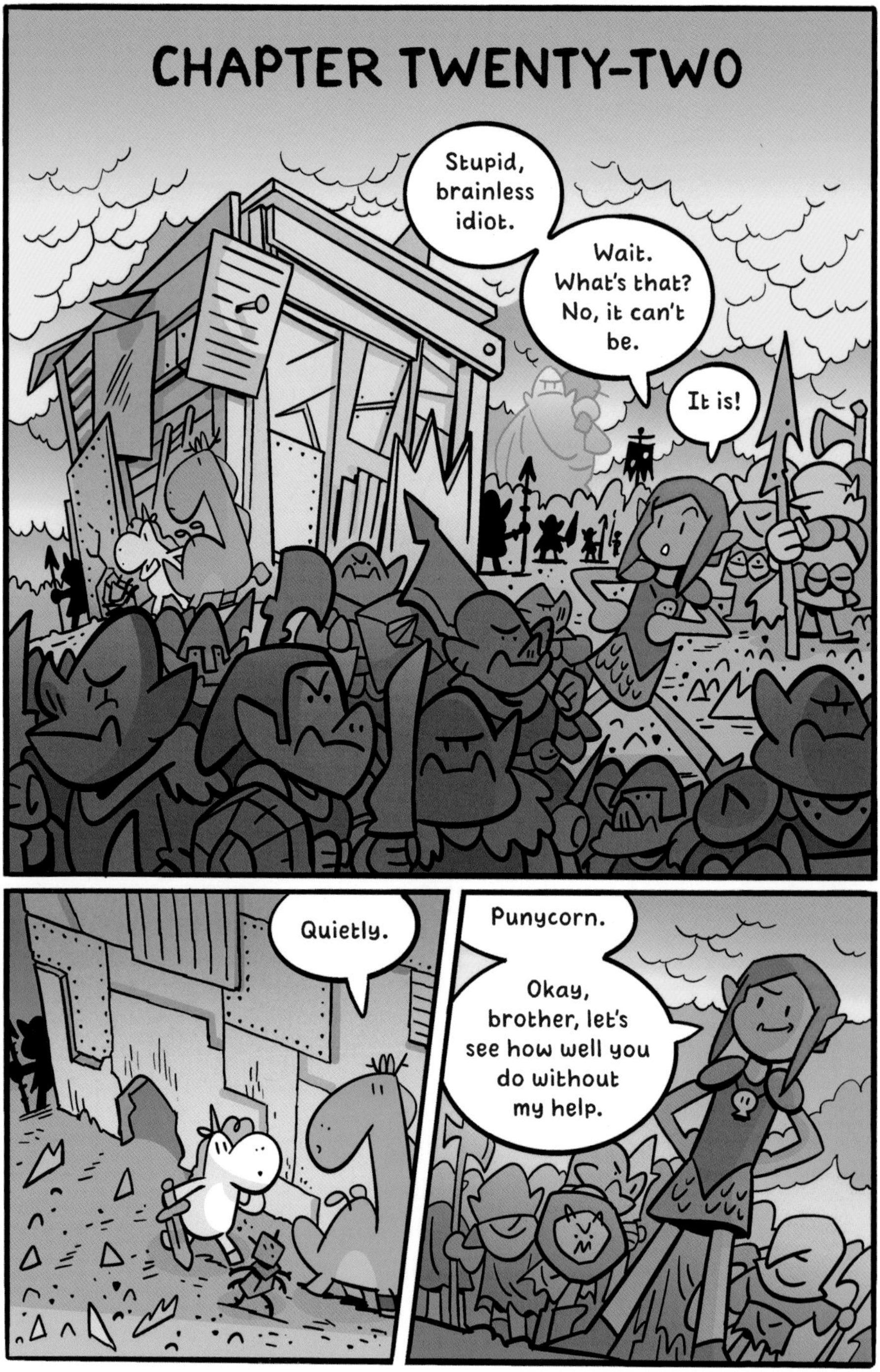
Stupid, brainless idiot.
Wait. What's that? No, it can't be.
It is!
Quietly.
Punycorn.
Okay, brother, let's see how well you do without my help.

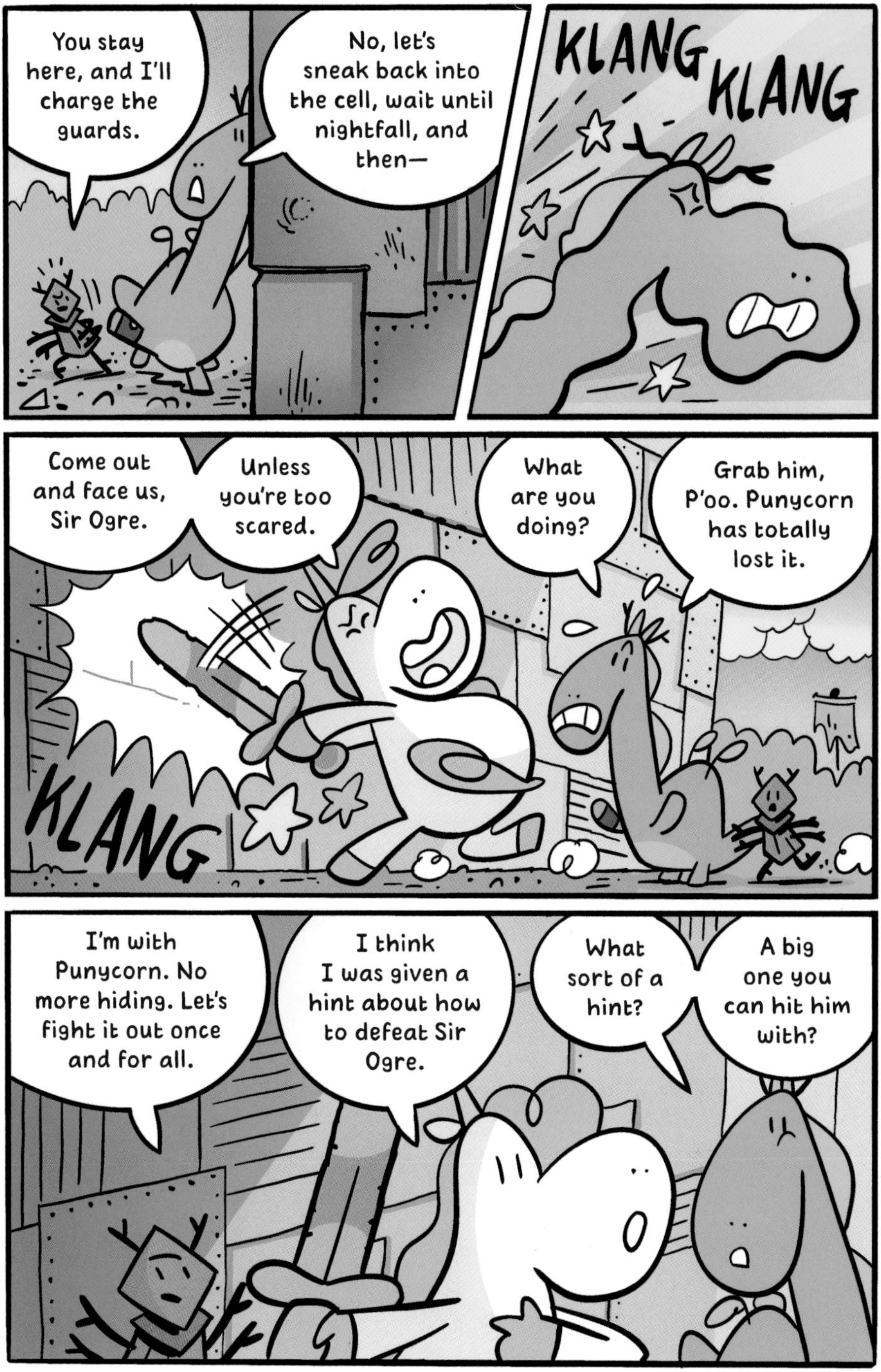
You stay here, and I'll charge the guards.
No, let's sneak back into the cell, wait until nightfall, and then—
KLANG
KLANG
Come out and face us, Sir Ogre.
Unless you're too scared.
What are you doing?
Grab him, P'oo. Punycorn has totally lost it.
KLANG
I'm with Punycorn. No more hiding. Let's fight it out once and for all.
I think I was given a hint about how to defeat Sir Ogre.
What sort of a hint?
A big one you can hit him with?

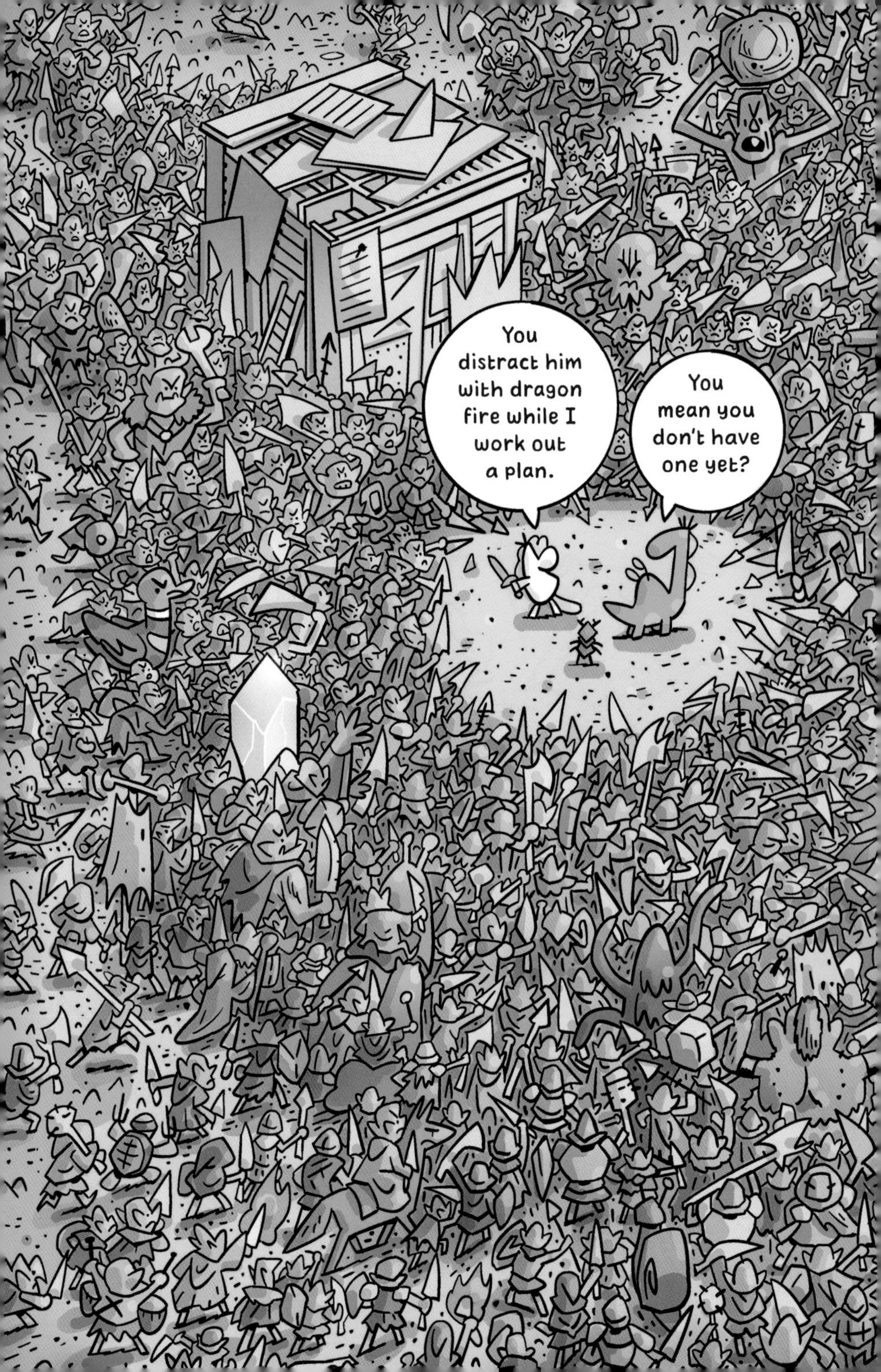
You distract him with dragon fire while I work out a plan.
You mean you don't have one yet?

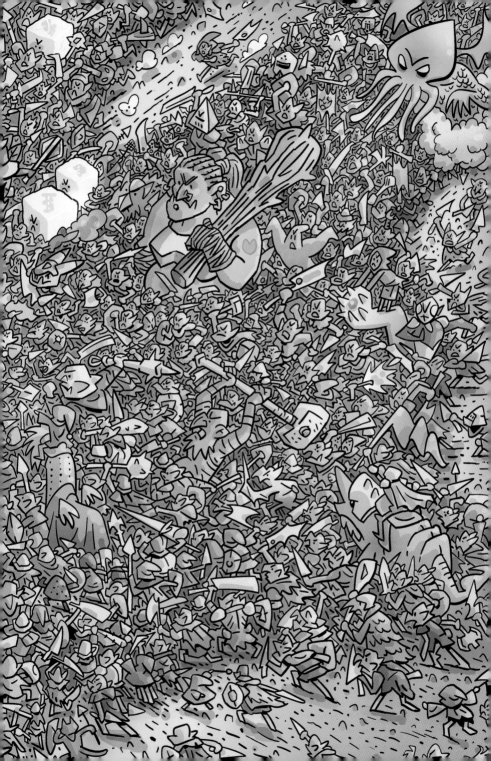

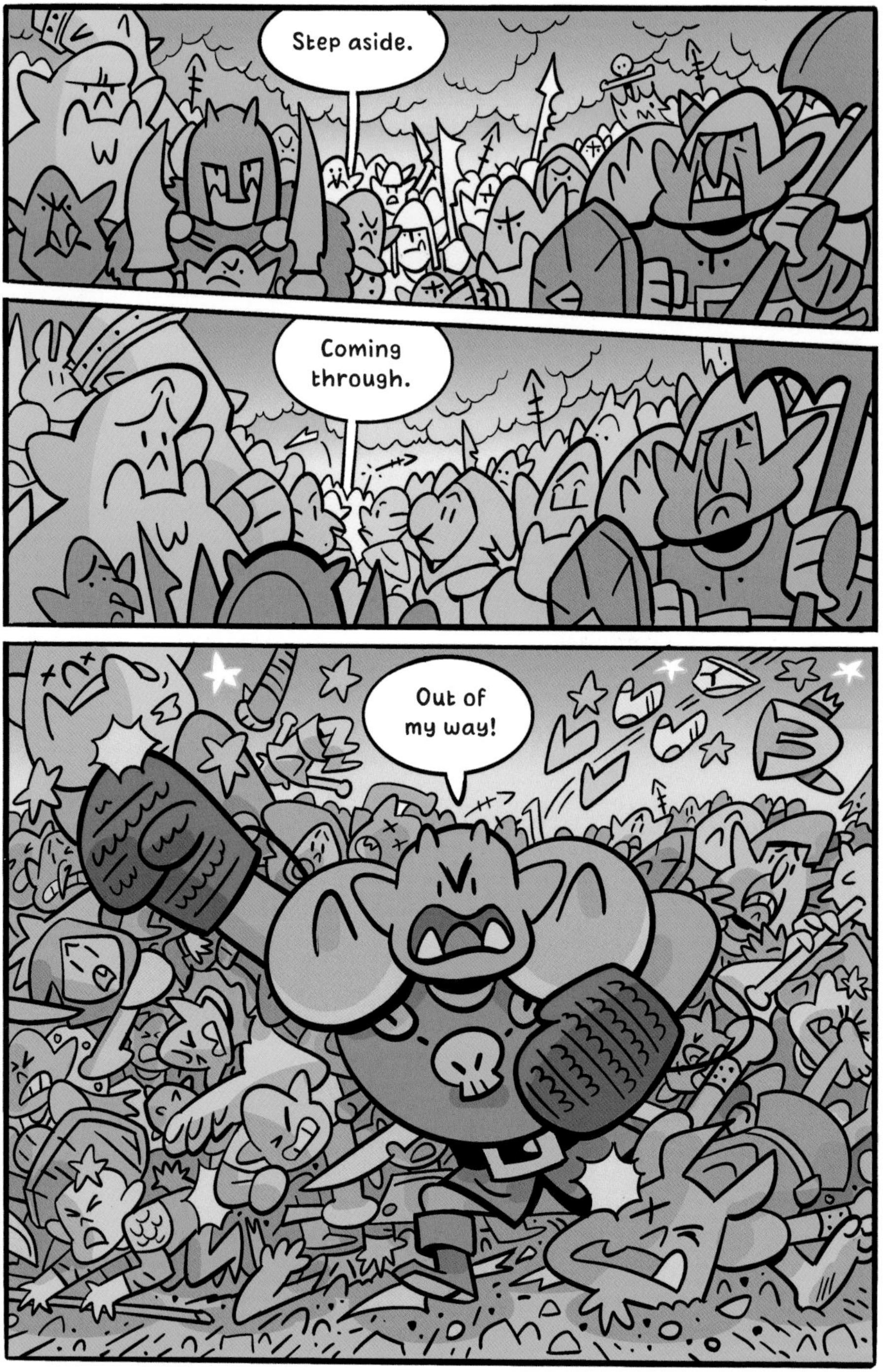
Step aside.
Coming through.
Out of my way!

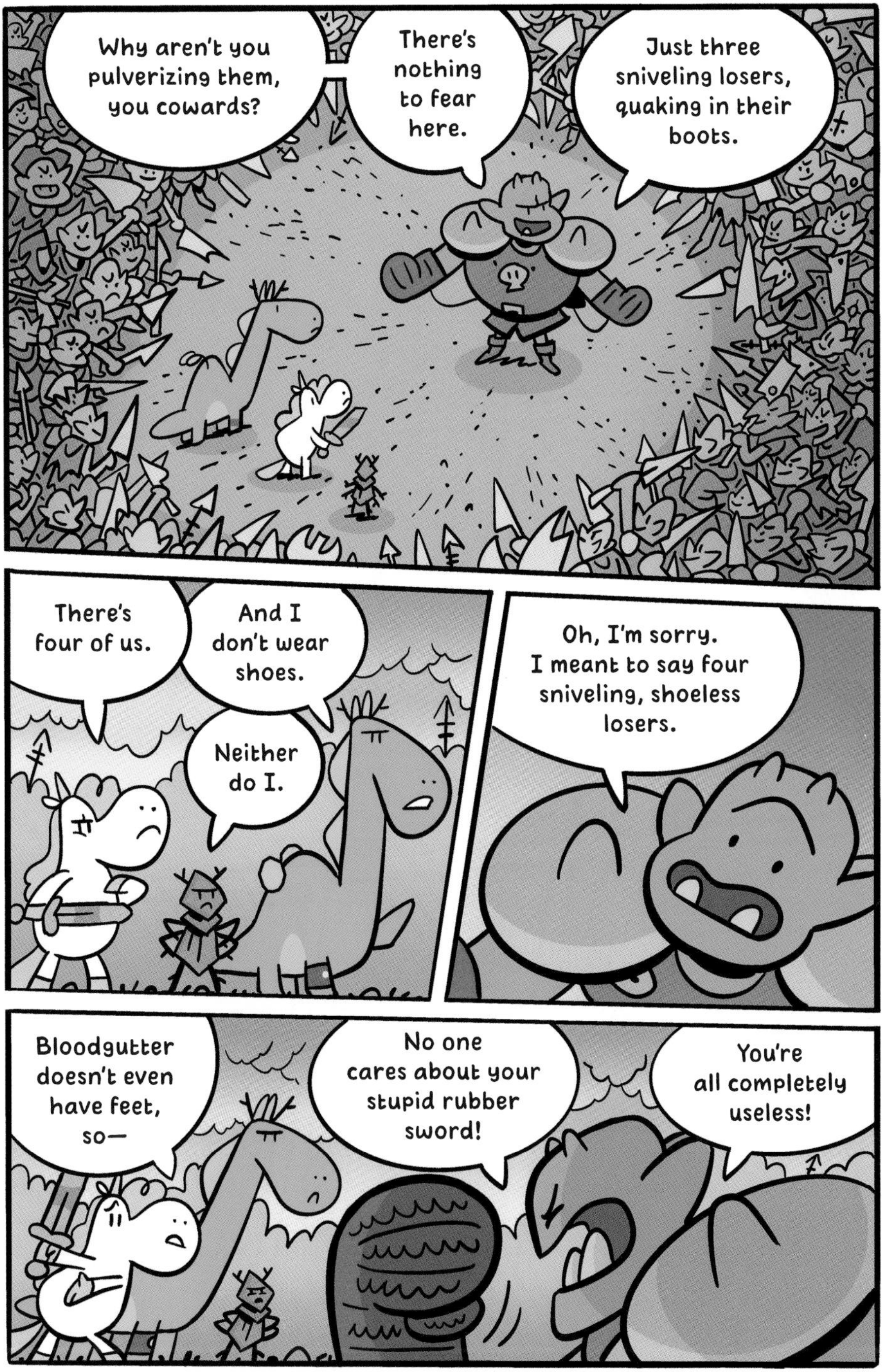

Why aren't you pulverizing them, you cowards?
There's nothing to fear here.
Just three sniveling losers, quaking in their boots.
There's four of us.
And I don't wear shoes.
Neither do I.
Oh, I'm sorry. I meant to say four sniveling, shoeless losers.
Bloodgutter doesn't even have feet, so—
No one cares about your stupid rubber sword!
You're all completely useless!

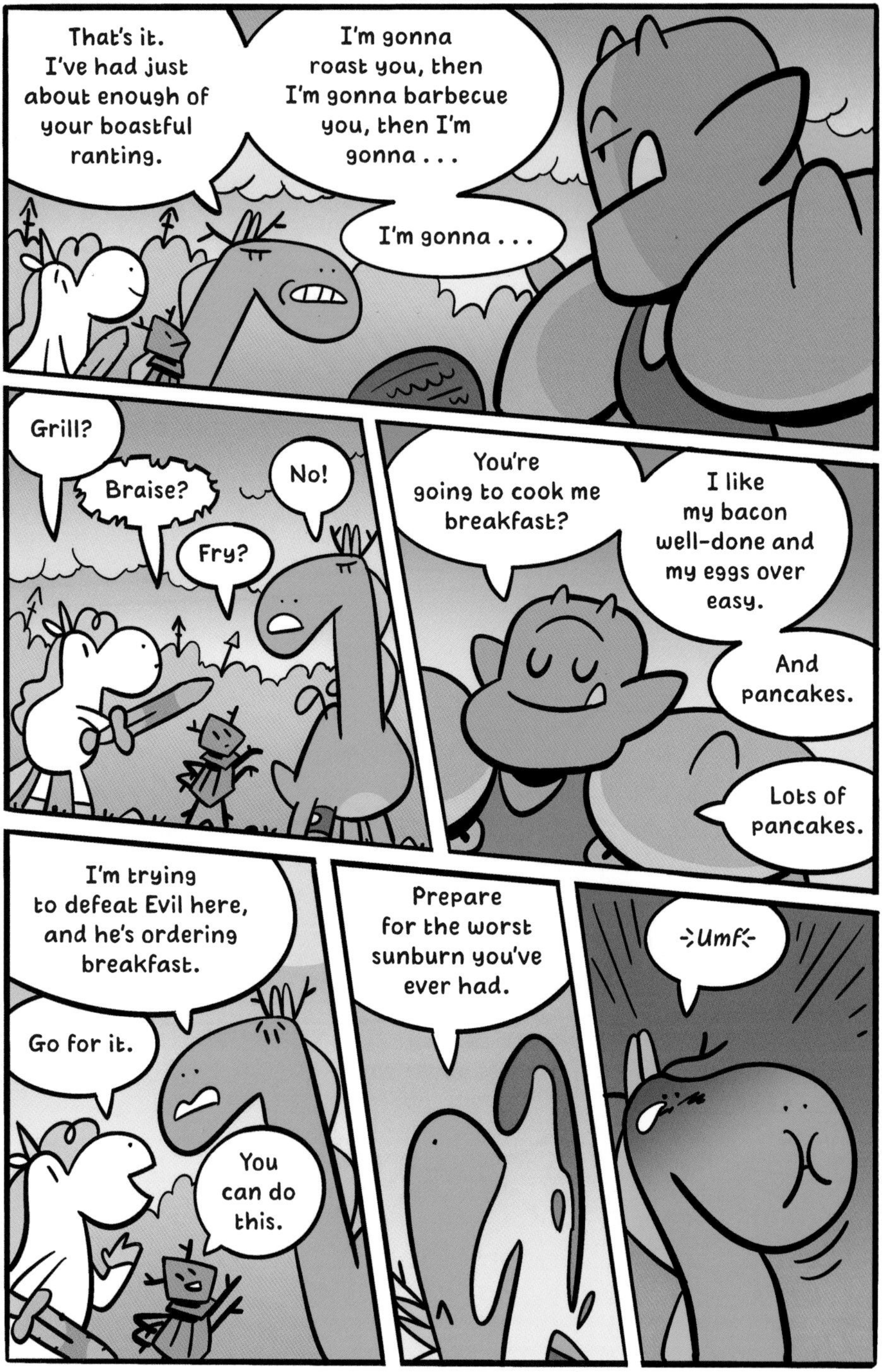
That's it. I've had just about enough of your boastful ranting.
I'm gonna roast you, then I'm gonna barbecue you, then I'm gonna . . .
I'm gonna . . .
Grill?
Braise?
Fry?
No!
You're going to cook me breakfast?
I like my bacon well-done and my eggs over easy.
And pancakes.
Lots of pancakes.
I'm trying to defeat Evil here, and he's ordering breakfast.
Go for it.
You can do this.
Prepare for the worst sunburn you've ever had.
Umf

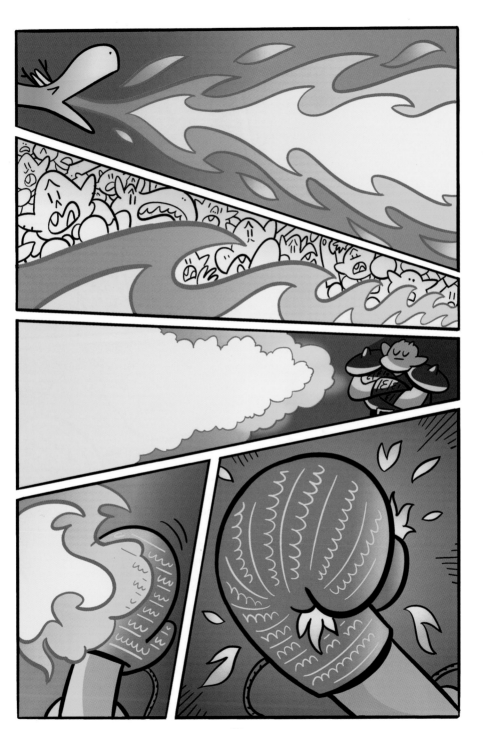

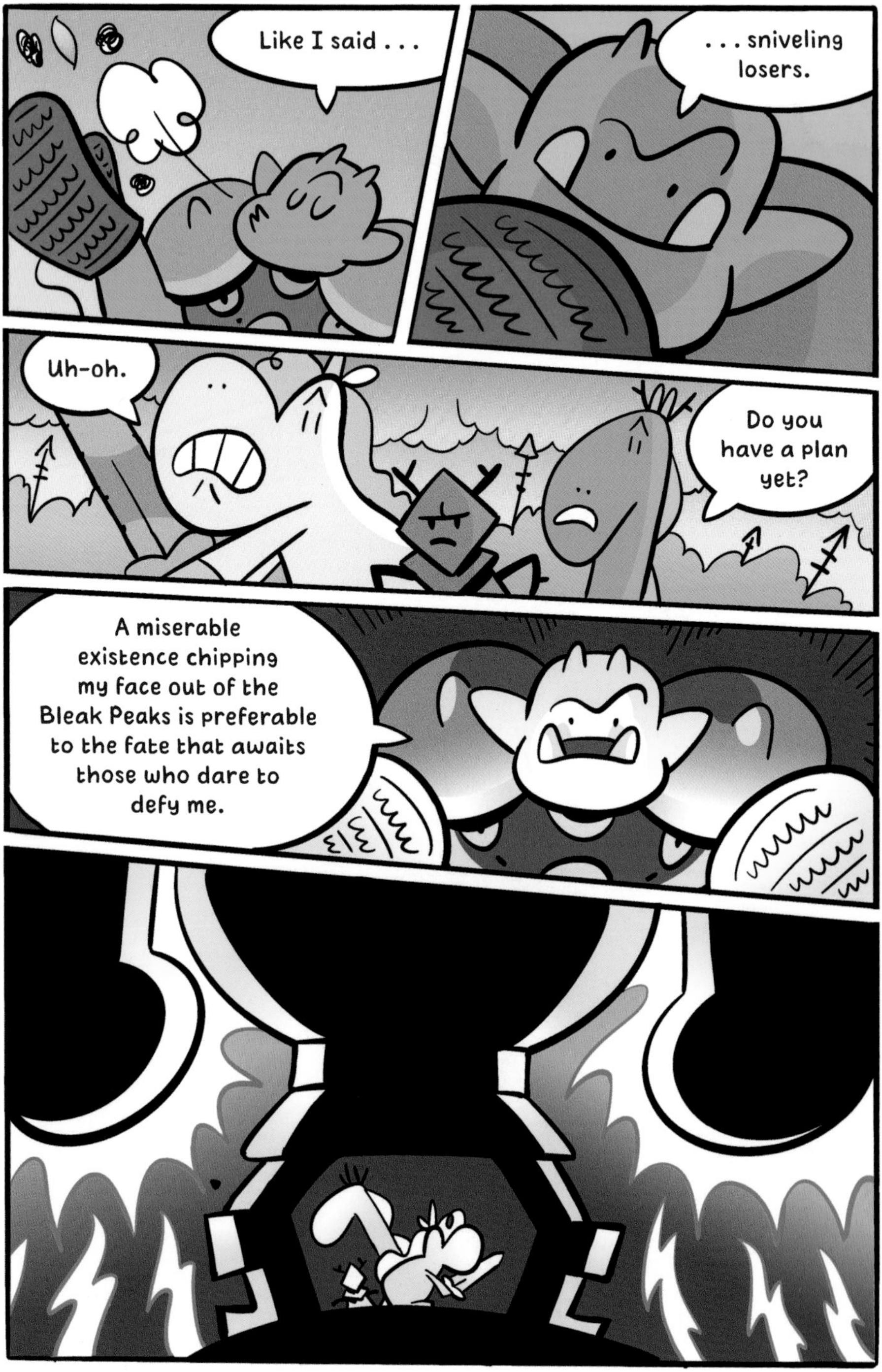
Like I said . . .
. . . sniveling losers.
Uh-oh.
Do you have a plan yet?
A miserable existence chipping my face out of the Bleak Peaks is preferable to the fate that awaits those who dare to defy me.

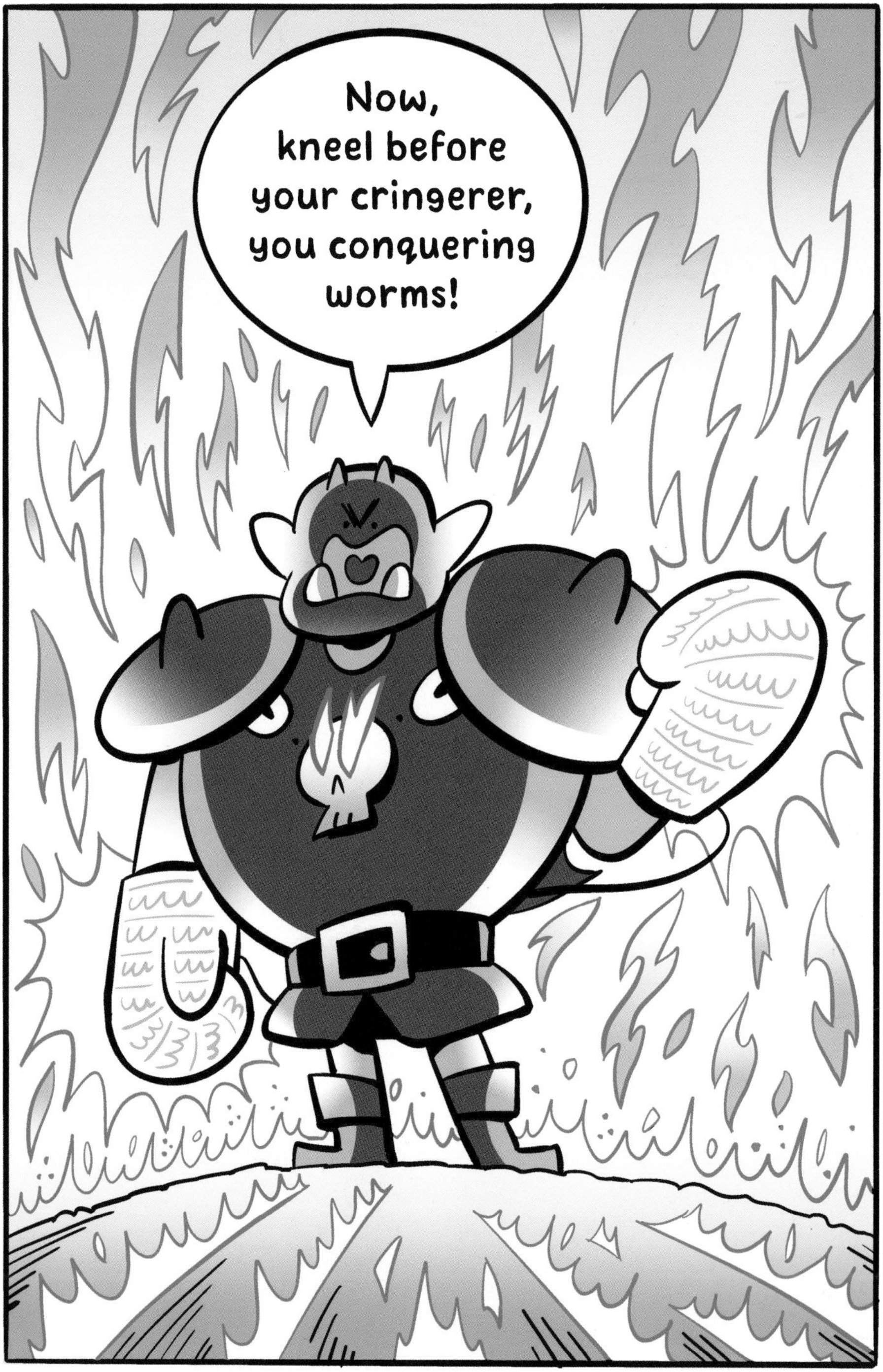
Now, kneel before your cringerer, you conquering worms!

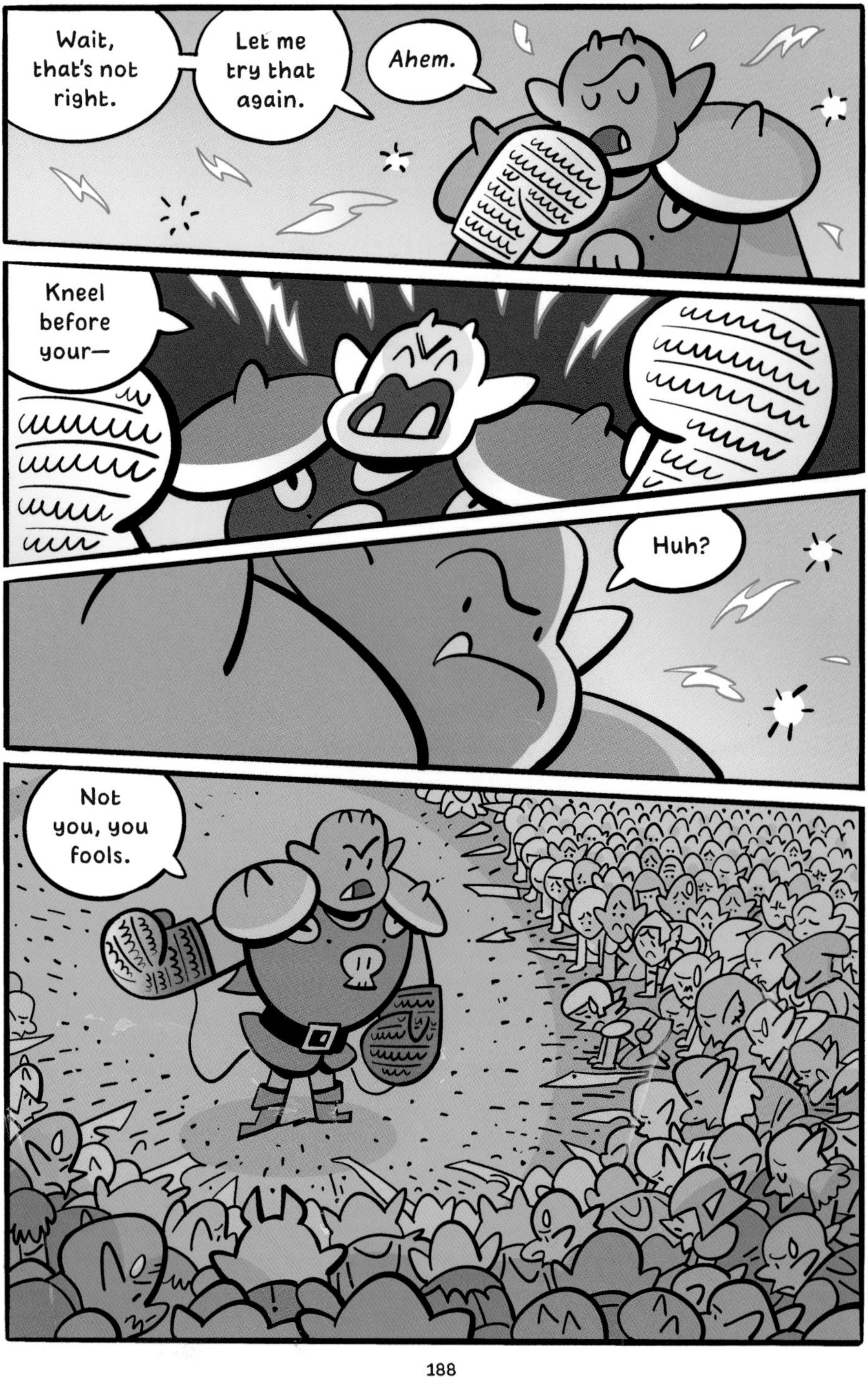

Wait, that's not right.
Let me try that again.
Ahem.
Kneel before your—
Huh?
Not you, you fools.

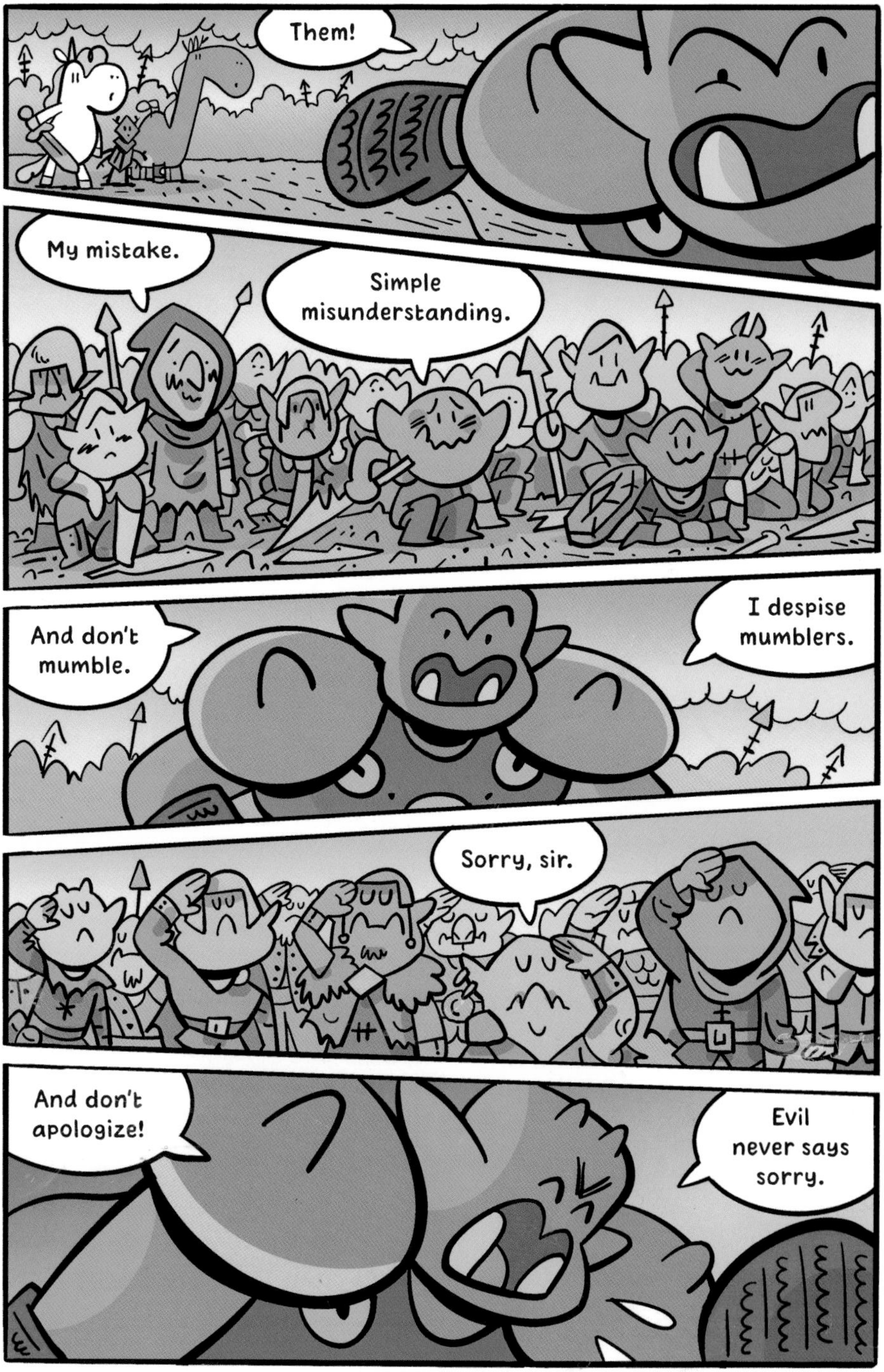
Them!
My mistake.
Simple misunderstanding.
And don't mumble.
I despise mumblers.
Sorry, sir.
And don't apologize!
Evil never says sorry.

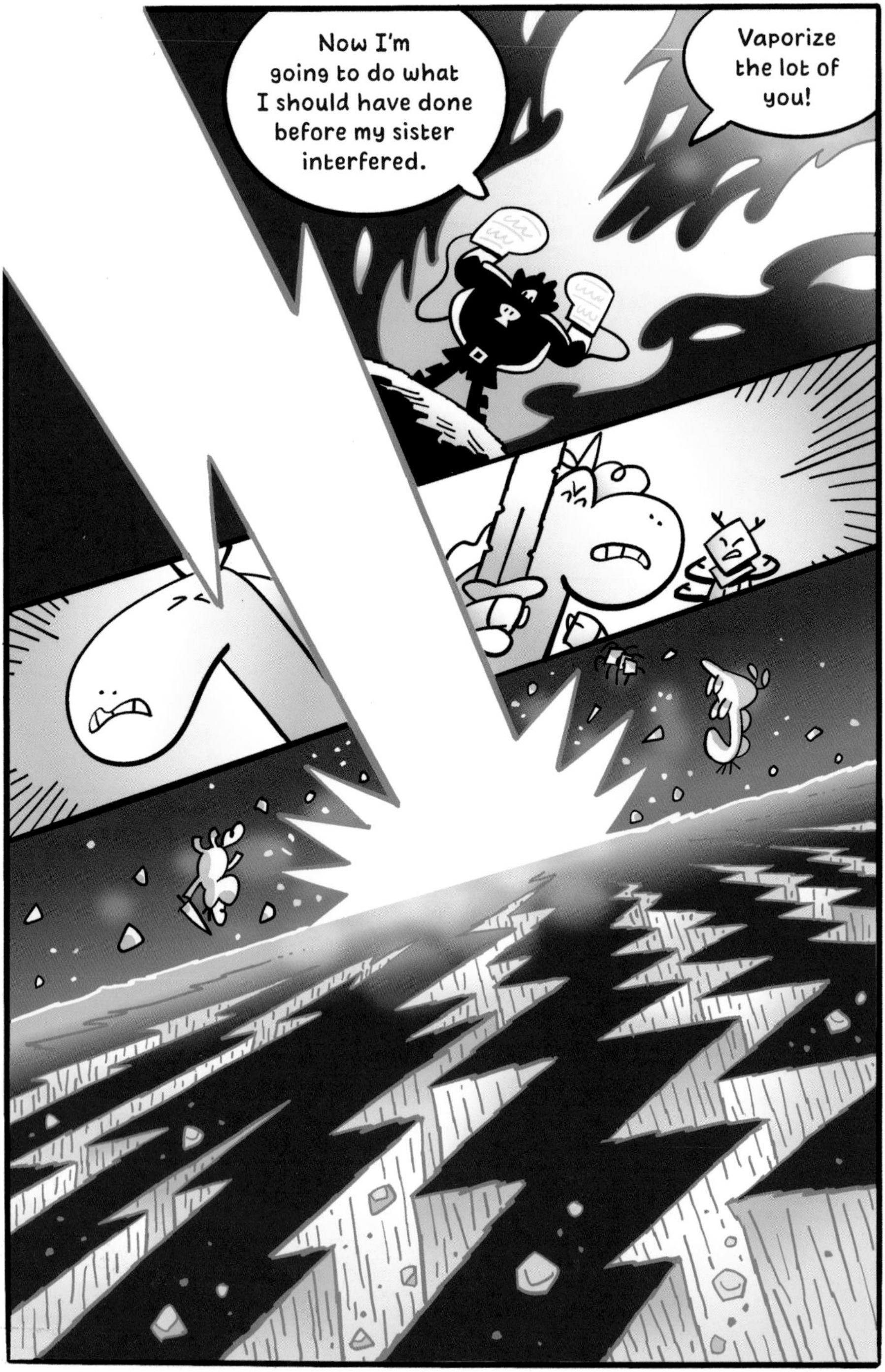
Now I'm going to do what I should have done before my sister interfered.
Vaporize the lot of you!

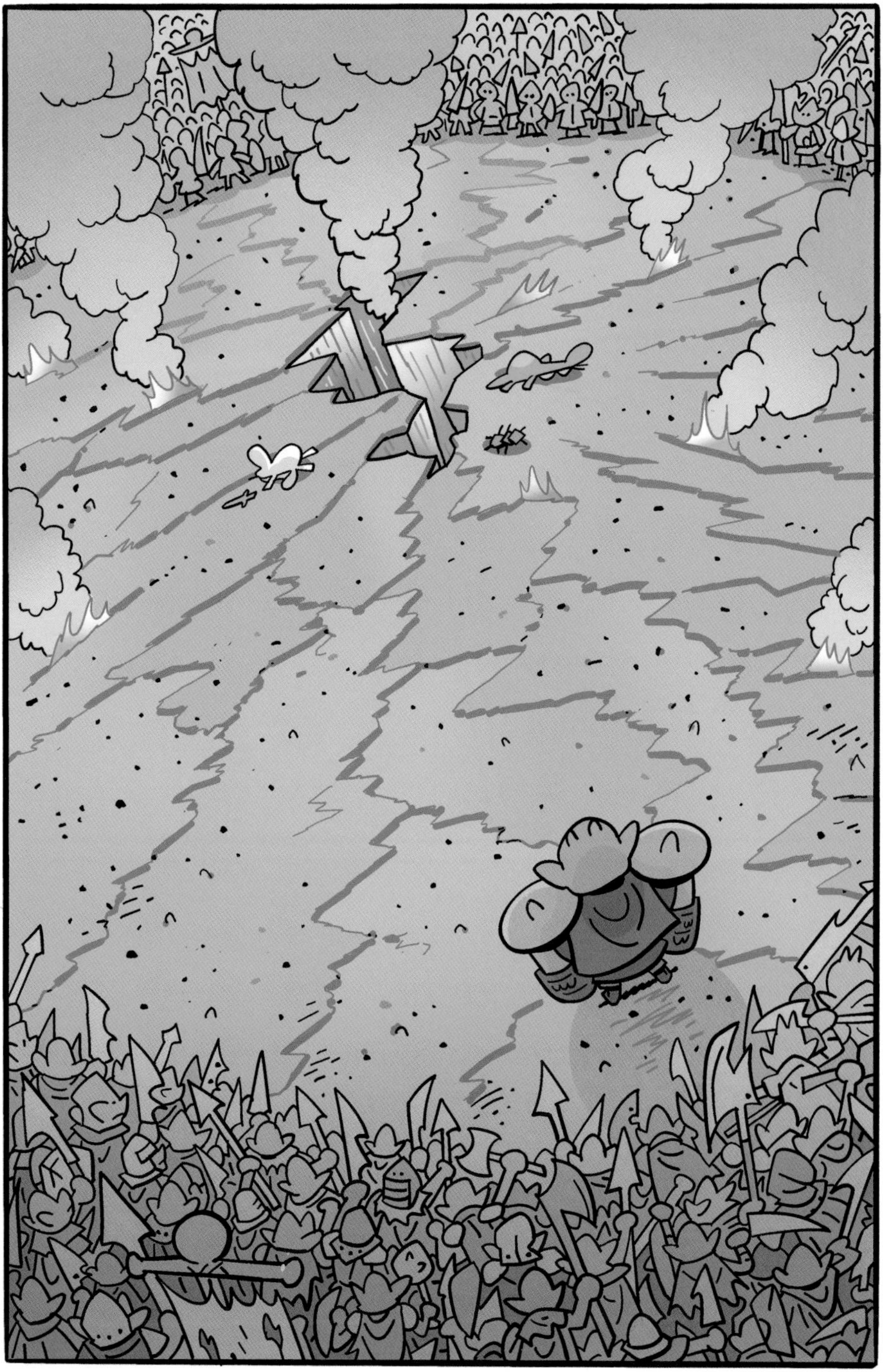

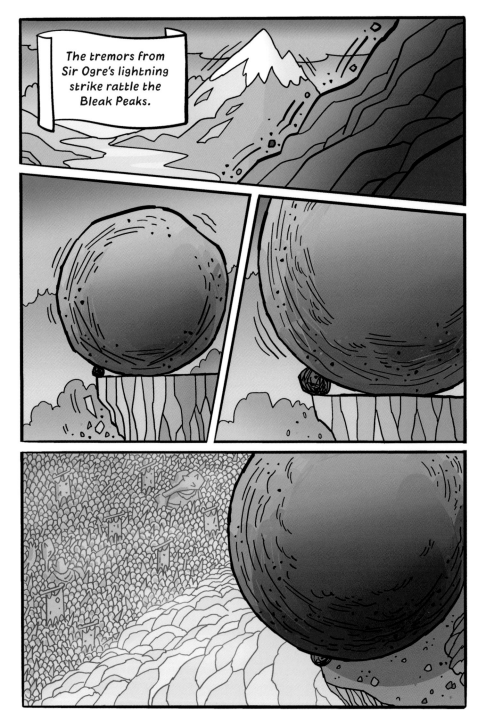

The tremors from Sir Ogre's lightning strike rattle the Bleak Peaks.

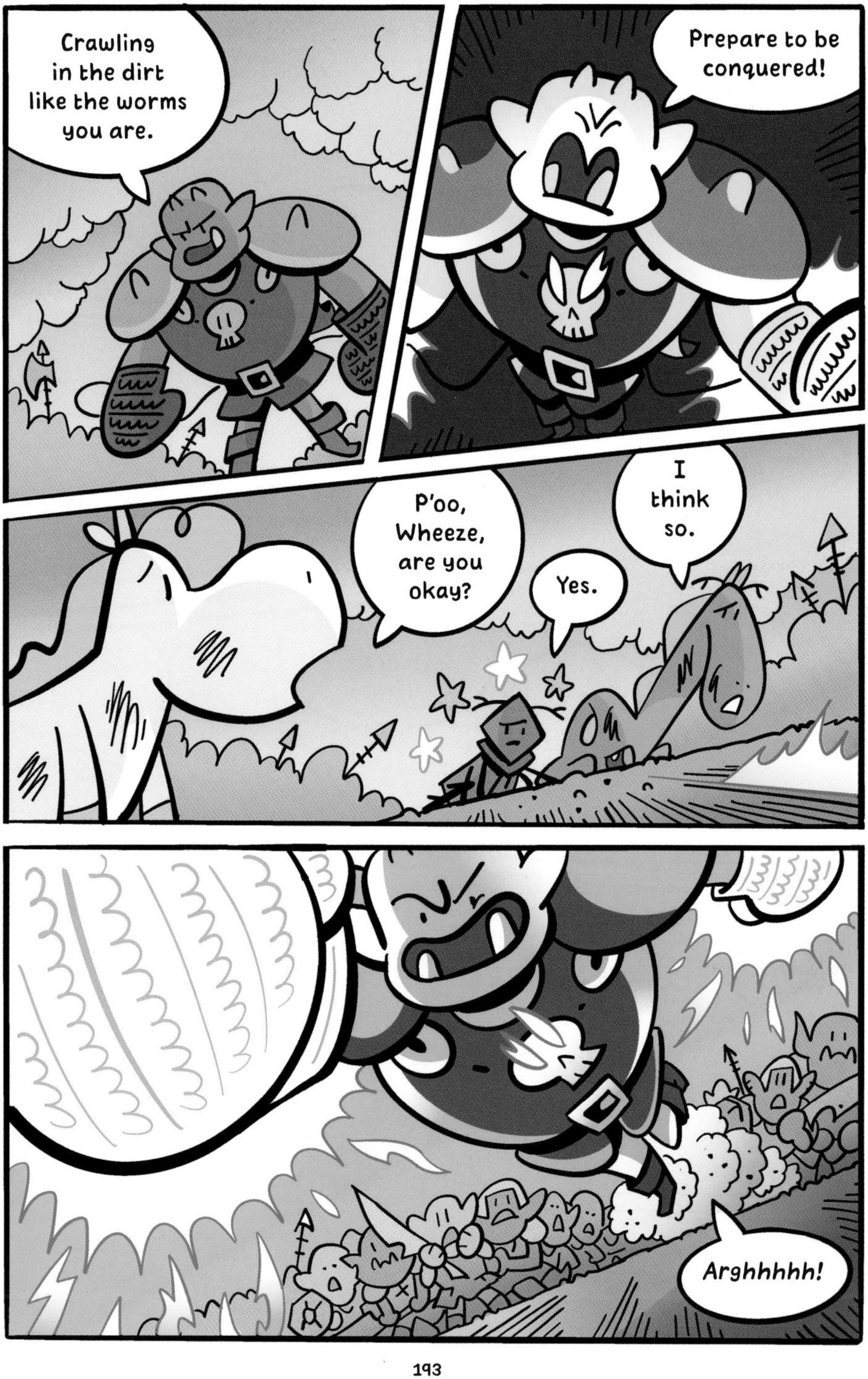
Crawling in the dirt like the worms you are.
Prepare to be conquered!
P'oo, Wheeze, are you okay?
Yes.
I think so.
Arghhhhh!

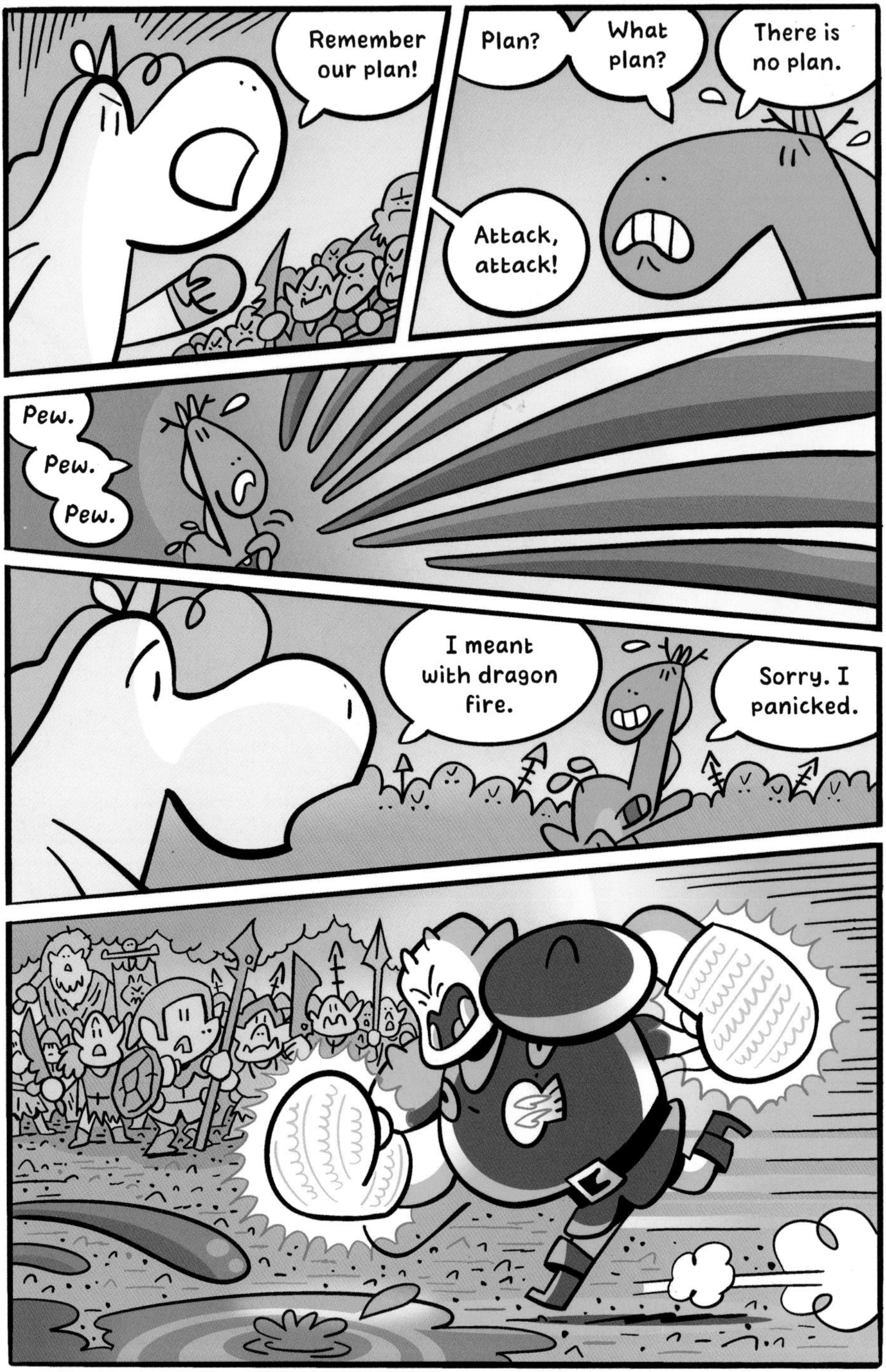

Remember our plan!
Plan?
What plan?
There is no plan.
Attack, attack!
Pew.
Pew.
Pew.
I meant with dragon fire.
Sorry. I panicked.

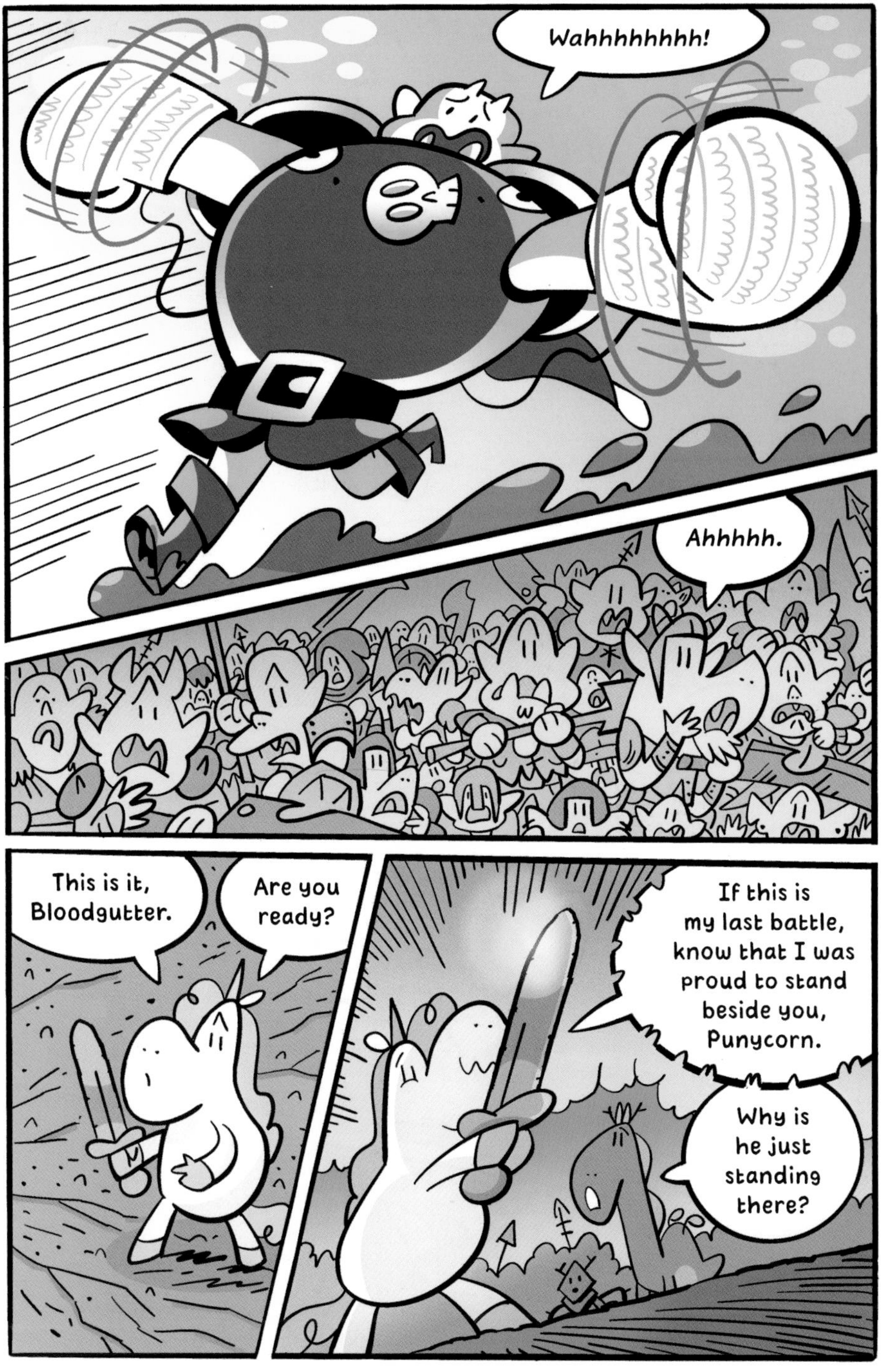
Wahhhhhhhh!
Ahhhhh.
This is it, Bloodgutter.
Are you ready?
If this is my last battle, know that I was proud to stand beside you, Punycorn.
Why is he just standing there?

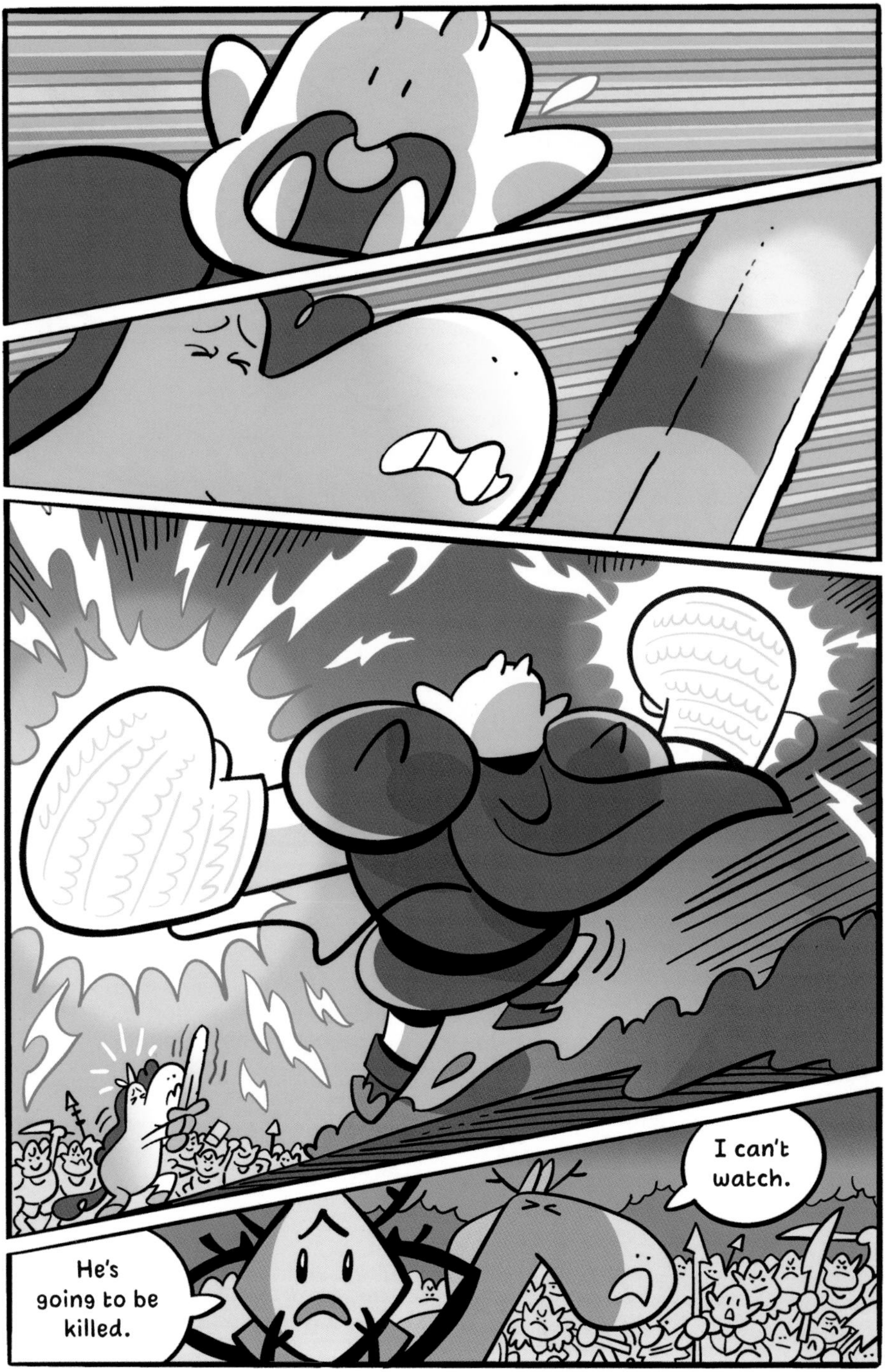
I can't watch.
He's going to be killed.

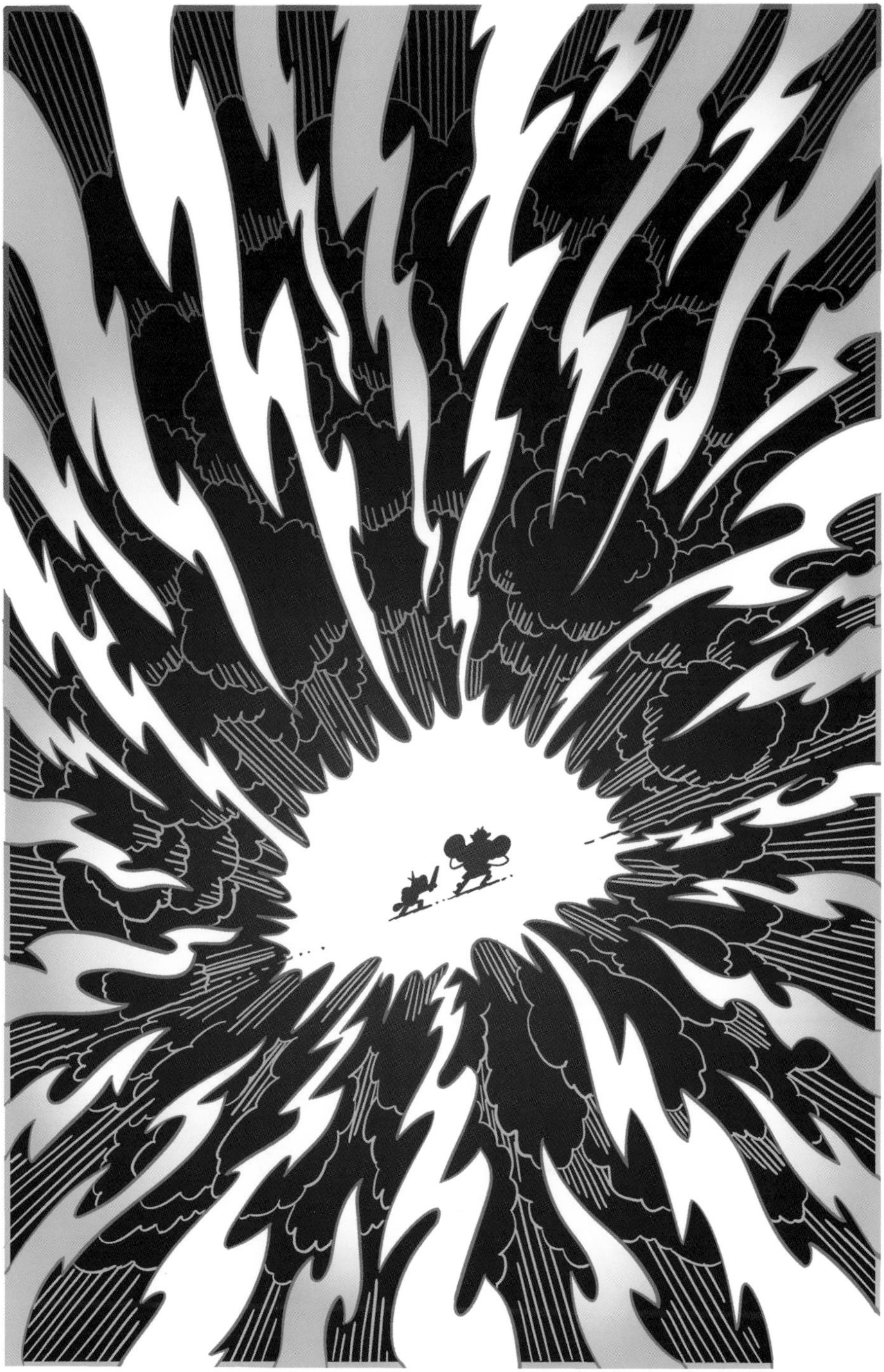

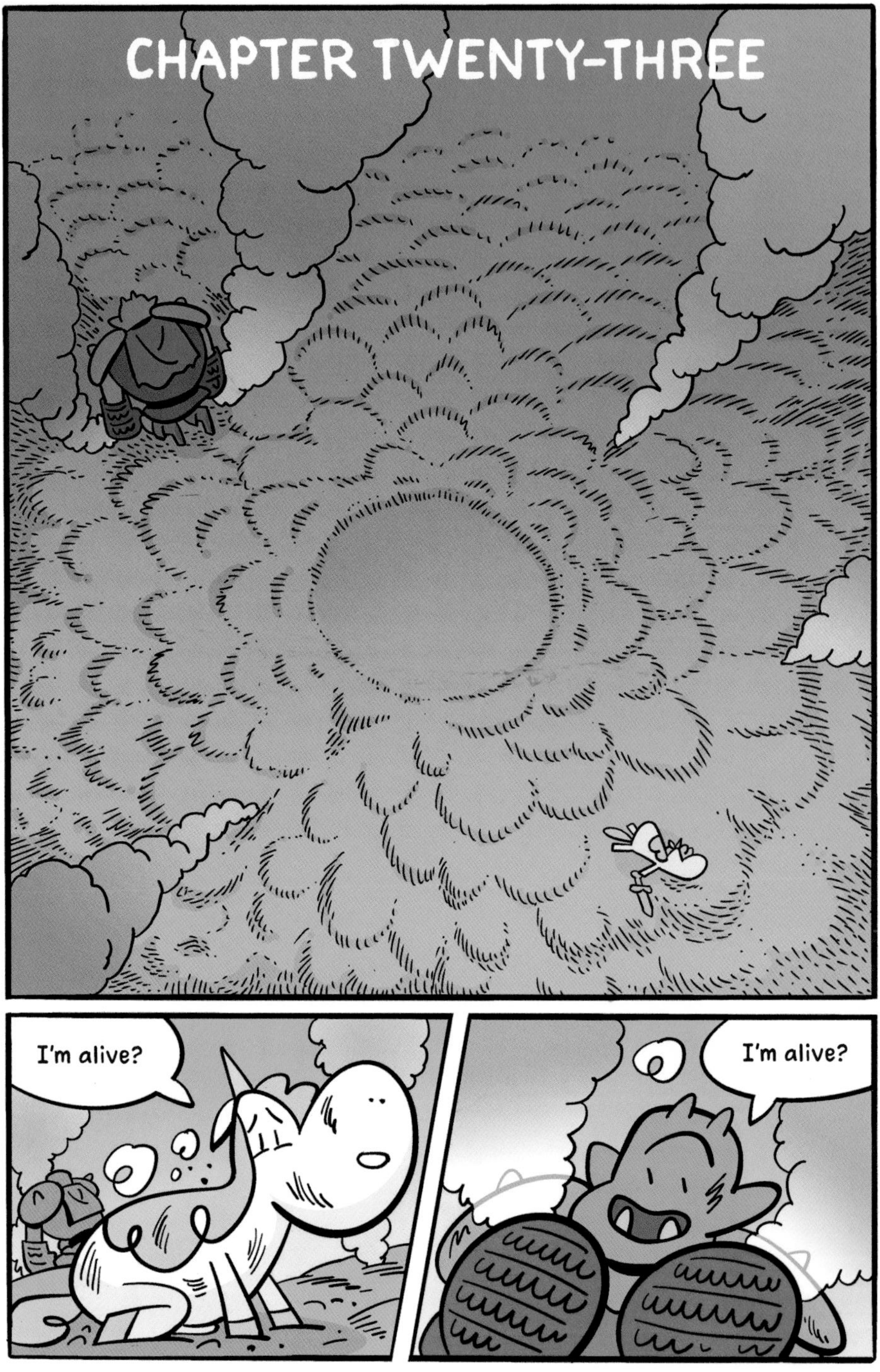
CHAPTER TWENTY-THREE
I'm alive?
I'm alive?

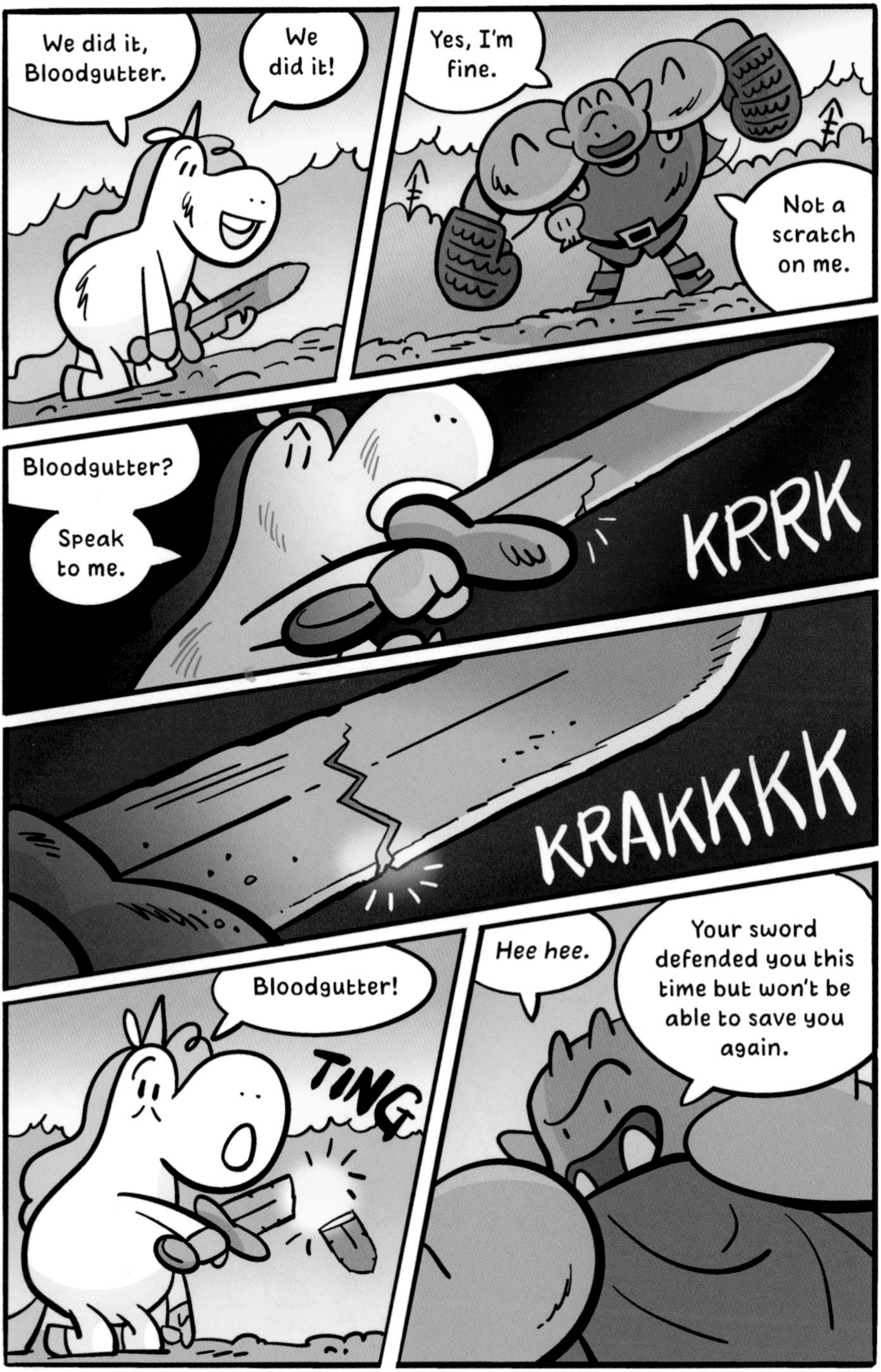
We did it, Bloodgutter.
We did it!
Yes, I'm fine.
Not a scratch on me.
Bloodgutter?
Speak to me.
KRRK
KRAKKKK
Bloodgutter!
TING
Hee hee.
Your sword defended you this time but won't be able to save you again.

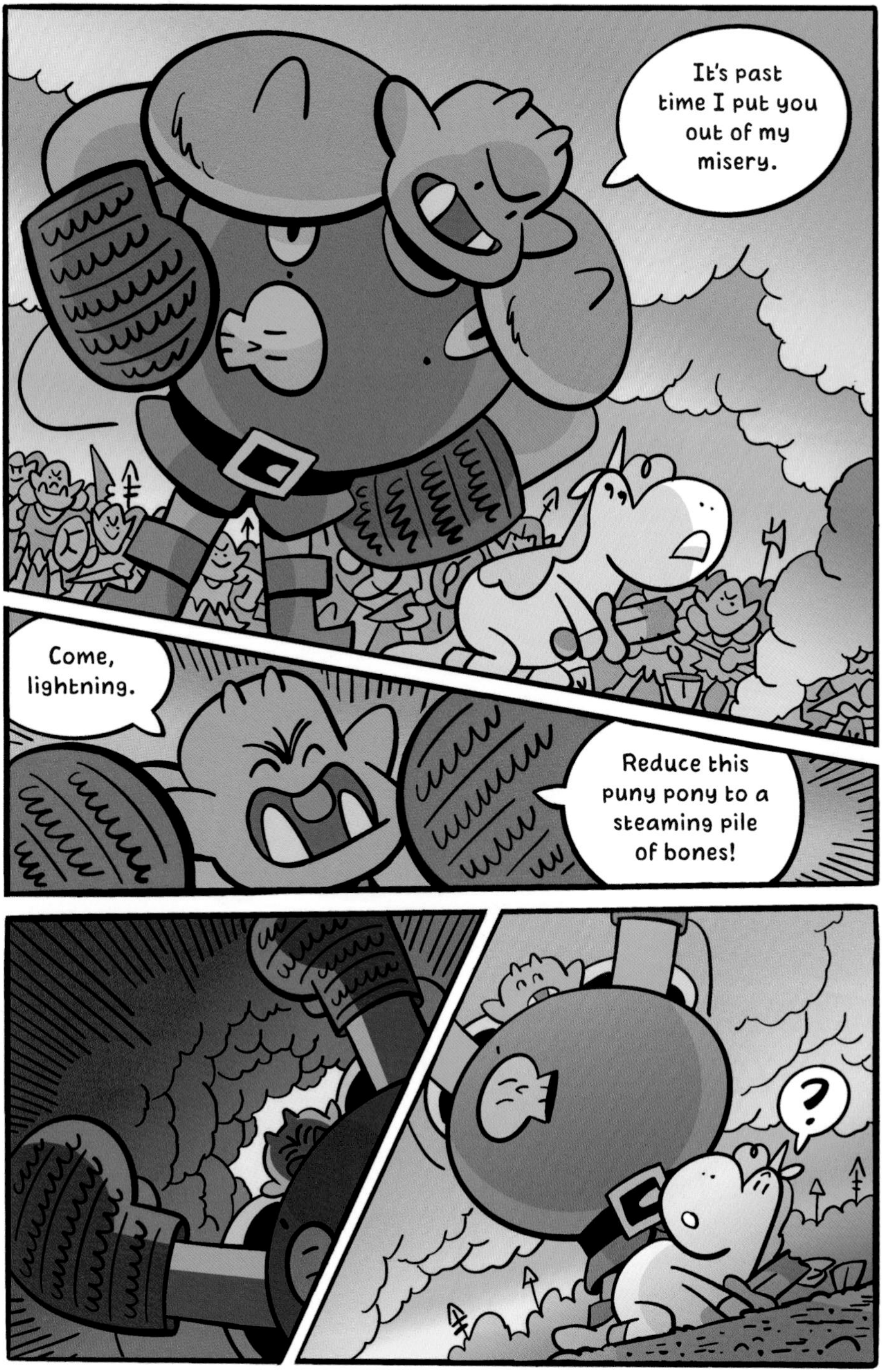
It's past time I put you out of my misery.
Come, lightning.
Reduce this puny pony to a steaming pile of bones!
?

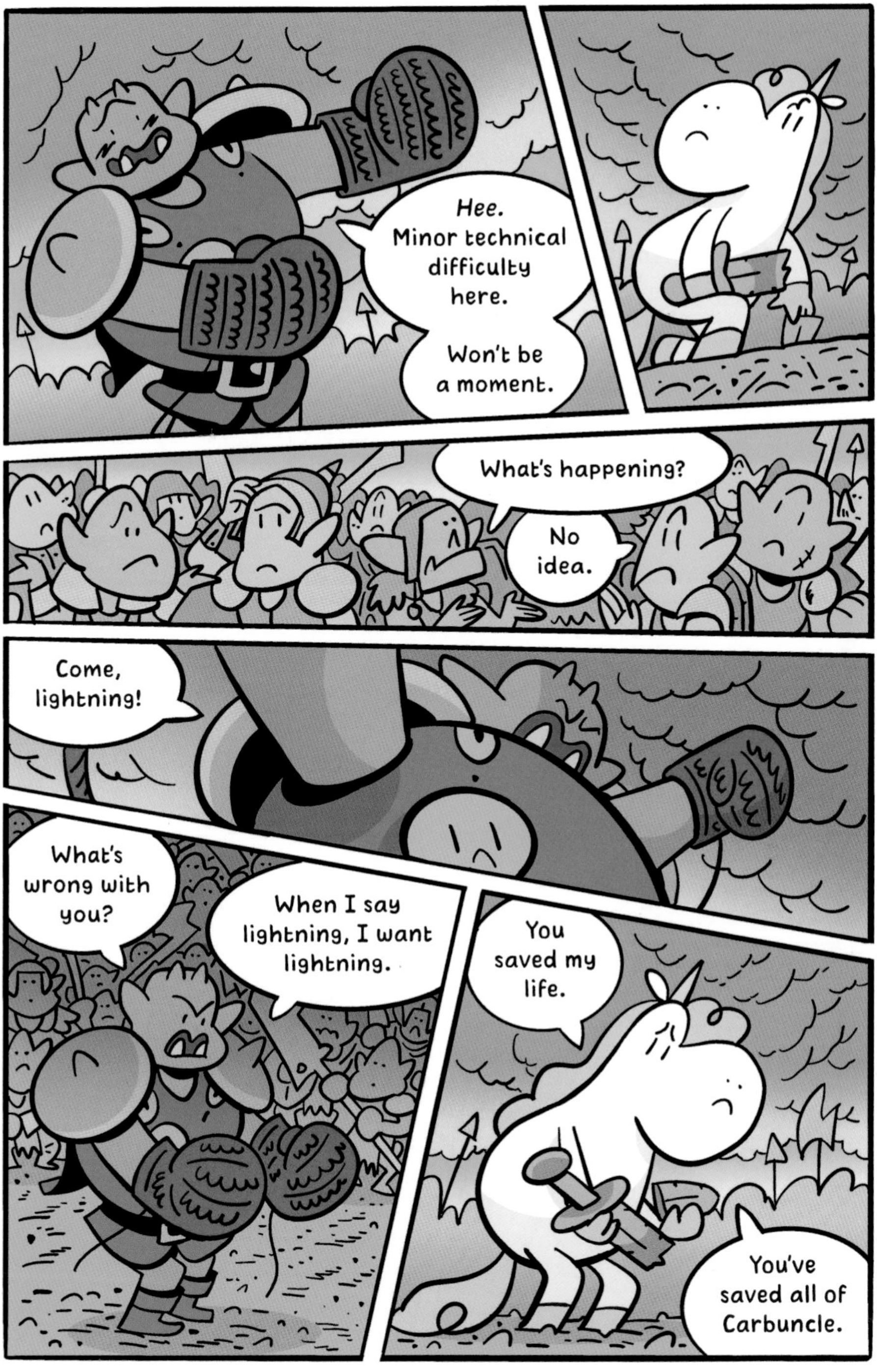

Hee.
Minor technical difficulty here.
Won't be a moment.
What's happening?
No idea.
Come, lightning!
What's wrong with you?
When I say lightning, I want lightning.
You saved my life.
You've saved all of Carbuncle.

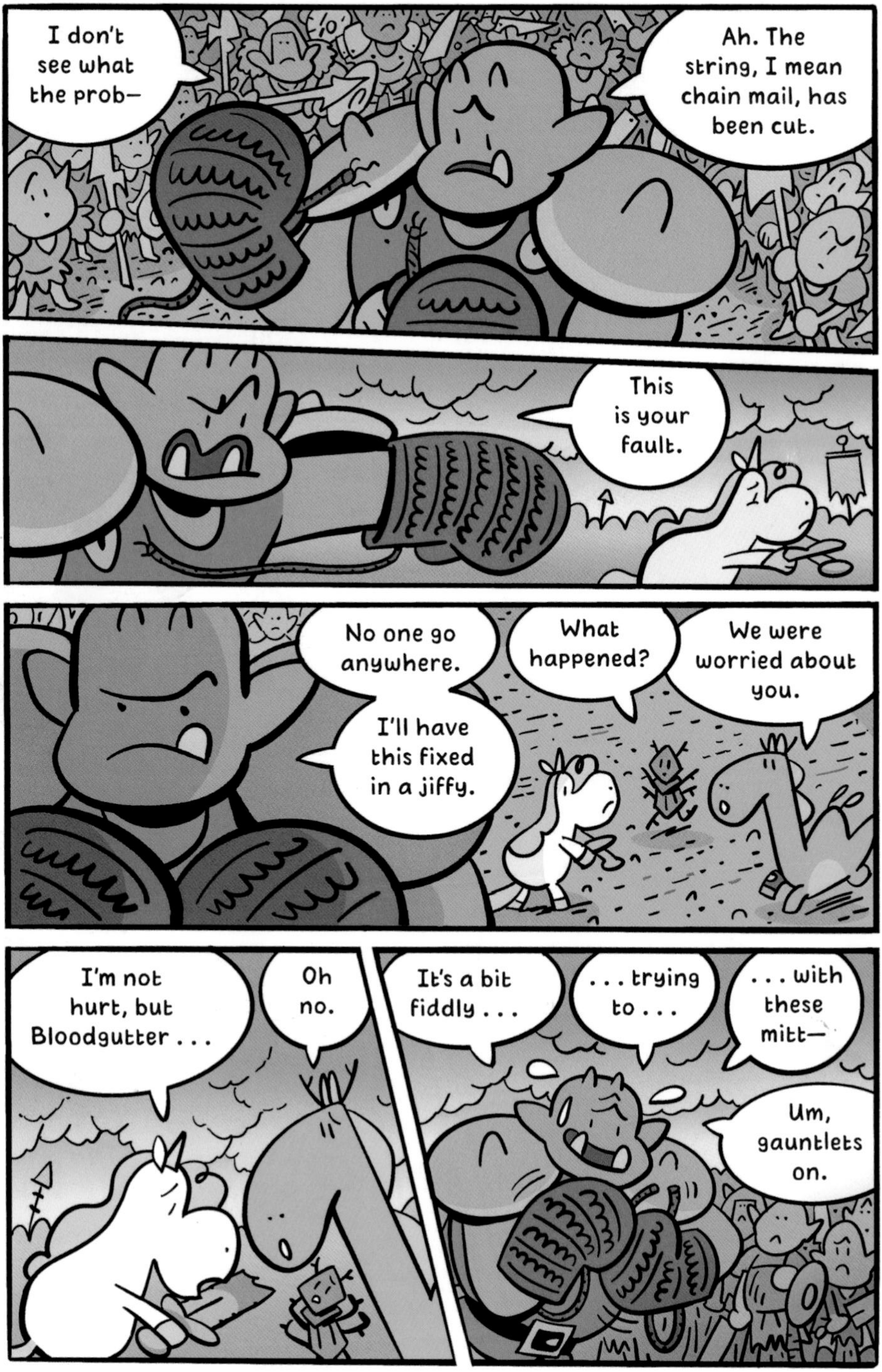
I don't see what the prob—
Ah. The string, I mean chain mail, has been cut.
This is your fault.
No one go anywhere.
I'll have this fixed in a jiffy.
What happened?
We were worried about you.
I'm not hurt, but Bloodgutter . . .
Oh no.
It's a bit fiddly . . .
. . . trying to . . .
. . . with these mitt—
Um, gauntlets on.

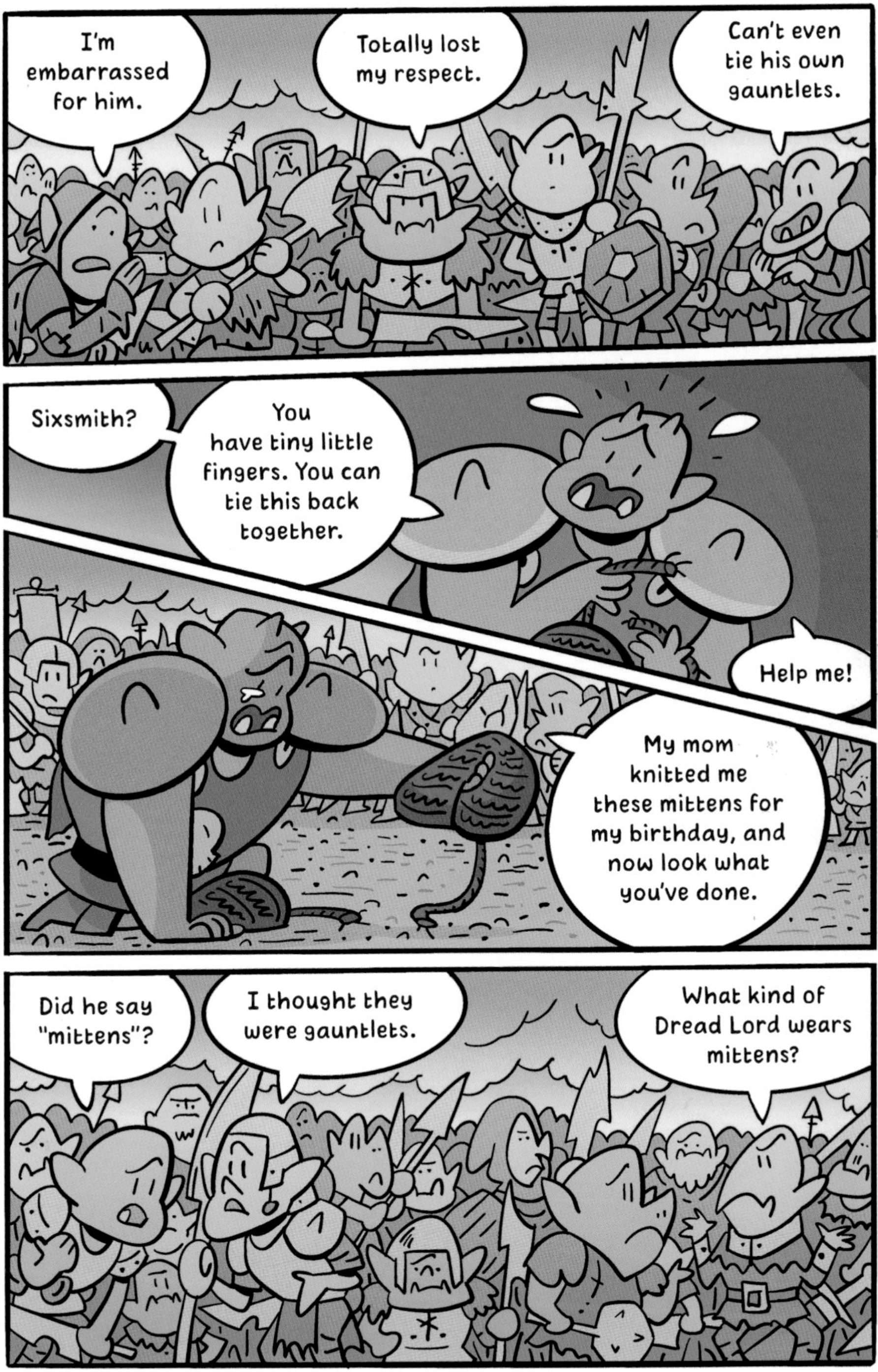
I'm embarrassed for him.
Totally lost my respect.
Can't even tie his own gauntlets.
Sixsmith?
You have tiny little fingers. You can tie this back together.
Help me!
My mom knitted me these mittens for my birthday, and now look what you've done.
Did he say "mittens"?
I thought they were gauntlets.
What kind of Dread Lord wears mittens?

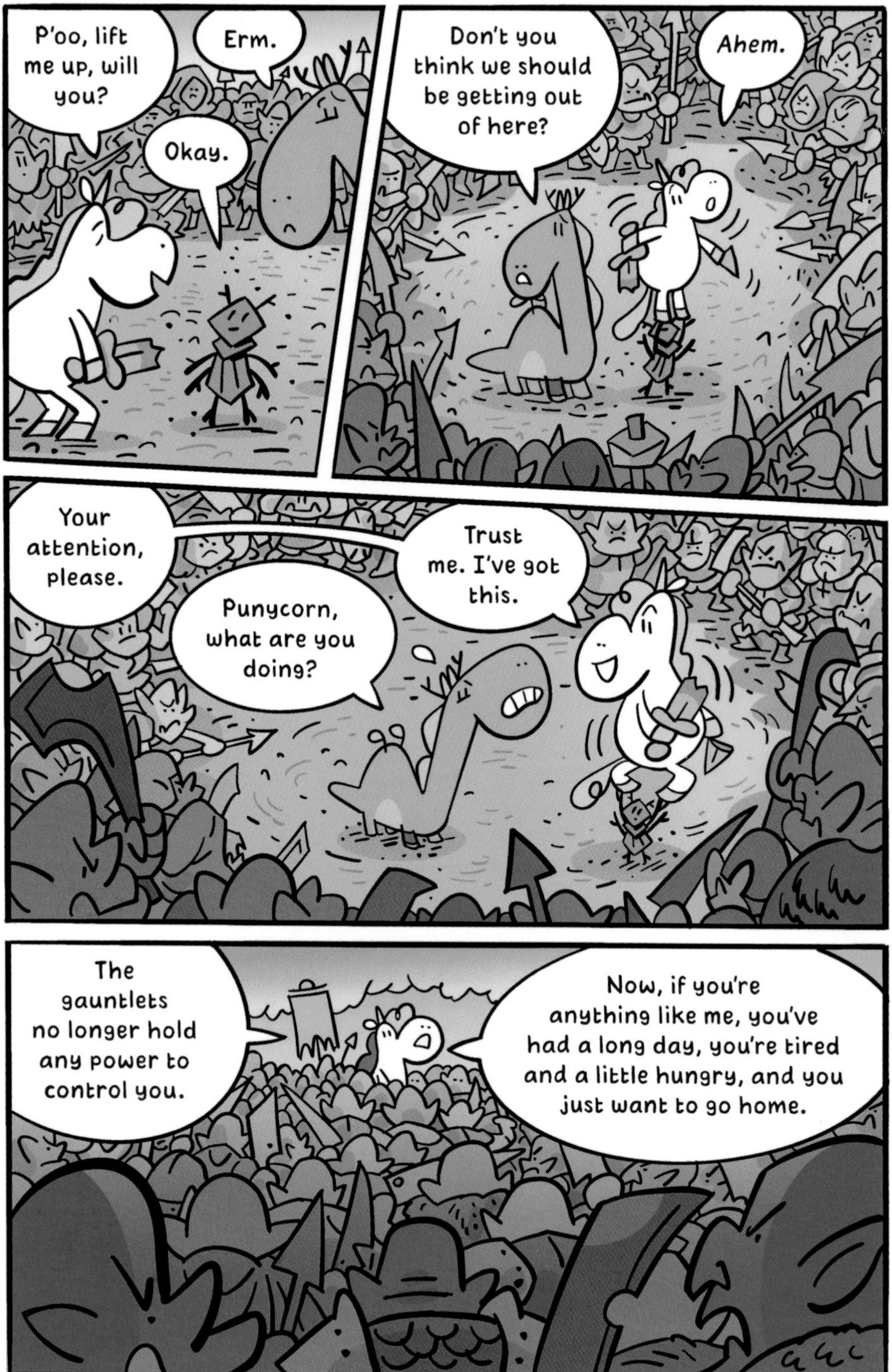
P'oo, lift me up, will you?
Erm.
Okay.
Don't you think we should be getting out of here?
Ahem.
Your attention, please.
Trust me. I've got this.
Punycorn, what are you doing?
The gauntlets no longer hold any power to control you.
Now, if you're anything like me, you've had a long day, you're tired and a little hungry, and you just want to go home.

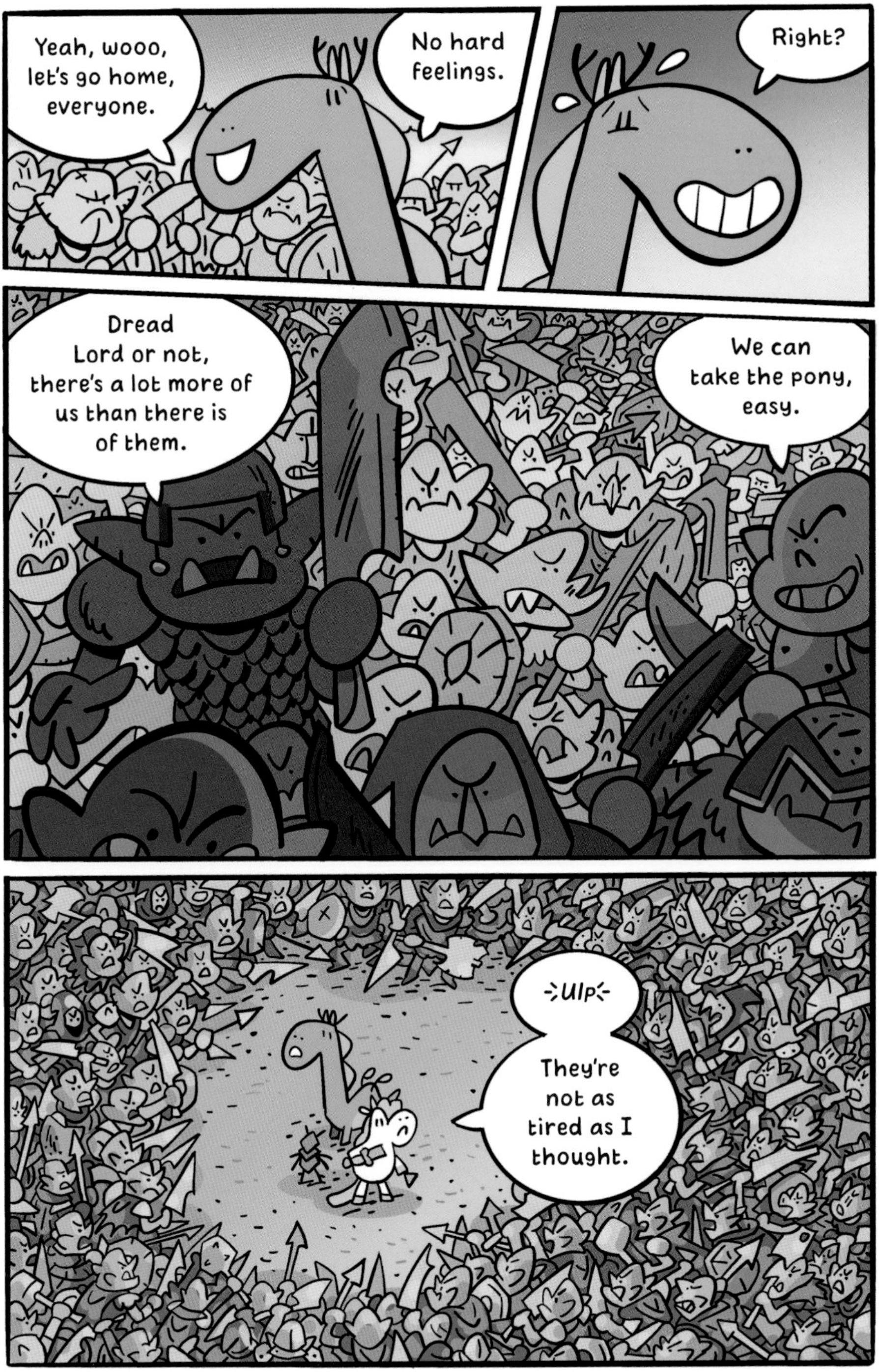
Yeah, wooo, let's go home, everyone.
No hard feelings.
Right?
Dread Lord or not, there's a lot more of us than there is of them.
We can take the pony, easy.
-Ulp-
They're not as tired as I thought.

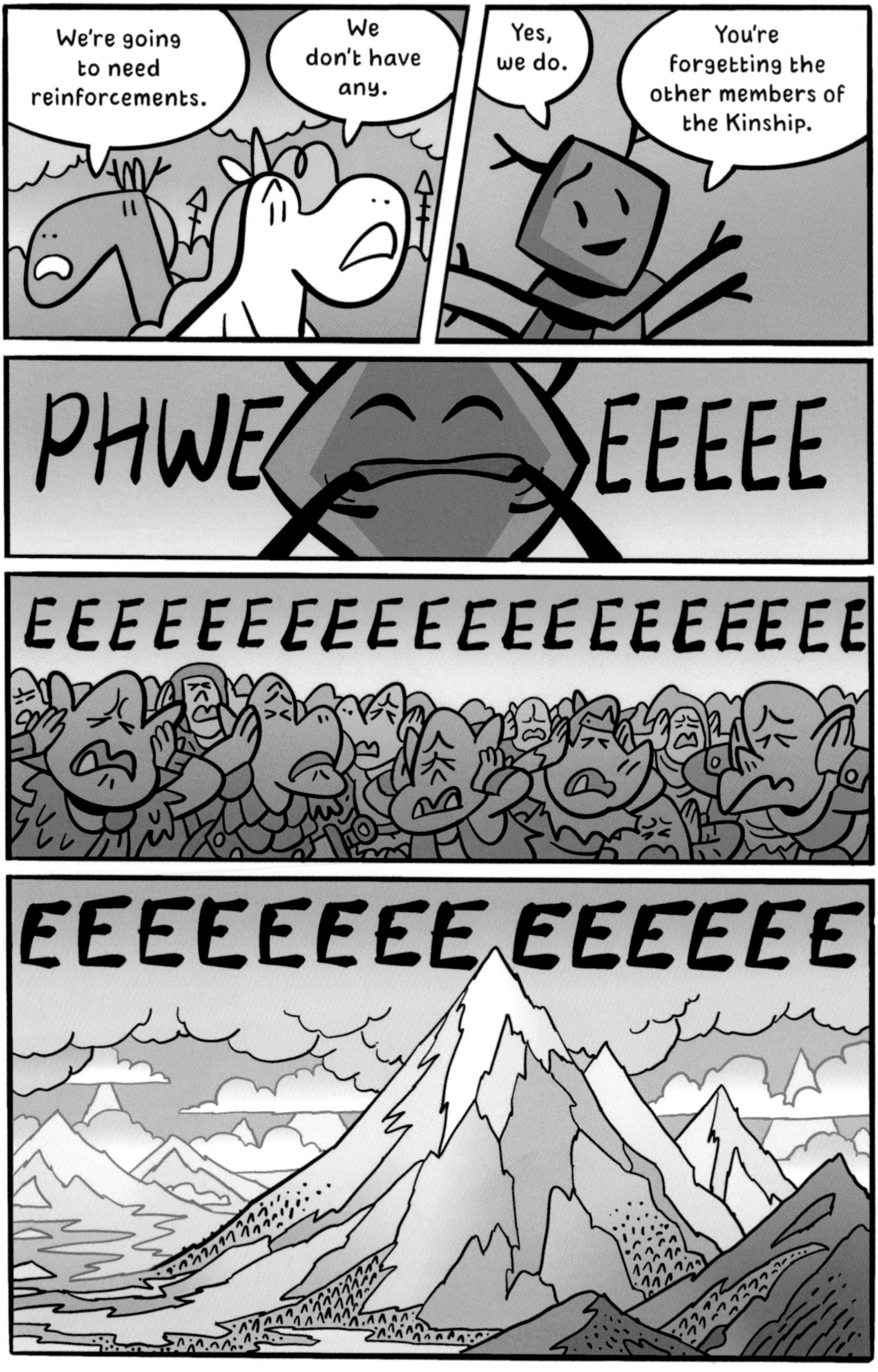
We're going to need reinforcements.
We don't have any.
Yes, we do.
You're forgetting the other members of the Kinship.
PHWEEEEEE
EEEEEEEEEEEEEEEEEEEE
EEEEEEEE EEEEEE

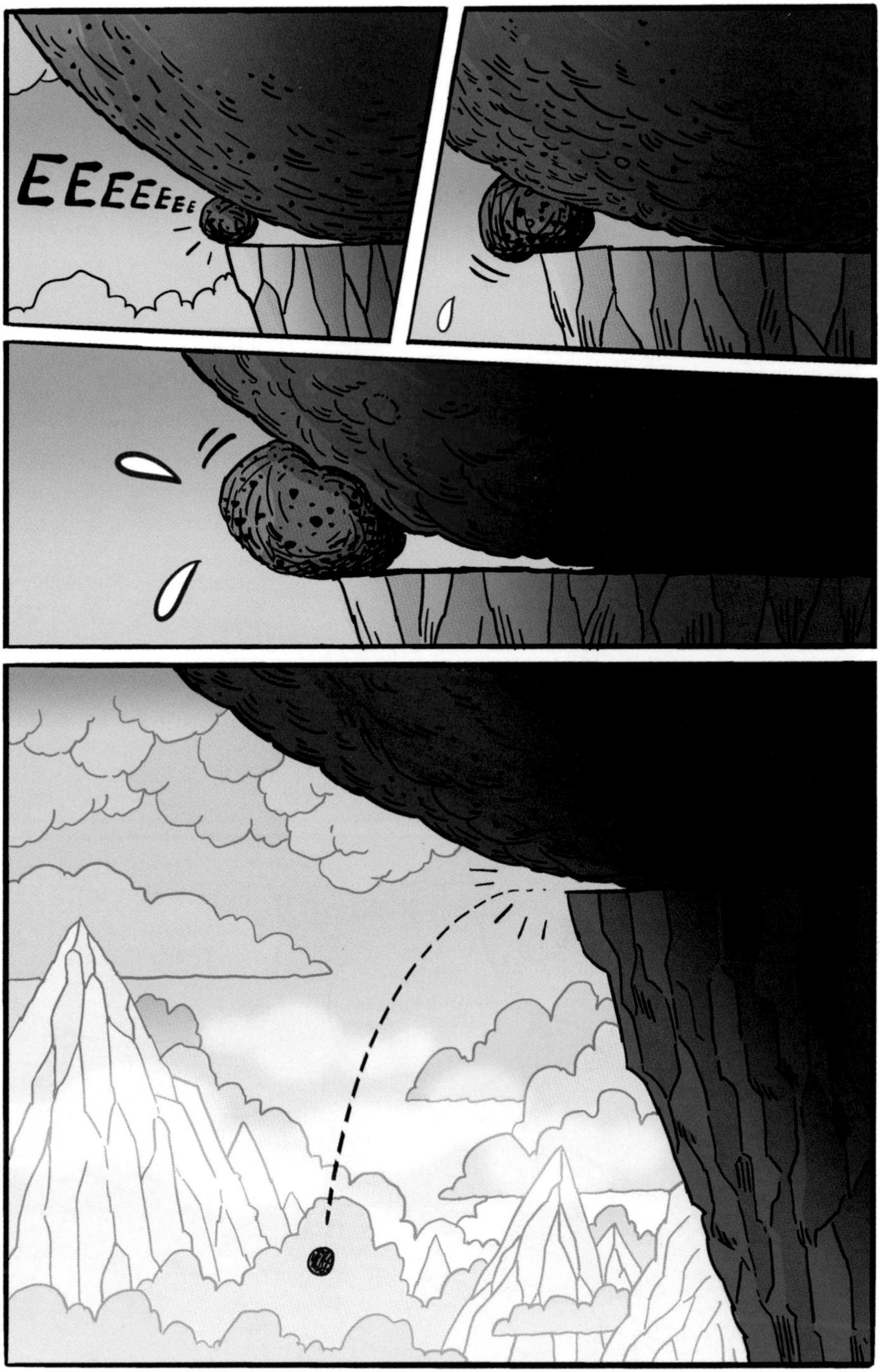
EEEEEEEE

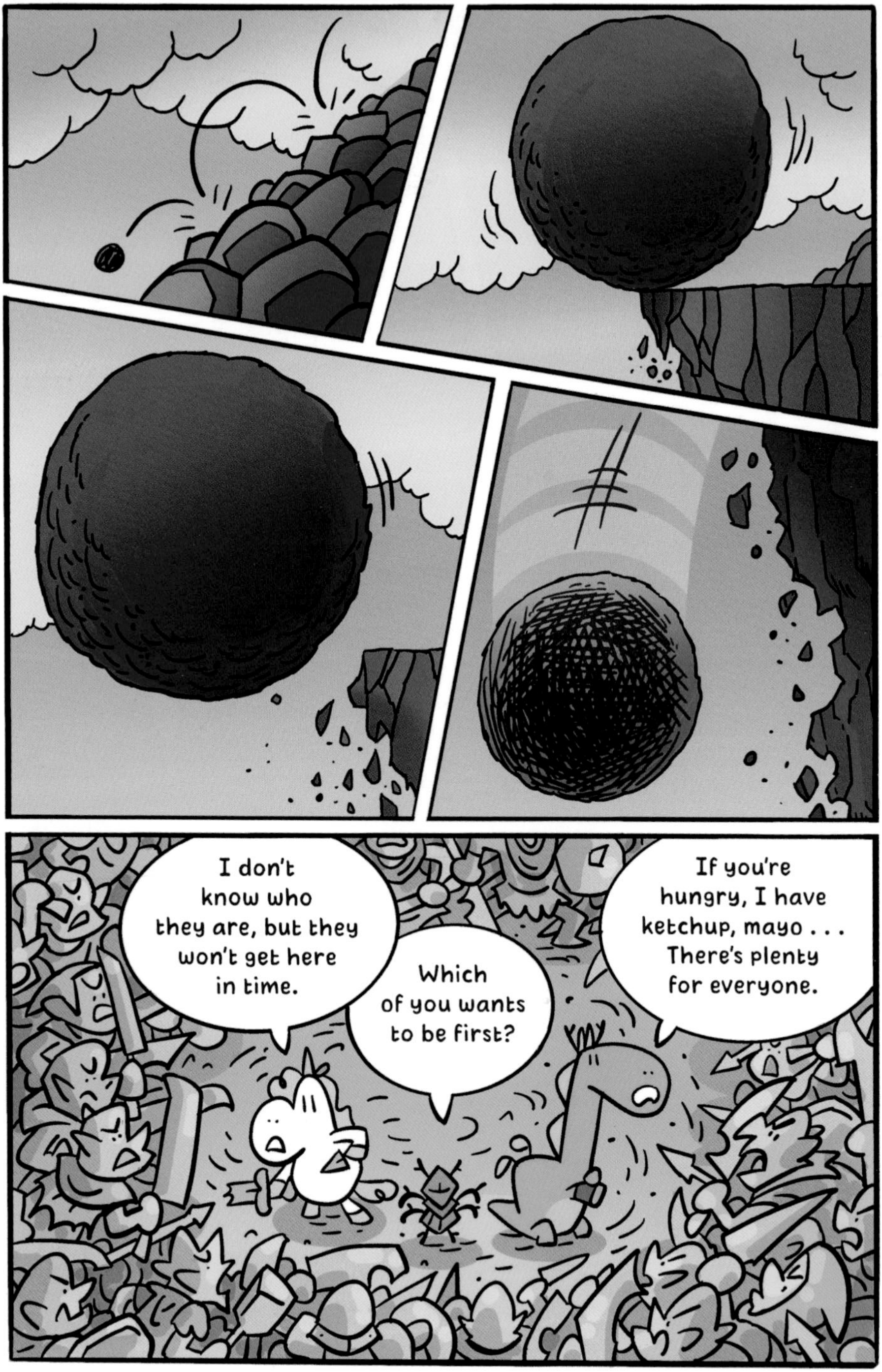
I don't know who they are, but they won't get here in time.
Which of you wants to be first?
If you're hungry, I have ketchup, mayo . . . There's plenty for everyone.

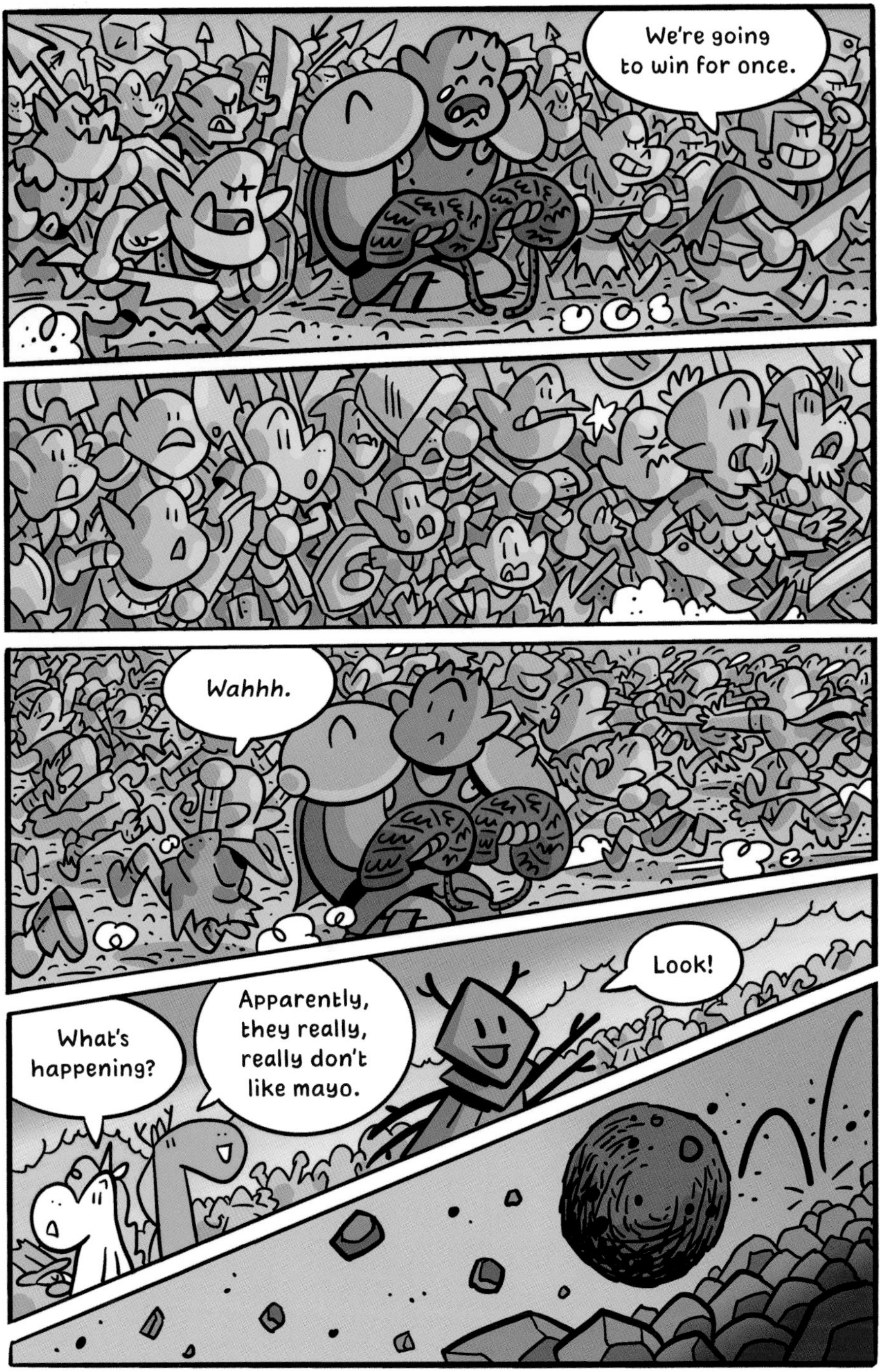

We're going to win for once.
Wahhh.
What's happening?
Apparently, they really, really don't like mayo.
Look!

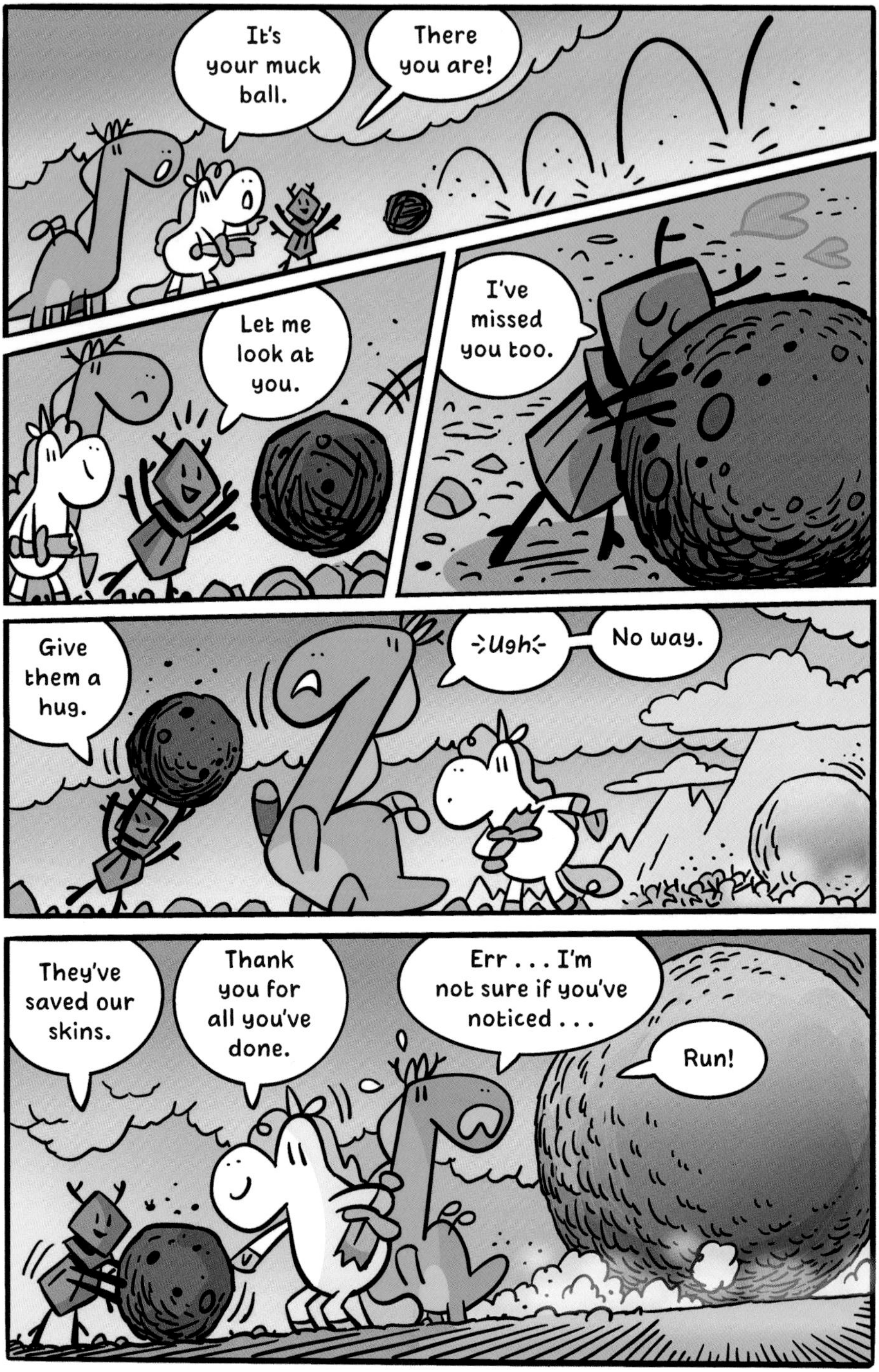

It's your muck ball.
There you are!
Let me look at you.
I've missed you too.
Give them a hug.
-Ugh-
No way.
They've saved our skins.
Thank you for all you've done.
Err . . . I'm not sure if you've noticed . . .
Run!

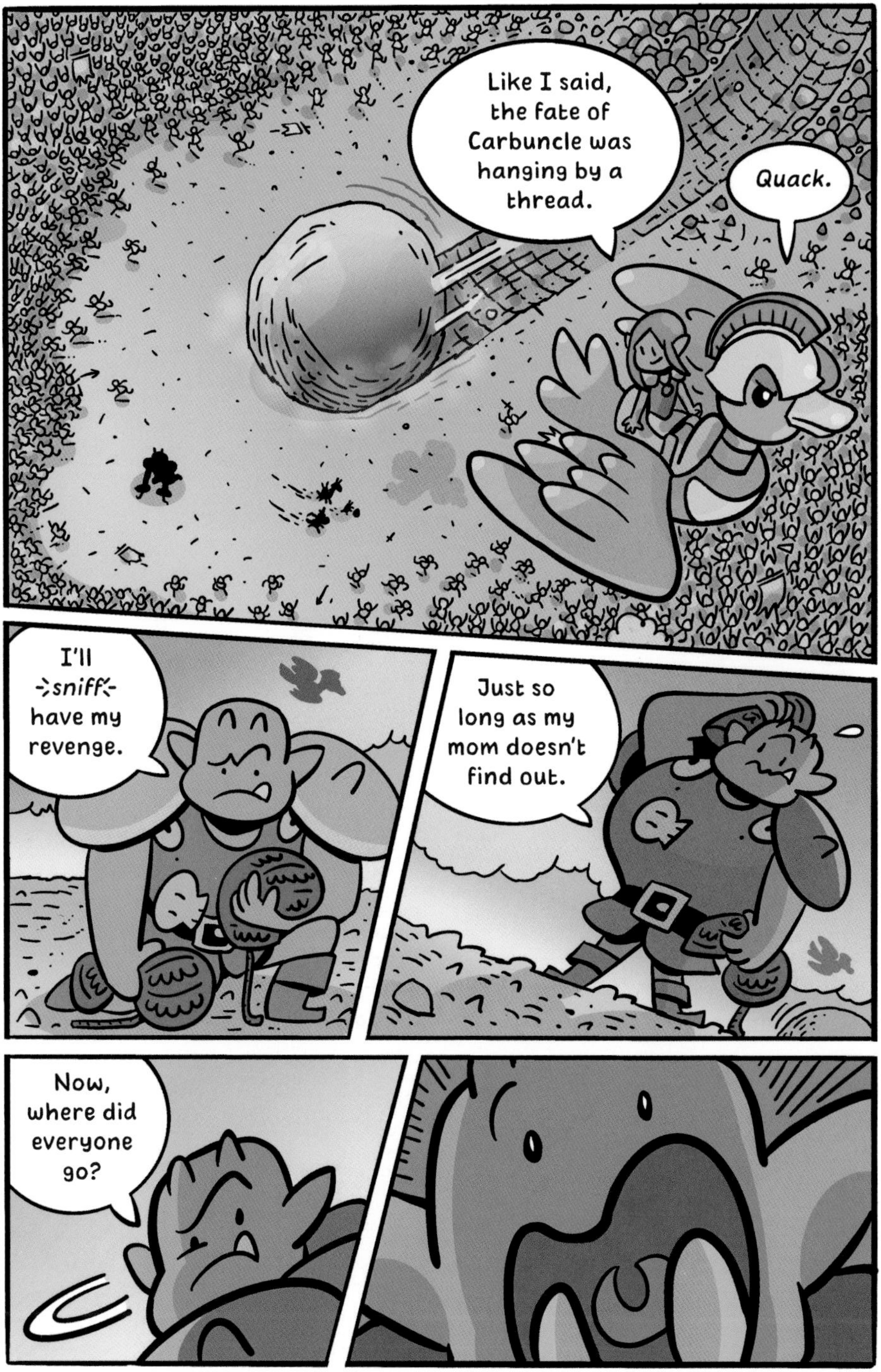
Like I said, the fate of Carbuncle was hanging by a thread.
Quack.
I'll -sniff- have my revenge.
Just so long as my mom doesn't find out.
Now, where did everyone go?

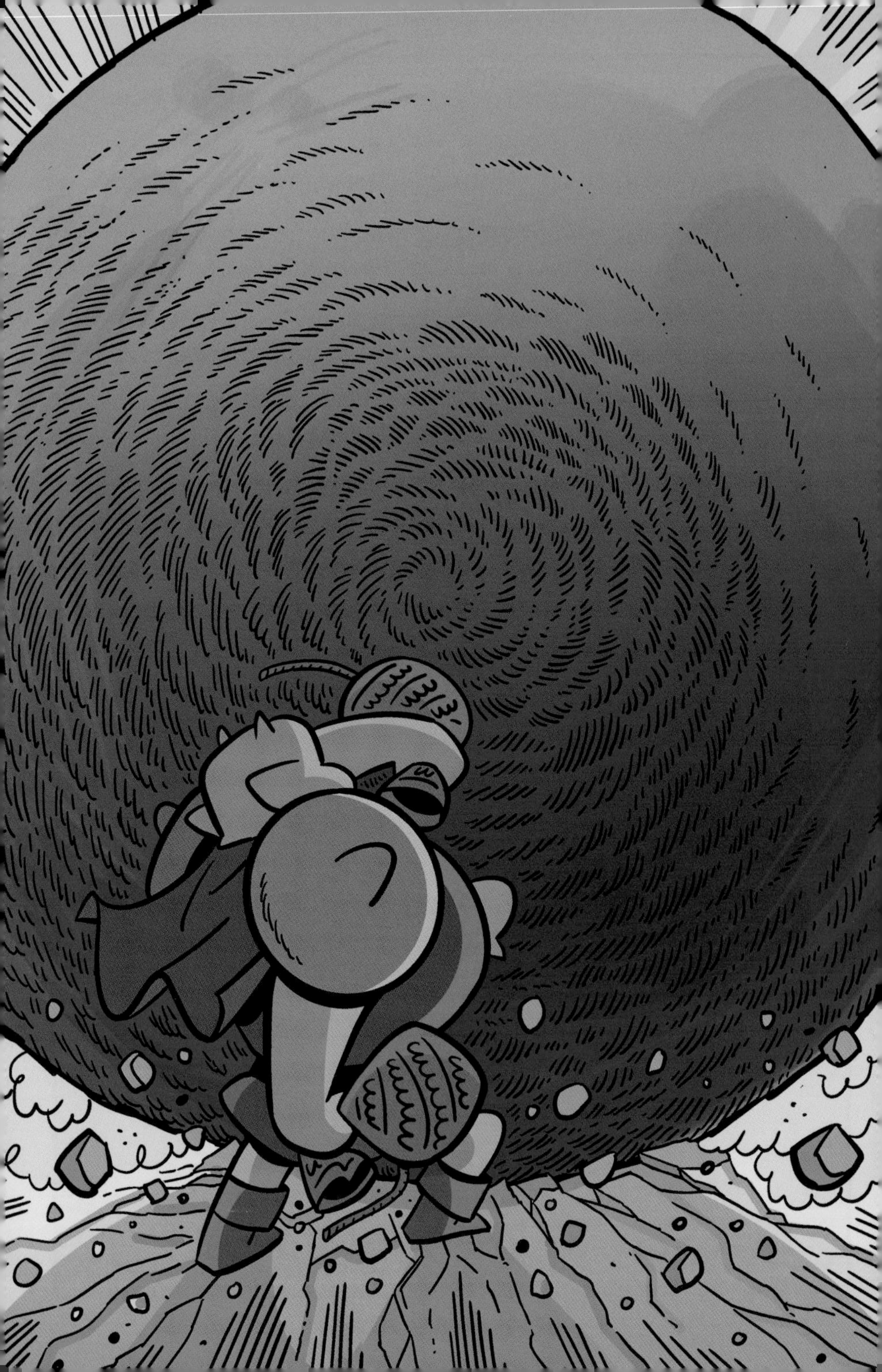

CHAPTER TWENTY-FOUR

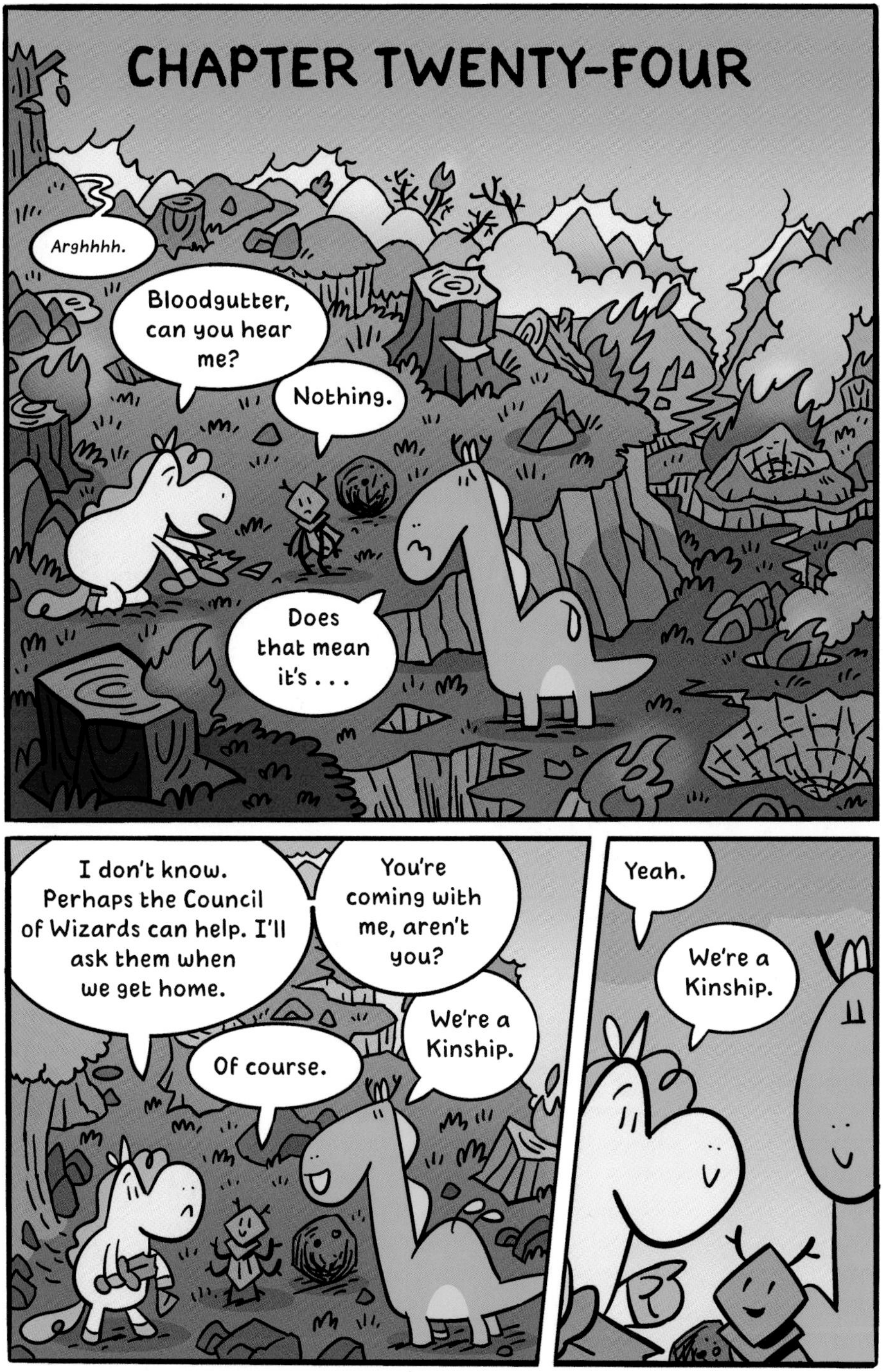
Arghhhh.
Bloodgutter, can you hear me?
Nothing.
Does that mean it's . . .
I don't know. Perhaps the Council of Wizards can help. I'll ask them when we get home.
You're coming with me, aren't you?
Of course.
We're a Kinship.
Yeah.
We're a Kinship.

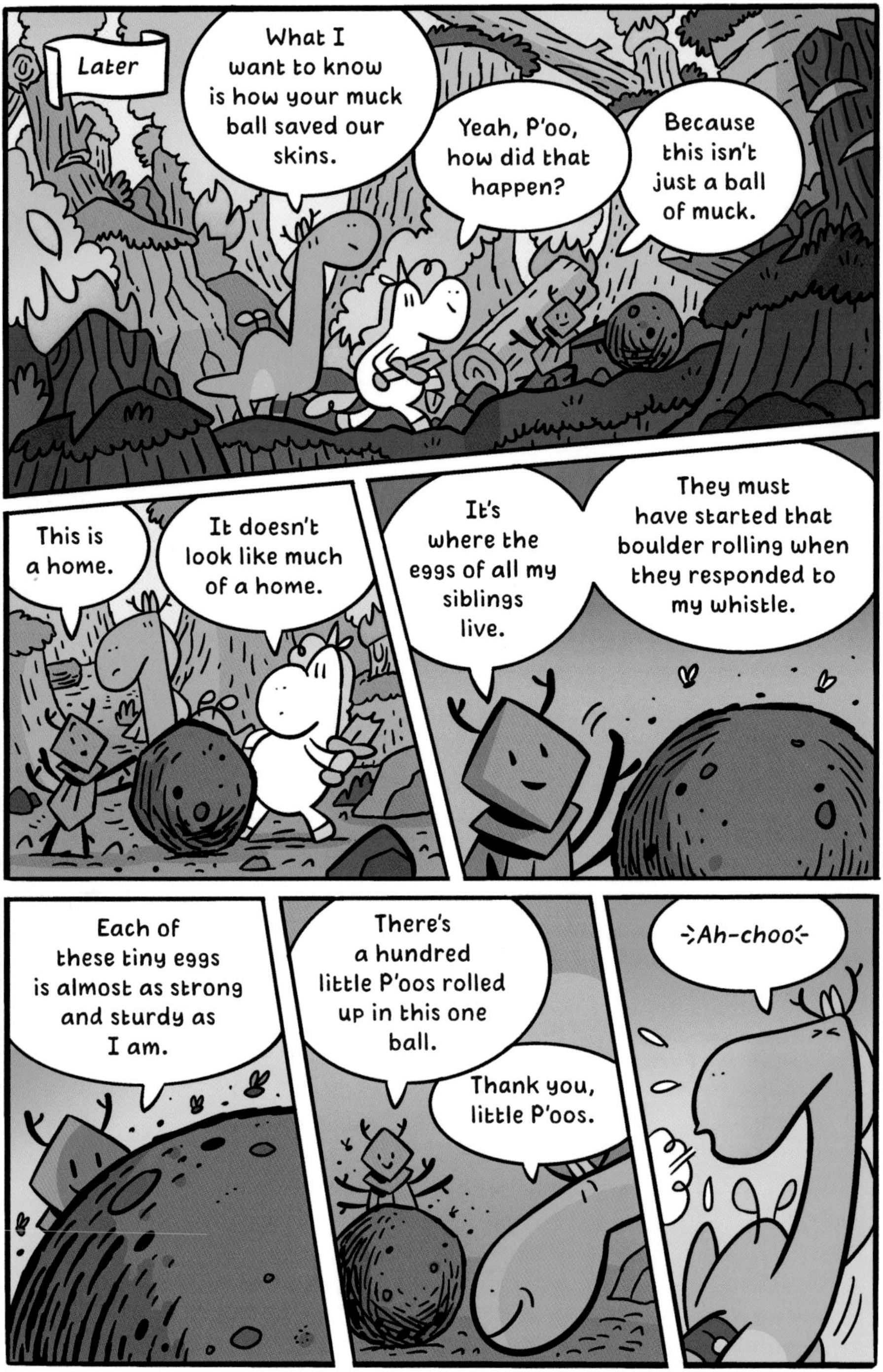
Later
What I want to know is how your muck ball saved our skins.
Yeah, P'oo, how did that happen?
Because this isn't just a ball of muck.
This is a home.
It doesn't look like much of a home.
It's where the eggs of all my siblings live.
They must have started that boulder rolling when they responded to my whistle.
Each of these tiny eggs is almost as strong and sturdy as I am.
There's a hundred little P'oos rolled up in this one ball.
Thank you, little P'oos.
Ah-choo

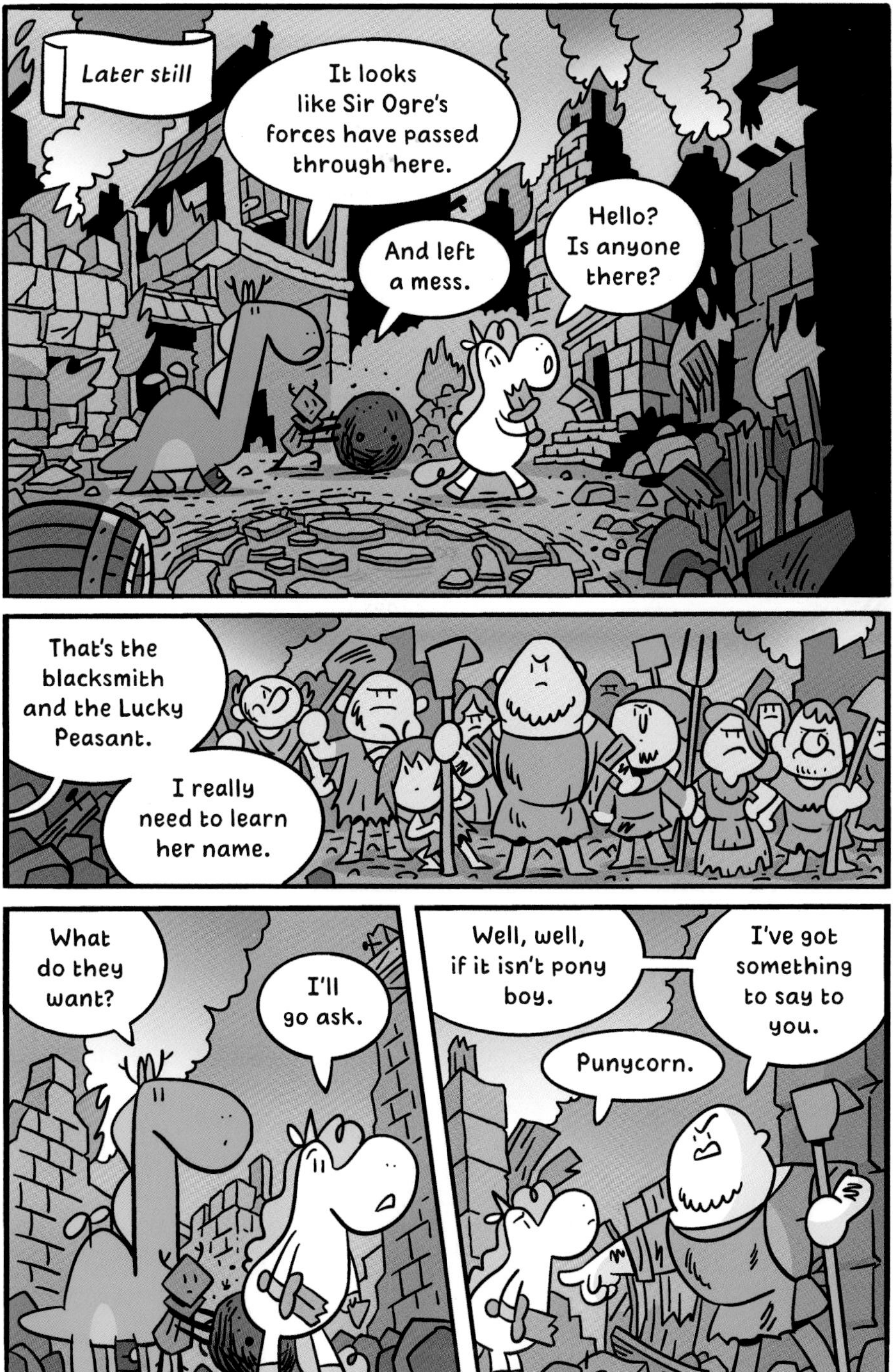

Later still
It looks like Sir Ogre's forces have passed through here.
And left a mess.
Hello? Is anyone there?
That's the blacksmith and the Lucky Peasant.
I really need to learn her name.
What do they want?
I'll go ask.
Well, well, if it isn't pony boy.
I've got something to say to you.
Punycorn.

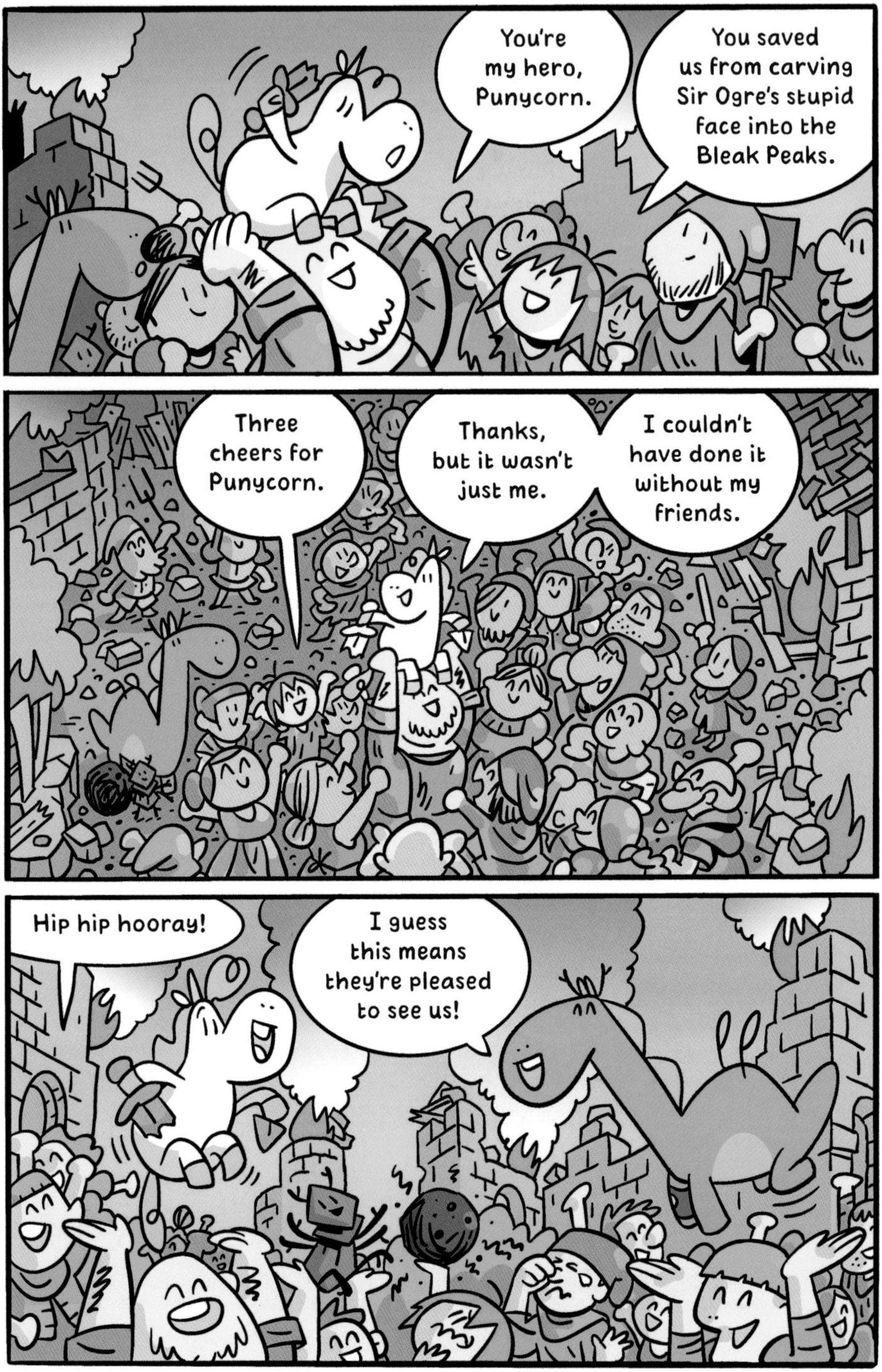
You're my hero, Punycorn.
You saved us from carving Sir Ogre's stupid face into the Bleak Peaks.
Three cheers for Punycorn.
Thanks, but it wasn't just me.
I couldn't have done it without my friends.
Hip hip hooray!
I guess this means they're pleased to see us!

CHAPTER TWENTY-FIVE

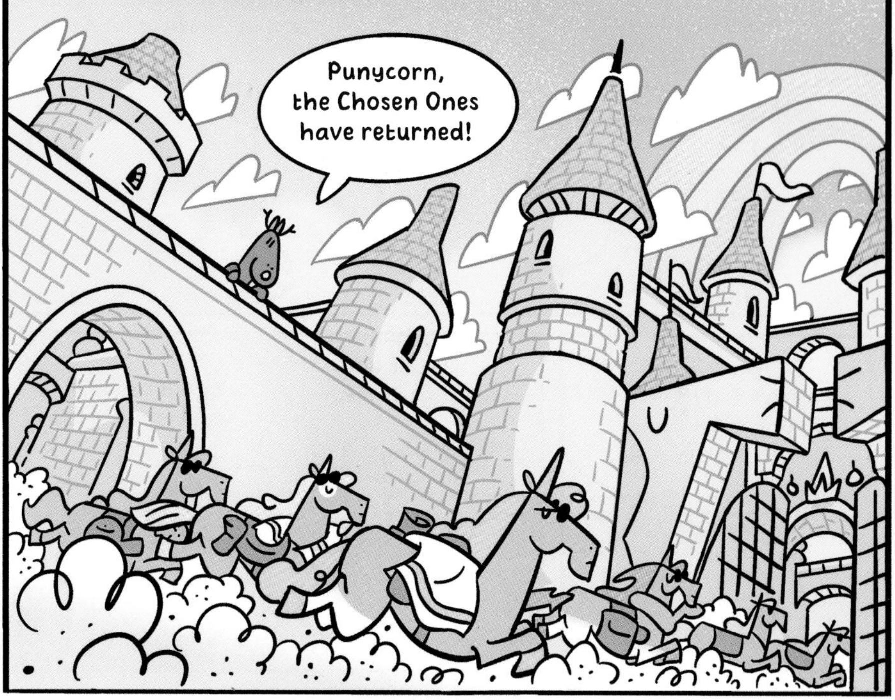
Punycorn, the Chosen Ones have returned!

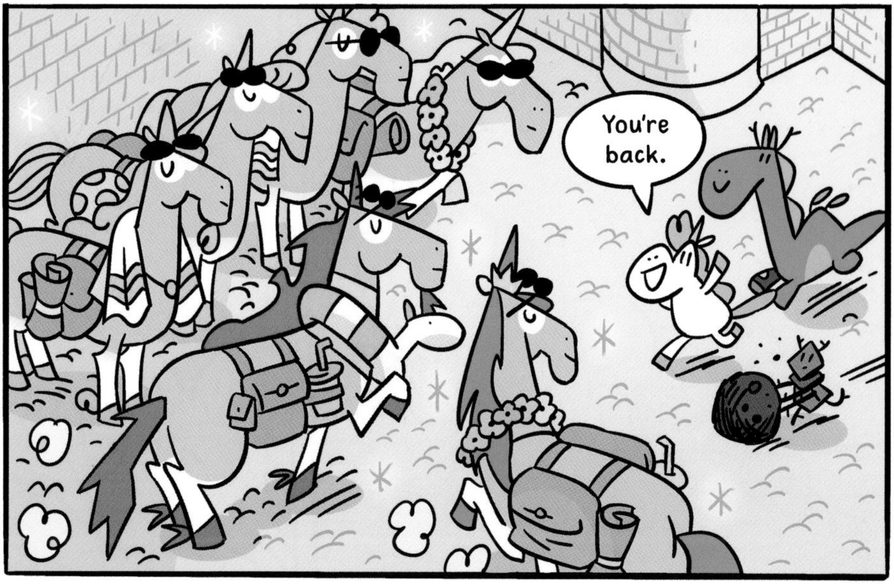
You're back.

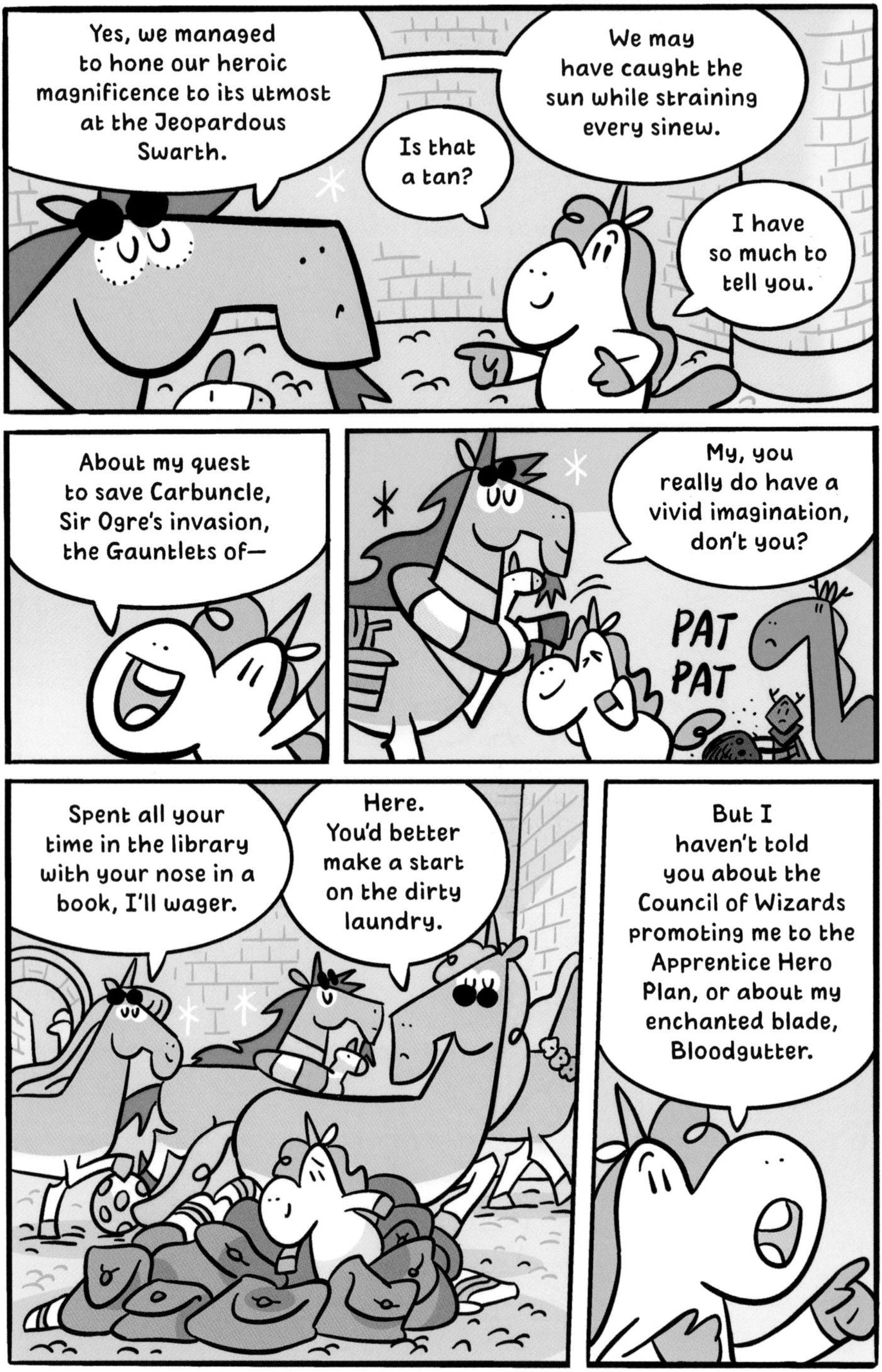

Yes, we managed to hone our heroic magnificence to its utmost at the Jeopardous Swarth.
Is that a tan?
We may have caught the sun while straining every sinew.
I have so much to tell you.
About my quest to save Carbuncle, Sir Ogre's invasion, the Gauntlets of—
My, you really do have a vivid imagination, don't you?
PAT PAT
Spent all your time in the library with your nose in a book, I'll wager.
Here. You'd better make a start on the dirty laundry.
But I haven't told you about the Council of Wizards promoting me to the Apprentice Hero Plan, or about my enchanted blade, Bloodgutter.

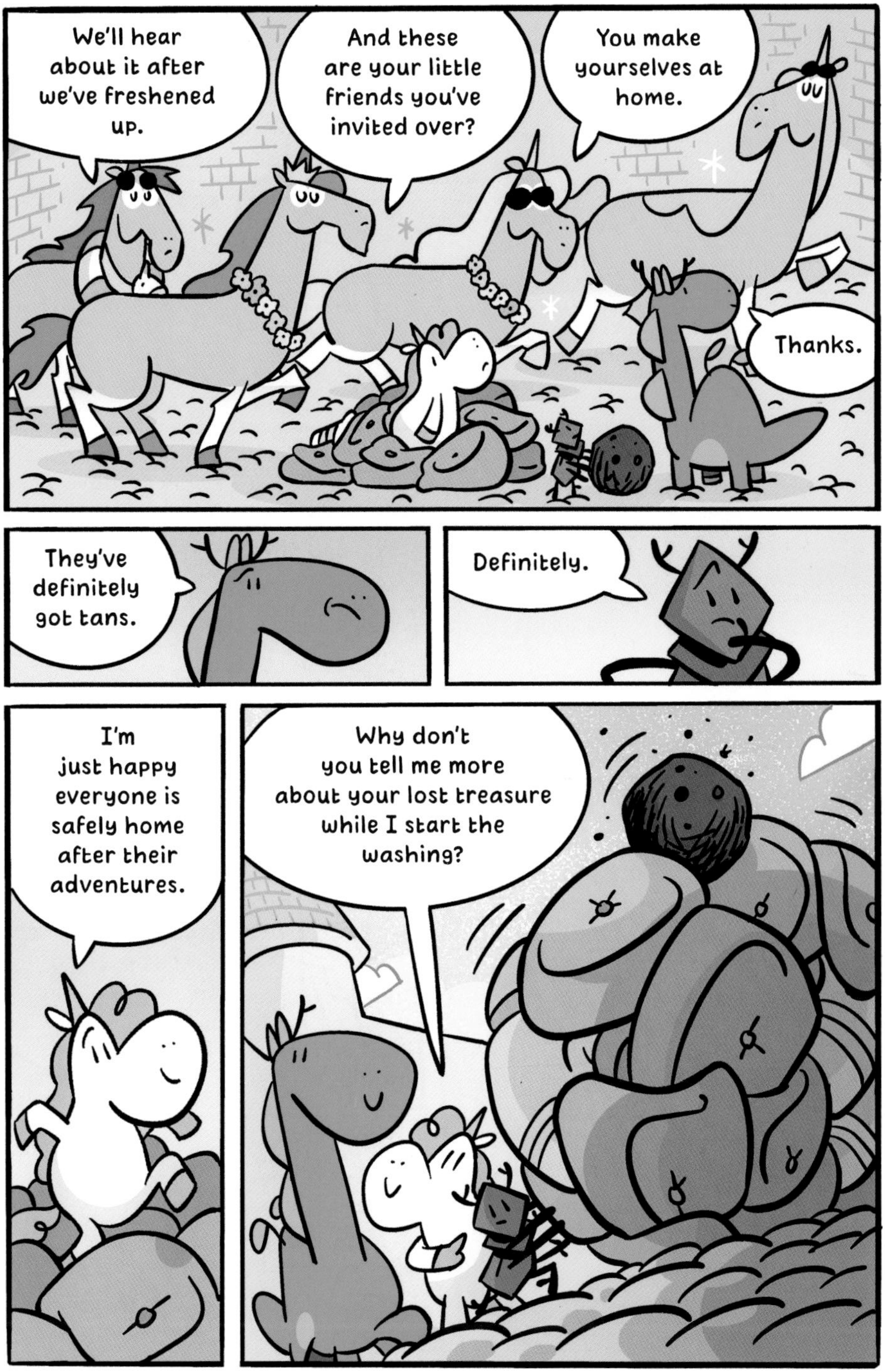
We'll hear about it after we've freshened up.
And these are your little friends you've invited over?
You make yourselves at home.
Thanks.
They've definitely got tans.
Definitely.
I'm just happy everyone is safely home after their adventures.
Why don't you tell me more about your lost treasure while I start the washing?

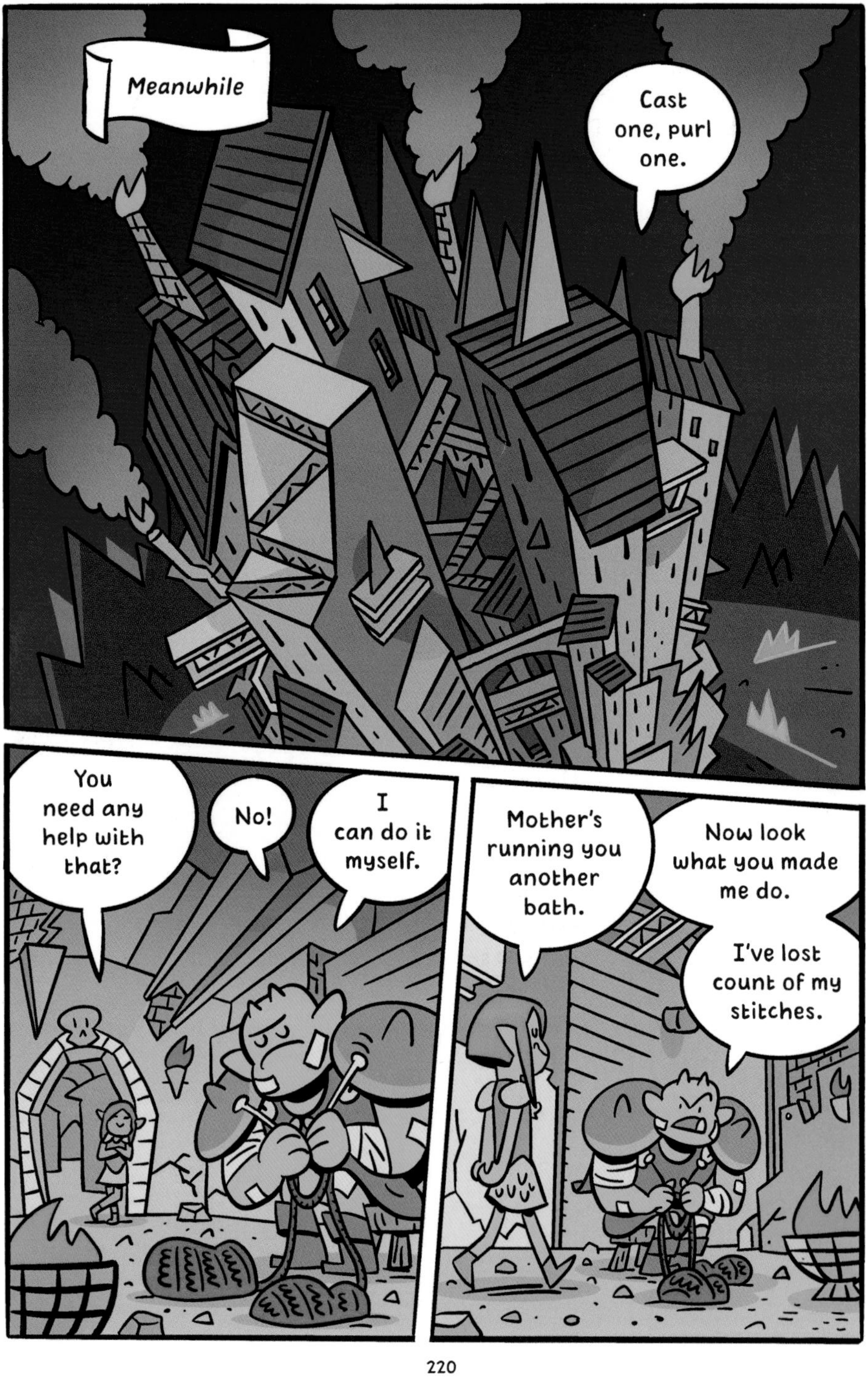
Meanwhile
Cast one, purl one.
You need any help with that?
No!
I can do it myself.
Mother's running you another bath.
Now look what you made me do.
I've lost count of my stitches.

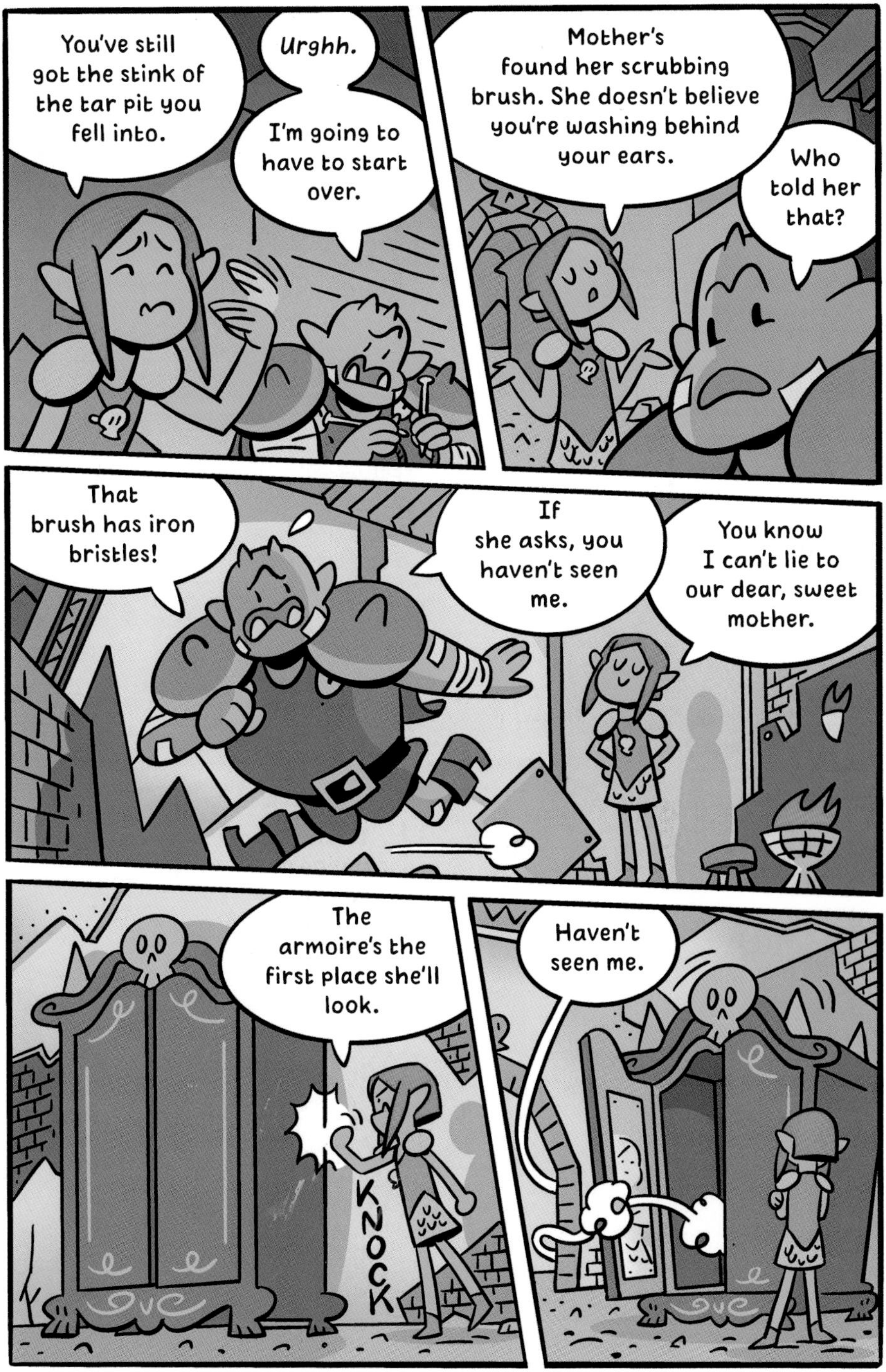
You've still got the stink of the tar pit you fell into.
Urghh.
I'm going to have to start over.
Mother's found her scrubbing brush. She doesn't believe you're washing behind your ears.
Who told her that?
That brush has iron bristles!
If she asks, you haven't seen me.
You know I can't lie to our dear, sweet mother.
The armoire's the first place she'll look.
KNOCK
Haven't seen me.

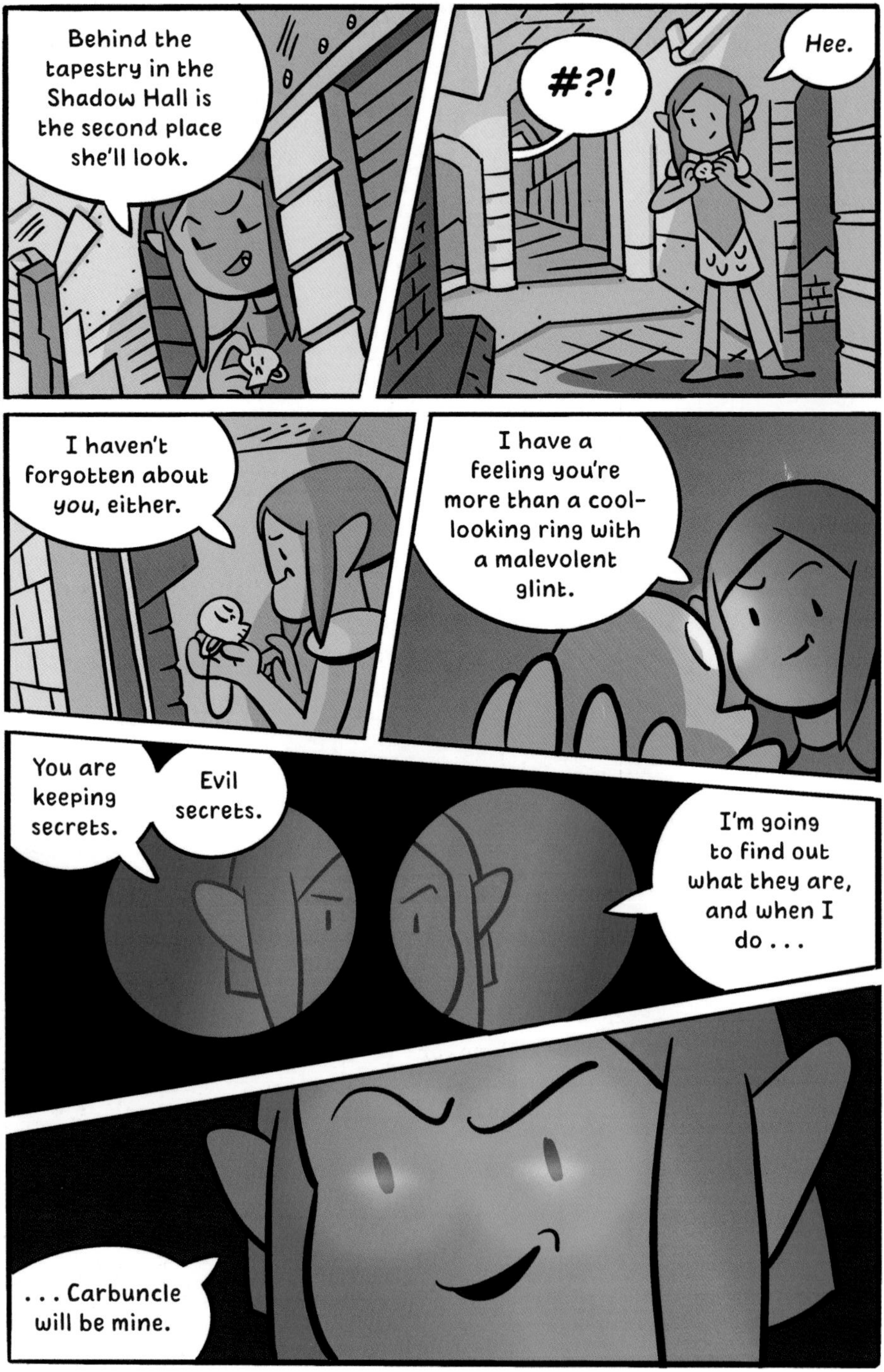
Behind the tapestry in the Shadow Hall is the second place she'll look.
#?!
Hee.
I haven't forgotten about *you*, either.
I have a feeling you're more than a cool-looking ring with a malevolent glint.
You are keeping secrets.
Evil secrets.
I'm going to find out what they are, and when I do . . .
. . . Carbuncle will be mine.

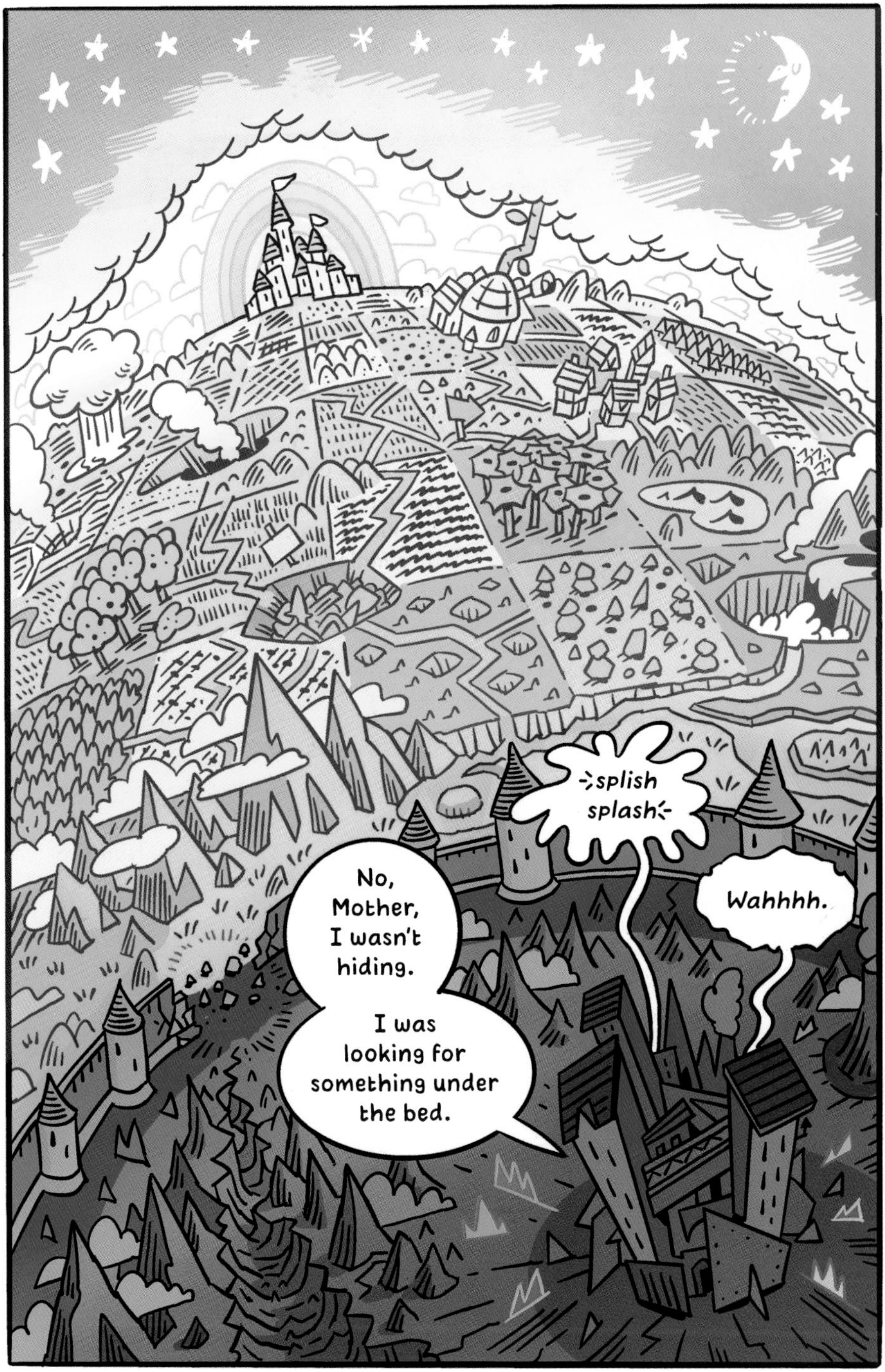
No, Mother, I wasn't hiding.
I was looking for something under the bed.
splish splash
Wahhhh.

WATCH FOR THE NEXT ADVENTURE:

and the PRINCESS OF THIEVES

To Janna, who championed Punycorn
from the beginning.
—A.W.

Clarion Books is an imprint of HarperCollins Publishers.
HarperAlley is an imprint of HarperCollins Publishers.

Punycorn
Copyright © 2023 by Andi Watson

ISBN 978-0-35-857199-5

The artist used pens, pencils, paper, Procreate on iPad, and
Photoshop CS6 to create the illustrations for this book.
Design by Celeste Knudsen

23 24 25 26 27 GPS 10 9 8 7 6 5 4 3 2 1

First Edition

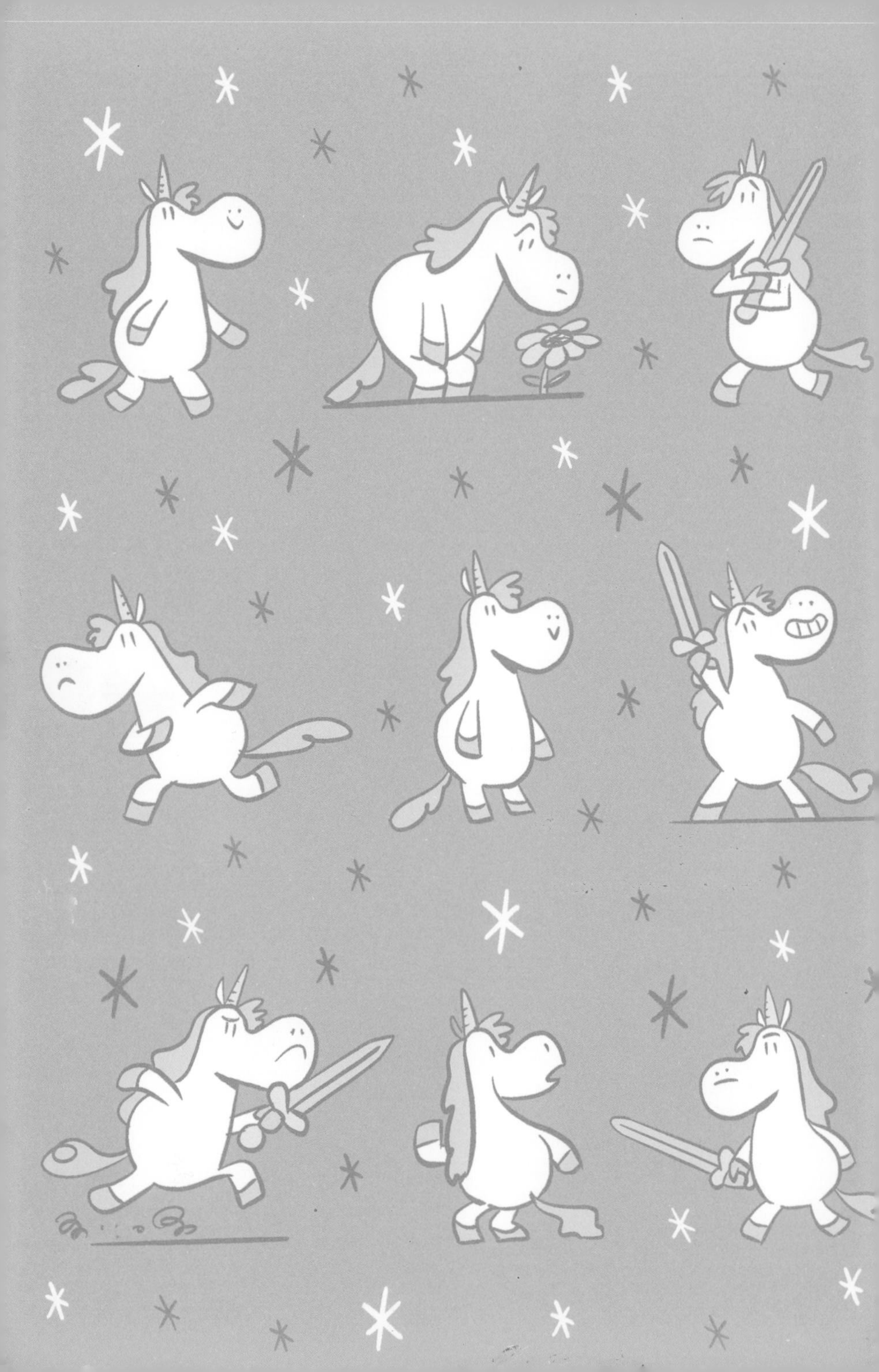